life. This particular story does just that . . . A master of her
genre, McInerney invites you into this charming and addictive
tale of love and family values'
U Magazine

'An exquisite novel, which combines well-crafted characters
with a captivating story . . . McInerney's latest offering is
guaranteed to enthral her legions of adoring fans'
Ulster Tatler

'If you're looking for a good family saga to get stuck into,
then Monica McInerney's books are just for you'
Image

'A heartwarming, romantic and funny story about love,
family and relationships'
Irish Independent

'McInerney's great skill lies in creating well-drawn and
realistically flawed characters. Her books are well-written,
compelling   'y life'

Lola's Secret

Monica McInerney grew up in a family of seven children in the Clare Valley wine region of South Australia. She has worked in children's television, arts marketing, the music industry, public relations and book publishing, and lived all around Australia, and in Ireland and England. She is the author of eight previous novels, including, most recently, At *Home with the Templetons*, *Those Faraday Girls* and *Family Baggage*. *Those Faraday Girls* was the winner of the General Fiction Book of the Year at the 2008 Australian Book Industry Awards. *Lola's Secret* is the sequel to *The Alphabet Sisters*. Monica and her Irish husband currently live in Dublin.

For further information please visit
www.monicamcinerney.com

Also by Monica McInerney

At Home with the Templetons
Those Faraday Girls
Odd One Out
Family Baggage
The Alphabet Sisters
Spin the Bottle
Upside Down Inside Out

Short stories
All Together Now

Lola's Secret

MONICA McINERNEY

PAN BOOKS

First published 2011 by Penguin Australia

This edition published 2012 by Pan Books
an imprint of Pan Macmillan, a division of Macmillan Publishers Limited
Pan Macmillan, 20 New Wharf Road, London N1 9RR
Basingstoke and Oxford
Associated companies throughout the world
www.panmacmillan.com

ISBN 978-0-230-76158-2

For my beautiful aunt Marcelle Lemm,
and in memory of my other Hogan aunts,
Jacqueline Galliford and Margaret Johnson

CHAPTER ONE

Even after more than sixty years of living in Australia, eighty-four-year-old Lola Quinlan couldn't get used to a hot Christmas. Back home in Ireland, December had meant short days, darkness by four p.m., open fires and frosty walks. Snow if they were lucky. Her mother had loved following Christmas traditions, many of them passed down by her own mother. The tree decorated a week before Christmas Day and not a day earlier. Carols in the chilly church before Midnight Mass. Lola's favourite tradition of all had been the placing of a lit candle in each window of the house on Christmas Eve. It was a symbolic welcome to Mary and Joseph, but also a message to any passing stranger that they would be made welcome too. As a child, she'd begged to be the one to light the candles, carefully tying back the curtains to avoid the chance of fire. Afterwards, she'd stood outside with her parents, their breath three frosty clouds, gazing up at their two-storey house transformed into something almost magical.

She was a long way from Ireland and dark frosty Decembers now. Sixteen thousand kilometres and about thirty-five degrees

Celsius, to be exact. The temperature in the Clare Valley of South Australia was already heading towards forty degrees and it wasn't even ten a.m. yet. The hills that were visible through the window were burnt golden by the sun, not a blade of green grass to be seen. There was no sound of carols or tinkling sleigh bells. The loudest noise was coming from the airconditioner behind her. If she did take a notion to start lighting candles and placing them in all the windows, there was every chance the fire brigade would come roaring up the hill, sirens blaring and water hoses at the ready. At last count, the Valley View Motel that Lola called home had more than sixty windows. Imagine that, Lola mused. Sixty candles ablaze at once. It would be quite a sight. Almost worth the trouble it would cause . . .

'Are you plotting mischief? I know that look.'

At the sound of her son's voice, Lola turned from her seat at one of the dining room tables and smiled. 'I wouldn't dream of it. You know me, harmless as a kitten.'

Jim simply raised an eyebrow, before pulling out a chair and sitting down opposite his mother. 'I was talking about you with Bett and Carrie today. We've all agreed it's not too late to change your mind.'

'About what? My lunch order? It's Friday. I always have fish on Fridays.' Another tradition from her days in Ireland, even if she'd long ago stopped following any religion.

'About you sending us away and taking charge of a fifteen-room motel on your own for five days. At Christmas. At the age of eighty-four.'

'You make me sound quite mad.'

'I don't, actually. You manage it perfectly well on your own.'

Lola stood, reached for her stick and drew herself up to her full five foot nine inches, fixing her sixty-four-year-old son with the gaze that had worked to silence him as a child, but hadn't had much effect for many years now. There was a brief staring contest and then she started to laugh. 'Of course I'm mad, darling. You don't live as long as I do if you have any sense. What's the point? Hips giving up, hearing going, wits long gone —'

'So you admit it, then? Will I call off our driving trip? Tell Bett and Carrie to cancel their holidays too? Say that you'd gone temporarily insane and you didn't mean it?'

'And what? Let you and Geraldine down? Let down my poor adorable granddaughters and their even more adorable children, not to mention their handsome husbands and their handsome husbands' families? Never. In fact, why don't you leave now, all of you? Begone. Leave an old lady in relative peace. Literally.'

'That's what I'm worried about. What if we're not leaving you in peace?'

'It's the middle of one of the hottest summers on record. We haven't had a drop of rain in years. The Valley is beautiful, yes, but as dry as a bone. Who on earth is going to choose to spend Christmas in a parched country motel?' She opened the bookings register to the week of December twenty-fifth and placed it in front of her son. 'See? Not a sinner. Or a saint. It'll just be poor old me rattling around the place on my own, while the turkey stays happily frozen in the coolroom, the puddings soak in their brandy for another twelve months and you and Geraldine and the girls hopefully get to have a proper Christmas break.'

Jim flicked through the pages, frowning. 'It's odd, isn't it? This time last year we were much busier. I thought we'd have at least one booking, that you'd have someone to talk to.'

'I'll be grand, darling. I'll have the radio for company. They have lovely programs on Christmas Day for lonely, abandoned old women like myself.' She laughed at the expression on his face. 'I'm teasing you, Jim. Don't get guilty on me and insist on staying, please. You know I enjoy my own company. Now, shouldn't you be helping Geraldine pack your bags? Getting the tyres pumped up? Checking the oil? A driving holiday won't organise itself.'

Jim was still distracted by the empty bookings register. 'That's the last time I try an online advertising campaign. Everybody kept telling me it's the only way people find motel accommodation these days, but it obviously didn't work for us. Our computer problems haven't helped, either.'

'Never mind, darling. Worry about your advertising next year. Off you go and leave me alone. I have eighty-four action-packed years I want to sit here and reminisce about before I go do my shift at the charity shop.'

'I think you should cut down your hours there, by the way.'

She put her fingers in her ears. 'Not listening, Jim. Reminiscing.' She shut her eyes, tight, like a child, until he left the room.

After a moment, she opened one eye to be sure he'd gone.

Thank God. Any longer and she'd have been forced to tell him the truth. That in fact his online advertising campaign had worked wonders. She'd been receiving email enquiries all week. Not on the motel computer, of course. It had been broken – been 'down', in the computer parlance she loved using – for the past four days. Her official story to her fortunately distracted son and his wife was that the server was having problems. ('Server!' she'd said, pretending more amazement. 'In my day that word meant maid or waitress!') The truth was she'd pulled out the internet cable on the office computer. Hidden it, too, to be doubly sure they stayed offline. The last thing she needed was Jim or Geraldine seeing the emails asking for more information about their Christmas special offer. As it happened, they didn't know much about what that Christmas special offer comprised, either. Why bother them, when they were in almost-holiday mode? When even the hint that there could be a Christmas guest or two at the Valley View Motel might make them change their minds about going away?

Lola had given her plan a great deal of thought. Firstly, Jim and Geraldine badly needed a break. Or, more accurately, Jim was due a break and Lola badly needed a break from her daughter-in-law. She loved Jim dearly but there had never been any love lost between herself and Geraldine. It had never been open warfare, for Jim's sake – more subtle, underlying hostility. Lola herself could talk to a stone on the road if the occasion warranted it, yet in all the time they'd known each other – almost forty years – she and Geraldine had never managed a single lively, interesting conversation. The tragic events in the family nearly five years earlier had prompted a thaw, a brief closeness between the two of them, mothers both, but it hadn't lasted. Lola thought Geraldine was a po-faced, humourless milksop, and Geraldine thought – well, really, who cared what Geraldine thought of her? As Lola liked to say airily whenever she caught Geraldine giving her a disapproving glance, 'Don't worry, dear. You'll be able to pack me off to a home for the bewildered any moment now. I'm sure I lose more of my marbles every day.'

Lola's opinion of Jim and Geraldine's daughters was a different story. She didn't just love them. She adored them. Anna, Bett and Carrie, her three Alphabet Sisters.

Theirs had been an unconventional childhood, living in motels, moving from town to town. Lola had taken over their care while their parents both worked. She'd revelled in all three girls, filling their lives with fun, adventure and especially music. She'd even coaxed them into a short-lived and frankly unsuccessful career as a childhood singing trio called, of course, The Alphabet Sisters. A young Anna had taken it seriously, Bett had cringed through it and Carrie had basked in the attention. Lola herself had been thoroughly amused and even more entertained. Everything about her three granddaughters had amused and entertained her.

But where there had been three, now there were two. Like a line from an old poem, so true and so heartbreaking, still. It was almost five years now since her oldest granddaughter Anna's death from cancer at the age of thirty-four. Years of pain, sorrow, tears. Lola knew they were all still coming to terms with it, each in their own way. Even now, thinking of Anna sent a too-familiar spike of grief into her heart, less sharp now, but ever present. She knew Anna was gone, visited her grave once a month if not more often, yet sometimes she found herself reaching for the phone to call her, wanting to tell her a story or be told a story in return. Share a memory. Laugh about something. Simply hear her beautiful voice one more time.

Lola knew it was no coincidence that her other two grand-daughters had stayed in the Valley, close to the family motel, since Anna's death. There'd been a need to be near each other, to talk often and openly about Anna, to cherish and celebrate good times and happy events. The missing link was Anna's daughter Ellen, now aged twelve, who lived in Hong Kong with her father Glenn. In the years since Anna's death, Glenn's work as an advertising executive had taken him and Ellen to Singapore, Kuala Lumpur and now Hong Kong. It hadn't been easy on any of them, Anna's only child being so far away, but they had all understood that it was best for her and for her father to be together.

A family never completely got over a loss like theirs, Lola knew. The Quinlans hadn't. Instead, they'd changed shape. It was the only way they'd been able to go on. And what better way for any family to change shape than with the arrival of babies, to help fill the gap Anna had left behind? Lola smiled even at the thought of her great-grandchildren. Carrie and her husband Matthew now had three children, Delia, aged four and

a half, Freya, three, and two-year-old George. They'd kept up
the family tradition of alphabetical names. Ellen had already
bagged the 'E' spot. Lola's middle granddaughter Bett and her
husband Daniel were the proud if exhausted parents of seven-
month-old twins, Zachary and Yvette. They'd kept up the family
naming tradition, too, although from the other direction. The
twins were, in Lola's opinion, the two most glorious babies on
the planet, but heavens, the racket they made! Like echo cham-
bers – one making a noise would set off the other.

An old friend of Bett's had invited them to celebrate Christmas with her and her husband at their beach house near Robe,
volunteering their teenage children for twin-sitting, meaning
sleep-ins for Bett and Daniel. Lola had seen the longing in Bett's
eyes at the idea of it. Lola also knew that Carrie and Matthew
and their little ones hadn't spent a Christmas with his family
in New South Wales yet. It was definitely time they did. The
two girls had also expressed concern that Lola would be on her
own in the motel at Christmas, but she'd argued just as forcefully with them that it was what she wanted. 'I've had zillions of
family Christmases,' she'd said. 'Let's all try something new this
year. And I've been managing motels since before you were born.
I can easily handle a few days on my own.'

She checked her delicate gold wristwatch. Good, nearly ten
a.m., the time she'd arranged to be collected for her stint at the
charity shop. Her alleged stint. Oh, she would do a bit of sorting
and selling while she was there, but, frankly, she had bigger fish
to fry these days. One step through the ordinary faded curtain

at the rear of the shop and it was like being in a NASA control room, not a country thrift shop storeroom. There was not just a computer, but a modem, scanner and printer. Even a little camera.

'Ladies, we have ourselves a portal to the world wide web,' Lola had announced the first day it was in operation, enjoying the look of surprise her young friend and computer guru, Luke, gave her. But of course she knew about the world wide web. And emailing. And blogging. She spent hours during the night listening to the radio, poring over newspapers, watching TV documentaries – how could she not know about new media? She'd been dying to give it all a try herself. And once the equipment was in place, she'd taken to it like a, well, not duck to water . . . What term would be more appropriate? Bill Gates to money-making? Luke had been amazed she'd heard of Bill Gates, too. Honestly, did he think she'd spent the past eighty-four years in an isolation unit?

She couldn't wait to get onto the keyboard again today. She had so much to do. Catching up on the motel Christmas situation was a priority, but she also had an email to write to Ellen in Hong Kong. Lola didn't get to see her nearly as often as she'd like, once a year at most, but the letters, phone calls and latterly emails they exchanged kept the bond between them strong. They had a regular correspondence going these days. Lola had even learnt how to email photos of herself to Ellen. At Ellen's request, in fact. For some reason, Ellen seemed to find Lola's fashion style amusing.

Wow, Really-Great-Gran! she'd written in her last email. Pink tights and leopard-skin dress as day-wear? Watch out, Lady Gaga!

Lola googled this Lady Gaga and rather than being insulted, had been inspired. Which reminded her – she wasn't fully dressed yet. Fine for around the motel, but not spruced up enough for the shop. She made her way to her current room – number eleven of the motel's fifteen rooms, the one with the beautiful view over the hills with just a glimpse of a vineyard. It was part of her arrangement with Jim and Geraldine, that she lived in her pick of the motel's rooms rather than share the managers' quarters with them. She'd just finished adding the final touch to her day's outfit of purple pantsuit and gold belt – a large pink flower pinned in her short white hair – when she heard the sound of young Luke's old Corolla straining its way up the drive. Ah, that lovely boy. So reliable. So clever too.

It was twenty-three-year-old Luke who'd organised the entire computer setup in the charity shop. After finishing his apprenticeship with a local electrician, he'd moved to Adelaide, trained in IT and was now rising through the ranks of a successful computer installation firm. The shop computer was what he called his 'after-work work', a labour of love whenever he was back in Clare visiting his mother Patricia, another of the volunteers. There'd been opposition at first from some of the other ladies, but once they'd seen it in operation, well, it had become quite a computer club. Lola had needed to set up a schedule to be sure she got enough time for her own activities. Between Lola's oldest friend Margaret and her online bridge club, Patricia and her

Etsy handicrafts addiction, and another volunteer, Kay, with her eight hundred Facebook friends, it was sometimes hard to get even an hour at the computer to herself. There was also Joan, who loved posting videos of her cat on YouTube, another lady who skyped her son in Copenhagen every Saturday, and even Bill, the shop handyman, who made a big deal of not having a TV at home but spent hours each week watching reruns on TV network websites. Remarkable all around, really. Their average human age was seventy-five. Average computer skills age mid-twenties, according to Luke. 'You oldies pick things up quickly, don't you?' he'd said admiringly, early on in his training sessions. 'I wasn't sure you'd get a handle on all of this.'

'I'll have you know I used to run my own accountancy business,' Margaret announced, piqued.

'I was CEO of a local council,' Joan said.

'These hands helped more than a thousand cows give birth,' Kay the dairy farmer said, holding them up.

Luke had looked quite shocked.

As Lola pulled the door to her room shut behind her now and made her way to the front of the motel, she thought she saw Geraldine look out the dining room window. She gave her daughter-in-law a cheery wave. If Geraldine saw her, she didn't respond. No manners as well as no personality, Lola thought. 'Bye for now!' she called to whoever else might be watching. 'Off I go into town. Off I go to do some useful charity work.'

An hour later, Lola's mood wasn't so bright. She'd been mistaken about the response to the Valley View Motel's online Christmas offer. Yes, there had been more than a dozen enquiries via email, but not a single follow-up booking. God forbid she *would* actually have to spend Christmas alone. She peeked through the curtain separating the office from the shop itself – only one customer browsing and Margaret was well able to handle her.

Lola frowned as she checked the emails again. No bookings at all? Why ever not? She clicked on one of the queries at random, and noticed the mobile number under the person's name. Was it standard business practice to make a follow-up call? Perhaps, perhaps not, but how else was she to find out? She took out her mobile phone. Luke had been astonished to see that as well. 'You use a mobile?'

'Only for the time being. I'm saving up for an iPhone,' Lola told him. It was true, she was.

Her call was answered on the third ring. Lola put on her most polite voice. 'Good afternoon. My name is Lola Quinlan and I wonder if you can help me. I'm doing a marketing survey into a recent online advertising campaign. No, please, don't hang up. I won't be long. Let me cut to the chase. You enquired about but didn't book the Valley View Motel. Why not?' She listened for a moment. 'But it's *not* expensive. Not compared to other places. Really? You did? For three nights and Christmas lunch included? My word, that is a bargain. I'd have gone there instead myself.' She made three more calls. Two gave her the same answer – they'd found cheaper packages elsewhere. The third person had decided to stay home for Christmas.

Lola clicked on the different computer files until she found the wording for her Valley View Christmas Special online ad. Jim had given her his version before he'd sent it to the online accommodation sites. She'd tinkered with it a little bit before sending it out to some more sites of her own choosing, but obviously she'd not tinkered enough. Luke had given her a lesson in something he called meta-tags, words that people might use when going searching – 'surfing, you mean', she'd corrected him – online. She'd rewritten Jim's ad until it included nearly every Christmassy word she could think of. *Christmas. Pudding. Santa. Carols. Holly. Come stay in our lovely ho-ho-hotel!* The Valley View was actually a motel, but still . . . The special offer included three nights' bed and breakfast and a special three-course Christmas lunch – *turkey and all the trimmings!* She'd also added a line about a surprise gift for everyone. They would be surprising – so far they included a travel clock, a wooden picture frame, a jigsaw puzzle that she hoped had all its pieces and a rather alarming red tie, all chosen from the bags of donations left for the charity shop. Lola had paid for them, of course. Above the odds, too.

She peeked through the curtain again. The customer had left and Margaret was now dusting the bookshelves. 'Everything okay, Margaret?' Lola called out.

'Counting down the minutes, Lola,' Margaret called back.

Drat, Lola thought. She'd hoped Margaret would forget about her turn. She quickly sent an email to Ellen, sending her lots of love and asking for all her news, then turned her attention back to Christmas. She shut her eyes to concentrate hard for a moment, trying to remember marketing tips from the online course she'd completed the previous year. Eye-catching headings, tick. Clear concise offers, tick. Irresistible offers. That was obviously where she'd gone wrong. Her current offer was too easy to resist. What would make something irresistible?

If it was free?

It took her only a minute to compose the new ad. Just as well, she only had eight minutes left before she'd have to hand the computer over to Margaret and her online bridge game. If Lola had followed Luke's instructions correctly, the next group of people who emailed asking for extra details about the Valley View Motel's Christmas package would receive this automated email in return:

CONGRATULATIONS!
You are the lucky winner of the Valley View Motel's special Christmas package draw! Three nights' accommodation, breakfast each day and a slap-up Christmas lunch – all completely free! Simply reply to this email within twenty-four hours and include your contact details and I'll get right back to you.

For extra authenticity, she added her own signature – she'd recently learned to scan it – and her mobile number. She pressed send, sat back and smiled. The bait was out there. All she had to do now was wait.

Chapter Two

Guest 1

Neil didn't even know for sure where the Clare Valley was. He knew it had something to do with wine. He knew it was in South Australia somewhere. Beyond that, he didn't know, didn't care. He'd picked it, and the motel, at random. Simply logged on to a last-minute accommodation website and scrolled through until one caught his eye. It didn't matter to him what the view from his motel window was like, how many stars the motel had earned, whether they had in-room dining or an outdoor swimming pool. All he knew was that on Christmas Day he wanted to wake up as far away from home as possible. Not just from Broken Hill, but from his life, from every single atom of his stupid, wasted, pointless life. Leave it behind, and never come back. He sent off an enquiry email and was about to turn off the computer when he saw he'd received a reply already. The subject line read: CONGRATULATIONS! It was a long time since he'd been congratulated for anything he'd done. Frowning, he clicked on it.

Guests 2 and 3

As Helen heard the sound of the front door opening, she hurriedly clicked 'close' on the computer screen, clicked again several times until an innocuous shopping website appeared in front of her and then turned and gave her husband an innocent smile. He didn't smile back. He didn't smile very often any more.

'Good day at work, darling?'

'Fine, thanks. Any post?'

She'd keep her voice cheerful. If it killed her, she wouldn't let it show how much his distraction and depression day after day affected her. The doctor had told her to be patient. To offer stability. To keep the house quiet. He's going through a normal reaction to a traumatic incident, he told her. The shock may have passed, but the mental scars take longer to heal. 'You love him, don't you?'

Back then she hadn't hesitated to nod. If she was asked that same question now, though? Did she still love Tony or was what she felt closer to pity, or exasperation? She had to keep trying, though. Weary inside, but hoping she sounded enthusiastic, she tried her latest attempt to make things right for him.

'I was thinking about Christmas today,' she said. 'Only three weeks away. Where does the time go?'

He didn't answer, just kept walking through to the kitchen.

It was his silence that hurt. She'd tried – she was still trying – so hard, every day, to be patient, loving, understanding. But the lack of communication was contagious. There was now so much she wanted to say to him – that she was worried for their marriage, worried for his mental health, for her mental health – and for so many reasons she couldn't say any of it.

And how could she tell him she'd realised that afternoon she couldn't bear another Christmas like the previous year? He hadn't bought any presents. He'd said sorry, he just hadn't been up to it. Don't worry, she'd said, as cheerily as she could, handing over the too many presents she'd bought him, trying to over-compensate as always. The rest of the day had been as hard. The two of them sitting silently in the dining room for lunch. The afternoon and evening in front of the television. There had been nothing and no one to distract them. Both their children were working overseas, their daughter Katie in London, their son Liam in Barcelona. They hadn't come back last Christmas, instead arranging to meet one another for what they called an orphans' gathering in Munich. 'You don't mind, Mum, do you?' Katie had said. 'It's just one day. And it's so amazing over here. It's like Christmas should be, all cold and snowy, and the decorations look so beautiful and the Christmas markets . . .'

'Of course I don't mind,' she'd said. Of course she minded. She wanted them back. She wanted her husband back. She wanted to turn back time to before the accident at work that had changed her husband from the cheerful, enthusiastic person she'd married into this morose, silent man. She'd tried everything, from sympathy to plain speaking. 'It wasn't your fault, Tony. You didn't kill Ben.'

'But I did. I was his boss. I should have made sure he was safe.'

Back and forth they'd gone, him blaming himself, her trying

to soothe him, until they'd run out of words. Run out of conversation. Today, she'd found herself in tears about it again. She knew she had to do something, anything, as soon as possible. She also knew that if they were going to have another Christmas without their children, she just couldn't have it here. She'd decided she and Tony would go away for Christmas Day, maybe even for a few days. She'd find some way to pay for it. Money was tight, certainly. The deeper Tony's depression, the more his car repair business's output suffered. If it wasn't for the money she made working as a part-time teacher, they'd be in financial trouble. But if she had to break into what was left of her own savings, she'd do it.

She hadn't asked Tony for his opinion or for any ideas about where he'd like to go. She knew there was no point. So that afternoon she'd gone online, googled 'Christmas breaks and hotel specials' and, after a quick perusal of what was available, she'd found a motel in the Clare Valley of South Australia. It seemed perfect. A manageable five-hour drive from their home twenty kilometres inside the Victorian border. It would be even quicker to fly, but Tony had developed a fear of flying in the past year. Perhaps it was just an excuse not to go and visit their children overseas – another of her suggestions to cheer him up. She'd read through the Valley View Motel description – just an ordinary country motel by the sound of things, nothing special in itself, but there seemed to be plenty in the area to visit, historic buildings, lots of small wineries . . . Neither of them had been to that part of the country before, either. That might give them something to talk about, even for a few minutes. She missed their conversations. They'd always had lots to talk about and laugh about . . . Yes, forget the expense, the bother of driving, the cost of accommodation, petrol, all of it. *She* needed to get away, even if it didn't do Tony any good.

She checked where he was now. Once upon a time, he'd go straight from work out into the garden to his vegetable patch, or even announce that he'd cook dinner. Tonight, he'd gone into the living room and turned on the TV, his usual after-work ritual these days. Sometimes she was lucky if she got four words out of him in an evening. The sight of him there in the armchair now, staring ahead, almost broke her heart. She had to do something, change *something* in their lives.

Three clicks of the computer mouse later, she was back on the Valley View Motel website. She didn't bother reading the description of their Christmas special offer again, but just went straight to the enquiry form, quickly filling in the fields: one room, two people, their names and contact details. She pressed send, then walked into the living room, forcing a pleasant expression onto her face.

'Tony?'

'Hmm?'

He wasn't listening properly either, she knew that. He hadn't listened for months now. She forced the bright voice out of herself. 'Darling, I've had an idea. About Christmas . . .'

On the computer in the room behind her, an email appeared in the inbox. The subject line was CONGRATULATIONS!

Guest 4

There had to be some place in Australia that didn't insist on pretending it was wintertime or that it made sense to serve turkey and roast potatoes in the middle of a boiling hot summer, surely? Somewhere you could get a salad for lunch if you wanted? Some place cool? Green? Forget the tropical islands. Martha had made the mistake two years earlier of booking a Christmas break at one of the Queensland resorts, certain that sense would prevail there and she'd be offered seafood, cool cocktails and summery music, not carols extolling snowy days and Santa's reindeer. No such luck. She'd arrived to find the resort covered in fake snow and the bar staff wearing a peculiar combination of beach wear and Santa hats, smiling gamely over the relentless sound of piped Christmas carols.

Martha sighed in recalled exasperation, and clicked through several more hotels listed on the screen in front of her, dismissing each option as it appeared. No, she'd been to Byron Bay before. She also went to Sydney enough for work. Ditto Tasmania and Western Australia. Her recruitment consultancy business kept her travelling thirty weeks of the year away from the head office in Melbourne. Perhaps she should just stay still for Christmas. Turn the airconditioning up high in her small but expensive Carlton terrace and cook a seafood lunch . . . No, no way. She needed a change of scene. She kept clicking through the options, sighing loudly at the wording of many of the ads and descriptions. She couldn't abide bad grammar, or lazy —

'Is it okay if I head home now?'

'You've finished that report?' It came out sharper than she'd intended. About to apologise, Martha remembered her first boss and mentor's advice: never apologise, never explain. It was his life's philosophy. One that had served him well, and paid off even better, she knew. It had done the same for her in turn. Her business was booming, her bank account not just healthy but overflowing.

At the door, her secretary nodded. 'It's printed and in the file on your desk.'

Martha hadn't heard her come in. She'd probably been shouting down the phone at one of their suppliers at the time.

'Good.' A pause. 'Thank you.'

Her secretary still didn't leave. Martha waited, her impatience surely visible on her face. 'Yes, Alice?'

'I just wanted to say happy Christmas.'

It was only the start of December. 'You're a bit early, aren't you?'

'I'm taking a month off this year. Do you remember? I put in the special request, and you signed it. I've arranged a temp, as you requested. She'll be here first thing Monday, by eight —'

'Oh, right. Yes. Fine. Well, have fun.'

It was only after the door had shut and she heard the faint ping of the lift bell down the corridor that Martha remembered her secretary wasn't just taking a long holiday. She was getting married the week before Christmas and going on honeymoon to Thailand. It was too late to go chasing after her now. And not the right thing to do in any case. It was important to keep the boundaries between employer and employee well defined. Never apologise, never explain.

She turned back to the problem at hand. Where to go for her own Christmas break? Somewhere away from the city. She was sick of traffic and noise and people. If she couldn't avoid the turkey and trimmings, surely she could at least find somewhere cool and green? A film her father used to love came into her head suddenly. *How Green Was My Valley*. Pushing down the memories it threatened to bring up, she googled 'Valley' and 'Christmas' and 'hotel'. Four pages of entries appeared. She clicked on the first one. Valley View Motel, Clare Valley. Two valleys. That sounded twice as cool. That would do. What did she care anyway? Christmas only lasted one day and she intended to have her laptop with her and be working for most of it. It didn't matter where she was.

She scanned the information. Fine, yes, in the country, self-contained rooms, just a two-hour drive from Adelaide, the nearest city. Not that she'd be driving herself. As usual when she travelled interstate, she'd arrange for a car to collect her so she could work during the journey. She hoped her secretary's temporary replacement would be competent enough to arrange that for her. More to the point, she hoped her secretary had left all the correct contact details for her preferred chauffeur company. If not, Martha would just have to call Alice, holiday or not. And perhaps take the opportunity to wish her well for her wedding and honeymoon. Or perhaps not. Never apologise . . . She barely read the rest of the entry, her decision already made. She'd go to the motel for Christmas Eve and Christmas Day and return home on Boxing Day. Two nights away was more than enough, even if it was a three-night break on offer. She wouldn't join the other hotel guests for Christmas lunch either. She knew she'd prefer to eat on her own in her room. She clicked on the enquiry form, filled in her details and pressed send.

She'd just opened the folder of spreadsheets in front of her when she heard the sound of an incoming email. She looked up at it. The subject line was CONGRATULATIONS!

Guests 5, 6 and 7

In her bedroom, Holly pulled her two younger sisters close. Not close enough. The shouting outside their door was still audible. The shouting, the swearing, the blaming. It had been going on now for almost thirty minutes. Yesterday it had lasted only ten. The day before that, more than an hour.

'With any luck they'll lose their voices soon,' she said, in the most cheerful tone she could find.

Belle was already crying. Once she started, Chloe usually followed. Sure enough, within a minute, both of Holly's little sisters were crying.

'Did I show you that Christmas card on the computer?' she said brightly. 'It's like magic. Come and look.' Perhaps the sound of the electronic carol would block out the sound of their parents' arguments for a few minutes.

The distraction worked, at first. Holly urged her sisters to follow the on-screen directions, clicking here and there, helping to build a virtual snowman, giving him a carrot for a nose, coal for eyes. Ludicrous, really. Outside, the Adelaide sky was bright blue. There was as much chance of snow as there was a chance of their parents talking nicely to one another and making Christmas something fun rather than a battleground. She tuned in for a moment to their fighting. It was about money, by the sound of things. Unpaid bills. Who worked harder. Who earned more. Who was lazier. Who was fatter. Who did more around the house. Shouts and accusations, getting louder and louder.

Holly pulled her sisters in even tighter beside her. 'Come here, littlies.' They were much younger than her. Holly was nearly seventeen, Chloe was eight and Belle had just turned six. The large age gap hadn't been by choice, Holly knew. Her mother had talked to her about the four miscarriages, how much she had wanted each lost child, how she'd thought Holly might be her first and last child and then Chloe had arrived, followed two years later by Belle. Sometimes Holly wished that all those other babies had survived too, and that she lived in a house filled with brothers and sisters. Perhaps if the house was full of kids, her mother would have been happy. Perhaps if there hadn't been that long gap between her and Chloe and Belle, her father wouldn't have started working so hard. Perhaps. If only. I wish.

It was as if Belle had read her mind. 'Let's make a wish each. Me first. I wish we could see snow this Christmas.'

'We'll sing "White Christmas" anyway, I promise,' Holly said. 'And "Jingle Bells" especially for you, Jingle Belle. Your turn to make a wish, Chloe. Can you put a carol in it somehow?'

Chloe gave a little jump as something crashed to the floor outside. 'I wish we could have a silent night this Christmas.'

She was trying to make a joke but none of them laughed. Holly leaned forward and turned up the volume on the radio beside the computer, hoping the cheery pop song might drown out the argument that was now following the smashed vase or glass or cup. 'Congratulations, Chloe. Your wish has just come true,' she said firmly. 'Let's do it, will we? Head off somewhere and have our own quiet Christmas? Tell Mum and Dad we're not coming back until they stop fighting?'

Two little faces looked up in amazement. 'Could we? Really?'

Could they? Really? She thought quickly. She had her driver's licence. She'd got it as soon as she turned sixteen. Strictly speaking, she wasn't supposed to be driving without a fully licensed driver in the car with her, but, strictly speaking, children were supposed to have happy Christmases and not be thinking about running away from their endlessly warring parents . . .

Was she actually doing this? Thinking about running away with her two sisters for Christmas?

Yes, she was. And for the first time in weeks, the tight feeling in her chest lessened a little bit.

'Wouldn't that be an adventure?' she said to Belle and Chloe. 'A proper Christmas adventure.'

'But where will we go?' Belle asked.

'That's where the adventure begins,' Holly said, as she typed the words 'hotel' and 'Christmas' into the search engine.

Before she pressed 'go', Belle hopped off her lap and ran into her bedroom. She was back moments later holding the bear-shaped moneybox Holly had bought her for her birthday five months earlier. She'd found it in a charity shop for ten cents. All it had needed was a bit of a clean. Belle loved it. She not only kept every bit of spare change she ever found or earned inside it, she also slept with it in her arms each night.

Now, though, she pulled at its belly until a gap appeared and a tumble of coins waterfalled onto the floor. 'Let's use this money. I've been saving up for something exciting and this sounds perfect.'

'I'll get mine too.' Chloe was back minutes later with her savings, kept in a little pink purse covered in red hearts. That had been a present from Holly too, also bought in a charity shop.

Holly didn't have the heart to tell her sisters that all their money, even added to Holly's own small savings from her job in a city-centre bakery, wouldn't pay for lunch in a motel, let alone a night or two. But they were so happy she didn't have the heart to stop the fun yet.

'Great,' she said brightly. 'But we'll use my money for the boring things like motel rooms and food, and your money for ice-creams and chips only, okay?' They both clambered back up beside her, their little bodies pressed on either side. 'Now, what are your ages again? I've forgotten.'

'Six!' Belle said.

'Eight!' said Chloe.

'Which equals fourteen. Right, then. Let's choose the four-teenth motel on this list. You both count for me.' Down they went, bypassing motels in Queensland, Tasmania, Melbourne, Mildura, down, down until they reached number fourteen. Holly nearly laughed. Some adventure. They'd chosen a motel less than two hours' drive away. Still, she'd go along with it.

'The Valley View Motel,' Belle read aloud. 'Click on it, Holly.'

'Click on it, Holly,' Chloe echoed.

Up came the motel website. 'There's a pool!' Belle said. There was, only a small one, but it looked blue and inviting. The photos of the interior showed a brightly lit function room and a cheerful dining room.

'What would we have for our Christmas lunch?' Belle asked. Belle was very interested in food. She'd told Holly that when she grew up she was going to open a chain of bakeries called Belle's Buns. Holly had found it hard not to smile.

Holly clicked on the sample menu and read it aloud.

'Yum,' Belle said, sighing at every description.

'I hate prawns,' Chloe said, looking worried.

'I'm sure you could have something else. Vegemite on toast, maybe?'

'On Christmas Day? No way!'

'That's a poem,' Belle said. 'On Christmas Day, no way, hooray!'

The two girls laughed. Chloe pointed to the screen. 'Is that where you book? Go on, Holly, please.'

Holly couldn't stop their fun yet. She scanned the website. There was a Christmas special on offer, three nights' accommodation and a Christmas lunch. She'd send off an email and then later tell the girls that she was sorry, the motel was so good it was already booked out, but they'd have a pretend motel themselves here on Christmas Day. She'd set it all up herself, with a little counter for them to check in at. She'd make up their twin beds to look identical like they would in a motel. She'd even pretend to be their waitress and cleaner if she had to . . .

She filled out the online form. 'They'll probably give us a family room,' she said, now wishing it was all for real. 'With a big TV. And a big bed for me and tiny beds in cardboard boxes for you two.'

'I'm not sleeping in a cardboard box,' Belle said. 'Chloe and I are going to sleep in the big bed with you.'

'Maybe Mum and Dad can sleep in the cardboard boxes,' Chloe said. 'But only if they've stopped fighting and we've told them they're allowed to come. It's a secret till then, anyway, isn't it, Holly?'

'It sure is,' Holly said. 'Now, who'll press send?'

Both girls did, their fingers on the mouse together.

'Right,' Holly said, standing up. Her sisters slid off the seat beside her. 'Enough computer for today. Homework time.'

Holly was in her bedroom helping Belle with her reading ten minutes later when Chloe came running in. The fighting had stopped in the living room. Now there was just something that felt like a cloud of hostility and anger in the house, like a fog leaking into corners. Holly smiled at the funny expression on her little sister's face. Her cheeks were red, her eyes were wide and yet her mouth was clamped tight. 'What's up, Chloe?'

She said something but with her hand over her mouth.

'Chloe? What is it? Good or bad?'

'Something on the computer,' Chloe said, in a whisper. 'Holly, hurry. Come and look.'

Holly followed her, puzzled, with Belle close behind.

Chloe had already opened the email that had come in. The message was up on the screen. The subject line was CONGRATULATIONS!

Chapter Three

In Hong Kong, the temperature outside the high-rise building was a warm twenty-two degrees. Inside the luxury apartment on the twentieth floor the air was cool and the mood frosty. For the fifth time, Glenn knocked on his twelve-year-old daughter's bedroom door.

'Ellen, please. I'm begging you.'

Silence.

'Just say hello. A quick hello.'

Silence.

'She's dying to meet you again.' He winced even as he said the word dying. The wrong choice. So very much the wrong choice. 'Please, darling. Talk to me.'

Ellen didn't actually need to tell him how she was feeling and why she wouldn't come out of her room. For the past six weeks she'd taken every opportunity she could to tell him how she felt about his new girlfriend and how she felt about his new girlfriend's daughter. 'I don't care that you think you love her. I don't care that her daughter is the same age as me. I don't care if you think she's been lonely too. I don't want to meet her again, or meet her stupid lonely daughter, and if you cared about me, you wouldn't be going out with her either.' That conversation had ended with a slammed door. Another day of silence.

He'd seen a counsellor. Tried to explain the situation as succinctly as possible. 'My wife – Ellen's mother – died almost five years ago. I thought Ellen and I had a good relationship. I'd seen other women in that time, Ellen knew that, but when I met Denise, it was different. I followed all the guidelines, didn't bring her home to meet Ellen until I knew it was serious between us.'

'And what happened at that first meeting?'

It had started well enough. Until Ellen noticed how affectionate Glenn and Denise were. She stood beside the photo of Anna that was centre stage in the living room.

'I don't need a new mother,' she said to Denise, ignoring Glenn.

Denise had glanced across at Glenn before smiling a little nervously. 'I don't want to be your mother.'

'Good. I don't want you living with us either.'

'She's still sad, still grieving,' the counsellor said. 'You just have to be patient.'

Glenn had been as patient as he could. Loving. Understanding. But he'd also been lonely. Ready to meet someone new. He'd tried everything he could to ease the way with Ellen, to talk about his dates as friends, to mention casually if he was going out to dinner. She seemed fine if it was casual, if he saw anyone once or twice. But the change was immediate if he even hinted that it was more than that.

'You've forgotten about Mum already? You told me she meant everything to you. If you lied about that, how do I know you won't lie to me about everything else?'

Was it just that she was nearing her teenage years? Would that account for the transformation from his sweet little Ellen into this outspoken, sometimes downright rude brat? Time and time again he was tempted to shout back at her. Slam doors as loudly as her, too. He'd been forced to seek advice from female colleagues who were also the parents of teenage girls. 'Don't rise to her bait. You have to stay the adult in the relationship.' Easier said than done. He'd even joined some online forums for single parents, but retreated quickly when they seemed to be thinly disguised dating sites. Finally, he'd resorted to asking his elderly mother for advice. Calling her in her luxury retirement home in Queensland (paid for by him) she'd been blunt, as always. 'Chart a steady course and always tell her the truth. Teenagers can sniff out a liar a mile off. What trouble you save yourself now will only come back tenfold to haunt you.'

Tell Ellen the truth? How could he, when he'd been lying to her since Anna died? He was already having enough trouble with his daughter. If he told the entire truth, who knew what monster he might unleash? Because what Ellen didn't know, and perhaps never should or could know, was that he and Anna had been having serious marriage problems before she died. Not just usual day-to-day issues. They had been on the verge of separation, moving swiftly towards divorce.

It had been going wrong between them for years. Perhaps

both of them had been too busy, Anna with her voice-over career, Glenn with his rising status in the advertising world. Perhaps they hadn't paid each other enough attention, their daughter giving them enough conversation topics to paper over the cracks. But then Ellen had been badly hurt, bitten by a dog while playing in a nearby park. Anna had been with her, her attention diverted as she took a phone call. It had happened in an instant, a jagged gash on Ellen's cheek, screams, shouts, blood, a rushed trip to hospital. The subtle tension between Glenn and Anna erupted immediately into full warfare. It was Anna's fault for being distracted. It was Glenn's fault – he was never home and when had he ever taken Ellen anywhere? The atmosphere between them had turned to ice. The bad scar on Ellen's cheek was a constant reminder, not just of the incident, but of the gulf between them. As home life became tense, he'd spent more time at work. He found himself drawn towards a colleague, and with an ease and swiftness that surprised him, he'd started an affair. He wasn't proud of his behaviour, but it seemed to him that Anna didn't care what he did any more. Ellen had still been their only talking point, but the blaming and guilt loomed beyond any polite surface words. Separation and divorce seemed the only possible outcome.

He could still remember how he'd felt the day Anna phoned him with the news of her cancer diagnosis. She had been in South Australia, at the family motel. She'd been there for weeks by that stage. Officially, it was to give Ellen a break from difficulties at school. The other children had been teasing her about her scar. Unofficially, they had both known it was a trial separation. Their personal animosity had been pushed aside in that instant. He had done all he could to make her final weeks peaceful and to make life as calm for Ellen as possible. He'd been truly devastated when Anna died, grieving their broken marriage as much as her passing. But as time went by, his feelings slowly changed. He saw the situation more clearly. Their marriage had been coming to its end. He knew Anna had found love elsewhere too, with a man she'd met while staying at the motel. If she hadn't become sick, if she hadn't died, what would have happened to their marriage? Would they have still been together now? He seriously doubted it. They'd learned too many ways to hurt each other. It was difficult to admit, but it was the truth.

But not a truth he could share with his daughter. Not now, perhaps not ever. What was the point? Ellen was only twelve years old. She'd already experienced more pain than any child should. He couldn't expect her to understand the complexities and intricacies of her parents' marriage.

Yes, when he was alone, he could reason it all out easily. It was only now, when he found himself shouting into a slammed door, his blood pressure rising, his fists clenched – in frustration rather than anger – that it was hard to stay calm. He counted to ten. He tried to keep his voice low and measured.

'Ellen, please. Think about it. I'd like us both to have Christmas with Denise and Lily. It would be fun. I know it.'

'Go ahead and have fun. But I'm not coming.'

'I can't leave you here on your own.'

'I don't care if you do.'

'Right. Sure. As if I would leave a twelve-year-old girl on her own on Christmas Day.'

'It's obvious you don't care about me, so you may as well.'

'Fine, then. I'll do exactly that. Leave you here for the day alone. And what will you do? Stay locked away in your room? Starve?' He winced again. Why was he choosing all the wrong words today? For two days last month, after another fight about Denise, Ellen had stopped eating. Worried she was on the verge of an eating disorder, he'd been about to coax her to the doctor when she'd started eating normally again.

She was silent for so long now he thought for a moment she'd moved away from the door, climbed into bed perhaps. About to walk away himself, he heard a smaller, softer voice, muffled but still audible.

'I want my mum.'

All his anger fled. His shoulders slumped, his hands unclenched, he leaned his head against the door. 'I know you do, sweetheart. I know.' He could hear her sobbing begin. 'Ellen, open the door please. Come out here and talk to me. Let me give you a hug. Denise and Lily will be here any minute —' The wrong thing again.

The sobbing stopped. 'I don't care, I told you. I don't want to meet them again and I don't want to spend Christmas with them. Ever!'

His temper flowed back, patience and understanding instantly wiped away. 'Fine. Fine, Ellen. You've made yourself perfectly clear. You've made your bed, and now you can lie in it. Neither of us will have Christmas with Denise and her family. You win. We'll stay here and we'll have a horrible lonely time and I hope that will make you happy, because nothing else seems to!'

His shout was met with silence. He felt a rush of fury combined with self-loathing. Oh, yes, he was really being the adult in this relationship. He placed his hand on the door, took a deep breath, spoke again, in quieter, calmer tones. 'Ellen, I'm sick of this. Day after day, all this fighting. But I can't do it any more tonight. Stay in there, Ellen. Stay in there until you realise just how hurtful and selfish you're being —' he hesitated for just a moment, 'and how much your mother would hate to see it. Think about that.'

He heard her gasp, followed immediately by more sobbing. He'd gone too far. He ran his fingers through his hair. 'Ellen?' No answer. 'Ellen?' Nothing. 'I'm sorry. I'm sorry for saying that. But —' He ran out of words then, too. Holding his hand against the door for one more minute, knowing there was no sense knocking again, no sense trying to talk reason to her, even less chance of stopping her crying, he had no option but to walk away, to go and sit in the living room and stare out across the skyline.

Denise was due any moment. He'd promised her everything was going to be all right with Ellen, that she was just going through a stage. He'd sensed Denise's subtle withdrawal from him recently, perhaps a slight doubt about him, about them, the thought that perhaps it was all too much trouble, more trouble than it was worth. It was then he'd realised how much she meant to him. He didn't want to lose her. He didn't want to upset Ellen. But he was in an impossible situation. It seemed he couldn't please one without upsetting the other. And what a mess he'd made of it all just now.

For God's sake, he thought, standing again and pouring himself a glass of wine from the bottle chilling ready for Denise. He was a businessman. He had a staff of forty working efficiently and profitably for him. He'd managed equally successful offices in Singapore, Kuala Lumpur, Sydney. He was renowned for his quick decision-making, his strong work ethic, for being tough but fair. He had enviable client lists, more work than his agency could handle. Yet he was no match for a twelve-year-old girl, even if she was his adored daughter. What else had his mother said to him in her recent pep talk? *Think of it as a campaign, darling. Step by step, battle by battle, you'll both get to Armistice Day eventually.* If he had just won this latest battle, it was a hollow victory.

The doorbell rang. Finding a smile from somewhere, he walked over, trying to decide how to break the news of this latest setback to Denise.

In her room, Ellen didn't know whether she wanted to stop crying or sob even louder. She didn't know whether to feel good that she'd made her dad lose control like that, made him actually apologise to her, or to feel guilty that she'd upset him so much that he had lost it. She didn't know how she felt about anything any more. It was like a whole mass of feelings was all churning inside of her, out of her control, like a volcano inside her body that erupted again and again, without warning. Always at her father. She picked up the photo – a copy of the one in the living room – and put it on her bedspread, stroking the glass softly. Her mother smiled up at her. She was smiling in all the photos Ellen had of her around the apartment. Ellen only wanted to remember her mother as being happy. Sometimes, in the middle of the night, she would remember other things about her too. The games they played. The stories Anna read her. And then, no matter how much Ellen tried to block out the memories, she would remember her mother when she was so sick, in those final weeks. Ellen remembered it all. The whispering, at first. Everyone kept whispering and they would stop talking if they saw Ellen was listening. Then one day she was taken to her and Lola's favourite spot at the motel, the bench that looked over the vine-covered hill, and her dad and her auntie Bett told her everything. That her mother was very sick and that she wasn't going to be better and the time they had now was very precious and special.

Ellen wasn't sure any more if she remembered the actual funeral or all the times she had replayed it in her mind, adding little details here and there. For the first two years after Anna died, Ellen and her dad had gone back to the Clare Valley on the anniversary of her death. But not the third year. Ellen had been sick with tonsillitis and they'd agreed it was best to stay home in Singapore. On the fourth anniversary, they'd been in the middle of their move to Hong Kong, for her dad's job. There had been many conversations between Lola and Glenn, and as many conversations between Ellen and Lola.

'Do you think about your mum every day, darling?' Lola had asked.

'Of course,' Ellen answered.

'Where?'

'Wherever I am. At school, at home, in the park.'

'You see, darling. Your thoughts happen inside you, no matter what's outside you. Perhaps it's time for you to start your own special ceremony for Anna, wherever you are at the time, rather than thinking it can only happen here, at her grave, or at the motel where she died.'

Ellen liked that her great-grandmother wasn't scared to use words like 'grave' and 'died'. Too many people used strange words with her when they heard that her mother was dead. Passed away. Gone to heaven. In God's arms. Final resting place. Lola had also gently explained that, in her opinion, Anna was far, far away from the Clare Valley now, in any case. Part of the sky, the stars, the moon, even. 'That's the wonderful thing, Ellen. Your mum can be wherever you want her to be, because she's wherever you are, in your thoughts.'

That fourth year Ellen and her dad made their own ceremony in Hong Kong, high up in the hotel they'd been staying in until their apartment was ready, looking out over Victoria Harbour. There were skyscrapers all around them, a bustle of ferries, freighters and little boats in the water far below, so many at once it always amazed Ellen that they didn't keep crashing into each other. They sat at a table right by the window, so high that Ellen felt a bit sick looking down. Her dad ordered two elaborate cocktails for them both, his with champagne, Anna's favourite drink, and Ellen's with three different fruit juices, four curly straws, umbrellas and enough fruit that it was more a fruit salad than a cocktail. They made a toast, to Anna and to each other and to everyone back home in Australia, and then her dad let her ring the motel on his mobile phone.

The whole family was there. She'd talked to Lola and her grandpa and grandma and her two aunties, Carrie and Bett. They all cried and laughed, the way they did whenever they spoke about Anna. Ellen talked to her little cousins too – well, she hadn't talked to Bett's twins exactly, as they weren't born yet, but she insisted Bett hold the receiver against her stomach and she'd shouted down the phone to them.

Six months after that, she and her dad flew to Adelaide and drove up to the Valley to see everyone, and to meet Zachary and Yvette. All her memories rushed back at her again that day too, seeing Lola, the motel, her grandparents. She didn't want to leave. But Lola took her to their bench and talked to her in that lovely way she did, saying that even if Ellen was on the other side of the world, it didn't matter because they all thought about each other all the time, many times every day, even sometimes in the night, and all those thought-waves shot across the sky. They didn't even need phone lines or satellites or submarine cables. They were magic, and any time Ellen felt an itch, or she sneezed, or hiccupped, or her eye twitched, it was because at that exact moment, all the way across the seas and the countries, Lola or Bett or Carrie, or all three of them, were thinking about her. Ellen was old enough to know Lola was joking, but still, back home in Hong Kong, it was like a little secret any time she did sneeze or hiccup . . . Maybe there was some truth in it.

There was a knock at the door.

Her father again. 'Ellen, Denise is here. With her daughter.'

All her guilt flew out the window immediately. 'I don't care! Go away!'

'Ellen, please. I'm sorry. Please.'

'No!'

She could imagine how horrified Lola would be if she heard Ellen talking to her father like that, but right now, she didn't care. It was how she felt. Angry and sad and lonely and everything, all mixed up together. And homesick, a feeling like being homesick, for her mum. And for Lola. And for all her family, there, thousands of kilometres away while she was stuck here, stuck in Hong Kong with her dad being evil and some hideous, horrible witch. Not just a witch, a *bitch* of a woman out there with her fake smiles and fake nails and everything else fake about her trying to push her way into their lives. Well, it wasn't going to work. Not if Ellen had anything to do with it. She would never, ever, ever be nice to Denise. She'd already had one mother, the best, kindest mother in the world, and she didn't need another one.

She put the pillow over her head to try to block out the sound of her father's voice. After a minute, he went away. She closed her eyes tight and tried to do what Lola had suggested – fill her head with only good thoughts and good memories. Trying not to cry, trying to ignore the murmur of voices from the living room that she could hear despite the pillow, she did everything she could to think of only good things – Lola, her auntie Bett, the funny twins, Carrie and her noisy, happy family. It didn't help. It just made her wish even more that she was there with them, having fun, laughing and joking and feeling safe and happy and loved. All the things she didn't feel now.

CHAPTER FOUR

At home in her renovated farmhouse south of Clare, Carrie was wishing she had never met Matthew, never married him and definitely never had three children with him.

'Delia, stop hitting your sister. Freya, turn that TV down, George is asleep. And, Delia, put your toys away please. I've asked you five times already.'

'Four.'

'What?'

'Pardon, not what. Four times. You've asked me four times, not five.'

'And I'll ask you fifty times if I have to. Go. Now. Do it.'

'Why are you always so cross?'

'Why are you always so naughty?'

'We're kids. Kids get naughty.'

Carrie did her best not to scream. Where was Matthew? Off at work, allegedly. How convenient that he always had a lot of work to do whenever she happened to mention that the house had to be cleaned, or the garden needed weeding. Or, like today, when she'd sighed and said she wasn't sure how on earth she was going to finish making all the relishes and chutneys she'd promised for the school street stall on the weekend, as well as plan for their Christmas trip to visit *his* family.

'You'll manage, Carrie. You're great at that stuff.'

His compliments had long lost their lustre. At first, she'd fallen for them. 'What's the point in me cooking dinner?' he'd say. 'It's never as nice as your cooking.' 'How come I can never get my shirts as white as you can?' She'd enjoyed the praise until she realised it was a way of him wriggling out of ever doing his share. She'd had to force him to cook dinner even occasionally, and force herself not to complain when it was invariably barbecued sausages and oven-baked chips. And why did he have to make such a song and dance of it any time he did do some housework? 'I've emptied the bin. Look, Carrie.' 'I've just swept the verandah.' 'The grass looks great now I've mowed it, doesn't it?' What did he want, a medal? She did all of that and more every day but she didn't present him with a printed list of completed chores every night when he walked through the door, did she?

He seemed to take great delight in stirring up the children, too, coming in most nights from work around seven, just as she'd got them fed and bathed and about to settle into quiet pre-bedtime activities. She'd asked him time and time again to keep his voice down, not to start tickling little George or playing chasey with Delia and Freya. 'Not play with my kids at the end of a long day? They love playing with me, don't you, kids?' Of course they agreed with him, and of course they hung off him, squealing with fake terror at his wild piggy-backing, shrieking with pretend-fright when he found them during games of hide and seek, dragging him by the hand to show him this or that. 'Watch me, Daddy!', 'Look at me, Daddy!' Carrie knew she should have stood by smiling, enjoying the sight of father–children bonding, been glad that she had a husband who took such pleasure in his children. So why did she feel only a burning combination of jealousy and resentment? Because as soon as Matthew came in, the children couldn't care less about her. She became their maid, their cook, their cleaner, relegated to second-hand citizen.

She loved them still, of course she did. Always. Hugely. She loved Matthew. Of course she did. Didn't she? But sometimes . . . More than sometimes, more often than not lately, she wished she could spray them all with some sort of immobilising potion, not just the children, but Matthew too, just for a day or two, to give her some breathing space. In her day, in her life, in her head. It was the constancy of it all that was killing her. The relentlessness of it all. The feeling of never finishing anything properly. Of being a mouse on a wheel, except the wheel was a conveyor belt of housework, children's demands, children's arguments and tears and squabbles. She couldn't even have a shower without one of them either coming into the bathroom to ask her something, or standing outside knocking until she was forced to turn the water off. 'Mum?' 'Mum?' Their voices were an endless soundtrack in her head. Delia had wanted to get a cat, and Carrie had shocked her and herself by her vehement '*No!*'

One more voice in the house, asking, begging, pleading for attention and food? At least the cat would have washed itself. Perhaps she should have turned into a cat-lover rather than a mother. But knowing her luck, she'd have ended up with a house full of cats, and turned into a mad old lady smelling of . . .

'Mum, Freya bit me!'

'So bite her back,' she said to Delia. The mobile phone rang in her handbag. Someone else wanting something from her? She had nothing else to give. She let it ring out. When it rang again a few minutes later, she let it go unanswered then as well.

In her small cottage on the northern edge of Clare, Bett put down the phone, cursing under her breath. Where could Carrie be? She had just one last-minute favour to ask her younger sister, something she'd never done. Right now, though, she had no choice. The friend she'd lined up a week ago to be her babysitter this afternoon had just rung, full of apologies, to say her elderly mother had twisted her ankle and needed to go to hospital. 'Of course I understand,' Bett had said, also assuring her she'd easily find a replacement.

Who, though? Carrie was the obvious choice. Not that Bett could tell her why she needed a babysitter. As she tried her sister's number again, she decided to say she had a medical appointment. There was still no answer.

'Damn,' she said, loud enough to get the attention of Yvette, wide-eyed and alert as ever, in her bouncer on the floor beside her. Next to her, in his chair, Zach was on the verge of sleep, his eyes fluttering. 'Sorry, sweethearts,' she whispered. 'Mummy's not cross, I promise.'

Tiptoeing out of the room with the phone, she dialled another number. Jane, her nearest neighbour. Bett could probably have shouted across the dry yellow paddock that separated their properties, the sound carried so well on hot days like today. As Jane answered, Bett sent up a prayer of thanks. Her neighbour was a stay-at-home mother too, but unlike Bett, she was rarely at home, filling her and her daughter's days with a constant schedule of playgroups and outings around the Valley.

'Of course I can mind the twins,' she said, even before Bett had finished asking. 'See you soon.'

It was all Bett could do not to throw her arms around Jane and kiss her when she arrived, smiling, her equally smiley three-year-old daughter, Lexie, beside her. Bett signed a hello and got a hello back, a quick movement of her little fingers. Lexie made another sign and Bett looked to Jane for a translation.

'She wants to know how you are.'

Bett gave her a thumbs up and got a thumbs up and big smile from Lexie in return.

'Thanks so much, Jane,' Bett called from her bedroom a moment later, trying to zip up the one good summer dress she'd found on the rail. 'The twins are due a sleep, but when —'

Jane interrupted her. 'When they wake up, would I look after them and perhaps feed them and change them if they need changing?' She laughed. 'Bett, I know what babysitting means. Go. You look like you'll burst a gasket if you don't get out of here now.'

Bett did kiss her that time. Five minutes later, having pulled a brush through her short, dark-brown curls, cursed her size sixteen figure, wished she had her sister's petite blonde looks, found a lipstick that had something left in the tube – too red for this time of day, let alone for a sleep-deprived thirty-six-year-old, but beggars couldn't be choosers – and changed her clothes after discovering a splodge of unidentified something on the left shoulder of her first dress, she was on her way into town, driving too fast.

She made herself slow down. It was difficult. She'd got into the habit of doing everything too fast these days. Dressing, showering, sleeping – they all seemed to happen in record time. Conversely, things she did wish could be over in an instant – crying sessions, sleepless nights with two unsettled babies – seemed never-ending. She couldn't understand it. Time felt as if it had taken on a different shape in the seven months since the twins had arrived.

She thought of Jane, so happy, so relaxed, taking in her stride the fact that her daughter had been born deaf. She and her husband had just got on with it once the diagnosis was made, both of them learning how to sign, teaching Lexie as soon as she was old enough. Bett had never once heard Jane complain, or express anxiety about how life might be for Lexie. And here Bett was with two healthy babies, doing nothing but stress and worry. She should be grateful, shouldn't she? Happy every moment of every day? And yet . . .

Even keeping to the speed limit, she managed to arrive into the main street of Clare fifteen minutes early for her appointment.

She found a parking space and sat for a moment to collect her thoughts.

She'd set up today's meeting a week before. It was with the editor of the *Valley Times*, the newspaper she'd worked at for more than four years, right up until she'd left for maternity leave eight months previously. Officially, she was supposed to be on leave for another five months. Unofficially, she was beginning to worry for her sanity. Seriously worry.

She hadn't talked about it with Daniel yet. When did they get the chance to talk about anything much, apart from the twins? It wasn't that she regretted having them, not for a second. She didn't. They'd talked about starting a family from the earliest days of their marriage, and had been overjoyed when she finally fell pregnant. Her pregnancy hadn't been easy, bad morning sickness combined with day-long tiredness. But then to learn that she was having twins! It seemed like the most wonderful present anybody could ever get.

And it was. It *was*. She loved her babies so much, with a fierceness that surprised her. She'd done everything she could for them. Breastfed even when it seemed so painful and strange. Stayed up all night if she had to. Slept for only an hour here and there for weeks on end. She hadn't brushed her hair or changed out of pyjamas for the first few months. It had all been worth it, to be with the two of them, to see Daniel with them, to be able to think 'we're a family'. It felt magical, amazing, special. Precious.

She'd also loved being at home initially, being a full-time

mother, with no office politics or deadlines, the world simplified to the day-to-day, hour-to-hour practicalities of caring for two small babies that she adored. That euphoria had lasted for the first three months, even if it had taken the occasional buffeting from a kind of exhaustion she'd never thought she'd feel. Until, recently, something had started to change. When she looked at her son and daughter, the overwhelming love was still there, but underneath it was a new, different but equally strong sensation. It felt like claustrophobia. As if the walls were closing in on her. It wasn't only unsettling. It was becoming frightening.

Something had changed with Daniel, too. She'd started to feel something other than rushes of love when she looked at him. To feel jealousy instead. But how could that be? She loved her husband, didn't she? His kindness. His humour. His lanky body, his kind eyes, his dark shaggy hair. How amazed he looked, every time he held his son or daughter. How happy he was.

That was it. She was jealous of how happy he was. It's all right for *you*, she kept hearing a voice say at the back of her mind. It *was* all right for Daniel. She'd never seen him so content. He loved his new job, as photo editor and production manager on a rural newspaper based in Gawler, less than an hour's drive from their house. Off he went every morning, transparently happy to have that time in the car on his own, listening to music, or the news, or just silence. Back home, she was buried alive in nappies, in mess, in dirty clothes, dirty dishes, sterilisers, bibs, noise and chaos. She still wasn't sleeping properly. She was eating badly and too much, putting on weight, not losing it. It'll get better, won't it? she kept asking herself. Once the babies were a bit older? Less helpless? Less dependent?

But what if it didn't? What if the older they got, the bigger they got, the hungrier they got, the more of her they needed? What if this was all that her life would ever be from this moment on? What if this was the truth of motherhood, the feeling that she was slowly drowning, slowly losing herself, slowly shedding any independence, leaving her old, free, happy life behind her, tangled on the ground, like a snake and its skin?

Night after night, it was all she could think about. It was as if she could see her life in split-screen – how it should be and how it was. In the 'should be' section was a happy, smiling Bett, loving wife, mother of two adorable babies, content with all the riches in her life, organised, cooking nutritious meals, exercising daily and yes, having regular, terrific sex. In the 'how it is' section . . . she didn't even have to imagine it. That's how it was. Chaos, exhaustion and about as much sex as she was having exercise. None.

A week earlier, a solution had come to her in a middle-of-the-night flash of insight. All she had to do to fix things was return to work part-time. Just for a couple of days a week. One day. A couple of hours a week even. Just enough to get a bit of her old life back, regain some control. She hadn't discussed it with Daniel yet. But in her daydreams, he'd agreed immediately. He thought it was a wonderful idea. He wished he'd thought of it first. He'd go part-time too, so they could take turns caring for the babies. It was the perfect solution all round, he'd tell her.

It wasn't just Daniel's reaction she imagined, either. She pictured telling her sister Carrie too.

'It's fantastic, Carrie,' she'd say. 'I've got the work–life balance I've always really wanted. When I'm with the twins, I'm really with them one hundred per cent, but my time at work gives me the independence and space I need too. It's the best of both worlds.' It didn't seem to matter that Bett didn't speak in glib soundbites like that in real life. Then she would ask Carrie the big question. 'And you're happy being a stay-at-home mum? Great! Good for you! If that fulfils you, that's great, really. It comes down to personal choice, doesn't it?'

There was always a whole range of imaginary reactions from Carrie. The tearful one: 'I'm so jealous of you, Bett. How have you managed to get everything sorted out so well?' Angry: 'Not everyone has a husband as supportive as Daniel, Bett. You don't have to rub it in.' In one daydream, Carrie even stormed out, leaving Bett to explain to imaginary onlookers. 'Sorry, she's finding motherhood a bit tricky.'

Bett sighed deeply, hating herself for even thinking this way. When had she turned into this person? This tired, bitter, competitive creature? She'd hoped living close to Carrie again and having children at the same time would bring the two of them together. Instead, it had become a whole new battleground. A point-scoring battleground.

Why was she surprised? It had always been that way between them – even as children, Carrie had been the confident one, Bett more anxious, Carrie free with her opinions and advice,

Bett uncertain. The tensions had built between them over the years, coming to a head seven years before, in a domino fall of events – Bett's fiancé Matthew falling in love with Carrie at first sight, their engagement breaking up, sparking a feud between the three sisters that had lasted more than three years. Now, it seemed almost silly. She'd been fooling herself that she had ever been in love with Matthew. She knew what she now had with Daniel was the real thing. But at the time, it had seemed like the biggest betrayal in the world, with both her sisters taking sides against her. They hadn't spoken for three years. Three whole years. If it hadn't been for Lola forcing them back together, giving the three of them precious time together before Anna fell ill, it could have been much worse . . .

But had she and Carrie learned nothing from Anna's death? Hadn't they promised in the days, weeks and months afterwards to never let anything come between them again, to cherish each day, to keep reminding themselves how fragile life was, how important family was?

Those promises had faded into memory. Worst of all, Bett knew in her heart that she was the loser. She was the Bad Mother and Carrie was the Perfect Mother. If only Carrie would ring now and again to say she was at the end of her tether, that her three kids were driving her crazy, that she was tired, that she and Matthew hadn't talked about anything but bottles and nappies for weeks, let alone kissed, let alone the rest of it. But that wasn't Carrie's life. All she ever told Bett was how perfect things were at home.

Bett and Daniel had started fighting about Carrie lately too.

They'd had a row about her as recently as this week. She'd been telling him what Carrie had told her, that she and Matthew had hired someone to do her 'big wash' once a week – the sheets, towels and baby clothes. How much time it saved.

'That's wonderful for Carrie and Matthew,' Daniel had said, in the mild tone she should have registered as a warning sign. 'Perhaps when we have as much money as Carrie and Matthew we can hire a staff of helpers too. I'm working all the hours I can, Bett, but it's a small paper and unfortunately it just doesn't pay as much as a state-wide vet business. Perhaps you should have married Matthew after all.'

She'd been too shocked to answer. In the five years they'd been together, Daniel had never referred to her past history with Matthew. She'd wanted to go to their bedroom and burst into tears, but then Yvette had woken and started crying and Zachary had followed suit. She and Daniel had taken a baby each and the conversation they might have had, the apology she might have made, the make-up sex they might have enjoyed didn't happen. But the words, the accusations, were still in the house, festering. One more middle-of-the-night worry. Her marriage was in serious trouble.

It was another reason to get out of the house and go back to work. Wouldn't that give her something more to talk to Daniel about? Turn her, even in a small way, back into the Bett he'd fallen in love with and married? Because she knew she wasn't that person any more. She'd completely understand if he did want to leave her. She hated herself at the moment too.

Another piece of helpful advice from Carrie flashed into her mind. 'Make sure to have some you-time with Daniel, won't you?' she'd said. She'd given Bett a head-to-toe look. 'Even if you just change into something nice before he comes home each night, it'll give you a lift too. I know it sounds all 1950s and *Stepford Wives*-ish,' she'd given that trilling laugh that set Bett's teeth on edge, 'but really, it works. If you pretend you're happy and in control, sometimes it will really feel as though you are.'

If I pretend I'm driving an axe into your head, will it feel as if I really am? Bett had thought.

Stop it! she told herself now. Forget Carrie. Forget Daniel, even. The twins are safe with Jane. You've got the afternoon to yourself. Use it. Live in the moment, or whatever that saying was. Easier said than done. She took three deep breaths and told herself exactly where she was. In her car, in the main street of Clare, on a stinking hot day, wearing entirely the wrong clothes but at least they were clean, just ten minutes away from the meeting with her editor. Step One of her Save My Life plan.

It was far too hot and she was far too edgy to sit quietly in the car and compose herself, though she knew that was exactly what she should do. What she really needed was a dose of her grandmother. A good, soul-clearing, stress-relieving rant to Lola about Carrie in the first instance, and possibly even about Daniel too, if there was time. Starting the car again, she drove fifty metres down the street, easily finding a parking spot. She just hoped today was one of Lola's days in the charity shop.

It was. Through the front window she could see the tall, erect figure of her white-haired grandmother standing behind the counter arranging a tray of jewellery. Thank God. Bett walked inside to the cool relief of the airconditioning and started talking even before the door shut behind her. 'Carrie's at it again, Lola. I swear, if she gives me one more bit of advice, I'll —'

'Do what, darling?' Lola said with a welcoming smile. 'And please speak clearly. I'd like my customers to hear too.'

Bett looked around. There were two people browsing in the corner of the shop, both now obviously listening. Bett blushed and came up to the counter, mouthing a 'Sorry' before leaning across and kissing her grandmother's powdery cheek. 'Hello, Lola,' she said, more quietly. 'Sorry again, Lola.'

'Hello, Bett. Forgiven, Bett,' Lola whispered back. 'But what will you do to Carrie? I'm dying to hear now.'

'I don't know,' she said, whispering too. 'Stuff Zachary and Yvette's nappies down her —' She stopped there. 'Except she'd take the opportunity to tell me that her talented trio were out of nappies in record time.' Bett sighed deeply, pushing her fingers through her curls. 'How does Carrie do it, Lola? How does she manage to infuriate me so easily? Sometimes she doesn't even have to speak, just a look does it.'

'Years of practice? Bett, if you and Carrie weren't fighting about child-rearing, you'd be fighting about something else. You've been like that all your lives. Why you thought both of you having children would bring you closer together, I don't know. Face facts, darling. She's going to keep giving you advice you don't want to hear, and you're probably driving her crazy as well. That's just the way it will always be. You need to get over it.'

Bett blinked. 'Get over it?'

'That's right. Offer it up. Stop complaining. And more importantly, stop annoying me in the middle of my working day.'

Bett started to smile. 'It's that consoling nature of yours that I love so much.'

Lola winked. 'And it's everything about you that I love so much. Except when you start having middle-of-the-day pity parties like today. What have you really got to be unhappy about? Hasn't the worst thing happened to us already? Didn't we all promise after Anna died to be happy and grateful for everything we had? Or did I dream that?'

'You didn't dream it.' Bett was shocked to feel a sudden welling of tears. It only ever took a mention of her sister to feel the rush of grief again. 'Anna wouldn't have been like Carrie, would she, Lola? Wouldn't have rung me up to tell me how much better a mother she was than I'll ever manage to be?'

'Yes, probably. Or she'd have said you're making too much of a fuss, you've had twins not sextuplets. And you'd complain to me about her as well. You know I'm right, so take that outraged expression off your face. What are you doing in town anyway? Have you left the twins at home alone? That's it. I'm having you arrested for abandonment.' Lola frowned. 'You haven't, Bett, have you? Or left them in the car? It's forty degrees out there.'

'Of course not. They're home, safe, with my neighbour. I've got an appointment.' Bett wasn't ready to confide all in Lola either yet. 'A doctor's thing, I mean. A check-up thing.'

'At what time?'

'Three.'

'In which case you'd better go or you'll be late. As I will be if you don't get out of my sight. You're not the only one with an appointment today.' Lola checked her watch. 'Starting in five minutes, in fact. And I'm not completely prepared so I need you to leave so I can have a moment to collect myself.'

'You're eighty-four years old. Who could you have an appointment with?'

Lola raised a well-defined eyebrow. 'My undertaker? Don't look so shocked. I know that's what you're thinking. It's a charity shop committee meeting, as it happens.'

'I'd like to be a fly on the wall for that.'

'No, you wouldn't. Believe me. It's vicious.' She touched her granddaughter on the cheek. 'Go, darling. And please, cheer up. Be grateful for what you have. And try not to hate your sister too much. Use your energy for something more fun.'

Outside in the heat again, Bett felt so much better she decided to walk to her meeting. Lola was right. She had been having a pity party. And she'd been overreacting about Carrie too. She was just a bit tired. A lot tired. All right, completely tired. Perhaps the real problem was she just wasn't seeing enough of the outside world. Look how much even a brief conversation with Lola had cheered her up. She was being unfair to Daniel too, going behind his back and making meetings about possible part-time work. It wasn't what they'd decided as a couple, as parents. Of course she couldn't expect him to go part-time and share the childcare. And they certainly couldn't afford a crèche or a nanny. And that wasn't what they wanted, either. No, she had to live with things as they were. It wasn't fair to ring Jane up at the last minute either, when she was busy with her own daughter. She'd cancel the meeting, and go right home now. Back to her babies. The babies she loved. And to the washing. And the ironing. And the cooking. And the cleaning . . .

She started to feel the tight sensation in her chest again.

No, she was right to be having this meeting. She *had* to change something before she went mad. Before one day the worst thing happened, that she got so overwhelmed she made a serious mistake with her babies, had an accident with them, hurt them in some way. Or she started crying and couldn't stop. Or she —

Her mobile phone rang, breaking into her thoughts. How long had she been standing here? Had she been talking to herself, in public, on the main street? Had it come to that?

'Earth calling Quinlan?' It was her editor Rebecca on the phone. Bett looked across the road. Rebecca was standing in front of the *Valley Times* office, smoking a cigarette and waving across. 'Are you going to stand there all day or come and see me? Time's money and I'm short of both.'

Even the sound of her familiar voice, her familiar joking made Bett feel good. *This* she could handle – the banter, the teasing. She knew how to be a journalist, too. She knew how to interview people, write stories, meet deadlines. It was being a mother, even an incompetent mother, that was so difficult.

She practically ran across the road to her friend.

Chapter Five

Back in the shop, Lola wished she had been joking to Bett. But it *was* vicious in the charity shop committee meetings these days. In years gone by, they had been fun. Lately, it was as if there had been a hostile takeover. These things came in cycles, she knew that, people moving into town, getting involved in sudden rushes of community enthusiasm, ruffling feathers and upsetting everyone before moving on to greener charitable pastures. She'd seen people come and go on the committee, some helping, some hindering, and had mostly let it wash around her. Lately, though, her patience had been growing thin. Thinner by the day.

Was that another symptom of old age that nobody mentioned? There was the public face of being old: the wrinkles, the deafness, the fading eyesight. The obsession with health problems and doctor's visits. The sudden close relationship with one's local pharmacist. What Lola was noticing lately, however, was a change in her own personality. It wasn't fear of death looming closer, though heaven knew she didn't want it to come any day soon. It was impatience mixed with exasperation. An urge to act, and act now! Quickly, before it was too late.

She wished sometimes she had friends in Clare who'd known her all her life, who would answer truthfully if she was to ask them whether she had always been this way. Jim had, of course, known her for the longest, for his whole life, literally, but she would never ask him. She didn't need to. She knew he loved her, and he knew she loved him. Theirs was the simplest of relationships. She wouldn't change a bone in his body, and she felt sure he wouldn't change a bone in hers.

Geraldine was another matter. Geraldine would cheerfully have her deboned in the blink of an eye. She knew Geraldine saw her as the mother-in-law from hell, interfering, bossy, meddling, overbearing. A whole thesaurus entry, in fact. And very possibly, just perhaps, some of those words might be accurate descriptions of how things had been in the time they'd known each other. But Lola only ever behaved that way if she genuinely felt she had to, if she saw something drift, or a problem start to form that she could avert through action. Was that being overbearing or being proactive? Proactive, of course. Sensible. Practical. Otherwise what would happen around her? Chaos? Mayhem? Yes, Lola thought. Perhaps that had always been her main personality trait. She was A Fixer.

She had a dim memory of her teachers in Ireland scolding her, using words like incorrigible and unmanageable. And certainly, she and her husband had shared a fiery, if thankfully brief, relationship, before she had left him as quickly as possible, preferring the difficult life of a single mother to the even more difficult life of being shackled to a bully, a weakling and a drunk. But if she hadn't had that desire to change things, to make her life better, to make Jim's life better, the best it could be, then where would she be today? Beaten down? Dead even, from exhaustion and sorrow? She'd had to act, and act now!

Hmm, perhaps this impatience trait wasn't a sudden thing after all, she thought. More memories floated in, backing this new, slightly alarming theory. All right, perhaps it had been a tiny bit annoying for Geraldine sometimes to see her mother-in-law not so much 'fixing' as 'interfering in' some of their family situations. The ridiculous feud between Anna, Bett and Carrie of a few years back, for example. But if it hadn't been for Lola's plotting and plan-hatching, the three girls might never have talked to each other again. How much more of a tragedy would that have been, if Anna had fallen ill while they were still estranged? Not that Geraldine had ever thanked her. Nor had Jim, but he was her son. He didn't need to thank her.

The difference in this personality trait of hers now was the depth and scope of her feeling. Previously, she'd been happy to confine her fix-it-ing to her own family and perhaps one or two close friends. These days, she was feeling an urge to fix the whole town and everyone in it. The state. The country. The world. Was it normal? Was it a rush to get things done before the Grim Reaper came a-reaping?

She'd raised the subject with her friends and fellow charity shop ladies recently. They already had so much in common, and

not just the fact they were all widows. She'd come at it in a cir-
cuitous way, asking whether they felt they had changed at all
mentally as they got older. And not in a forgetful way that might
hint at Alzheimer's or anything similar. Purely from a personality
point of view. A sudden urge to Get Things Done.

Margaret – a grey-haired sixty-seven-year-old – had given it
some thought. No, she'd decided. If anything, she'd become more
relaxed. 'All the hard work's done. I'm coasting down the hill
now,' she'd said. Patricia, a beautifully groomed fifty-seven, had
dismissed the idea immediately too. In her opinion, her personality was now set in stone and she liked it that way. 'I don't like
physically aging, but there's no way I'd go back to all the angst-
ridden thoughts of my thirties or forties. It's a miracle I've got this
far, when I think of all the things that could have happened to me.
I might have been hit by a bus. Or fallen out of a plane. Even got
run over by a train.'

'I hadn't realised you'd been starring in silent movies,' Lola
said.

'You know what I mean. People die in odd accidents every
day. Electrocution by toaster. Drowning in paddling pools. Spider
bites in toilets. I've made it this far. I plan to take it easy to the
end now too. No point tempting fate or putting myself at risk.'

'You don't have the urge to try something new? Use what time
you have to do something, I don't know, spectacular? Important?
Life-changing?'

'Like what? Skydiving?' Patricia laughed. 'Win a poker tour-
nament? Of course. I just do it all online.'

The conversation had immediately turned to their various online activities. Lola was left vaguely dissatisfied. She'd wanted to be told that the way she was feeling was normal. But it seemed she was on her own.

She sighed now. Once upon a time, she might have brought up the subject with Bett. Of her three granddaughters, she'd always been closest to her middle one. But Bett had moved into that chaotic land known as Parenthood, and while Lola knew she would have tried hard, listened as best she could, perhaps even made suggestions, only a percentage of her would have been paying attention.

Lola knew from her own experience with Jim, and then the girls themselves, that one's mind was never truly one's own once children came along. Yes, on the surface, conversations took place, opinions were offered and listened to, but underneath it, at all times, there was a constant soundtrack of maternal worries, organisational lists being made, scenarios being played out. Parenthood was exhaustion mixed with elation, anxiety with contentment. It was why mothers naturally gravitated to other mothers. There was a shorthand language, a mutual understanding.

But if Lola did ask for Bett's opinion, she knew Bett would encourage her. 'I'm sure there's nothing you couldn't do if you set your mind to it, Lola.' The same advice Lola had spent many years giving her three granddaughters, and now, even Ellen and the other great-grandchildren too.

But what was there for people her age to set their minds to? Those who weren't ready to play bowls, or be admitted into old folks' homes? Who didn't only want to reminisce, but also wanted to look forward, to plan, to hope? She ran through a mental roll call of famous people her age who were still active, still filled with energy. Clint Eastwood. The Queen. Rupert Murdoch. Marvellous. All she had to do was direct a few films, become a monarch and run a global media empire and she'd sleep easy at night.

A sudden call from Margaret broke into her thoughts. 'She's here!'

Drat, Lola thought. She'd hoped they might have had a last-minute reprieve, a call to say her car had broken down or her drains needed fixing. Sadly not. 'Coming,' Lola said, with a sigh.

'She' was Mrs Kernaghan. Her first name was believed to be Barbara, but from her first appearance at the charity shop three months earlier, she'd made it clear she wasn't to be treated as 'one of them'. She'd introduced herself as Mrs Kernaghan and Mrs Kernaghan she'd remained at all subsequent fortnightly meetings.

Lola had had her measure from the moment Mrs Kernaghan stepped into the shop. Lola had moved so many times herself over the years that she recognised the key types of new arrivals. The ones seeking a sea change. Those searching for a fresh start in a country town. The city ones making a show of bringing their expertise to their simple country cousins. What people forgot was that the town had got on perfectly well before their arrival and would continue to prosper after they left.

Mrs Kernaghan was clearly a fierce combination of all the

types. She also managed to get under Lola's skin in the first minutes of their meeting. Their committee of five had been sitting around the table in the back of the shop. Patricia was unofficial chairwoman, introducing everyone to the new arrival. Mrs Kernaghan acknowledged each name with a regal nod. When it was Lola's turn, the nod changed into an even more condescending smile, as she made a show of taking in Lola's outfit from head to toe. 'Good heavens,' she said, eyebrows raised. 'Are you on your way to a fancy-dress party?'

Someone – Kay, perhaps – had gasped. Margaret leapt to her defence. 'It's not fancy dress. Lola always dresses up like that.'

She did. That day's outfit hadn't been out of the ordinary by any means, either – pink culottes, silver strappy sandals, an electric-blue tunic topped with a shimmering silver lamé bolero. A flower in her hair. Three strands of coloured glass beads and large plastic daisy clip-on earrings. Lola had always enjoyed dressing the way she did. It cheered her up and she knew it cheered up others too. Amused them as well, she suspected. But she'd never been publicly criticised before.

Mrs Kernaghan's rude remark and mocking expression had instantly reminded Lola of other soul-sapping people she'd met in her life: bullies at school, her husband with his constant drip-drip-drip of low-level insults, government officials when she had been trying to find her feet as a single mother and a business-woman. The sneerers. The pessimists. People throughout her life who'd told her again and again, in many different ways, 'You can't do that', 'That's not how things are done', 'Who do you think you are?' She'd made a point of being polite and then completely ignoring them. That evening, and in subsequent meetings, she tried to do the same thing with Mrs Kernaghan.

It proved difficult, unfortunately. Mrs Kernaghan was soon a regular fixture at the shop, sweeping in unannounced, issuing decrees and then sweeping out again. She prefaced everything with her business, fashion and artistic credentials – for twenty-five years she and her late husband had, among their many other business interests, owned a number of high-end fashion boutiques in leafy, wealthy suburbs of Adelaide and Melbourne, as well as upmarket art galleries in Sydney and on the Sunshine Coast in Queensland. If Lola, and her friends Patricia, Margaret, Joan and Kay, happened to be rostered on during Mrs Kernaghan's visits, they would listen to her commands and then do nothing about them, except perhaps laugh and roll their eyes afterwards. Some of the volunteers, however, found her impossible to ignore. There was a chaotic week when she bullied two of the more elderly volunteers into rearranging the shop's contents by size, rather than colour. She apparently helped with the first rack, before pleading an urgent appointment and only returning at the end of the day to ensure she was happy with their work.

'This place is still a mess and we've a long way to go, but it's a start at least,' she'd apparently said.

If she was happy, no one else was – their customers in particular.

'Where's the fun in going to your own size rack?' one said loudly.

'I already know I'm size sixteen and above,' another said, 'I don't need anyone else in the shop to see me at that rack.'

'It was so much more restful in here when it was arranged by colours,' another sighed.

Lola had worked until nine p.m. the following night, personally moving everything back. Two days after that, there was a showdown of sorts with Mrs Kernaghan.

'It took me hours to organise it properly into sizes,' she said to Lola, voice raised and hands on hips. 'I have more than twenty-five years' retail experience and I know what I'm talking about.'

'It took our oldest volunteers, *not* you, those hours, and then it took me even more hours to return it to the way it was,' Lola said calmly. 'Thank you for taking such a keen interest but we prefer it this way.'

'You're all wrong, then.'

There was a peaceful fortnight when she stayed away from the shop, but Lola had heard from two impeccable sources (Kay and Margaret) that Mrs Kernaghan had phoned to confirm she'd be attending today's meeting.

Sure enough, it was Mrs Kernaghan arriving now, all fuss and bustle. Lola greeted her cheerfully, then greeted the three other volunteers who came in behind her even more cheerfully and far more sincerely. Five minutes later, with tea poured and biscuits offered, the meeting got underway. The subject was a vote on whether the shop should participate in the Main Street Traders' Christmas Window competition. A recent initiative, it was growing more popular each year. This year, for the first time, a prize was on offer: $500 for the best display.

'What do you think, everyone?' Kay asked. 'Shall we give it a go?'

Mrs Kernaghan answered first. 'We hold a prime real estate position in the town. Of course we should.'

We? She'd only been in the town for three months. Lola dug her nails into the palms of her hands to stop herself from answering back. Hadn't she just been thinking that she needed to tone down her personality? Was now the time to start? Even if sitting here saying nothing was a kind of torture?

Mrs Kernaghan continued. 'I've already given this a great deal of thought, based on my own extensive retail and artistic experience, and I'd like to propose a modern approach to our window display. I've done a preliminary sketch. Here, there's a copy for each of you.'

She passed them around. The sketch wasn't preliminary. It looked like it had been done by an expert, either a set designer or an architect, all firm lines and detail. There wasn't a Christmas tree, brightly wrapped present or Santa Claus to be seen. In the centre of the page was a female figure in silhouette, with dozens of multicoloured strands wound around it in intricate patterns. Mrs Kernaghan's signature and a copyright symbol took up the bottom right-hand corner.

'Very nice,' Margaret said tentatively.

'Very nice,' Joan agreed.

They both looked to Lola. Lola was having trouble holding

her copy while digging her nails even more fiercely into her palms. On the verge of agreeing that she thought it was very nice too, she decided she couldn't lie. 'I'm sorry, Mrs Kernaghan, but I'm not sure what it's supposed to be.'

Mrs Kernaghan lifted her chin. 'It's a visual interpretation of the summer heat, rendered primarily in traditional red and green Christmas colours, with the addition of splashes of gold, white and blue highlighting the burning centre of the sun against the wide summer sky. The figure at the centre is a metaphoric representation of us, the human race, battling against the harsh elements ever present in the Australian landscape.'

'Oh,' Kay said.

Nope, Lola thought. In her opinion, Mrs Kernaghan's drawing looked like a store dummy tangled up in a few coloured bedsheets. She did one more nail-dig and tried to be diplomatic. 'Mrs Kernaghan, I think our Traders' Association was thinking more along the lines of nativity scenes. Or three wise men. Or Christmas on the beach, Australian-style.'

Beside her, Margaret and Joan were nodding enthusiastically. Joan had even arrived that morning with her family's old nativity set. Joseph was held together with yellowing sticky tape and there were only two wise men, but she'd been very proud that she'd managed to find any survivors at all, after more than forty Christmases with her rambunctious family of sons.

Mrs Kernaghan thumped her hand on the desk. Margaret and Joan jumped. Lola had to fight an inclination to slap her.

'What's the slogan for the Main Street Traders?' Mrs

Kernaghan said, too loudly. 'Tell me that? Exactly! They don't have one, do they? But I'll tell you what it should be. Moving forward. Looking forward. A slogan of go-getting energy. And that's what our window should demonstrate! That we have ambition, attitude and energy.'

Lola kept her voice level with some difficulty. 'Mrs Kernaghan, we're a charity shop. We sell old things cheaply and then give the proceeds to people in need. We're not here to make huge profits or win awards.'

'What kind of attitude is that? I say, let's push the boundaries, use my display and if I – sorry, if we – don't win this year, then you can all go back to your old ways for next year's competition.'

If Lola had to bribe the traders to award the charity shop final place, she would. 'Excellent idea,' she said brightly. She ignored Joan and Margaret's surprised look. 'And I also think we should be sure to put "Designed by Mrs Kernaghan" in large letters at the bottom of the window, so everyone knows it was your work, don't you think?'

Mrs Kernaghan preened.

Half an hour later, Lola was alone in the shop again. Mrs Kernaghan had left immediately after the meeting. She always had somewhere better to go, yet found the time to tell them about it. Lola had even heard a whisper she was thinking about running for mayor. She'd definitely get Lola's vote. With any luck, her mayoral duties would keep her so busy she'd have to stay away from the shop.

Margaret, Joan and Kay hadn't wanted to leave afterwards. 'The hide of her!'

'Who does she think she is?'

'Why did you just give in, Lola?'

'I don't know,' she said honestly.

After another five minutes of their outrage, Lola had been glad to say goodbye to the three of them too. Not only because the meeting had been unpleasant and all their complaining was starting to give her a headache. The truth was she wanted to get on to the computer before her shift was over. It was two days since she'd had a chance to check her emails and she was getting twitchy.

Now, she felt the familiar tingle of anticipation as she opened up her email account. Four new emails and none of them spam! She quickly read through them, her smile growing wider with each one. They were all responses to her Christmas bait! No, not bait, how could she call it that? Her Christmas special offer was a much nicer way to put it. Thoughts of Mrs Kernaghan and unfathomable window displays disappeared in an instant. Now she really had something to plan and look forward to.

She swiftly printed out all four emails. Much as she loved the computer, information still didn't feel real unless it was on paper. Reading each closely, she realised with another dart of pleasure that her guests were coming from all over the country. A man called Neil from Broken Hill in New South Wales. A couple called Helen and Tony from a town in Victoria – she'd look it up later on Google maps. A woman called Martha from

Melbourne. And a family of three from Adelaide, an adult and two children. Seven in total, the perfect number. She'd easily be able to manage them.

She quickly wrote back to all four.

Marvellous news! Congratulations again on your good taste and good luck. I'll be in touch again this week to confirm arrangements.

She added her scanned signature and a little smiley face – she'd grown to like emoticons – and sent them all off. She also removed the automatic reply function to her online Christmas ad, and to make doubly sure she'd get no more guests, she removed the ad as well. She checked her watch. Drat it. She only had ten more minutes until her shift finished, Joan returned to take over the shop and Luke arrived to drive her back to the motel. Still, it was enough time to send one more email. An important one, too, to Ellen in Hong Kong. She hadn't heard anything back from her last email yet. Something must be up. She did a swift calculation of the time in Hong Kong. Not that it mattered if Ellen was home from school yet or not. From what Lola gathered, her great-granddaughter and her smart phone were joined at the hip or the mouse or whatever the right term was. Hopefully she'd get the email wherever she was. Luke had tried to talk her into trying something he called 'gee-mail' chat for her communications with Ellen, but Lola preferred the formality of emails. She also liked to keep Ellen on the straight and narrow with her spelling. None of this abbreviation business for them.

You're too quiet over there. What's up, darling? She pressed send and waited. A minute later, there it was. An email back from Ellen.

Nothing.

Lola quickly typed a one-word answer – Liar – and pressed send again.

Don't call me a liar.

I think you're lying so I'm calling you a liar. What's wrong, my Ellie?

Nothing. Why do you think there is?

Lola typed as quickly as she could. Because your emails have been either non-existent or really boring recently so either you've become boring, in which case I hope one of my other great-grandchildren grows up quickly and starts entertaining me, or else you're upset and your energy is going into that rather than composing amusing emails to send to me.

Lola waited for another few minutes but there was no reply. She typed again. Darling? Are you all right over there?

A minute later, another email. I'm trying to be funny for you but it's too hard. I'm too upset.

Lola didn't hesitate then. She dialled Ellen's number. 'What's wrong, darling?'

'Nothing. Everything. I hate it here.' Ellen sounded very young and upset.

'Why?'

'My dad.'

'Is he starving you again? Beating you?'

'It's not funny, Lola. It's her, anyway. Not him.'

'Her?'

'Dad's girlfriend.'

'She's starving and beating you?'

'He wants us to spend Christmas with her and her daughter. In some big house on some island near here.'

Ah, Lola thought. That relationship was getting serious, then. Before she had a chance to reply, Ellen spoke again.

'How dare he, Lola? How can he do it to me and to Mum?'

'Oh, darling. He's not "doing" anything. He's trying to make a new life for himself. He can't stay sad forever.'

'I can! I'm always sad. He's not allowed to be happy yet. If he's already able to be with someone else, he must never have loved Mum. And if he didn't love her, then what am I doing here with him? I hate it here. I hate, hate, hate, *hate* it here. I want my mum.'

Lola couldn't stop a sudden welling of tears. Outside, she heard the shop door open. She'd have to be quick. 'Darling, please, don't get upset. And don't worry. I'll think of something.'

Ellen sniffed. 'What? You'll come and rescue me? You told me your legs would explode with clots if you had to take a flight any longer than two hours.'

'There are many ways to skin a cat and to sort a problem. Leave it with me. I have to go now, but I want you to smile at yourself in the mirror until it feels real. I also want you to apologise to your father.'

'For what? It's his fault.'

'I have a feeling there's been some shouting, has there? Some sulking?'

A pause. 'A bit.'

'Is his girlfriend there at the moment?'

'Yes. And her stupid daughter.'

'How do you know she's stupid if you haven't spoken to her?'

There was no answer.

'Ellen, I'm going to give you the same advice I've just given your beloved aunt Bett. Get over it. And here's some extra advice just for you. *Pretend* you're getting over it if you have to. Your mother was an actress and a good one, and I'm sure you have some acting genes in your beautiful self too. Use them now. Make Anna proud of you. Go out there and apologise. Say a polite hello to your father's visitors. If that's all you can manage, fine, go and hide back in your room again. That will do for today.'

'I *can't*.'

'You can and you will or after I die I'll make your mother come with me and we'll both haunt you for the rest of your life.'

'Lola!'

'I mean it. Be polite, even for five minutes. And stop worrying about Christmas. That's days away yet. We'll sort it out.'

'We?'

'You. Me. Your dad.'

'Promise?'

'I promise.'

'I love you, Lola.'

'Not as much as I love you. Now, out you go, my darling. And don't forget to smile.'

Lola had just hung up when she heard what was unmistakably a loud miaow. Surely not? She peeked through the curtain. Yes, surely. Joan hadn't just brought in her camcorder with her latest cat video to upload. She'd brought the cat itself. Lola liked cats, but this really was one of the ugliest creatures she'd ever seen. Ginger. Bad-tempered-looking. It reminded her of . . . Yes, it reminded her of Mrs Kernaghan.

Joan appeared in the doorway, beaming. 'Lola, I hope you don't mind. It's just I was telling Boo-Boo about all the funny cat videos on the internet and I swear he miaowed that he wants to see them too.'

He'd enjoy playing with the mouse if nothing else, Lola thought. She stood up. 'All yours, Joan. Happy viewing, Boo-Boo.'

She was already deep in thought about Ellen by the time Luke arrived outside to collect her.

CHAPTER SIX

As usual for a Wednesday night, Carrie and the children were at the motel for an early dinner, before Carrie left to play netball while her parents babysat. Her few hours of sanity a week, she called it. They didn't eat in the dining room with the guests, but in the kitchen, helping themselves to samples of different dishes from the menu – prawn cocktail, Wiener schnitzel, spaghetti bolognese. Lola didn't like to see it. She much preferred the children to learn good table manners in the restaurant itself, rather than stand around the large kitchen table reaching across each other. But Geraldine had introduced the idea, presumably as a way of them being together while she prepared meals for the motel guests. For once, Lola had let it be. The children were now playing in the function room, demolishing the chairs and tables by the sounds of things. Lola tried not to wince as another crash echoed through the wall. There was a pause and then a wail.

'The little darlings, what are they doing in there?' she said.

'Building cubby houses, I suppose,' Carrie said, flicking through a magazine and not looking up.

'You don't want to check on them?'

'They'll come to me if they're really hurt.' Carrie waited until her mother had gone out into the dining room carrying two plates. It was a quiet night in the restaurant. It usually was, mid-week. 'Lola, I need your advice before this all blows up into another feud. She's driving me crazy.'

'Your mother is?' Why did that make Lola feel so good?

'Not Mum. Bett, of course. What's wrong with her at the moment?'

Lola trod warily. 'What do you mean?'

'She's so snappy and defensive all the time. And she won't even listen when I'm trying to be helpful. It's like she's deliberately doing the exact opposite of what I tell her just to annoy me. I thought that both of us having kids would bring us closer together but instead it's even worse. I mean, we got through all the Matthew business, though frankly sometimes lately I've wished he had married her and not me . . . Okay, okay, I won't go into it, but —' She gave a big dramatic sigh. 'I thought we had both turned a corner in the past few years, and thank God you brought us together when Anna —' She stopped again and sighed once more. 'I wish Anna was here, Lola. She'd never have treated me the way Bett does. She'd have been much —'

'Oh, God, not you too.'

'I beg your pardon?'

'Moan, moan, moan. Either get over it or get on with it, would you?'

'Lola!'

79

'Don't look so shocked. I said the same thing to your sister when she was complaining about you too.'

'Bett was complaining about me? How dare she? It's all her fault.'

'It's no one's fault. I mean it, darling. Build a bridge. Get over it. Or offer it up. Was there one other piece of advice I gave Bett?' Lola pretended to think, head on one side. 'No, that was it. You need to stop complaining about each other, darling. Face facts. You're one sort of mother and Bett is another and I suspect never the twain shall meet.'

'But the difference is I know what I'm talking about. I've got three, she's only got two. And it's not as if I'm offering untrialled advice. She wonders why they don't sleep properly. You should see what she feeds them!'

'Vodka and beetles? Excellent, that's what I suggested. Carrie, I'm not listening any more. Actually, yes I am. I think one of your beautifully fed and perfectly behaved children has just fallen off a table.'

As if on cue there was a shout from next door. 'Mummy, Delia pushed me!'

Carrie ran out of the room just as Jim came in from the bar. There was another loud squeal from the function room, either from Carrie or one of her children.

Lola winced. 'Do you suppose Matthew really does have late clinics three times a week or is he hiding somewhere?'

Jim smiled. 'Far be it from me to even speculate. All okay, Lola? Can I get you anything?'

'A piggyback to my room? Soundproofing *in* my room?' She smiled, then winced again at another wail, this time definitely from a child. 'Good Lord. If Carrie comes looking for me and mentions the word babysitting, can you please tell her I've gone back to Ireland for a very long holiday?'

Jim winced too as a trio of thumps joined the crying. 'Our three girls were never this noisy, were they?'

'Never. I stickytaped their mouths most days.' She did like it when Jim asked her about the girls' upbringing. She glanced at the clock. Not even seven thirty p.m. But still, time enough for her to slip away. She gave a ladylike yawn. 'I feel old age taking me over, darling. My bed calling me. Give Carrie and the children my love, won't you? Tell them I just can't wait until next Wednesday night and we get to do this all over again.'

After the noise in the main building, her room felt like even more of a haven than usual. She'd personalised it with a few of her favourite things – a scarf, a vase, an antique table lamp. She'd become quite settled here in room eleven, in fact. In years gone by, she'd moved from room to room of the motel, sometimes evacuating at short notice if a large group booking came in. Recently, the bookings had slowed down. Not great for Geraldine and Jim's bottom line but good for her peace of mind. Another symptom of old age? The urge to nestle away?

Not that she'd ever really needed familiar furniture or paintings around her to feel at home. Two or three ornaments, a few favourite outfits in the wardrobe – generally made of chiffon or silk so they were easy to fold and pack – and in later years, necklaces and the flowers she liked to pin in her hair. Everything else she needed for a happy life was stored away in her head and could be brought out for mental viewing whenever she liked. That was one of the great things about living to this age, she thought, if one was lucky enough to keep one's memory and wits. It was like having access to the world's largest DVD store. All she needed to keep herself entertained was a moment with her eyes closed, a rummage through eight decades of memories and away she could go, replaying happy times, sad moments, tear-jerkers and romantic comedies alike.

Although not that many romantic moments, unfortunately. After her marriage ended, she'd only ever had one more serious relationship. He had been a fine man. Fifty years later, she could still recall his face, even his voice. What a sweet ten months that had been, an unexpected love affair, with an unfortunately sudden ending. He'd be long dead now, of course. Most people of her vintage were. For a time, Lola had kept an eye on funeral notices, until they became more like a roll call of her friends than a casual reading. She could almost conduct funerals herself she had been to so many. Anna's, of course, had been the saddest. The hardest. Every moment seared into her memory . . .

Enough! Enough sad thoughts. Keep going, keep looking forward, keep planning. Christmas was fast approaching, and she had an extravaganza to organise. Sitting around reflecting on life and death wasn't going to get the turkey stuffed or the presents wrapped, was it? And once she'd spent a bit of time on her

Christmas plans, she could turn her full attention to Ellen and her predicament.

She took out a notepad and started to jot down her ideas to make the Valley View Motel Christmas not just special, but very special indeed.

An outdoor Christmas lunch, she decided. She knew the perfect spot. A grassy area to the side of the motel, between a willow tree, a gum tree and an unidentified one that had long green leaves. She called it the long green leafy tree. The ground beneath them was hardly a verdant paradise at the moment, but in town the previous week she'd seen something marvellous in the hardware shop window – fake grass, sold in rolls. Surely they'd loan her a few metres, to create that oasis look for her guests? As for the table setting – lots of colour, she decided. It didn't have to be matching crockery either. And a table centre-piece, of course. She'd read a biography of one of the Mitford sisters, who'd reported casually that for one dinner party she'd placed a glass box filled with live chickens in the centre of her grand dining table. Lola had immediately made a mental note. That would certainly be a talking point for her Christmas guests. Something more local than chickens, though, perhaps. A kooka-burra in a cage? No, she didn't like birds in cages. A couple of black snakes? A jar of red-back spiders? There was plenty of time to decide.

Now, the food – she had an idea or two about that too. No point only serving a traditional turkey and plum pudding lunch, not these days when people had so many fads and likes and dislikes. She'd ask each of her guests – Neil, Martha, Helen and Tony, Holly and her daughters – what their favourite foods were, their favourite drinks, even their favourite jokes, and she'd give them exactly that. What fun! She could picture the lunch already, even imagine the conversation, the laughter and the joke-telling. Unfortunately, she couldn't picture anyone cooking and serving the food, and truth be told, cooking had never been her strong suit and she was a bit too weak in the wrists these days to carry out plates. But she'd work something out.

She was now too impatient to wait until her next turn at the charity shop computer. Going to her wardrobe, she pulled out a box she'd labelled *Boring letters and bills etc* and rummaged inside until she found the internet cable she'd hidden there. Hopefully Jim and Geraldine would be too busy trying to keep Carrie's children out of the hospital emergency department to notice that Lola was in the office. Not only that, but at the computer, which appeared to be connected to the internet again. If they did happen to come in, she'd just say she was – what? Sleepwalking?

Worry about that when it happens, she decided. Five minutes later, she was in the darkened office, the only light coming from the computer screen. The internet was working, she was glad to see. Amazing what a cable could do. She opened a new Word document, having decided to draft the questions before moving on to her email. What name to give the document? she wondered. Something innocuous, in case someone did happen to use the computer and wonder what she was up to? No, to hell with innocuous. She named the file *Lola's Secret*.

She needed to tread lightly with the questions to her guests. Find out as much as she could, all under the guise of a friendly country motel's excellence in customer service. She shut her eyes, picturing that scene under the trees, and her fingers flew across the keyboard.

Once the questions were done, it took her only a few minutes to open up her email account and compose a covering message to them all. Luke had taught her to send what he called blind emails when she was doing a group message. 'People don't like their email address being sent out to strangers,' he'd explained.

Dear Special Guest, she wrote.

Thank you again for responding to my advertisement and warmest CONGRATULATIONS again on being the lucky winner of a three-night Christmas package here at the delightful Valley View Motel. I guarantee it will be a Christmas to remember!

To assist me and my team (that made Lola laugh), would you please advise me of the following:

She swiftly cut and pasted her questions from the Word document. It really wasn't good manners to brag, even to oneself, but she was getting very good at this computer carry-on, she thought.

Favourite colour

Favourite food

Favourite drink

Favourite Christmas carol

Favourite Christmas joke

Age

Occupation

Reason for spending Christmas at the Valley View Motel

The last three questions weren't strictly to help with the Christmas lunch, but Lola had become curious about her guests. Especially about the two single ones. It was far too early to be thinking along such lines, but one possibly single male, a possibly single female – well, why not think about a little matchmaking while she was playing Christmas hostess? And perhaps the two children would be the right age to enjoy some of the collection of games and toys belonging to Ellen that they always kept on standby for other guests.

I assure you that all information received will be used strictly to enhance your enjoyment of Christmas at the Valley View Motel and will be deleted from our records afterwards. I look forward to hearing back and congratulate you again – here's to a very merry Christmas indeed!

Lola Quinlan

Proprietor

She had just sent off the emails when a sixth sense made her turn around. Geraldine had come in silently behind her. It was one of the many things Lola disliked about her daughter-in-law – her habit of wearing sensible shoes that gave her a creepy, gliding way of walking. Lola herself preferred high-heeled shoes whenever possible. Far more flattering and to hell with comfort, that was her opinion. Their fashion choices were yet another gulf between herself and Geraldine – her daughter-in-law had always favoured conservative clothes like crisp shirts and neat skirts, as well as minimal makeup and short, no-nonsense practical haircuts. Lola had never understood why.

'Hello, dear,' Lola said, turning in the swivel chair so that her back hid the screen. Had Geraldine done her silent sneaking in time to see the email? Worse still, in time to see that Lola had signed herself proprietor? Lola knew Geraldine felt very strongly about that. Lola had formally retired on her seventieth birthday, handing full ownership of the motel over to Jim and his family. 'Though I will stick my beak in now and again, I hope you know that,' she'd said.

'I'd be astonished if you didn't,' Jim had laughed. Geraldine hadn't even smiled.

'How are Carrie's little darlings?' Lola said to her now. 'Swinging from the chandeliers, I suppose?'

'Jim's reading to them. Is the internet working again?'

Lola turned back to the computer, swiftly closing her email program. 'Gosh, yes. It seems to be. Isn't that marvellous? Mind you, it took them long enough to fix it. When did I ring to register the fault? A week ago? Or was it a month ago? I really can't remember.'

'Six days ago,' Geraldine said. 'I need to do some online ordering, Lola. Would you mind?'

'Mind?' Lola was being deliberately obtuse. She knew Geraldine wanted her off the computer and out of the office. She just wasn't sure whether the file marked *Lola's Secret* was hidden. She decided to try to buy some time. 'Oh, you want to use the computer? Silly me. I tell you, I'm losing more marbles every day.

It seems to take ages for anything to sink in with me. I swear sometimes I'd forget my own head if it wasn't attached. Do you know, yesterday I spent nearly half an hour trying to get into the wrong room, convinced there was a problem with my key. And all along I was at completely the wrong door! Imagine!'

Geraldine didn't answer, just waited. Lola had a suspicion that if the chair had an eject button, it would have been pressed by now and Lola would be sailing through the roof and up into the sky in cartoon-fashion. She had no choice. If she turned back to hide her file, she would only make Geraldine even more suspicious. She stood up, making a show of how hard it was, even though she'd had a good day flexibility-wise. 'Not just my mind going either these days. Sometimes I can barely move, my joints hurt so much. Not long now, Geraldine, and I'll have shuffled off this mortal coil and you'll have the place all to yourself.'

Anyone else would have laughed at that, or protested. Not Geraldine. 'Thanks, Lola. I'll turn the computer off after I finish my order, will I?' It was a statement more than a question.

'Of course, Geraldine. Save power whenever possible. That's always been my number-one rule of efficient housekeeping.'

The next morning, before Lola had had a chance to get dressed and go over to the computer again, Jim appeared at her door. His broad open face was sunburnt, as always, his tall stocky figure well turned out in a crisp white shirt, ironed trousers and shining shoes. Even as a little boy, he'd been neat and tidy. It had always amused Lola. He certainly hadn't inherited that trait from her.

He was carrying a tray, with her favourite breakfast – a mushroom omelette. Beside it was a large pot of tea and two cups.

'Darling!' she said, beaming at him as she pulled a purple silk dressing-gown over her bright-yellow silk pyjamas. 'How thoughtful. It's not my birthday, is it?'

'No, it's not. But I just wanted to spoil you.'

'You have been well brought up. Who did that? Oh, that's right – me. What a lovely treat. And did you make this yourself?'

'With my two hands, yes. And three eggs and a cup of mushrooms.'

Lola took a bite. 'Perfect, dear Jim, thank you.'

'When is your birthday, Lola?'

She stopped mid-bite and smiled at him. 'You are funny today.'

He waited.

'It's in February, darling. Don't you remember? That old lady blowing out eighty-four candles in the dining room nearly a year ago? That was me.'

'Of course.' He cradled a cup of tea in his hands.

'What is it, Jim?'

'Nothing.'

'Nothing? So it's perfectly normal that you bring me breakfast in my room, sit there sighing and looking anxious and ask me when my birthday is? Are you worried about something?'

He nodded.

'Something about me or about you?'

'Both of us. It'll affect both of us.'

Lola frowned. 'Are you worried about *your* memory? Is that why you asked about my birthday?'

'Not my memory, Lola. Yours.' He held up a hand as she started to protest. 'Geraldine noticed it first. She thinks you're getting forgetful. That you've become secretive. She said she found you in the office last night and that you were behaving very strangely.'

'Really? What was I doing? Speaking in tongues?'

'She said you were at the computer, writing reminder notes to yourself.'

'To myself?'

Jim spoke quickly. 'Lola, I know she shouldn't have looked at your files but she was worried. She said you'd made out a questionnaire to remind yourself what your favourite food is, favourite drink, carols, songs, colour, everything. She saw it on a documentary, that this is what people are advised to do when they've been diagnosed with early dementia. And she said you told her you'd forget your own head if it wasn't glued on.'

'Attached. I said attached, not glued.'

'She also said you told her you keep forgetting which room is yours. And that you can barely walk some days.'

Lola sat more upright, and put down the knife and fork. 'Dear Geraldine. So thoughtful. And what else? Did she have a suggestion or two as to what the next best step for me might be?'

'Lola, don't be like this. You know how much I love you, we all love you, but you're eighty-four. You've had a busy, active life —'

'But I'm too old now and it's time to have me put down?

Perhaps Matthew could do it. Family rates and all that.'

He seemed relieved to laugh. 'Lola, please. I'm sorry to have just blurted it out, but is there something you're not telling me?'

'There are a hundred things I haven't told you. A million, probably. You're my son. The last thing you need to know is the contents of your mother's brain.'

'Is it getting too much for you here, is that it? Too many people around? Having to move rooms now and again? Look, I know you know your own mind better than anyone, but would you be happier if you were in your own place, a room that could be yours permanently, with all the support around you that you could possibly need?'

'What are you talking about, Jim?'

He reached down beside him. She had thought he was carry-ing a newspaper. It was a bundle of brochures for local old folks' homes. 'We're not rushing you into anything, I promise. But Lola, perhaps some time in the future, it's something you might want to think about.'

She kept her temper with great difficulty. She wanted to stand up, push the now dry-tasting mushroom omelette onto the floor, call her son a traitor and then go and hunt down his fool of a wife and . . . What? Lock her in the coolroom? Instead, she dug her nails into her palms again, slowly counted to five and kept her voice even. 'How wonderful. How thoughtful of you both. And where are you putting me? Should I start packing now?'

'We're not "putting" you anywhere. And of course we don't have a date in mind. I've made a mess of this, haven't I? Lola, look, I wanted to wait until after Christmas to bring this up with you, but there's something I need to tell you.'

Lola knew then what he was going to say. 'You and Geraldine are leaving, aren't you? Or you want to.'

He looked shocked and then instantly relieved. 'Have you heard us talking about it?'

'No.' But suddenly many things made sense. The lack of repairs recently, for example. Their decision not to host Christmas parties in the function room this year . . .

'We're ready to move on, Lola. We stayed here after Anna's —' He stopped. Jim could still barely say his daughter's name. 'But it's not got any easier for Geraldine, no matter how much time passes.'

Lola felt a momentary bond with her daughter-in-law.

Jim kept talking. 'At first she wanted to stay here because there were so many good memories of Anna. It felt right to be here where she spent her final days, to be close to her grave . . . It helped us both, I know. But in the past six months, Lola, something has felt different. For Geraldine more than me. It's making her sadder. She thinks of Anna every day —'

'That will happen wherever she is.'

'But she needs a new start. New surroundings. We're going to look for a new business to run when we're on our driving holiday around the state. In the Riverland maybe. Or perhaps the Adelaide Hills. We don't know exactly where yet. As close to Clare as possible, but enough distance to make it feel new.'

'Have you told the girls?'

'Not yet.'

'Need to work out what to do with the old bat first?'

'Mum, please.'

He only called her Mum occasionally. At times like this when he was upset.

Lola sat upright. 'Let's be as clear as we can about everything, Jim, shall we? Geraldine isn't inviting me to come and live with you in your new motel, is she?'

'Of course you'd be welcome. You're my mother.'

'Jim, tell me the truth. Would she prefer it to be just you and her?'

A nod. Then another flurry of words. 'We're thinking about just a small B&B. Perhaps not even a restaurant, just a breakfast room. We're not getting any younger either. We'd like to slow down a little. Find a new business just for a few years, perhaps, and then think seriously about retirement. I'm nearly sixty-five, after all.'

'My little Jim, imagine.' She took in his worried expression then and her heart softened. It wasn't Jim's fault he'd married an old cow. 'Darling, thank you for being so honest. And so straightforward. There's no rush, is there? You're not about to pack up before Christmas?'

'No, of course not. We're thinking in the next six months. Perhaps putting the motel on the market in the new year.'

'So I've time to enjoy one last Christmas here?'

'Of course! We'll cancel our holiday if you want. I'm sure Bett and Carrie would too. We could have one final family Christmas here together. Is that what you mean?'

'No!'

He looked shocked at her vehemence.

'No, darling, of course not. The peace and quiet I'll have over Christmas will be exactly what I need to make up my mind about the next best step for me. An old folks' home here in Clare, perhaps. Or perhaps I'll toss a coin to decide whether I go and live with Carrie or Bett and their babies. What's one more drooling face to wipe or nappy to change?'

'Lola!'

'I'm joking, darling.' She leaned across and patted his hand. 'I'm so glad this is out in the open. And my lips are sealed for now, I promise,' she said, making a zipping motion. 'I won't even mention it to Geraldine. It's our little secret.'

'Thanks, Mum.' At the door, he stopped and turned. 'Can I ask you one more thing?'

'Of course you can.'

'What was that list for?'

'The list?'

'The one called "Lola's Secret". Listing all your favourite things?'

She produced the best smile she could. 'You've spoiled everything. I was going to give it to you as a hint for what I wanted for Christmas. I guess it'll just be bath salts again now.'

He shook his head, smiling as he walked away.

Lola kept the smile on her face too, but only until he was out of sight. Then she stepped back and slammed the door as loudly as she could. She hoped Geraldine heard it.

CHAPTER SEVEN

Guest 1

It was a week now since Neil had been outside his flat. That wasn't unusual. What was the point of going outside? What was the point of anything these days?

A knock at his bedroom door. 'Neil?'

It was his flatmate Rick. He ignored him.

'Neil, your mother's on the phone again.'

He still didn't answer.

A harder knock, more of a thump. 'Neil! Jesus, mate. You can't stay in there forever.'

He didn't plan to stay there forever.

Another thump. 'You're not the first person in the world to lose your job or your girlfriend. Come on, mate. Pull yourself together. Your mother's really worried.'

He didn't reply. He knew that if he stayed quiet for long enough, he'd eventually be left alone, by Rick and by his mother. She'd been trying his mobile that morning as well. He'd let those calls go to voicemail. Maybe it was annoying, for his flatmate, for his mother, for everyone who knew him. Well, too bad. They'd be rid of the annoyance of his presence soon enough.

He turned up the volume on his computer to drown out the sound of Rick talking deliberately loudly on the phone outside his door. 'He's in there, Mrs Harris, but he won't answer. I'm sorry.' Perhaps he'd send his mother an email, get her off his back that way, before she got it into her head to drive the three hours from Wilcannia to visit him. He could hear her voice in his head enough already. He didn't need to see her. He already knew what she'd say. The same thing she'd said to him, over and again, the last time he'd made the mistake of answering when she rang. 'It's Christmas time, Neil. Please come home. A family should be together at Christmas.'

'Why?' he'd asked her. 'What makes Christmas better than any other time?'

She hadn't had an answer for that. He'd said goodbye then, telling her there was someone at the door. There might have been. A takeaway delivery, probably. He wasn't eating a lot these days, but what he did eat arrived at the house in plastic containers, ordered online. He lived most of his life online. What was the point in going outside when he could do everything from here? This way he was the one in control. He could decide who he spoke to and who spoke to him. If he didn't like what he was reading, or hearing, he just had to change websites or blogs or press delete. It was . . . What? Better? No, *safer*, that was the word. He'd tried life out there, tried it and didn't like it. It was much easier in here.

He hadn't cut himself off from the world completely. If anything, spending so much time online made him more tuned in to world events and new music than he'd ever been in the 'real' world. There were even a few people he spoke to, kind-of friends, he supposed he could call them, that he'd met via chat rooms and blogs. Not that he'd talked to them recently. They'd started asking too many questions. If he wanted to be interrogated, he'd ring his mother, or go outside his room and see his flatmate. And he didn't want to be interrogated. He didn't want to do anything, not any more.

His life had been good once. He'd worked in lots of different jobs, most recently as an upholsterer, played a bit of sport, did what most twenty-eight-year-olds did around Broken Hill, drank too much some nights, smoked some dope now and again, nothing serious. He'd even had a girlfriend for a few months. Until, piece by piece, it had all started to collapse around him. The job went first. Completely out of the blue. His boss had called him in from the workshop, his face all serious. 'It's not you, Neil. You know I think you're a bloody good worker. It's just the orders have dropped off, and it's last in, first out.' He'd heard the same phrase again and again the following weeks, as he applied for other jobs. 'Sorry, mate. The orders have dried up. We'll let you know if anything comes up.' If anything *had* come up, they hadn't let him know.

A month after he lost his job, he'd been drinking at home on his own, run out of beer, got in his car to go to the bottle shop and had a crash. Nothing serious. All he'd done was hit a tree.

The only person he'd hurt was himself, a stupid knee injury from slamming his foot so hard on the brake. At least he'd managed to start the car and get it safely home before the cops arrived and he got breathalysed. Some luck. But the car hadn't driven properly since and he couldn't afford the repairs. His knee was still sore, and he didn't have the money for a physio. So he'd had to give up the footy too.

His girlfriend pulled the plug next. She'd used almost the same words as his boss. 'It's not you, Neil, it's me. I want to go travelling, see the world, not settle down yet. You're getting too serious for me.' He'd pleaded with her, but it had been no use. Her mind was made up, she told him. Then change your mind, he begged. Please. She wouldn't, no matter how many times he asked, how many times he called her. She was the only good thing in his life, he told her. It was the truth. No job, no car, no sport – she was all he had. He tried another tack, writing her letters, sending her emails. Couldn't he go travelling with her? It didn't have to be serious between them. He'd lighten up, he promised, but couldn't they at least stay together? He didn't think he could live without her.

She stopped answering his calls after that. She didn't reply to any emails or texts either, no matter how many he sent and what time he sent them. He'd gone around to her house one night, one last-ditch effort. Her flatmate was stony-faced when she eventually answered the door. 'You're too late,' she'd said, sounding almost happy about it. His ex-girlfriend had left for London the previous day. 'You need help,' the friend said, before shutting the door in his face.

His own flatmate started criticising him. 'You're so serious these days, mate. Cheer up.'

His mother started ringing too often. He'd made the mistake of calling her one night when he'd been drinking, telling her everything about the breakup, the job, how he was running out of money. She'd threatened to visit again. He'd had to insist she didn't. Told her he needed to work it out for himself. The next day a cheque had arrived, sent priority post. A note from her in it. She'd obviously decided all he had wrong with him was a broken heart. If only it was that simple. 'You'll meet someone else,' she'd written. 'There's plenty more fish in the sea. Don't worry. You're still young.'

Sure. Don't worry, be happy. He had so much to be happy about, so much to live for, life was so full of wonders.

Bullshit. Life's hard and then you die. And if you don't want to hang around and wait for it to happen, wait for life to drag itself out day after day, then you make it happen, don't you? Bring it to an end yourself.

What was the alternative? Get another job, lose that one? Find another girlfriend, break up with her too? Go through this pain again? Forget it. What was the point? So why not die before life gets even harder?

He'd done his research. He spent hours on the web. He made his decision. He'd use tablets. Quick, painless. No blood, no guns. There had been site after site giving him advice. He chose the place next. A motel, he decided. Not here in the flat. He owed Rick that much. He chose it at random online – the town, the motel, the dates, everything. It was only after he sent the enquiry email that he realised the date he'd booked. Christmas Day. Ho ho ho.

When he got that email straight back telling him his stay would be free, that he'd won some online competition, he took it as a sign. He was doing what he was supposed to do. If the motel was free, there'd be no bad scenes money-wise afterwards, his mother being chased to pay some outstanding bill. He'd also leave a note for her, explaining everything. He'd already tried to write it, several times. He wanted her to know it wasn't her fault. It had nothing to do with the kind of mother she'd been, the fact that his parents had divorced years ago. None of that mattered these days. Everyone he knew came from broken homes. Bad phrase. His home hadn't been broken. His mum had done the best she could for him and his little sister. Told them nearly every day how much she loved them. If anything, she laid it on a bit thick sometimes. That was one of the reasons he decided to leave home when he did. She'd been so proud when he started getting trade work, even prouder that time he came home for his summer holiday two years earlier and surprised her by re-covering the old sofa in the back room. She'd carried on as if he'd redecorated the entire house. 'All I did was fix up a sofa. That's what I do. That's my job these days.'

'It's beautiful, Neil. It really is.'

She'd been so happy that day. So proud of him. But he couldn't think about her. She'd understand. She'd have to understand. She'd have no choice. Just like him. He had to do what he'd decided to do. He was too sick and tired of living like this.

He checked his emails now and frowned. A new one had just come in. Another one from the motel, from someone called Lola Quinlan, asking him to list his favourite food, drink, his age and occupation. For fuck's sake – whatever happened to anonymous motel bookings? Who cared what his favourite things were? It wasn't as if he'd be joining everyone for lunch, was it? Sitting around pulling crackers and telling jokes and singing 'Jingle Bells' with complete strangers? He wanted to just catch the bus there, book into his room and be left alone so he could do what he'd gone there to do. For his sake, for their sake, for everyone's sake. So long. Goodbye. Forever.

He looked at the email again and felt another surge of rage. One more person nagging him, demanding attention and answers. His flatmate and mother were bad enough. He pressed delete. Forget it. He'd go somewhere else, where he wasn't going to be interrogated.

Then he remembered it was free.

He clicked on the trash file and retrieved the email. If he didn't go to that motel, he'd have to find somewhere else. Maybe even pay a deposit with money he didn't have. He'd already spent most of his dole money. What did it matter what he said back, anyway? It wasn't as if he'd be eating or drinking anything there, anyway.

He wrote back one line, No favourites, and pressed send.

Outside, he heard Rick say something, call goodbye, maybe,

and then the sound of the door being pulled shut behind him. Good. He was alone again.

Guests 2 and 3

In their suburban home, Tony and Helen had been fighting for the past ten minutes. Helen had made the mistake of telling him about the email she'd received from the Clare Valley motel that afternoon asking for their favourite food, drink, carols etc., in preparation for Christmas. She'd answered on behalf of both of them, sending the email straight back, impressed at how organised this Lola Quinlan was. She'd told Tony all about it, hoping to get him even slightly enthused. Instead, he'd said again that he wouldn't go.

'Why not?' she asked again.

'I told you. Just because.'

'That's no excuse. Why not?'

'We can't afford it. Business hasn't been great this year, you know that.'

'But it's *free*, Tony. I told you last week, I won a competition. I showed you the email. So you can't use that as an excuse.'

'We'll still have to pay for most of our meals.'

'I'll pack sandwiches if I have to. I'll go without you.'

He shrugged.

The shrug triggered it. She burst into tears. It was the first time since everything happened that she'd cried in front of him. Now, once she'd started, it felt like she would never stop. He didn't move. He just stared at her, shocked, but he didn't move.

She made herself calm down, roughly wiped the tears away. But she had his full attention, for once. She had to use it. She had to talk to him, had to try to make him understand. 'I can't go on like this, Tony. I've tried to be patient. Give you the time you need, the space you need, the understanding, everything. But what about me, Tony? What about us?' It all surged up from inside her, the hurt and frustration finally overtaking the sympathy she'd felt. 'You think more about that man than you think about me, your wife, or your kids. Is it making you feel any better to wallow in this guilt day after day? Making anyone else feel better? No, Tony. It's only doing bad things, stopping you from celebrating the fact you're alive and punishing all of us who live within sight or sound of you.'

'My life's been a living hell the past year, Helen.'

'And so has mine, Tony, so has mine.'

'You weren't there that day. You didn't hear Ben scream. If I'd been a minute earlier, I might have seen it start to happen. Even thirty seconds earlier, I could have stopped the van from falling on him —'

She'd heard every detail of the accident so many times she'd had nightmares herself about it. The simplest of workplace errors, a chain not fastened properly before the car was hoisted onto the ramp. 'But you *weren't* there in time, Tony.' Her tone was much gentler. 'You weren't. And it doesn't matter how many times you go over and over it, how many days and nights you lock yourself away from the world, from me, how unhappy you make yourself, you're not going to bring him back to life.

He's dead, Tony. It was an accident. A terrible, tragic accident. And it wasn't your fault. You read the coroner's report. It was an accident. You weren't to blame.'

'It was. I was his boss. I should have trained him better.'

'You did train him. You taught him all the safety rules. And that morning, Tony, for a reason we'll never know, Ben ignored the rules and he paid the worst price possible for it. But *he* ignored the rules, Tony, not you. It wasn't your fault.' She took a step towards him. 'You can't just let it go round and round in your head forever. It's been more than a year, Tony. And nothing has changed. Can't you see that? Is this it? Is this what life is going to be like for us now?'

'At least we're alive.'

'Yes, Tony, we're alive. But it's no life. Not for either of us.'

They didn't talk for the rest of that night. He went into the living room and turned on the TV, though she knew he wasn't watching it. Helen washed dishes, filled more time cleaning out cupboards that didn't need cleaning, knowing the sound of the dishes and glasses being moved would be annoying. She wanted to annoy him. She wanted to keep talking to him, shout at him, get some new reaction out of him. Anything but this . . . this *nothing*, night after night.

Twice Helen went to the computer to send an email to the motel. She'd keep it brief. Explain that unfortunately they were now unable to take up the offer of the free Christmas stay. Thank you anyway. Happy Christmas.

The first time she was stopped by another sudden rush of

tears. Guilt of her own, for not being understanding enough, then guilt for the anger she kept feeling towards Tony. One of her friends had gently suggested that she should perhaps go and talk to someone. A professional.

'It's Tony who needs it, not me.' He'd tried one session with a counsellor, in the early months after the accident, but the appointment had lasted less than fifteen minutes. Tony had walked out. The counsellor hadn't known what she was doing, he said. He'd refused to go back again, no matter how much Helen urged him.

'I think you both need it,' her friend said.

Helen had changed the subject.

But was that what she needed to do? Go and talk to someone, try to explain just how bad it had been? Or should she stop wishing she could turn back time, not just to before the accident, not just to back when Tony was interested, interesting, engaged with life, with her, with their children?

Because she wanted to go back even further than that, she realised. Back to when Katie and Liam were still living at home, when they were a family, when the very best moment of her week was Friday night, when the kids were home from school, Tony back from work. She'd have made something simple but good for dinner and they would settle back, the four of them, for a family night in. Those had been the happiest nights for her, safe and happy at home with a husband she loved, and the two happy, healthy children they loved and had raised together. The family they'd created.

The family that was now – what? Changed forever? Her

husband was a different man, a stranger to her. Her two children were on the other side of the world. She thought of all the love she'd poured into them, the fun they'd had, even the difficulties they'd got through – exams, job searches, broken hearts. She remembered pretending she was so happy and so excited they were going to live overseas when in her heart she hated the idea of not seeing them every week . . . All of those thoughts and feelings and emotions, all she'd done for them, so willingly – she'd do it all again tomorrow – yet here she was, alone, unhappy, and so, so sad.

If Tony heard her crying again, he didn't come in to see her. She stayed there, in front of the computer, until the sobs eased, until her breathing calmed, feeling so tired, as if the tears had used up all the energy she had. That was it, she realised. She'd run out of the energy she needed to keep Tony on an even keel, to try to cheer herself up. To do anything except a few hours teaching a month and the day-to-day drudgery of housework, meals, washing, cooking. Her life had shrunk to the inside of this house now, too. Was that all that was left for her? Was it time to think about finding a full-time teaching job? What was the alternative? Endless days here at home, tidying rooms that were already tidy, waiting for the sound of Tony's key in the lock, feeling the mood in the house drop several degrees as he brought an almost visible cloud of unhappiness and misery in with him?

She was dreading Christmas Day especially. She must have been mad thinking a change of location would make any difference. They would just be miserable there instead of here. Any hopes of a merry country Christmas gathering, drinks with other guests, even a singalong, had faded. She'd been too optimistic. Even if she did get Tony to go there, he wouldn't engage with anyone else. He barely spoke to her any more. He was hardly going to strike up lively conversations with fellow guests, lead everyone in a carol-singing evening, offer to carve the turkey, barbecue the prawns.

They'd have to stay here. Perhaps she would make a Christmas lunch for the two of them. Perhaps not. At the moment, she didn't have the energy to think about even preparing a tray of sandwiches. She'd get something ready-made, they'd watch a few TV movies, talk to their son in Spain and daughter in England and then call it a day. What was the point in doing anything else?

She turned back to the computer again to write an email to cancel the booking. She was stopped again. As she opened up the folder, an email from her daughter appeared in her inbox, as if on the other side of the world Katie had known she was thinking about her. It was a cheery, enthusiastic email, filled with news about her weekend, her social life, the week ahead at her work in a bank in London, the bands she'd seen, the market she'd gone to, the cold weather, the talk of snow. How much she loved the lights and the decorations, how Christmassy it felt, like being in a film. How much she was looking forward to going away with friends to a rented country house in Norfolk for Christmas: It's going to be like something from *Pride and Prejudice* or *Upstairs Downstairs,* by the sounds of things! she'd written. All we're missing is the maids. Liam is really jealous. I think he has to work all over Christmas. What are your and Dad's plans? A barbie on the beach? Picnic at the park?

Two days before, Helen might have written back about the Valley View Motel, how she'd booked it on the spur of the moment and then learnt she'd won a competition. Katie would have loved hearing all about that. It wasn't the case now. She wrote back, forcing herself to sound cheerful.

Good morning, darling. A real-time email! Your Christmas sounds like it will be wonderful. No, no big plans here. A quiet day here at home, just your dad and me. You'll have your mobile with you, won't you, so we can at least ring you on the day?

She pressed send and waited, still marvelling at the wonders of this technology, that she could be talking to her daughter thousands of kilometres away. Her answer came back within two minutes.

Of course! It's surgically attached to my hand. Just to warn you, my friend said that the mobile coverage isn't great there at the best of times, and there's snow forecast, so don't worry if you can't get through to me, I'll trudge through snow and across fields if I have to, to find a spot that works. There's no way I'd miss talking to you at Christmas. Better go, Mum, late for work. Love you. xxxx

Love you too xxx Helen wrote back.

After even that brief email exchange, Helen felt cheered up. Only slightly, but enough. She allowed herself a secret wish that both her children would surprise her with emails or phone calls to say they'd decided to change their plans for a working Christmas in Spain and a country mansion Christmas in England, that they were coming home for a proper Australian family Christmas and could Helen and Tony come and get them at the airport on Christmas Eve . . .

She stopped the fantasy there. Who was being the selfish one now? She was, wanting her children to put their adult lives on hold so she could have the pleasure of their company, their liveliness around her. This was empty-nest syndrome, magnified by what had happened to Tony. She had to pick herself up, keep going, try to be more patient, more understanding. It wasn't going to help anyone if she and Tony kept arguing, if —

'Helen?'

She turned. Tony was at the door.

'I'm sorry.'

It was the first time he had apologised for anything, for a long time. She was so shocked she didn't answer.

'You're right,' he said. He stepped into the room. 'I have to move on. It's just . . . I just wish —'

He started to cry. For the first time she could remember since their children were born, her husband of thirty-five years, a grown man, sobbed in front of her. She didn't hesitate. She moved across to him, took him in her arms, soothing him with words, stroking his hair, holding him as tight as she could.

'I'm sorry, Helen,' he kept saying. 'I'm so sorry.'

'It's fine, Tony. It's fine. It's fine.' Over and over again, the same words, until she sensed his tears start to slow, felt his breathing change, grow calmer.

'I wish . . .' Again, he couldn't finish the sentence.

'Things could be different?' She spoke softly.

He nodded.

She held him tight again. Yes, she wished everything was different too. Not just for them, but for Ben's family especially. If she and Tony were finding the thought of Christmas difficult, how on earth were they feeling? But she knew more than anything that this wasn't the time to mention them.

He moved back slightly from her. She reached up and wiped a tear from his cheek. In that moment, she knew for sure she still loved him.

When he spoke again, his voice was soft. 'If you really want to go away somewhere for Christmas, let's go.'

'What do you want to do?'

She saw him begin to shrug, that simple gesture that had begun to hurt her so much, a physical representation of how little he cared about anything these days. Then he stopped it, straightened his shoulders, only slightly. 'I'd like to give that place a go. That motel. It might do us good.'

It was only a small step, but it was a step. 'Thanks, Tony.' She didn't need to say anything else. Not yet.

'Can I get you a glass of wine, love?' he asked. 'Cup of tea?'

'Tea would be lovely, thanks.'

She turned off the computer and followed her husband out to the kitchen.

Guest 4

Martha walked into the office, having to duck under loosely hanging Christmas decorations. If she had her way, she'd ban them from the workplace. It was hard enough to keep everyone motivated and productive in December as it was. Every time she walked past people's desks she'd hear snatches of conversations about holiday plans, Secret Santa gifts and Christmas parties. She was feeling uncomfortably like Scrooge, muttering 'Bah humbug' under her breath, but the truth was, if she heard one more thing about Christmas, she'd scream.

Even her temporary secretary had got into the spirit that morning. Aged in her fifties, she was old-fashioned in appearance and manner. 'And will you be joining your family for Christmas, Miss Kaminski?'

'No,' Martha had said. 'And please, call me Martha.'

'I'm afraid I can't. I'm an old-school secretary. Are you from Melbourne?'

'No.'

'Young people like you move around so much these days, don't you? I do admire you. So where are you from, if you don't mind me asking?'

'Actually, I do mind. Could we please finish these letters?'

Martha sighed inside as she saw two bright spots of colour appear on the temp's cheeks. What was the lady's name? Gwenda or Brenda . . . Glenda, that was it. She turned the conversation back to business, loading the older woman with enough work to keep her busy for not just that afternoon but most of the next day too.

She wouldn't apologise for her sharpness, even though she could see Glenda was put out. What on earth had she thought Martha would do? Lean back in her chair, put her feet up on the desk and spill her soul? 'Of course I don't mind you asking, Glenda. I was brought up in Brisbane, where my father, who's originally from Poland, ran his own furniture-importing business and my mother, whose parents were from the Ukraine, managed a local fabric store. I'm the eldest of three children, one brother, one sister. And for the past three years, since an almighty fight with my father one Christmas Eve, I've had nothing to do with my family. So no, I don't think we'll be meeting up for Christmas this year or in fact for any year coming. I had one Christmas on my own at home, another in a horribly expensive and expensively horrible resort, and I wouldn't recommend either option. So this year I'm going to some place in South Australia I've never heard of before, to some motel that could be either a kip or a country delight, and frankly, I don't really care either way, as I plan to take my laptop with me and work as much as possible and be back here behind my desk the day after Boxing Day. What was the fight with my father about? I won't go into details if you don't mind, but I can tell you that it lasted for thirty minutes, involved a lot of shouting and that I still believe he had absolutely no right to say what he did about the way I run my company *or* my life. And I didn't appreciate the others sticking their noses in either. And yes, I am in my late thirties and still single, and no, I don't have a house full of cats. Please feel free to tell the rest of my staff my personal business too, won't you?'

Martha almost felt like calling Glenda back and actually having that conversation with her. Instructing her to pass on the news to all the staff. At least that would stop them all speculating. She knew they were curious about her private life too. She'd overheard their conversations often enough. She also knew none of them liked her very much. The Dragon, one of them had called her. He hadn't realised she was coming down the corridor behind him. His face when he saw her was a picture. She didn't care. It was a workplace, not a knitting circle. If she wanted friends, well . . . If she worked better hours, she'd have more time for friends. She'd made the decision many years before that she wanted to succeed as a businesswoman. She'd always known that would take dedication and thick skin. Fortunately she had both qualities in abundance.

After finishing reviewing the week's new recruitment contracts, she took a moment to check her personal email account. There was one from the proprietor of the Valley View Motel, asking for details of her favourite things. She was impressed. A country motel with this kind of customer service? Perhaps it wouldn't be Three Days in Hicksville after all. Not that she planned on eating with any other guests, or singing her favourite carol or telling jokes. But she always did like questionnaires. She filled out the first part in record time, ignored the last three questions, pressed send, then took out her spreadsheets and started the following year's profit projections.

She was deeply immersed in the mid-year figures when the phone beside her buzzed. 'Yes, Glenda?'

'Your mother's on line three, Miss Kaminski.'

'What?'

'Your mother's on line three.'

For God's sake. Hadn't her usual secretary explained that Martha didn't take calls from her family? Any of her family? 'I'm not here.'

'But I told her you were.'

'Tell her you were wrong. Tell her I'm overseas.'

'But you're not. And it's your mother.'

'Take a message.'

A long pause expressed Glenda's displeasure. 'Very well.'

Martha called her in as soon as she saw the phone light go out. 'Glenda, my usual secretary should have explained. I don't take personal calls at work.'

'It was your mother.'

'Perhaps I'm not making myself clear. I don't take personal calls. Any calls. From anyone.' Her mother had done this every year for the past three years, started calling the fortnight or so before Christmas, leaving messages at home too, begging her to put the fight behind them, telling Martha that she was just being stubborn, as her father was stubborn, that they missed her, that if they couldn't gather as a family at Christmas time, then what chance did they have the rest of the year? Martha had ignored the calls each year. She would do the same this year. She turned back to her computer, hoping Glenda would get the hint. What temp agency were they using these days? Daft Personnel?

'Your mother gave me a message for you.'

Martha didn't turn around.

'Quite a long message. I took it down in shorthand. I can read it to you now, or I can type it up, whichever suits you better.'

Martha turned then, her expression murderous. 'Glenda —'

'Yes, I know you don't take personal calls. Strictly speaking, you didn't take that one, but I did and now I want to pass the message on to you so that my conscience is clear.'

There was a long moment when they just stared at each other, before Martha sighed. 'Go ahead.'

Glenda gave a small cough, then began to read from the paper she was holding. '"Martha, please. How many more years is this going to go on? I could lie and pretend that your father is ill, that we are all gathering at his deathbed and that you must rush home, but knowing you, you'd ring his doctor and get it verified before you came, and my story would be blown. So I'll tell the truth. It was a silly fight between two silly stubborn people who are more alike than either of them realise, but because of your stubbornness, all our Christmases for the past three years have been spoilt. Your brother misses you, your sister misses you, your nieces and nephew miss you. Your father misses you too, even if he won't admit it. And I miss you too, more than anyone. Please, Martha, come home for Christmas. I'll have a place set for you. You only have to stay for a drink if dinner is too much. But please, come home."'

It was all read out in an extremely dramatic fashion. Glenda smiled at Martha as she finished. 'I used to be in an amateur dramatic society.'

'I'm sure it was amateur.'

Glenda didn't react. 'So what shall I say back to her?'

'Nothing.'

'Nothing?'

Martha lost patience. She stood up. 'Glenda, how do I make myself clear? I didn't want to hear that message in the first place, and I especially didn't want to hear you acting it out. My mother doesn't speak anything like that.'

'No, you're right. She has a lovely quiet voice. I shouldn't have added my own interpretation, but the whole subject, a family rift, two stubborn people, what sounds like the age-old clash between generations . . . I suppose the drama of it appealed to me and I —'

'Glenda, do you mind?'

'So what shall I say back?'

'Nothing!' Martha practically shouted the word.

Glenda was unmoved. 'I can't do that.'

'I beg your pardon?'

'I promised your mother I'd ring her back. And I always keep my promises.'

'Glenda, I think it might be best if you don't work here any more. I'll call your agency now.'

'You'll have trouble getting anyone else.'

'I'm sorry?'

'You've got a reputation at the agency. No one likes coming to work here. That's why you got me. I'm older than the others. I've seen the best and worst of bosses already.' She smiled. 'I'm also very good at my job. I've finished your filing, typed and posted your letters and inputted this month's figures. You can't fault me on the work side of things.'

'That's why you're meddling in my private life, is it? Because you've got nothing else to do?'

'That's part of it. Mostly, it's because you seem lonely and I liked talking to your mother and she sounded at her wits' end about you.'

'Thank you, Glenda. That'll be all for now.'

'So I'll call and let your mother know that you haven't made up your mind yet?'

'No, Glenda. You won't.'

'You'll let her know yourself?'

'Neither of us will let her know anything.'

'How rude.'

'I'm sorry?'

'She's your mother. No matter what happened between you and your father, it's not very fair to punish your mother because of it. It sounds like she only wants the best for all your family. And it is Christmas time.'

'I don't like Christmas, Glenda. I never have.'

'So go and see them after Christmas. Before then, even. That might be a better way to do it, actually. People do tend to get worked up on Christmas Day, all the pressure to have fun, tempers fraying, too much alcohol . . . Is that why you had that fight with your father?'

'No, neither of us drink. We were fighting because —' She stopped abruptly. 'I don't need to tell you what we were fighting about.'

'No, don't. I'll ask your mother when I ring her back. I'll get an unbiased account then.'

Martha reached for the phone. 'I'm ringing the agency now. Cancelling my contract with them. Your behaviour is completely —'

'Unacceptable? I have heard that before. Please go ahead and ring them. But I mean it. You won't get anyone else to fill in at this short notice, from my agency or any other. This is peak season for temps. And your own secretary did have to give me a big briefing. If you sack me, I won't get to give my replacement a briefing and you'll be in chaos for the next month. But that's your call, of course.'

Martha counted to ten. It was all she could do. 'Thank you, Glenda. That's all for now.'

'I'll give your mother your best wishes, though, will I?'

'If that's what it will take to get you out of my office so I can do some work.'

'That's all it will take. Thank you, Miss Kaminski.' She closed the door gently behind her.

Guests 5, 6 and 7

Holly handed over a beautifully packaged, brandy-soaked plum pudding to her latest customer, who smiled with apparent delight when he noticed her nametag and remarked what a perfect name it was for this time of year.

'She's got a sister called Belle too. Short for "Jingle Bells",' the bakery owner June said cheerily beside her.

'And a brother called Rudolph?' the customer asked.

'No, no brothers,' Holly said, still smiling, even though she'd heard all the jokes before. 'And my surname isn't Berry, either. I promise.'

'You should change your name at Christmas time,' June said when the old man had finished giving them season's greetings and they were alone again. 'I'd go crazy if I were you.'

'Do you go crazy in June, June?'

June grinned. 'Good point. I guess I've handled it for the past fifty years. I can handle another few decades. Can you keep an eye out here while I go and wrap some more puddings? They're racing out the door today. What is it? Has everyone suddenly realised it's only a couple of weeks until Christmas?'

Holly knew it wasn't just people noticing the date. It was the wonderful quality of the puddings. June's bakery was small, and easy to miss on this busy Adelaide city-centre shopping strip, but she was such a skilled baker of not only puddings, but also cakes, buns, bread, even scones, that they had a stream of regular customers at all times of the year, not just Christmas. Holly had worked there for two years, originally part-time after school and full-time for the past ten months. She loved everything about her job, from the baking to the selling – the smell of the spices, the feel of the dough, the sight of it rising, the warmth and colour of the shop itself, with its plump buns, colourful cakes, all made from June's own recipes. Holly was slowly learning them all, gaining confidence under June's patient, careful teaching methods. 'You've a gift for this,' June had said to her the previous week after Holly produced a batch of flawless sponge cakes. The compliment had kept Holly going for days.

She used the brief quiet period now to tidy the small cluster of tables and chairs that took up one end of the bakery. June was a stickler for keeping everything spotless and organised. Holly was back behind the counter, crouched down wiping the glass shelves when she heard the door open.

A child's voice spoke. 'Can we please have five scones, one loaf of raisin bread —'

'And fifteen frog cakes?'

Holly peered out through the glass of the counter. Her two little sisters were standing there, beaming in at her. She stood up, nearly hitting her head on the shelf. 'Belle! Chloe! What are you doing here?'

'Mum wasn't there after school,' Chloe said. 'So we came here instead, like you told us to do if it happened again.'

Belle had her nose pressed against the glass. 'Can we really have fifteen frog cakes?'

'No, Belle, you can't,' Holly said. 'What happened to Mum? Where is she?'

'I don't know,' Chloe said. 'We waited for a while but she still didn't come so we just decided to leave and come here.'

'Did you tell your teacher you were going? No? Oh, Chloe. You should have. What if Mum turns up and you're not there?' Holly took out her phone and dialled. 'Mum, it's me. The girls are here . . . I know. Yes, they walked . . . No, but . . . did you tell them Dad was coming instead? Well, he wasn't there. No. Okay. Mum, please . . . Fine. Fine. Okay. Bye.'

'Is she cross with Dad again?' Chloe was very serious.

'Is she cross with us?' Belle was just as serious.

Holly suddenly wanted to pull both her sisters into a tight hug and never let them go. They were just little kids. They shouldn't have to ask questions like that. They shouldn't have had to walk more than two kilometres because their mother had forgotten to tell them their father was supposed to collect them. They shouldn't have to be told that he'd forgotten all about it.

'He's bloody useless,' Holly's mother had just shouted down the phone. 'I always pick them up. And for once, just once, I ask him to do it, and look what happens. I should have known he'd forget. His problem is he is so bloody caught up in —'

Holly had heard it all before, too many times. It was as if her parents had studied a handbook in how to behave badly. 1. Fight constantly. 2. Use children as pawns. 3. Make life so hard and so difficult, every day.

Holly crouched down to their level, deciding she wasn't going to tell the girls any more than they needed to hear. 'Now, I can't give you fifteen frog cakes and all those scones, because your dentist would kill me.' She heard a noise from behind her. 'And not only your dentist, but so would my boss.'

'I sure would,' June said, appearing from the storeroom with a box of puddings freshly tied in shiny red paper and green ribbons. 'Hello, Chloe-Belle.' She always called them the one name like that. They loved it. 'Have you skipped school again? That's it. I'm calling the police.'

'It's *after* school, June,' Chloe said.

'We're finished for the day,' Belle said. 'Until tomorrow. We go back tomorrow.'

'In that case you'll need something to give you energy for another day. Scone, bun or frog cake?'

'You weren't expecting them, were you?' June asked Holly in a whisper, once the girls were set up at one of the tables with milk, a green frog cake and a comic each. 'Trouble at home again?'

Holly nodded. For the first year Holly had worked with June, she hadn't said a word about her family situation. Until one day, having been up all night with the girls while her parents yelled at each other, she'd come in with shadows under her eyes. 'Are you sick?' June had asked in her blunt way. 'You look like death. You'll put my customers off their food.'

Holly had overreacted. 'Please don't sack me,' she'd pleaded, tears in her eyes. 'I love this job. Please, June.' June got her a glass of water, a chair and for the next fifteen minutes, listened to Holly pour out all that had happened, and kept happening, at home.

'Have they tried counselling?' June asked.

'They wouldn't. They wouldn't be able to stop blaming one another for long enough.'

'There's no one else you can live with, even for a little while? An aunt? Uncle? Grandparents?'

Holly shook her head.

'Could you leave? Get a flat on your own?'

'And leave Belle and Chloe behind? Never.'

'Why are your parents still together? Wouldn't it be easier on everyone if they just split up?'

'They tried it once, for a week.' It had been even worse, Holly told her. Her mother had insisted on taking Belle and Chloe and had gone to stay with a friend. Holly remained in the family home with her father, out of guilt, out of love, out of a combination of both. She'd rung her sisters every night and her heart had almost broken to hear the two of them so upset. She was the one who eventually made her mother come home, promising on behalf of her father that it would be different this time. It was different for two days. The fighting started again on the third day.

'You poor kids,' June said simply.

It had helped Holly just to talk about it. June rarely asked much, just a gentle enquiry now and again. She was very generous, though. If extra shifts were on offer, Holly was always the first one asked. And any leftover buns, bread and cakes always seemed to go to Holly too. 'The girls might like them for their school lunches,' she'd say.

A flurry of customers stopped their conversation for the next fifteen minutes. In the following lull, June walked over to the girls' table, praised them both for making their frog cakes last so long – they'd both taken just small nibbles from the edge, working their way into the centre. She put four containers of sugar sachets in front of them, asking their help to count them. 'There should be twenty in each bowl. Can you make sure of that for me?'

They started work immediately, counting aloud.

Back at the counter, June spoke to Holly. 'So, any special plans for Christmas yet?'

Holly shrugged, about to say no, not really, when Chloe piped up. 'Yes! A secret plan!'

'We're running away!' Belle added.

Chloe pouted. 'Belle! I was going to tell June! You've got a big mouth!'

'They're both joking,' Holly said quickly.

'We can tell June, can't we?' Chloe came over, all shining eyes and eager voice. 'We won a competition, June. We're going to a motel called Valley something. For three nights. There's even a pool.'

'Only two hours from here,' Belle said, coming over too. 'Holly's going to drive.'

'All five of you?' June asked. 'That'll be fun.'

Belle shook her head. 'Not Mum and Dad.'

'No, Belle,' Chloe said. 'They *can* come and sleep in cardboard boxes, but only if they're good.'

'Well, that sounds lovely,' June said, giving Holly a 'kids and their imaginations, hey?' look.

'Mad as snakes, the pair of them,' Holly said, busying herself arranging the puddings.

'So what *are* you all doing for Christmas, if you're not running away in a secret plan?' June asked again, once Chloe and Belle were back busily moving the remains of their frog cakes around their plates.

'I don't know yet,' Holly said. It was the truth.

That night it was quiet at home. Both her parents had gone out after dinner, separately, leaving her to babysit. There had been a brief argument between them about what had happened with the school pick-up that day, but Holly made sure neither Belle nor Chloe heard it. She'd kept them busy on the computer. Another email had arrived that day from the Valley View Motel. She hadn't had the heart to put an end to their excitement yet, so she'd asked the girls to help her fill out the brief questionnaire someone called Lola Quinlan had sent. The girls had loved doing it, calling out their favourite drinks, food and carols. Another question had asked their age. There was no problem with the girls. But Holly couldn't say she was seventeen. She picked a number at random, thirty-five, keeping up the charade that she was their mother. She answered the final question honestly, at least. Reason for spending Christmas at the Valley View Motel? Peace and quiet, she wrote.

She was about to go to bed when her mobile rang. It was June. Her boss rarely rang her after hours.

'June? Is everything all right?'

'No, it's not. That's why I'm ringing. Holly, tell me to mind my own business if you want, but I've been thinking about Christmas. Your Christmas. I can't stop thinking about it.'

Holly stayed quiet.

'Was what the girls said today true? Were you really thinking about running away?'

About to deny it again, Holly suddenly felt too tired. 'Yes,' she said. She told June what had happened, the three of them looking at the website together, sending off an email just for fun on Holly's part, and then the excitement of finding they'd won a competition.

'Oh, Holly. That would be a pretty tough Christmas, three kids away on their own like that. And your parents would be so worried, wouldn't they?'

Holly stayed silent again.

June's tone softened. 'Holly, the three of you can spend Christmas with us if you want. We've got heaps of room. There'll be heaps of food too.'

Holly's eyes filled with tears. How many times had she wished that June was her mum, that June's lovely quiet husband was her dad, that their three grown-up daughters were her big sisters, looking after her for once? But that wasn't the way it was. 'Thanks anyway. We'll be okay.'

'It's not right. A girl your age worrying about Christmas because her parents are too busy fighting. I'd like to bang their bloody heads together.'

That made Holly smile. 'I'd like to see you try. Thanks, June.'

'It'll work out, love.'

'I hope so,' Holly said.

Chapter Eight

The heat coming in through the open door of the charity shop was remarkable, like an oven on full blast. Lola fanned herself with the Senorita fan she'd unpacked that morning. It went very well with her outfit for the day – a Spanish-style ruffled top over what she believed was called a maxi dress these days, but she still preferred to call a kaftan. It was the coolest thing she owned, temperature- and style-wise. She'd have to raid the shop's racks again if this weather continued. And it would, according to last night's forecast. Another week of at least forty-degree temperatures was expected. At this rate, if it kept up till Christmas Day, she could just toss the prawns she planned to serve onto the asphalt and they'd cook in seconds.

It wouldn't just be prawns she'd be cooking, either. The emailed questionnaires to her guests had produced excellent results – that morning she'd received four replies. A brief one from the gentleman in Broken Hill, saying he didn't have any favourites. Perfect, she'd thought, a trouble-free guest. There had been a sweet note from the family of three, Holly and her two children, Chloe and Belle. Holly had put her age as mid-thirties, the girls were aged eight and six. They were very specific that their favourite cereal was Coco Pops, their favourite drink milkshakes and their favourite colours purple and pink. Martha in Melbourne liked seafood, fruit and New Zealand white wine. Lola had also heard back from the couple in Victoria – favourite food: simple and un-spicy, favourite colour: red, and favourite drink: white wine and beer. Unfortunately only two of her guests had answered her question about why they had chosen the Valley View Motel. Peace and quiet, the family said. A change of scenery, the couple wrote. No matter, she'd ask the others face-to-face when they arrived. It would make a great conversational ice-breaker.

She'd decided to keep all the information she was collating for her Secret Christmas in the most battered and innocent-looking notebook she could find, and carry it in her bag at all times. She most certainly wasn't going to risk picking up her emails on the motel computer any more, either. Not with Geraldine sniffing about for enough evidence to have her committed to an asylum or a nursing home, whichever had a vacancy first. Though perhaps Lola should be thanking her, rather than still feeling that strong desire to lock her in the motel coolroom for a few hours. At least everything about her and Jim's plans were now out in the open.

She hadn't told Patricia or her other friends the news yet. She knew they would be supportive and, if she told the story the right way, instantly outraged on her behalf against Geraldine. Perhaps they would be quick with suggestions, too. Patricia might offer a temporary room in her house. She had the space now that Luke spent most nights in Adelaide. Lola also knew that the sister in charge of the main old folks' home in the Valley was a cousin of Kay's, and would be very helpful with applications and the like. But it was too soon to talk about it yet. The truth was Lola still felt too shocked.

That was life for you, she realised. You could plot and plan and organise as much as you liked, but you never knew what was going to come flying out of nowhere and give you a big surprise or a nasty shock. She still hadn't decided whether Jim's bombshell news was one or the other. Possibly both.

Now, though, she had no choice but to put her living plans and even her Secret Christmas plans to one side. Today was all about the front window. She, Margaret and Patricia had already spent two hours removing everything from the display area. It had been so hot in there next to the glass they'd begun to feel like chickens in a rotisserie. Mrs Kernaghan was supposed to be helping too, but she'd rung five minutes before the agreed start-ing time to say that she'd been caught up at another unspecified and very important meeting and would be there as soon as she could.

Margaret passed over the last of the shirts from the display, leaving the shop's only and very old mannequin naked. She wiped a sweaty lock of hair from her forehead and clambered over the small barrier that separated the front window from the shop. 'It just needs a sweep now. If you pass me that broom, Lola —'

Lola shook her head. 'Mrs Kernaghan will be flying in on hers any minute now. She can do it.' So childish, but Lola was glad to see her friends giggle.

The door opened behind them, giving all three of them a minor fright, until they saw it wasn't Mrs Kernaghan, but Luke. He glanced at the empty window and the piles of old display material in Lola's arms and frowned. 'I would have helped you do that. Why didn't you wait till I got here?'

'Because your time is more valuable spent in Mission Control back there,' Lola answered. 'And in any case, we're doing this for the window display competition and the rules are strict. Displays to be mounted by staff only. Or volunteers, as in our case.'

'Why? In case someone cheats and flies in the Harrods window dresser?'

'Very funny. It's to guard against sabotage, actually,' Lola said. 'Last year, don't you remember, Len the butcher asked a group of high school students to do his display and it all went horribly wrong.' Poor Len hadn't realised they were all vegetarians. It took him days to scrape the Meat is Murder graffiti off the glass.

Luke held up a USB stick. 'Okay if I go through? It's the new program I promised I'd load up.'

'The bridge game?' Margaret's eyes lit up. 'Can I go first?'

'You'll be too busy here, Margaret,' Lola said. 'My poor arthritic knees have just started twitching a warning. I think our esteemed leader is about to arrive.'

Half an hour later, more than Lola's arthritic knees were

twitching. Her entire being was radiating with fury. She wasn't sure exactly how it happened, but within minutes of arriving Mrs Kernaghan had somehow managed to find herself a seat in the coolest part of the shop, directly under the airconditioner. She'd spent the time since directing – ordering, in fact – Patricia and Margaret around like a pair of stagehands. 'There's no point me getting in the window area myself. I need to stand back to make sure my internal vision is being replicated.'

On the bright side, Lola thought, at least she hadn't been asked to clamber up and down the ladder or over the barrier time and time again like an elderly Grand National horse. Her job description appeared to be official holder and fetcher. Mrs Kernaghan had arrived with a large basket of coloured chiffon and Lola's role was to hand the lengths of material to Patricia and Margaret as instructed.

'I might need a cup of tea soon, Mrs K,' Patricia said, wiping the sweat from her forehead. 'It's very hot in the window.'

'Good idea. A break will do us all good. Because I'm afraid we're going to have to start from scratch. It's just not looking as I imagined it at all.'

'How *did* you imagine it?' Lola asked. 'On hallucinogenic drugs?'

Patricia gasped. Mrs Kernaghan simply ignored her. As Margaret gave a sigh and prepared to climb back over the barrier and take down all the red, yellow and green fabric strips she'd just spent more than an hour painstakingly arranging around the store dummy, Lola decided enough was enough.

'Luke?' She called his name so loudly she was glad to see Mrs Kernaghan give a little jump beside her.

Luke's head emerged from behind the curtain. 'Yes, Lola?'

'You've helped me sort CDs here before, haven't you? And moved the clothes racks for me as well?'

'Well, a while ago. I'd have helped out more, but you know, with work and all the travel —'

'Darling, I'm not accusing you. I'm praising you. Because of course that means you are a volunteer as well. Which means that you are legally permitted to assist with the window display competition. Come here and clamber about for a little while, would you? Before your poor mother and poor Margaret collapse in the heat.'

'We were about to stop for a cup of tea,' Mrs Kernaghan said sharply. 'I thought it best to keep the momentum going until then.'

'Splendid idea,' Lola answered. 'Luke, keep the momentum going with Mrs Kernaghan for a little while, would you? I feel a three-cup pot of Irish breakfast tea coming on. We'll take breaks in shifts, Mrs Kernaghan, don't you think?'

In the back room, Lola was surprised to be turned on rather than thanked by her friends.

'Why wait so long to stand up to her?' Margaret hissed. 'What's wrong with you, Lola? Once upon a time you'd have eaten someone like Mrs Kernaghan for breakfast. Now you're letting her walk all over you and all over us.'

Patricia nodded. 'And I still don't have a clue what this display is supposed to represent.'

Lola gave an airy wave of her hand. 'It's about fire. Earth. Passion. Progress. I'll stand up to her tomorrow. It's too hot today. Lemon or milk, my dears?'

It was nearly four p.m. before Mrs Kernaghan pronounced herself happy with the way the window looked. They had attracted a lot of attention from passersby in the main street throughout the afternoon. Groups of schoolchildren giggling and laughing at Luke up a ladder covered in colourful chiffon. Several other onlookers from nearby shops. Mrs Kernaghan hadn't been happy to see them. 'Try and stand in front of it, Luke. I don't want them stealing my ideas.'

Lola, Margaret and Patricia were now seated in a row as close to the airconditioner as possible. Whether it was dehydration – she still hadn't stopped for a cup of tea – or a kind of creative mania, Mrs Kernaghan was now in full flight and, much as it pained Lola to admit it, proving to be an entertaining diversion on a hot afternoon. She was lucky that Luke had the patience of Job and also the fitness levels of a mountain goat. Anyone else would have snapped the ladder in two if they'd had to run up and down it so many times. Not to mention possibly suffocated Mrs Kernaghan in her own fabric creation.

Finally, she seemed happy. 'I need to view it as the judges will, though,' she said. 'Everyone, follow me.'

Everyone did. Again, a blast of furnace air as the front door opened. Moments later, they were all lined up in front of the window, staring in.

'Perfect,' Mrs Kernaghan breathed. 'It's everything I dreamed.'

She'd obviously been having nightmares, Lola thought. The previous window display of second-hand shirts, dresses, books and toys had been replaced with what looked like a snapshot from Dante's 'Inferno'. If this was a representation of Christmas, then Lola was, well, Lady Gaga. The display was a nauseating mixture of garish strips of material wound around their store mannequin. It looked like an Egyptian mummy with 1960s hippy leanings. Not only that, despite Mrs Kernaghan's sternest instructions and Luke's most patient attempts to follow them, the entire display appeared in danger of collapsing at any moment. Even their exit through the door had produced a current of air that was causing the chiffon to flutter and the dummy to teeter in a worrying way.

Before Lola could mention it, Margaret did. 'I think we might need to put another support up there, Mrs Kernaghan. Or change the design a bit. Otherwise, it'll wobble any time we open the front door.'

'We'll just have to use the back door. Another support will spoil the whole flowing effect and there is no way I'm changing the design. It's perfect. *Perfect*.'

'I don't think it's practical to use the back door,' Lola said, as mildly as possible. 'We're a shop.'

'We'll just have to limit the times we open the door, then. Wait until there are a few people and bring them inside in groups.'

Lola was conscious of Luke staring at her, expecting her to bite back. She wouldn't. It was her new approach. She was getting too interfering. She had to let others have their say.

'Are you all locked out?'

Lola turned to greet the new arrival, a young plump-ish woman in her early twenties, with brown curly hair and a shy smile. She was wearing a blue dress that matched her eyes. 'Emily, hello there! Don't you look lovely in your new uniform?'

Emily blushed, the colour obvious even against her heat-flush. 'Hi, Lola.'

'You know everyone, Emily, I think? Margaret, Patricia, Mrs Kernaghan, this is my dear friend Emily, once one of the finest waitresses we ever had at the motel, and now the manager of the finest gourmet food store in Clare. And you already know Luke, Emily, of course.'

'Hi, Emily.'

'Hi, Luke.'

Lola watched closely as two of her favourite young friends greeted each other. She wasn't imagining it. Emily was now blushing even more furiously and Luke had changed colour too, from white to red and back again. Either Mrs Kernaghan's display was making him bilious or something else was to blame. In Lola's experience, young men his age only blushed when they were nervous, and they were usually only nervous when they were face to face with someone they might just happen to have a little bit of a crush on. Lola was fairly certain she could rule herself and the other three elderly women out of the equation. He must have a crush on Emily! Lovely shy Emily! How wonderful! A little budding romance between two of her dearest youngsters! Just what she needed to keep herself busy in the run-up to Christmas.

No time like the present to get things moving, either. She whipped out her Spanish fan and waved it furiously in front of her face. 'I do believe I'm about to faint. Emily, would you please be able to give me a cool glass of water in your cafe? Luke, would you please escort me there? I'll be back as soon as I can, ladies. Congratulations again, Mrs Kernaghan. Your window is one in a million.'

Lola didn't think she imagined Margaret's muttered response. 'A million disasters, that is.'

She hid a smile as she continued down the main street, with Emily on one side and Luke on the other.

An hour later, Lola had taken off her shoes, lain down on her bed with the airconditioning at full tilt and begun to reflect on a good start to her matchmaking. She'd left Luke and Emily together at her cafe, insisting Luke stay and help Emily put up some new shelves, insisting equally forcefully that she was more than happy to catch a taxi back to the motel. Her eyelids had just begun to close and the pleasure of an afternoon nap was about to take her over when she was jolted awake by the bedside phone ringing.

'Lola Quinlan speaking.'

'Lola, it's Daniel.'

She sat up immediately, smiling into the phone. She was very fond of Bett's husband. 'How are you, darling? How are those two little angels of yours?'

'I'm not home yet, but I've just spoken to Bett and she said they're both fast asleep at the same time for the first time in months. I think they run on battery power. The only problem is we can't find the off switch. What will it be like when they're walking and talking?'

'Hideous, I expect. But fun too. What can I do for you, my dear? Are you planning a little surprise for Bett?'

'It's about Bett, but it's not a surprise. Not a good one any-way. Lola, can I come and see you on the way home from work? I need your help.'

He was there at the door less than half an hour later. He seemed as harassed as Bett had been earlier that week. Hand-some as ever, Lola thought, with his tousled black hair and dark eyes, but he also looked like he hadn't slept in months. 'I'm sorry to barge in like this,' he said.

'There's no one I'd rather be barged in on than you. What is it?'

'I'm worried about Bett, Lola. I didn't know whether to talk to you or to Geraldine, but —'

'You decided to start at the top? I'm attempting a joke, dear Daniel, to lighten the mood and relax you. What's wrong? Tell me everything.'

It poured out of him. His concern that Bett was exhausted. Not sleeping. Worrying too much, about every little thing the twins did, ate, touched or drank. 'I've read about postnatal depression. Is that what she has? She was so devastated by Anna's death, Lola, I'm worried the babies are too much for her, that she can't cope emotionally, let alone physically. I've tried to help,

I'm still trying, but —' His eyes filled with tears and he roughly wiped them away. 'I can't seem to do anything right. One minute she's happy I've got the new job, next she's sounding like she wants me to hand in my notice. But we can't afford it. Things are tough enough as it is, with the mortgage and everything else —'

'What happened with her at the doctor?'

'The doctor?'

'Bett had a doctor's appointment earlier this week.'

'She didn't mention it. Was it for her or the twins?'

'She was on her own when I saw her.'

Daniel went still.

'She assured me someone was minding them,' Lola said quickly. 'Your neighbour, I think she said.'

'Why didn't she tell me about it?'

'Daniel, I don't know. Go and talk to her. Ask her.'

He stood up, reached for his car keys, then stopped. 'I thought it was supposed to be easier than this. More fun.'

'It will be.'

'She's changed.'

'She's a mother now, Daniel. Everything changes when that happens. You're different too. You're parents now. That's a big deal. But keep talking to each other about it. That has to be your starting point.'

It wasn't until he had driven away that she realised he'd been so preoccupied he hadn't said goodbye.

She'd barely lain down when the phone rang again. She answered it as cheerily as possible.

'Lola, hi. It's Matthew.'

'Matthew, how are you?' She liked Carrie's husband too, though not as much as she liked Daniel. Was it all right to have favourite grandsons-in-law? She'd certainly felt that Matthew was the wrong person for Bett, and had been as surprised as everyone else when he and Carrie became a couple, but in the years that passed, she'd come to the conclusion that they were probably just right for one another. Carrie was a dear, when it suited her, but she was also spoilt. Her looks were to blame, probably – those blonde curls and blue eyes meant people treated her in the same way they treated kittens, as something to be admired and cosseted. Matthew had a solidity about him, in personality and physique, which was probably what Carrie needed. He just didn't have that sparkle in the eye that Lola liked to see and that Daniel definitely had. Still, it was always nice to get a call from him. 'How can I help you, dear?'

'It's about Carrie. Lola, can I come and see you after work?'

Had she hung up a *Marriage Guidance Here Tonight* sign outside her door without realising? 'Of course.'

He got straight to the point as soon as he arrived an hour later. 'I'm worried about Carrie, Lola. She's started getting obsessed about Bett again. Talking about her all the time.'

'Obsessed about Bett again? When did she get obsessed with Bett the last time?'

Matthew shifted uncomfortably. 'When, you know, a few years ago. When they were still feuding —'

'Over you? Of course, darling. How could I have forgotten?

And do you think that's happening again? That Bett's back in love with you?'

'She was never in love with me. That's not the problem now either. Lola, Carrie's just not herself any more. She hasn't been since Bett had the twins. She's cranky all the time. She talks about Bett constantly, about her kids, our kids, who's doing what, eating what, how they're sleeping. About who's the better mother. It's turned into some kind of competition between them and I don't know what to do about it. What do I do?'

'Nothing.'

'Nothing?'

'It's between them, Matthew, between Bett and Carrie. If you interfere, you'll only make it worse. As for Carrie's crankiness, you'll just have to try and weather that as well. What more could you possibly do to help her? You already cook four nights a week, don't you?'

'Me? Cook?' He looked even more uncomfortable. 'I try, of course. I mean, I do the occasional barbie, but Carrie's always been the one more interested in that side of things.'

That side of things? Lola thought. Feeding her family? She continued. 'And you give the kids their baths each night, don't you? So that Carrie gets an hour to herself at the end of the day?'

His silence and the expression on his face told her all she needed to know. So Carrie had been lying about that to Bett. This wasn't the time to challenge Matthew, though. She smiled at him instead. 'Really, darling, I wouldn't worry. You have three children under five. Life is just going to be a bit chaotic for a few years. Keep up the good work. Oh, and bring home a bunch of flowers now and again. From a florist, not a service station. That always works wonders. Start tonight, in fact. There's a good boy.'

She had him bundled out the door and into his car before he realised what she was doing.

She'd hoped to spend tonight making plans for her Christmas guests. It seemed she had business closer to home to attend to first. Poor Bett and poor Carrie. Who would be a mother in this day and age? So much pressure from so many sides, to do everything brilliantly – be the perfect mother, perfect wife, to choose between holding down a full-time job, a part-time job or being an at-home mother, to stay engaged with the world and also be guilt-free, while managing to cook gourmet meals, keep the house spotless and also stylishly decorated, and, oh yes, wear fashionable clothes on your slim post-baby body. Simple.

Impossible, more like it. Lola tried to remember her own first years as a mother. Had there been that pressure from other mothers around her when Jim was young? If there was, she couldn't remember it. Perhaps it helped that they moved around so much, and she was never in the one spot long enough to join a peer group and feel their pressure. It existed now, though. She read about it in newspapers and magazines, and saw it for herself among motel guests or customers at the charity shop. An old lady learnt a lot about the modern world through the joys of eavesdropping.

Lola knew there was no point bemoaning such competitive

behaviour, or declaring loudly and often that everyone should just get on and be more understanding of each other. Human nature was human nature. Bett and Carrie were perfect case studies. If they weren't being competitive about who was the better mother, they'd have been competitive about their jobs, or their houses or their husbands. It was just the kind of relationship they had. Lola had seen it between them as children. They'd been two little savages sometimes, fighting over the same doll, pulling each other's hair, pinching one another when they thought Lola wasn't looking. Anna had been a buffer of sorts between them, in childhood and later. And now with Anna gone . . .

What *was* it with sisters? Kay in the shop was the same about hers, Lola recalled. In her late sixties, a mature, retired woman, and yet she still often complained about her little sister – aged fifty-nine – and how annoying she was whenever she came to visit. Joan too. She had two sisters and alternated between talking about them as the most angelic, entertaining beings in the world and being infuriated by them. Another of the shop volunteers hadn't spoken to her sister in more than thirty years, since an argument over a damaged David Cassidy record, of all things.

Perhaps Lola should be glad she was an only child, much as she had begged her parents to give her a brother and a sister. She had been like a zoo exhibit in Ireland at that time, the only one in her class without at least four siblings. 'It must be so wonderful,' one of her classmates sighed once. 'You never have to share anything. It's all yours. You're *allowed* to be selfish.'

What could she do for Bett and Carrie now? she wondered. Listen whenever they needed to moan? Praise them effusively at regular intervals? She did that already and it hadn't seemed to help. What they probably both needed more than anything was an extra pair of hands at meal and bath times, a full-time cook and cleaner, a nanny on standby, more money, more sleep, more time to themselves and more understanding husbands. That was some wish list. All out of the question, too, unfortunately, so far as being anything Lola herself could supply. Twenty years ago, perhaps, but the sad truth was she no longer had the stamina or the strength to mind babies and little children on her own. Jim and Geraldine offered to babysit, she knew, and already had that once-a-week arrangement with Carrie and her trio on netball night, but they were running a business themselves, and had little spare time as it was. One of the hard facts of parenthood was that sometimes the only people who could do it were the parents themselves.

Perhaps what Lola could do was try to mend some of those broken fences between Bett and Carrie? Remind them of the fun times they'd had, performing as children together, or more recently, when they'd staged her musical 'Many Happy Returns'. They'd got on well then, hadn't they? Under duress, but Lola could clearly recall laughter and camaraderie between them. Was that the solution this time, too? Write a musical as quickly as she could, one with lots of bit parts for babies and toddlers and four-year-olds and veterinarian husbands and photographer husbands, so their entire families could be involved too?

Lola imagined the scene in the rehearsal room and actually shuddered. No, that most definitely wasn't the answer this time. But something would occur to her, she knew it. Something important, something special, to help bring Bett and Carrie together, to help them put their differences aside . . .

And what better to aid the thinking process, Lola decided, than a very large, very cold gin and tonic.

CHAPTER NINE

Singing along to the radio as she folded two large baskets of laundry, her beautiful babies gurgling to themselves in their high-chairs beside her, Bett felt as though the world around her had changed from grey to colour. It was the happiest she'd felt for a long time. Her meeting with her editor earlier that week couldn't have gone better. Afterwards, Bett had gone to one of the main street cafes and enjoyed a leisurely pot of peppermint tea and a slow read of two – two! – glossy magazines. She'd never known three hours to last so long. The twins were just waking from a nap when she arrived back home, right on six p.m. as arranged. Jane said they'd behaved like angels and had told Bett – truth-fully, she insisted – that she was more than happy to babysit any time she needed.

'But you've got your hands full already.'

'Lexie is deaf, Bett. Not difficult, not a handful, just deaf.'

It was a gentle rebuke, but a rebuke nevertheless. They'd agreed to Jane minding the twins again for a few hours the fol-lowing week. Lexie had loved playing with them, Jane told her.

Beside her, Lexie nodded and smiled and signed a long complicated message that Jane translated. 'She said that they are the funniest babies she's ever met and when she grows up she wants to have three sets of twins.'

Today had been great, too. Yvette had slept and fed like a dream. Zach too. He was even looking for more after usually being a slow eater. While they bashed their spoons against their highchair trays, she made a big salad for Daniel and her to eat out on the verandah later. She'd decided that was the perfect setting in which to break her news. And what great news. Rebecca had rung that afternoon to confirm the details. She wanted Bett to work a few hours here and there before Christmas, and then start back one full day a week in the new year.

Bett couldn't wait to tell Daniel. For once, though, her imagined scenarios let her down. No matter how many times she rehearsed her announcement, she couldn't picture his reaction.

She tried again now. 'Daniel, guess what! I've been offered a part-time job back at the paper! All you have to do is go part-time too!' That was exactly the way to be. Upbeat but firm. And what would Daniel say in return? She didn't know yet. But it would be fine. Absolutely fine. He'd agree, of course. And before they knew it, the new arrangement would be working perfectly, the twins would be settled and very happy to have their mum *and* dad around so much, and tranquillity would descend on the house.

She tensed as she heard the sound of Daniel's car.

She didn't get time to serve the salad or even go out to the verandah. After swiftly kissing Yvette and Zachary and making sure they were both firmly fastened in their highchairs, Daniel took her hand and led her into the living room. He sat down next to her on the sofa.

'What is it, Bett?'

'What's what?'

'What happened at the doctor?'

'The doctor?'

'Didn't you have a doctor's appointment this week?'

'Who told you that?'

'Lola. Your grandmother. The one you called in to see before your doctor's appointment.'

This evening wasn't going the way she'd expected. Daniel seemed tense. She was tenser. 'It wasn't the doctor.'

'What was it, then?'

She couldn't tell him like this. 'I can't say yet.'

'Bett, I'm your husband. Are you sick?'

She shook her head.

'Then why were you in town?'

'I had to so some shopping.'

'For what?'

'Stuff.'

'Stuff? Bett, what's going on?'

She'd never been so glad to hear Yvette start to cry. She stood up. 'We'll have to talk about this later.'

She managed to keep herself busy with the babies for the next hour. She rang friends she'd put off ringing for weeks. She suggested they eat their salads in front of the TV news. All the time, she was conscious of Daniel watching her.

At eight o'clock he followed her into the kitchen. 'Are you going to clean out the cupboards next? Or do some scrapbooking? Or have you run out of ways to avoid me?'

She didn't answer.

'What is it, Bett?'

'Nothing.'

'I need you to tell me.'

'I'm no good at this, Daniel.'

'At what?'

'This.' She gestured with her arms, all around her. 'At being a mother. A wife and a mother. I'm not even a good sister. I can't do it.'

'You are doing it. You've been a mother, a very good mother, for seven months. A wonderful wife for how long now, nearly three years? So you're wrong so far.' He smiled at her.

'Don't patronise me.' Her shout shocked them both. 'I'm not, Daniel. I'm useless at all of it. I can't talk to you without fighting any more. I'm no good at being a mother. It's like slowly drowning. I can't keep on top of things. Jane minded them for one afternoon, with her own daughter as well, and she somehow managed to get them to sleep and do a load of washing. She even made biscuits for me, Daniel. She did more here in three hours than I've been able to do in months.'

'That's not true.'

'It is true. Everyone is better at this than me.'

'Who else?'

'Carrie, Daniel. *Carrie*.' She was shouting now and she didn't care. 'As she reminds me every single day, she has three children, not just two like I have, and yet she manages to run her house perfectly, dress her children perfectly, keep herself fit with her stupid walks and her stupid netball, and she gets Mum and Dad to babysit when I don't even dare ask, and as each day passes she just rubs it in more and more and as each day passes I get more and more jealous of her stupid, smug, perfect life and her stupid, smug, perfect self —'

'Bett —'

'I mean it, Daniel. You don't hear her. You don't hear her telling me what a mess I'm making of it all. She doesn't even need to tell me. I see it for myself every day. She's the perfect mother and I'm the disastrous one. And I'm starting to hate her for it. I mean it. I hate her. And she's the only sister I have left, and sometimes —' The tears came then. 'Sometimes I wish she was the one who died, not Anna. That's how horrible I am, Daniel. And I hate that about myself even more.'

Daniel didn't move, or speak. He just sat watching her.

'It's the truth, Daniel. I'm a bad person. A bad mother. A bad sister. And a bad wife. Do you really want to know what I did this week? I went back to my newspaper and I begged for a job. And they don't even need me in there, but I begged, because if I am here on my own, being a bad mother, for one more day, I am going to go mad. I can't do it. I'm no good at it. And I know I'm supposed to love them and do everything I can for them, and I do love them, so much, but why can't I do it properly? I mean it. What's wrong with me?'

'When were you going to tell me about the job?'

'Tonight.'

'When did you set up the meeting?'

'Last week.'

'And you didn't tell me?'

'I couldn't.'

'But I'm your husband.'

She didn't reply to that.

'What were you going to do with the twins?' he asked.

'I was going to ask you to go part-time and mind them too. I know we can't afford a crèche.'

She kept waiting for him to come over, to put his arms around her, to tell her not to worry, that they'd work it out.

He didn't. He stayed where he was. When he spoke, his voice was low. His expression wasn't angry. He looked tired and sad.

'I thought we had a good relationship, Bett. That we talked about things. That we'd made a family together and we would face everything, the good things and the bad things, together. But you obviously don't see things like that.'

She could only stare back at him. She knew she should say, 'No, you're wrong. Of course we're a family.' But she was too tired, too. Too sad. Too, too everything.

'I'll ask at work tomorrow,' he said.

'What?'

'I'll ask at work tomorrow if I can go part-time in the new year.'

'Just like that?'

'It's what you want, isn't it? That would make you happy? Make everything all right again?'

'Yes. No. I don't know.'

'Bett, you've been planning this for a week. You lied to Lola about it. So it must be important to you. If you want me to ask about going part-time, I'll do it. Do you want me to?'

She suddenly had no idea what on earth she wanted. All she could do was nod.

'Then I will.'

They washed up in silence. Any attempt at conversation from Bett was met by monosyllabic replies from Daniel. He didn't ask her any questions. She asked him three times if he was all right. He nodded each time.

'Just have a lot to think about,' he said.

She went to bed first and lay there crying. If he heard her, he didn't come in to soothe her as he had so many times before, to stroke her hair from her forehead, tell her he loved her, that he loved this family they'd made, tell her to stay in bed, have a good night's sleep. She heard the TV in the living room instead. He was watching a show that she had never known him to watch before.

She was asleep before he came to bed. When she woke twice during the night to see to the twins, he didn't offer to help as he always had before, though she could sense he was awake. When she woke up at six the next morning, moments before the babies began to stir, he'd already left for work.

CHAPTER TEN

More than two hours into her shift at the charity shop, Lola hadn't had a chance to sell so much as a second-hand tie, let alone check her emails or do any more thinking about Bett and Carrie. She'd been completely occupied dealing with the constant stream of amused traders, shoppers and passers-by demanding to know what on earth had taken up position in their front window.

'I know what it looks like, but what is it?' Len the butcher said.

Lola refused to rise to the bait. She parroted Mrs Kernaghan's words. 'It's a representation of the primal forces of nature and the age-old collision between the elements of fire, water, earth and air.'

'And that relates to Christmas how?' the hardware shop manager wanted to know. His front window featured a store dummy dressed in summer Santa gear – red cap, board shorts and zinc cream on his nose.

'You'd need to ask Mrs Kernaghan that.'

Only Mrs Kernaghan had mysteriously gone missing since

it became obvious that her window display was attracting more laughs than gasps of admiration.

Lola looked up now as the door opened again and a couple came in. Good, she didn't know them. Hopefully they were visitors to the town who wouldn't feel the need to pass any smart aleck remarks.

They browsed for a moment, whispering between themselves until the man came to the desk. He was empty-handed.

'Do you mind if I ask —'

Lola steeled herself.

'Is that material hanging on the dummy in the window for sale?'

'You want to buy it? What on earth for?'

He looked a little embarrassed. 'We're from the Riverland and we've had trouble with birds eating our crops. We've tried everything, then we read online that it might be worth trying another kind of scarecrow —'

'You think it looks like a scarecrow?' It was more like an escapee from the *Hammer House of Horror*, Lola thought.

'A bit,' his wife said, before adding hurriedly, 'In a good way, of course.'

Could Lola sell it? Not just the fabric, but the whole display? Tell Mrs Kernaghan someone had made an offer that was just too good to refuse? Pretend it was a gallery owner from Sydney who'd been impressed with her primal rending of abstract blah blah blah?

The couple took her hesitation as a no. 'Thanks anyway. It's given us some great ideas. We just need to get some fabric that colour.'

'Stay right there,' Lola said. Five minutes later she waved as they went off happily with the leftover material. Thank heavens it was gone. Even the sight of it in the box had been giving Lola headaches.

She'd just finished tidying the racks when the door opened again. Her polite smile turned to a genuine one. 'Emily!' she said as the young woman came in. 'What a treat. Please don't feel you need to insult me about the front window display, will you?'

'I think it's very eye-catching,' Emily said diplomatically.

'So is smallpox,' Lola said. She beamed as Emily reached into a bag beside her and brought out a flask still beaded with condensation from the fridge. 'Is that for me? Another of your experiments?'

Emily nodded. 'This heatwave is supposed to go for another couple of weeks, so I thought some new flavours might keep my regular customers happy. You don't mind me testing them on you?'

'I'm honoured,' Lola said. 'What's this one called?'

'Billy Goat Hill blend,' Emily said. 'You know, after the look-out point.' She named all her drinks after local landmarks.

'You don't think it sounds as if you've put a goat into a blender? I'm joking, darling.' She took a sip. 'Let me guess – a base of lemonade, a touch of mint, a hint of ginger and don't tell me, is that raspberry essence? Or is it strawberry?'

'Raspberry. Lola, you really are amazing. One of the wine-makers should hire you to be their taster.'

'I only ever let gin pass my lips, Emily. No point cluttering up my arteries with shiraz or riesling at this late stage. Delicious, dear. A fine addition to your already excellent array of refreshments.'

Emily poured the rest into Lola's glass and then gazed at the window display again. 'It is pretty horrible, Lola. I hope you don't mind me saying. Everyone's talking about it.'

'For the wrong reasons. Yes, I know. It's such a shame. A large cheque like that up for grabs. Think of the good use we could make of it. And one of the other shops will win it and, I don't know, spend it on neon signage or a new till or something.'

'You haven't thought about it accidentally collapsing? It does look flimsy.'

'Emily! What a cunning mind dwells beneath that innocent face of yours. Of course I have. I dreamt last night not of Manderley but of a quick splash of kerosene and a match. Whoosh, up it would go in seconds and then we'd really have a representation of nature's fiery elements. But our poor firemen are busy enough as it is in this heat. I couldn't possibly add to their workload.'

'I could trip and spill the Billy Goat Hill blend on it.'

'Mrs Kernaghan would only be pleased. More colour, more drama.'

The door opened, bringing in another customer and with her, a gust of wind that sent a long frond of chiffon whirling and waving. 'Emily, dear, grab that, would you?' Lola urged. 'The blasted stuff catches in the door every time. We begged Mrs Kernaghan to put up another barrier but apparently that would destroy the soul of the piece.'

'It's only a few days till the judging,' Emily said. 'You could take it all down after that, couldn't you?'

Lola shook her head. 'Unfortunately not. The rules state that entries must stay in place until Boxing Day at least. They're a tourist attraction, apparently. The others, perhaps. Ours is more of a tourist repellent.'

Emily grinned, then glanced at her watch. 'I'd better get back to the cafe.'

'No, not yet!' Lola had been hoping for a chance like this. The sole customer seemed happy browsing. Now, how could she put this diplomatically? She'd given it a lot of thought since she'd seen Emily and Luke blush in each other's company. But Emily was very shy and Luke even shyer. She would have to tread very warily and carefully, not scare the horses, as the saying went, to find out if her hunch was right. She lowered her voice. 'Emily, can I ask you a question?'

Emily whispered back. 'Of course.'

'Have you got a crush on Luke?'

Up came the blush. Bingo! Lola thought. 'Darling, don't be embarrassed,' she said quickly, as Emily put her hands to her cheeks. 'It's lovely news.'

'Is it that obvious? Oh, Lola, no. I'd hate him to know. I'd hate anyone to know. How did you guess?'

'An old dog like me knows lots of tricks, darling.'

'He doesn't know, does he? You haven't told him?'

'Of course not,' Lola said. Not yet, she thought. 'But I couldn't be happier with your choice. He's a lovely young man, so clever, so kind to his mother —'

'So good-looking too.'

Was he? Lola thought he was a dear boy but whether his particular mix of gangliness and that thatch of hair could be officially classed as good-looking, she didn't know. But Emily was blushing even more furiously now.

'What do I do, Lola?'

'Ask him out, of course.'

'Why would he want to go out with me?'

'Why wouldn't he go out with you, more to the point? You're a catch. A successful entrepreneur, sweet-natured —'

'I'm not pretty enough for him.'

'Of course you're pretty enough.' It was only a small lie. Emily wasn't chocolate-box Carrie-pretty, with her frankly plain face and a figure more stocky than model-style, but she had such a kind heart and such a beautiful smile. Qualities like that lasted longer than any good looks.

'Lola, I've had a crush on him for years. Ever since he took us to that disco that night. Do you remember?'

Lola remembered every moment. It had been in Emily's final year of school. A bully of a boy called Kane had picked four of the shyest, most awkward girls in his year and invited them to the end-of-term social with the express intention of standing them all up. In public. Until Lola got wind of his plan and turned the tables, contacting all four of the girls herself. It was Kane who looked the fool as Luke, in his much-loved and now scrapheaped orange Torana, drove the four girls to the social and waited as they made a triumphant entrance past an already humiliated Kane.

'You've been holding a candle for him since then? And done nothing about it? Emily, I take my hat off to your patient nature.'

'It hasn't been patience. I've had to be realistic. What chance would I have with him?'

'Why wouldn't you have a chance with him?'

'He's got everything – looks, a successful career . . . He must have women falling off him.'

Lola tried to remember whether Luke had ever mentioned a girlfriend, either here in Clare or in Adelaide. No, but then again, they did tend to talk computers rather than matters of a Cupid nature. But she hadn't been mistaken, had she? Luke *had* blushed when Emily arrived at the shop that day. Unless it *was* a heat rash . . . 'Leave it with me, Emily.'

'No, Lola. Please, don't! Don't say anything to him. I couldn't bear it.'

'You couldn't bear the possibility of going out with Luke? Has my hearing gone? Didn't I just hear you tell me that you've been carrying a torch for him for years?'

'Yes, but . . . I have to go. Thanks for tasting the drink.' She almost ran out of the shop, the gust of hot air sending the window model teetering even more wildly than usual. Lola had to almost run to catch it just before it toppled.

Geraldine was alone in the kitchen when Lola returned to the motel later that day. There were always several hours in a motel's daily life when all was calm. When the morning cleaning of rooms had been done, the part-time staff had gone home, the dinner preparations finished and it was just a matter of waiting for the first dinner guests to arrive. In all her years in motels and guesthouses, the afternoon had always been Lola's favourite time. She liked the combination of smug organisation and happy anticipation. Would some last-minute guests arrive? Would it be a busy night in the restaurant? Would everything run smoothly or would one of the young waitresses from the town drop a plate or mix up an order? Of course, years had passed since she'd truly had to worry about the motel's operations. That was all Jim and Geraldine's responsibility now, but it was always nice to reminisce.

Geraldine didn't look like she was enjoying a feeling of organisation or anticipation. As usual, she was busy doing something. If she wasn't rearranging the coolroom, she'd be sterilising the stainless steel worktops. Or cleaning the cutlery. Or bleaching the napkins. Today she looked like her life depended on getting the oven as clean as possible, hands in gloves, strong-smelling chemicals and sponge at work.

It had been a sore point when the three girls were younger. They'd wanted their mother to find time for them, to take an interest in them as much as the motel work. But Geraldine had never been that kind of mother. Lola had seen it immediately, when Jim and Geraldine first had their children. Some women were natural mothers. Some women seemed more shocked by the role. Geraldine had been . . . matter-of-fact was the word Lola would have used. Distant. Not cruel. Not unloving. But from their youngest days, it was Lola to whom Anna, Bett or Carrie would come if they wanted fun, or play times. Geraldine cared for them practically, cooked for them, dressed them, took them to school and collected them afterwards if she was free, but Lola knew she was the one who'd fed their imaginations, brought the laughter and music into their lives. Jim had helped, of course. Jim had been – he still was – a doting father and now a doting grandfather. But he'd been busy with the motel work too. It was why Lola had been so glad to be around, to be the constant in the three girls' lives.

How did any parent, married, single, widowed or whatever, manage to give a child everything he or she needed? It was impossible. Perhaps communes were the way to go, Lola thought, a place where children ran wild but free, calling in to many caregivers throughout their days. Or perhaps the best model was life in African villages. Lola had seen fascinating documentaries about their way of childrearing, where many people played a part in a child's care and development. Perhaps she had done her own Irish-Australian motel version of just that. In retrospect, yes, she had. She'd wondered now and again whether Geraldine had resented her presence all those years. Perhaps. But if so, Lola didn't feel any real sympathy for her. What was done was done. And the recent admission from Jim that Geraldine had been snooping on the computer, that she'd been secretly planning

Lola's swift removal to an old folks' home, hadn't made her feel any more sympathetic or disposed towards her daughter-in-law. Still, one needed to keep up appearances, for everyone's sake.

She smiled at her daughter-in-law now. 'Geraldine, dear, how are you? Busy as ever, I see. Aren't you marvellous?' And the award for Most Polite Mother-in-Law goes to Lola Quinlan, she thought.

'I'm fine, thank you.'

No question in return, despite the fact they hadn't seen each other for several days. They hadn't spoken since the night in the office and Jim's bombshell news, in fact. But right then, Lola decided it was time they did.

'So you've decided to move on from here?'

Geraldine's head shot up. 'I thought —'

'Jim asked me not to discuss it publicly yet? Yes, he did. But really, dear, isn't it too much of an elephant in the room? Elephant in the motel, even? You've been feeling this way for a long time, he tells me.'

Geraldine still hadn't stopped cleaning. The sight of her rubbing at the stove, using it as an excuse not to meet her eyes, suddenly infuriated Lola. This might be the last chance she and Geraldine ever got to speak honestly to each other. She used the voice she only ever used on teenage boys swearing or jostling in the charity shop. 'Geraldine, would you please stop cleaning for one minute and talk to me?'

It worked. Geraldine's expression was one of shock but she at least put the sponge down.

Lola continued. 'We haven't talked much over the years, I know. But perhaps we should.'

'Why?'

'Why?' Lola laughed. 'Because I'm Jim's mother.'

'I married Jim, Lola. Not you and Jim.'

'Buy one, get one free,' Lola said. When Geraldine didn't smile, she stopped the joking herself. 'And you've always resented that, haven't you?' She waited for Geraldine to change the subject, to prevaricate. Instead, she was shocked by her reply.

'Always, Lola. Yes.'

Lola hesitated for just a second. 'I see. And why is that?'

'Because I wanted my own life. With my own husband and my own children. I had enough of sharing when I was a child.'

Lola looked at her blankly.

'You don't even remember, do you? I was one of eight, Lola. The seventh of eight children. And while some people love big families, I hated every minute of it. The noise, the clamour, how hard it was to make yourself heard, to get any time. And when I met Jim, I felt like I had found the most peaceful person on earth. He never shouted, he never grabbed at things. He would talk to me, not at me —'

'I did bring him up well.'

No smiling then, either. 'He's his own person, Lola. He always has been. Even if you haven't wanted him to be.'

'I beg your pardon?'

'Jim loves you. Adores you. Admires you. He knows how hard it was for you, raising him on his own after his father died, how hard you worked to put him through school. But when are you going to stop making him pay for your sacrifices? Let him live his own life? Work where he wants to work?'

'You are mistaken. Completely mistaken. Jim always wanted to go into business with me.'

'What choice did he have? What choice did I have? It was always a done deal. You were moving to this motel or that motel and you always made it clear that he had to come each time too. Even after he and I got married, after the children came along, nothing changed.'

'He always wanted to come. He loved running the motels with me. You're rewriting history. And don't tell me that you didn't need my help with the girls over the years. What were you going to do with them? Lock them in the linen room while you both worked all those hours?'

'Yes, we needed your help with the girls. And they loved you. And I know you loved them. All the attention you gave them —'

'It's just as well someone did.'

Geraldine stiffened. 'I've always been grateful for your help, Lola. But *I* am their mother. *I* am. Not you.'

'You've remembered, have you?'

'*No!*'

Lola almost took a step back she was so shocked at Geraldine's raised voice.

'I won't hear it, Lola. I won't have you criticising the way I've brought up my girls. Do you think I didn't notice, year after year after year? See you mentally criticising the way I was with them? I could only be the kind of mother that came naturally. I'm not you, Lola, full of games and adventures. But how dare you even think for a minute that I didn't love them, that I didn't want the best for them.'

'Geraldine —'

'No, listen to me for once. What chance did I have against you? You did your best to take them from me, didn't you? Did all you could to make them love you more than they love me? And perhaps you succeeded, with Bett at least. Are you happy now? One out of three? But I love my Bett, Lola. And I love Carrie, for all her faults too. And I loved Anna. I loved my Anna, my baby, my first girl, more than you will ever know. And I will never tell you how much because it's my story, do you hear me? My memories, my history with my daughter. And that's why we're leaving. Because the longer I stay here, with you – yes, Lola, with you – the more I feel you taking over Anna's memory. We talk about her when you want to talk about her. Ellen emails you more than she ever contacts me. Because you're more fun. You're Really-Great-Gran. I'm just boring Geraldine. But if I'm away from you, Lola, then perhaps, just perhaps, you will allow me to find the space to have my relationships with my own children and grandchildren before it's too late. As it was almost too late with Anna.'

Lola couldn't speak. Geraldine's accusations were too plentiful, too hurtful. She'd never had a conversation like this with her before. She could think of nothing more to say.

Geraldine didn't seem to care. 'So there it is,' she said, picking up the sponge again. 'That's why we're leaving, Lola. And that's why we haven't invited you to come with us.'

CHAPTER ELEVEN

Lola stayed in her room for the next two days. She told Jim she wasn't well, and told Bett and Carrie the same thing when they rang. It was the truth. She felt sick inside. Hurt and hollow and sick.

Luke rang. Patricia, Margaret and Kay rang. They wanted to share funny stories about the latest reactions to the window display, update her on their online adventures. Lola spoke only briefly, putting on a hoarse voice and apologising, saying she'd look forward to hearing all about it when she was better.

Emily dropped up to the motel with two more of her drink samples. When Jim phoned through to say she was there at the reception desk, Lola asked him to please apologise but she wasn't feeling well enough to talk to anyone yet. Emily left the drinks and a note:

We're missing you. I hope you get well soon. Emily xx
PS The blue one is blueberries and rosewater, the red one is pure strawberry. Full of colour and vitamins, especially for you. I'm calling whichever one you like best The Lola.

Jim brought her breakfast on a tray each morning, a sandwich at lunchtime and a salad each evening. She ate only a little of each, more for his sake than her own. She wasn't hungry. She was in shock. It was the only word to describe how she felt.

There had been anger at first, in the aftermath of her – her what? – with Geraldine. Her fight? Argument? Truth session? Anger, and astonishment. But after that first rush of reaction, more painful feelings had slowly crept up on her. Was Geraldine telling the truth? Had Lola tried to take over? Had she enjoyed knowing the girls preferred being with her? That they saw her as the fun one, the adventurous one?

Yes. Yes to all of those hard questions.

But only ever for the right reasons. Everything she had done had been for the girls. That was also the truth.

Wasn't it?

No, she thought again now, sitting in her room, the net curtains pulled across so she could see out but no one could see in. It wasn't the truth. It had been an unspoken competition between her and Geraldine from the moment Jim introduced her as his girlfriend. She'd wanted her son to have a lively, bright girlfriend and possible wife, one she could get on with, one she could be friends with, the daughter she'd never had. Instead, he had fallen in love with Geraldine. Quiet. Standoffish. Apparently without any personality whatsoever. Once, just the once, she had asked Jim what he saw in Geraldine.

'She's so peaceful.'

'Peaceful?' Lola remembered laughing. 'How boring, darling!'

Had Jim said any more about Geraldine after that? Had he told Geraldine that her future mother-in-law had described her as 'boring'? Regardless of what she had said, Jim had married Geraldine. And so their lives together had begun, the three of them moving and working together in motel after motel, soon followed by the arrival in quick succession of Anna, Bett and Carrie.

Lola could remember every one of their birthdays so clearly. The excitement, the happiness – one girl, two girls, a third girl! Her amusement at Jim's – yes, it was definitely Jim's, not Geraldine's – decision to name them alphabetically. It had been obvious very quickly that Geraldine found motherhood exhausting. No wonder. It *was* exhausting. Lola had had just the one and she'd been constantly tired for five years. Let me mind them, she'd say. Let me put them to bed. Give them their lunch. Their baths. You do the motel, I'll do the girls. Day by day, she'd taken on more of the caring role.

Deliberately? To deliberately displace Geraldine? To make herself indispensable, as she had been accused? Had she come up with fun activities, adventures, games, even the idea of the singing Alphabet Sisters as a ploy to make the girls love her more than they loved their mother, because she had never fully approved of their mother? Because she had always been disappointed in Jim's choice of wife?

Yes? No?

Yes.

But Jim and Geraldine had needed her, too. If she hadn't been there to act not just as unofficial nanny to the three girls, but as entertainer, as adjudicator, advisor, all the different roles she'd taken on with joy and with gusto, how could they have managed to keep working?

Or hadn't she given them the chance to find out?

Back and forth her thoughts went, anger at Geraldine's accusations, followed each time by an ever-strengthening voice hinting that there was truth in what she had said.

Lola stood up, walked over to her wardrobe and opened it. She'd culled her clothes to just a few outfits. If she ever felt the need for a change, she simply added a scarf or a wrap or some jewellery purchased from the charity shop. It was like having her own large dress-up box.

How long would it take her to pack now? To email her Christmas guests and say she was sorry, but the situation had changed and the Valley View Motel was no longer able to offer its Christmas special. She could do it all in an hour. Be on the bus to Adelaide that afternoon. And go where after that?

The phone rang beside her bed. She didn't answer it. She needed to hear only her own voice at the moment. Listen to her own thoughts. Try to make sense of this sudden, shocking turn of events.

She decided to talk to Anna. She'd started doing it in the past year, treating her eldest granddaughter as a kind of seer.

She spoke out loud. 'Well, Anna, what do you think?'

It took a little while to be able to imagine Anna's replies. Then it was as if she was there in the room too.

You never did like Mum much, did you? And now I guess you like her even less?

'No, I didn't and you're right, I certainly don't like her any more now.' A pause. 'But I do respect her.'

For insulting you? For pulling the rug from under your feet? For waiting all these years to tell you to keep away from her daughters?

'She didn't exactly put it like that. But it's good to see she does have some backbone. I just wish she'd shown it to, I don't know, Len the butcher rather than me.'

So what are you going to do? Stay in here sulking?

Lola smiled. Her imaginary Anna was asking exactly the kinds of questions Lola herself had asked her granddaughters many times in the past. 'Yes.'

That's a bit cowardly, isn't it? And selfish, worrying Dad like this? And Bett and Carrie? Not to mention all your friends in town.

'They'll survive.'

Of course they will. But they'll also keep worrying about you.

'I'm an old lady, Anna. Old ladies get sick.'

Except you're not sick. You're sulking.

'I'm not sulking. I'm thinking.'

Get over it. Stop having a pity party.

'How dare you!'

Sound familiar?

'Unfortunately, yes.'

Really, Lola, where's the surprise in all of this? You've never liked Mum and Mum has never liked you. The only difference is she's come out into the open and said it. You already know that she and Dad are going to leave the motel. Now, seriously, do you want to go with them? Start all over again in a B&B in the Riverland, or a small guesthouse in the Adelaide Hills or wherever it might be they end up next?

'You were eavesdropping on that conversation?'

I don't miss anything that goes on in this family. So, would you like to spend your last months or hopefully years with them, getting to know a whole new town, new people? Or would you rather stay here in Clare, with Bett nearby, Carrie nearby, the charity shop there as your social club, not to mention the computer setup out the back?

'You know about that too?'

I know everything, I told you. Let's be realistic here. You're eighty-four years old. You're in reasonable health, marbles still mostly intact, but you're not going to get any fitter or any younger. Now's the time to make a few decisions about your future.

'Perhaps they could sell the motel with me in situ. As a kind of added extra.'

That would look good on the website. Valley View Motel, with swimming pool, function room and ancient Irishwoman. You don't have that truth stick handy, do you?

Lola hadn't used the truth stick in years. It was a gimmick from the girls' childhood, a way of getting to the heart of any fight in seconds. She'd only ever had to point it at Anna, Bett or Carrie, say, 'Tell me the truth now, please,' and out it would pour, their honest thoughts about a situation, the real cause of their tears and disgruntlement.

'I don't need it. I'll tell you the truth anyway. Yes, I am sulking. Yes, I want to make Geraldine feel guilty. No, I don't want to live with Jim and Geraldine in some twee little B&B in a new town. No, I don't want to leave Clare. Yes, I will get in touch with the old folks' home. Happy now?'

Deliriously. Can I go now?

'Not too far, please, but yes, you can go.'

Lola sat there quietly for a few more minutes. She wasn't losing her mind. She knew she hadn't just communicated with Anna from beyond the grave. But she did feel curiously comforted, as if she *had* just had an honest conversation with her eldest granddaughter. As if much needed truths had been aired.

Now what, though? Should she stage a miraculous recovery? Go and apologise to Geraldine?

For what? For being herself? For loving her granddaughters? No, she wasn't going to apologise for that. She couldn't turn back time either. But she would talk to her daughter-in-law. She would let her know that she respected her opinion, even if it felt like ash in her mouth when she said it.

The phone rang beside her. This time she answered it. It was Bett. In tears.

'I've made a mess of everything, Lola. I need to talk to you. I know you're sick, but please, I won't stay long.'

'What is it? What's wrong?'

'My life. My marriage. Lola, I've ruined everything. Please, can I come and see you?'

Lola hesitated for a second. 'Shouldn't you talk to your mother about this first?'

'I don't want to talk to Mum. I want to talk to you.' She sobbed. 'Please, Lola.'

She'd tried. 'Of course, darling. Come now.'

The phone rang seconds after. 'Lola?' Carrie's voice was only just audible through the background noise. 'Are you having visitors yet? Matthew's being horrible and the kids won't stop fighting. If I don't get out of the house away from them all, I'm going to go mad.'

'Haven't you got friends you can visit?'

'They're all busy with their own horrible husbands and fighting kids.'

Lola tried again. 'Why don't you pop in and see your mother?'

'Why? You know she never has time during work hours. Please, Lola. Even for ten minutes? I've already told Matthew you need some more medicine dropped over.'

Lola asked Carrie to call by in an hour's time. She'd make sure Bett was gone by then. Her sixth sense told her the time wasn't right to have her two granddaughters under the same roof yet. It seemed 'Lola Quinlan: Grandmother' was back open for business. She checked her watch. She had about ten minutes before Bett's arrival. Not long, but long enough for what she needed to do.

She found her daughter-in-law alone in the kitchen. Good.

She'd have said this in front of Jim if needs be, but she preferred it this way. 'Hello, Geraldine.'

'Lola.' She looked up, warily. 'You're feeling better?'

'I wasn't sick. I was sulking after what you said to me.'

Geraldine blinked but didn't say anything.

Lola continued. 'I didn't like a single word of our conversation. And if I had my time over, nor would I change a single moment I spent with Anna, Bett, Carrie or Jim. I still don't completely understand what Jim sees in you and it's clear you don't like what the girls or Jim see in me. Am I right?'

Geraldine nodded.

'Good. But at least we now know where we both stand. And I admire your courage in telling me what you did. I'm glad you love your children so much. I do too. So we agree on that, at least. I also wanted to let you know what I'll be letting Jim know later today. I've decided to stay here in Clare. I'm going to start making some enquiries regarding old folks' homes and I'll be ready to move out as soon as you need me to in the new year.'

'I see. Thanks, Lola.'

'You're welcome, Geraldine.'

There was no hug, no smiles, no tears or reconciliation. But as Lola returned to her room, she knew it was the most important conversation she'd had with Geraldine in forty years.

Bett arrived minutes later. She was crying when she got out of the car, crying as she told Lola that Daniel had taken the day off and was home minding the children, crying as she explained that from January they were both going to work part-time and still crying when she told her that they'd done nothing but fight for the past two days and she was convinced the marriage was over.

Lola still didn't understand. 'But why are you so unhappy? Isn't it what you want? Daniel to go part-time so you can go back part-time too? Share the childcare? Isn't that the whole idea?'

More sobs.

'Darling, you have to stop crying. Or get someone to do subtitles. I can't understand tears and words together.'

Bett smiled for the first time, even if only briefly. 'I thought I wanted it. But Daniel hates the idea, I know. And he's only doing it for me. And that's not a good enough reason for him to do it.'

'He's hardly going to do it to keep the postman happy, darling. Of course he's doing it for you and for the twins. Why else would he do anything?'

'But I made him do it. I pushed him into it.'

'Now I'm completely confused. So you don't want to go back to work?'

'I do. I think I do.'

'Well, that's just as well because from what I think you just said in fluent crying, your editor wants you to start as soon as you can in the new year.'

'But I'm not ready. And it's too soon for Daniel to go part-time. He's only been in the new job five months, and I might have ruined everything for him too. See, Lola, I can't do *anything* without wrecking *everything*.'

'Good heavens,' Lola said.

Bett abruptly stopped crying. 'Good heavens what?'

'I've never been a believer in time travel but I truly think you've regressed at least thirty years in the past five minutes. What a load of nonsense you're talking.'

'It's *not* nonsense.'

'It is, darling. I'm sorry to be blunt, but it is. What are you doing sitting here talking to me about these things, anyway? You should be home saying them to Daniel, not me.'

'We can't talk any more.'

'Cat got your tongues?'

'There's never time, with the babies, his work, my housework —'

'Do you have time to eat? Shower? Dress yourself? Yes? Well, take time from those activities. Eat less. Shower more quickly. Wear the same clothes two days in a row.'

'I do all those things already. There's still no time to talk.'

Lola sighed. 'Bett, you gave birth to baby twins seven months ago, not to two huge millstones to hang around your neck. The wonderful thing about babies is they are portable. Not self-supporting yet, but I believe there's a marvellous invention called a pram. In fact, did I see you with one of those just recently? A double one even? Those things underneath it are called wheels. You and Daniel could push the pram along, with the babies inside, and you could talk at the same time. Isn't that extraordinary?'

'*When*, Lola? When would we get time?'

'What about every morning before he goes to work? Every evening before dinner? After dinner. During dinner if you're just having sandwiches. Twenty minutes a day, rain or shine. It'll do you and your figure good, your babies good, your marriage good.'

'Sure, Lola. It's that simple. A walk a day will fix everything. Thanks for your help.' She stood up.

Lola didn't move. 'You sulky little brat, sit down.'

Bett's mouth opened. She sat down again.

'I've just spent two days sulking,' Lola said, 'so I know a sulker when I see one.'

'What were you sulking about?'

Lola lied. 'The mess that Mrs Kernaghan made of our Christmas window display.'

'So take it down. Tell her something happened to it and you had to start again. I can't believe you let her get away with it anyway. It's horrible. And I'm not sulking now. I'm angry. It's a different thing.'

'Sulking is the first cousin of anger. And I can't pull down the display. The judging is in two days' time. We'd never get something up in its place in time.'

'So let that be your display.'

'An empty window? How festive.'

Bett stood up again. 'Christmas isn't a joyous time for everyone, Lola. Lots of people hate Christmas, spend it fighting with their families, or worrying about money. Some people can't afford even a present for their kids, let alone their husband or wife. You work in a charity shop. You know all this already. Len used sausages in his display, didn't he?'

Lola nodded. He'd wound them into wreaths. They looked disgusting.

'So why don't you use the idea of charity in yours?' Bett said.

'Next year, perhaps. It's too late for this year.'

'What have you always told me? That it's never too late to fix something that really needs fixing?' She leaned down and kissed her grandmother's cheek. 'I'm going to go home now and see Daniel. At least he doesn't tell me off as often as you do.'

'He wouldn't dare. He knows that's my job.'

Another smile from Bett. A proper one this time. 'I don't actually think you've been much help today, but thanks anyway.'

'You've stopped crying, at least. So what are you going to do when you get home?'

'What I've been told by my bossy grandmother. Drag my husband and my babies out for a walk.'

'Good girl. But make sure you pop in and say hello to your mother before you go.'

'Of course. I always do.'

'I'm glad.'

There wasn't time between Bett's departure and Carrie's arrival to do any more thinking about the window. But as Carrie sat there in Lola's room and ranted about Matthew, Lola's mind kept drifting towards what Bett had said. Was there a way around the current situation? She didn't necessarily actively have to ruin Mrs Kernaghan's display, but say, just say, that someone accidentally left the door open . . .

'Lola, are you listening to me?'

'Of course I am, Carrie.'

'What was I just saying?'

'You were talking about Matthew and how crazy he drives you and how he never does anything around the house and never cooks and how fed up with him you are and does he think all the washing just washes itself and that the floors are self-cleaning —'

'I didn't say that about the floors, but you're right, he never washes the floors, or the curtains, or —'

'Divorce him, Carrie.'

'And he won't even — What did you say?'

'Divorce him. You've never really been happy with him. File for divorce, go and live somewhere else with the three kids and hopefully you'll find another husband soon.'

'But I love Matthew. I don't want to divorce him.'

'So why have you been sitting here complaining about him for what feels like the last six hours?'

'Because that's what wives do about their husbands.' She stood up in a flounce. 'Your problem, Lola, is that your marriage didn't last long enough for you to start hating your husband.'

'No, Carrie. Unfortunately it didn't.'

'I'd better go. Matthew will be up the walls looking after the kids on his own.'

'So no divorce just yet?'

'Not yet. I'm going to give him one more chance. And I'm also going to call into the bookshop on the way home and buy him an idiot's guide to cooking.'

'That's my girl,' Lola said. 'Be sure to pop in and see your mother too before you leave.'

'Of course. Why wouldn't I?'

'Just checking,' Lola said.

Chapter Twelve

The next day Lola was up at dawn, turning on the TV in her room and waiting anxiously for the weather forecast. She didn't think she'd ever have thought this, but thank heavens the heatwave was continuing, and even better, strong winds had been forecast too. Terrible bushfire weather, but excellent for window display destruction planning.

Was there a moral dilemma in what she was about to do? Should she allow Mrs Kernaghan to have her time in the spotlight? She was a volunteer, after all, even if she'd never actually worked a shift in the charity shop. 'I'm more of a planner than a worker bee,' she'd said last time someone asked her to put her name down for the roster.

No, the display had to go, Lola decided. The shop had become a laughing stock. And it wasn't as if they had any chance of winning the competition, after all . . .

Patricia was already in the shop when Lola arrived. She was sorting through a bag of clothes that had been left in the doorway overnight. She pulled a face as she took out a dirty nappy. 'Can you believe people do this? They treat us like a rubbish dump sometimes.'

'Perhaps they've left their address in a pocket of something and we can return the nappy to them,' Lola said.

Unfortunately there were no identifying documents in the bag. Lola was glad, however, to see Patricia pull out several items that were worth getting cleaned and put up for sale. Perhaps the nappy had been placed in the bag by accident. Lola suspected not, but if she only ever thought the worst about people, well, it would be impossible to go on living . . .

Speaking of which. 'Patricia, I think it only fair to let you know that I intend to sabotage Mrs Kernaghan's display today.'

She was rewarded with a huge smile. 'Oh, thank God, Lola. We've all been so worried. We couldn't believe you'd just put up with it. It's so ugly and I know we haven't got a chance of winning and it's only a street traders' competition, but I hate that she thought she could come in and take over, just —'

Lola held up a hand to stop her. 'Patricia, I'm so sorry. I hadn't realised you all felt so strongly. I've been like a crocodile lurking in the shallows, keeping an eye on proceedings and wondering when or if to strike. I'm sorry I've caused you unnecessary worry.'

'I just hated the idea of her steamrolling us. Have you noticed she hasn't been near the place since she realised everyone's been making fun of the window?'

'I had noticed that, yes.'

'And the judging's tomorrow. More ridicule. I can't bear it. We haven't got time to put in a new display, have we? Although we could ask Joan to bring her nativity set back in, I suppose?'

'I've had an idea. Something one of my granddaughters said to me sparked it. Can I tell you about it?'

Patricia listened and started nodding even before Lola finished her story. Kay did the same when Lola told her. So did Margaret.

All they needed to do now was somehow destroy the current display.

'I'll do it,' Lola said.

'No, I will,' Margaret said.

'I'm the youngest,' Kay said.

'Let's all do it,' Patricia suggested.

As a quartet, they walked across to the door, opened it wide and secured it. The hot air rushed in. Margaret quickly reached up and turned off the airconditioner. 'It seems a shame to waste it. The electricity bill is going to be so high anyway.'

The first gust of wind set the chiffon spinning around the figure in what they all agreed was actually a dramatic and beautiful fashion.

'Perhaps we should have installed a fan in the window and had it swirling like this permanently,' Lola said. She noticed their expressions. 'Perhaps not.'

A second gust set the dummy teetering. A third made her rock forward, the fourth pushed her backwards.

In the end, it wasn't the fifth gust that made it happen. It was

Len coming across the road from his butcher shop to see what on earth they were thinking having the door open on such a hot day. He didn't listen as they tried to stop him. He rarely did. He simply walked in, talking loudly. 'Girls, have you lost your minds? You have to keep the door shut in weather like this!'

Afterwards, they agreed it was a combination of Len giving the door a good slam and one final gust of wind. The dummy began to rock, then spin, in slow motion at first, before it slipped sideways off its perch, bringing fifty strands of coloured chiffon with it. There was a moment's silence and then the dummy's head slowly and silently separated from its neck and rolled across the floor to Len's feet.

'Shit,' Len said. 'Did I do that?'

'It was industrial sabotage and there were four witnesses,' Lola said. She hurried to console him when she saw his expression. 'Len, I'm teasing you. The sad truth is that wonderful display has been an accident waiting to happen for days now. Thank God it was you standing there, young enough to leap out of the way. It would have been far worse if one of we elderly ladies had been in its path.'

'Or a baby in a pram,' Kay said.

'Or one of the competition judges,' Patricia said.

'Or a lawyer who could sue us,' Margaret added.

Len was quite agitated. 'I didn't do it deliberately. I didn't, I promise. What are you going to do now? The judging is tomorrow!'

'We'll think of something,' Lola said, gently steering him out the door. 'And don't worry about it for a minute. It was an unfortunate combination of the wind and the door-slamming, not your fault, and we'll be sure to tell everyone exactly that.'

The replacement display took less than five minutes to set up. It took longer to clean up the original one. Afterwards, all four ladies stepped out into the heat again and looked at their work.

'Much better,' Patricia said.

'Exactly right,' Kay said.

'We still won't win but it's what we should have done in the first place,' Margaret said. 'Well done, Lola.'

'Don't thank me. It was Bett's idea.'

Where that morning there had been a store dummy covered in multicoloured chiffon, there was now nothing. They hadn't put in a new backdrop, new display, new anything. The entire window was empty. All that was on show was a simple sign they'd written together on the shop computer and printed onto A4 paper.

Our Christmas display is empty. For too many families in our area, Christmas is a time of hardship. No food on the table, no presents under the tree, no tree at all. This year, the Clare Valley Charity Shop intends to produce as many Christmas hampers as we can. We need your help. We won't win the window display competition, but we hope to receive enough donations to fill as many as one hundred hampers to distribute to needy people in our area. If you can spare any canned goods or toys, books or gifts (new, please, not second-hand), we'd love to receive them.
Thank you
The Committee

'Perfect,' Kay said again. 'There's only one thing I'm worried about. Who's going to tell Mrs Kernaghan?'

As it turned out, none of them needed to. She saw it for herself. Lola got a phone call from Margaret that night. She'd been working the late shift and had faced Mrs Kernaghan's wrath.

'She was furious, of course. At first, at least. But she kept seeing people stopping to read the sign and come in to tell us what a good idea it was, and you should have seen her. She said that her initial display was just to attract attention and this had been the real intention all along. Shameless! And, Lola, there's already been donations left, cans of fruit and drinks, and Luke said he'd ask at work if we could have a pile of the cardboard boxes that the computers come in. They'd be just the right size for hampers.'

Lola already knew about the boxes. Luke had told her himself, when he called unexpectedly to the motel. She'd heard the knock, opened the door and there he'd been in all his gangliness, his hair even more unruly than usual, standing shyly smiling, holding a black bag in one hand, with a cardboard box at his feet. She'd barely had a chance to say hello before he started talking.

'Lola, I hope you don't mind, but I was thinking about when you were unwell and you didn't get a chance to go on the shop computer for a few days, and I know you told me there's a computer here at the motel, but you mightn't always . . . Anyway, I thought you might like this.' He held up the black bag. 'It's a laptop computer. And don't worry, I haven't bought it. It's an old one we had at work. No one was using it, so I've fixed it up and put new programs on it, and the internet might be a bit unreliable now and again, but I've installed a top-grade wifi system, and between that and the roaming broadband around here —' He stopped and laughed at her expression. 'You're not sure what I'm talking about, are you?'

'I think you lost me at "laptop", but please, do go on. But come in out of that heat first.'

He followed her in and started unpacking the bag and the box. 'Basically, it's a computer for your room, Lola. And I've also brought an old printer that I had lying around. Just for those days when you're not at the shop but feel like going online.' He plugged in cords and pressed buttons, explaining what he was doing in simple terms. Within minutes, there on her small desk was a working computer and printer. He turned and smiled. 'There you go, Lola. Now you can really take over the world.'

She'd planned to bring up the subject of Emily with him. To tease him a little, to see which way the land lay. But suddenly, inexplicably, she was so moved by his thoughtfulness that all she could do was wipe away the tears that had sprung into her eyes. 'Thank you, Luke. Thank you so very, very much.'

Now, after she'd finished talking to Margaret, she spent a happy hour surfing the internet in the comfort of her own room. She picked up all sorts of ideas for her Christmas lunch. Watermelon salad for starters, she decided. A grilled seafood main course. Chocolate-coated strawberries and cream for dessert.

There was still the minor matter of when she was going to find the time and the ability to prepare all these different menu items, but she'd worry about that later.

She was about to sign off and join Jim for a drink in the bar when she heard the sound she loved, the ping of an incoming email. It was from Ellen in Hong Kong.

Lola, are you there?

Lola quickly replied. Of course, darling. What's wrong?

I'm being mean to Dad again. I can't seem to help it.

If emails could come with sound effects, Lola knew she'd have heard tears. The internet was a wonderful way to communicate, but sometimes it just wasn't enough.

Are you near the phone?

Yes.

A minute later, Lola was on her bed, phone in her hand, trying to calm Ellen, who was now crying inconsolably. It appeared there had been another visit from Denise and her daughter Lily, which had gone even more badly than the last one.

'Dad said he's going to suspend my pocket money. And I'm grounded too. And it's not fair. It's how I feel, Lola. I can't instantly like Denise just because he does. Or be instant friends with Lily. I just can't!'

'Darling, I know. Did you try to be nice, like I asked? Did you say hello at least?'

Lola listened as Ellen told her everything, her story punctuated with sobs. She'd come out of her room this time, done her best to smile and be friendly with Lily, who was just a year younger than her. Until it became clear that Lily and Ellen's father were already the best of friends.

'He was joking with her, and he did that thing with her he does with me – you know, when he rubs the top of my head and ruffles up my hair? I always say I hate it when he does it but I don't, and he did it to her too, and laughed at something she said, and I knew then that she was like another daughter to him already, but she was much nicer, and I couldn't stand it, Lola. I know he doesn't want me there, that he has this new family ready to go to and I'm just in the way . . .' Her words dissolved into sobs again.

'Ellen, please, darling, stop crying. You need to stop crying. I can't help you if I can't talk to you.'

'You can't help me anyway. There's nothing anyone can do.'

'Where's your father now?'

'At work. I'm here with Lin, our housekeeper. And she's mad at me too.'

'What did you do to her?'

Silence.

'Ellen?'

Ellen started to cry again. 'I can't seem to help it, Lola. I'm just upset all the time and Lin asked me to tidy my room and I did and then she said would I tidy the living room too, my books and homework were in there, and I started to, I didn't mind doing it, but then she said that she had to get dinner ready, that Denise and Lily were coming over and Dad hadn't even told me —'

No wonder, Lola thought but didn't say.

'— and I got cross again and I might have thrown something on the ground.'

'Might? Something?'

'Did. A vase of flowers.'

'Ellen, this has to stop.'

'I want it to. I really want it to stop too, Lola. But how?'

How indeed, Lola thought. 'I'll call you back,' she said.

'She's just impossible, Lola,' Glenn said. He hadn't seemed surprised, only relieved, when Lola phoned him at his office. 'I've tried tough love, soft love, being upset, ignoring her behaviour, every parenting approach I can, and nothing seems to make any difference. We just can't stop fighting with each other.'

'She's about to turn thirteen. It's a tumultuous time for any young girl.'

'You think I don't know that? Lola, I'm at the end of my tether. I love Ellen, you know that. I love her dearly, and I loved Anna too. You know that, despite what happened between us before, you know, our separation —'

'Ellen still doesn't know about that, does she?'

'No. And how can I ever tell her now? She hates me enough as it is.'

'She doesn't hate you.'

'She does, or she feels the closest thing to hate towards me at the moment. If she were to learn that Anna and I had been talking about getting divorced, what would that do to her?'

'Are you serious about this Denise?'

'I am. I am, Lola.'

'And spending Christmas with her and her daughter?'

'I owe it to Denise. She's been so patient. She's tried again and again with Ellen. Lily has tried. They are very nice people, Lola. I don't know what Ellen has told you about them —'

'It's possibly best I don't repeat it.'

'They're still trying with Ellen. We're all trying. But I can't compete with Anna's memory. And I need to have a life too. Ellen is everything to me, but she can't behave like this. If she wins now —'

'Wins? It's a contest, then?'

'You know what I mean. We're at a stalemate. I've said if she doesn't come with me for Christmas, then I'm cancelling everything. Neither of us do anything. It will just be a normal, ordinary boring day.'

'Is that really what you want?'

'Of course not! I want to be with Denise and her daughter, having fun, and I want to be with Ellen and know she's having fun too. But that's impossible. If she joins us, I know she'll have a terrible time. And if she's having a terrible time, then I know I will too.' He sighed heavily.

'What if she were to get a separate invitation for Christmas? One that takes the pressure off you both, gives you a break, her a break and buys you all a little breathing space?'

'Invitation? From who?'

'Me, of course. I'm being purely selfish, Glenn. I'm holding the fort here at the motel for a few days over Christmas and

I fear I may have overstretched myself. I need an assistant. Preferably a twelve-year-old assistant who is also a blood relative and currently lives in Hong Kong.'

'But it's Christmas, Lola. A time for families. Ellen and I should be together.'

'You've fallen for all the advertising, too? Your own advertising? Glenn, Christmas isn't one universal happy day for everybody. There's too much pressure, too many demands. So why don't we give her a different kind of Christmas this year? You have your Christmas with Denise and her daughter. I'll have Ellen here with me. I'll spoil her in person. You spoil her from afar. We'll also tell her the truth, that I demanded you send her to me.'

'What? Tell her you rang me out of the blue and said you really need her help over Christmas and would I please put her on a plane to you?'

'Isn't that exactly what just happened? So you'll be telling her the truth. Think about it, Glenn. Talk to her when you get home from work. I'm in my room now for the night. Please tell her to feel free to call me to verify any facts.'

Ellen's call came exactly two hours later. 'Is it true, Lola? You really need me?' There were still tears but she sounded much brighter. 'I'd love to come. I'd *love* to. And Dad can have his Christmas with Denise and Lily and I don't have to, so we'll both be happy. Are you sure?'

'I'm not an escape route and this won't be a holiday, Ellen.

You'll be working hard every minute of every day you're with me. You do realise that?'

'Are you going to pay me or is it slave labour?'

Lola laughed. 'We'll decide that when I see you in action.'

'Thanks, Lola. Very, very much.'

'You are very, very welcome. But there is a condition attached.'

'Anything.'

'I want you to be polite to Denise and Lily from now on. More than polite. I want you to be well mannered and as friendly to them as I know you can be. I want you to behave in a way that would make me proud to see, and your mother, your grandparents, aunts and uncles proud to see. And that would also set a good example to your cousins if they were able to see you too.'

There was silence.

'Ellen?'

'How will you know if I've been good or bad?'

'I have a spy planted in your house. He's disguised as your father.'

'I'll try.' A pause. 'I will, Lola, I promise. It will be much easier now, anyway, now I know I don't have to spend Christmas with them.'

And so my evil plan has worked, Lola thought. 'There's just one other little matter we need to discuss. All of this has to be our little secret for now. If your grandparents and aunts knew you were making a surprise visit, they'd cancel their trips away and none of us want that. I'll work out the dates with your father so you stay on long enough to see everyone, I promise. You can be my special Christmas secret, and then I'll produce you out of a hat when they all arrive back in the Valley for New Year, okay?'

'That sounds *perfect*,' Ellen said. 'I'd love to be your secret.'

'Good girl.'

There were smiles in both their voices.

Chapter Thirteen

Guest 1

Neil came out of his bedroom. Rick looked up in surprise.

'Don't look so shocked.'

'I'm sorry, but I am. I haven't seen you in weeks.'

'I have to go to Centrelink.'

'I saw the letters they've been sending you. They hounding you a bit?'

A shrug from Neil. 'Usual bullshit. They'll cut off my benefits if I don't "present myself" for an interview.'

'Do you want to head out for a drink later?' Rick said. 'My shout.'

'No thanks.'

Rick waited until he heard the front door shut. Waited longer until he was completely sure Neil had gone. What he was about to do broke all the rules of flat-sharing. But how often did he get a phone call like the one he'd got at work the day before, from Neil's mum? She'd been in tears. 'I'm so worried about him, Rick. He tells me he's fine, but I know he's not. Is it drugs?

Is that what's wrong? Have you noticed him taking anything, or drinking too much?'

Rick told the truth. 'I don't even see him any more. He just stays in his room all the time.'

'Something's wrong, I know it is. Please, Rick, could you look in his room? He must go out some time.'

'He doesn't. Mrs Harris, I'm sorry, but he's in there when I go to work and he's in there when I come back. He's just going through a bad time, I guess. Wants to be alone.'

'He's been like this for months, though. Please, Rick, if you get the chance, would you just take a look? See if it's drugs, or alcohol? If I know, I can try to do something about it.'

'It's snooping.'

'Rick, please. I'm worried sick.'

He'd agreed, reluctantly. He'd been worried about Neil at the start too, all that time locked away in his room, but no matter how many times he'd asked him out for a beer, or to share something he'd made for dinner, the answer had been no. There were only so many times he could shout through the bedroom door at him, invite him to do stuff. He'd taken the hint eventually. Neil just wanted to be left alone. Fair enough. Rick felt like that sometimes too.

But Mrs Harris had been so insistent. Rick figured this morning would be his best chance. It could be days again before Neil left the house. He went to Neil's bedroom door, expecting it to be locked. Neil had been so secretive lately he was hardly going to leave it wide open. It *was* locked. What Neil probably didn't know was that Rick had a spare key. The lease was in his name, he had copies of all the flat keys. It felt bad, and wrong to do it, but he kept thinking of Mrs Harris. He got the spare key, came back and unlocked the door.

The first thing he noticed was the smell. Not of drink or drugs, but of a stale room, shut up for too long. The blinds were down. The only light came from the computer glowing in the corner. Beside it, a printer, also switched on, making a soft humming noise. There was a radio too. Switched off.

He didn't turn on the main light yet. There was enough coming in from the hallway. The room was surprisingly tidy. He didn't know what he'd expected – clothes everywhere, empty pizza boxes, rubbish. It looked . . . well, it just looked normal, he thought. Not like a drug den, anyway.

He'd better get started, he realised. He had less than an hour to find whatever it was he was supposed to be looking for. 'Sorry, mate,' he said aloud. 'This is for your mum.'

He looked in the bedside cupboard, the wardrobe, under the bed, under the pillow, wondering whether he should be wearing gloves to hide his fingerprints. He was careful at least to leave everything as he'd found it. There was nothing unusual – no bottles of vodka, no syringes, no cigarette papers, not even any dope. The most exciting thing he found was a couple of bottles of sleeping tablets in one of the drawers. Hardly anything to worry about, millions of people took those.

'Something's wrong with him,' Mrs Harris had said. 'He's different. If you can find anything at all that might give me a clue, please, Rick . . .'

'I swear, mate, your mum begged me to do this,' he said aloud again. He went over to the computer desk. Checked the drawers. Again, nothing unusual, pens, some envelopes. There were a few sheets of paper on the printer. He picked them up, gingerly, between two fingers. It was a printed bus ticket, with a sheet of terms and conditions attached. He frowned. Neil hadn't said he was going anywhere. Mind you, Neil hadn't said much about anything lately. Rick took it over to the doorway to get enough light to see it, still reluctant to turn on the main light. What he saw made him frown even more. According to this print-out, Neil was booked to go from Broken Hill to a place called Clare on Christmas Eve. There was no return ticket. Was he moving to Clare? Where was Clare anyway? There was another sheet of paper on the printer. Confirmation of a booking in the name of Neil Harris at a motel called the Valley View, also in Clare. For three nights, by the looks of it. Over Christmas.

He checked his watch. He'd been in here for fifteen minutes already. He had another forty minutes at the most. He quickly went to the front door and put the security chain on. If Neil did come back unexpectedly, hopefully the noise of the door rattling would buy enough time to get out of his room.

Was this enough to ring Mrs Harris about? The clue she'd been looking for? 'Your son's gone quiet and weird because he's been busy booking a one-way bus ticket to some place miles away.'

Maybe if he was able to find out what was in this Clare place, he might know what else he should be looking for and have something more interesting to tell Mrs Harris. Maybe there was a famous hippy commune there, or a cult, or a religious order he was planning on joining . . .

Neil had been doing all the booking on the computer. That was the obvious place to start. Unfortunately, Rick was good at repairing broken windscreens, but not so good on computers. He clicked on one symbol on the screen and then another. Nothing happened.

He rang his sister. She worked as a secretary. She'd know what to do. 'Quick question and I can't explain why yet. I'm at a computer. How do I get that web page to find things out on?'

'What?'

He repeated the question. She told him off for being so abrupt – he didn't mind, she was always telling him off about something – and then she talked him through the process, until he had a search engine page in front of him. He typed in the word Clare while she waited on the other end of the phone. Up came a tourist webpage. He clicked on it and had a quick look at the different sections. It was a winegrowing place. There were lots of vineyards, restaurants, old stone pubs, a few motels, a caravan park. Maybe Neil had applied for a job in one of the wineries or in one of the pubs or motels even? That would explain the one-way ticket. 'Funny time to go, though, at Christmas,' he said.

'What?' His sister was still waiting.

'Sorry, thinking aloud.'

'Fascinating. You're lucky I'm not busy today.'

Maybe that was it. Neil had applied for a job, got it, was

starting around Christmas and didn't know how to tell his mum. It could be that simple, couldn't it? And if so, would he have had to write a job application, maybe? Rick was really starting to feel like a detective now. Having fun, even. He checked his watch. Thirty minutes gone. He had about twenty minutes max to find —

'Can I go now?' It was his sister. 'Or do you want me to listen to your heavy breathing all morning?'

'Is there a way of finding out what someone's been doing on their computer?'

'Rick, what's going on? Have you joined the cops or something?'

'I'll explain later, I promise. Please, I haven't got much time.'

'You're in a hostage situation now?' She sighed, then talked him through it. How to go to Word documents. He followed her directions, clicked on a file or two. Nothing.

'Your mysterious subject might have deleted them already. You can check the websites someone's been visiting, if that's any help?'

He may as well while he was here. She talked him through that process as well. So simple, he was amazed. He should think about getting a computer himself. Yep, there it all was, under something called internet search history. A long list of all the websites Neil had been looking at recently. A very long list. He glanced down them, reading them aloud.

'Rick, I have to go. My boss has just come in —'

She was gone before he had a chance to say thanks. He kept

scrolling down through the list. No wonder Neil never came out of his room. He had too much to do in here. And no need to go outside the house either these days, Rick realised, if all of this stuff was at your fingertips.

There were bus company websites, yes. The same Clare Valley site Rick himself had briefly looked at. A website for a motel there too, called the Valley View. He checked the print-out. Yes, it was the same place.

He moved down through the list, feeling weird but unable to stop now. It was kind of like reading someone's diary, he thought, uncomfortably. There were a few porn sites. Music sites. There were loads of different chat rooms. He clicked on one. People talking to each other about everything under the sun, from films to music to computer games. A bit strange, in Rick's opinion, to talk to people by computer instead of stepping outside his bedroom occasionally and talking to his real flatmate, but that was still okay, wasn't it? Nothing for Mrs Harris to worry about there?

Then he reached another group of sites on the list. He clicked on one, then another, a third, a fourth. He wondered at first whether they were sites about new films. New computer games, maybe. Some kind of really weird porn sites, even. But the more he read, the more sites he clicked between, the more he realised what it was Neil had been doing in here for hours and days on end.

He'd been researching ways to commit suicide.

Rick's hands started shaking. He clicked off all the sites,

panicking now, pressing the close buttons as his sister had told him, backing out, site by site, away from Neil's secret life, swearing out loud, convinced Neil was about to come back in, catch him at it. Finally, the screen looked the same as it had at the start. He pushed back the chair. He wanted to get out of there as quickly as he could. He was reaching for his phone even as he pulled the bedroom door shut behind him, locked it and went into the kitchen.

'Mrs Harris? It's me. I think you should get here as soon as you can.'

Guests 2 and 3

The phone was ringing. Tony let it. Helen was at the shops. He'd got out of the habit of answering any calls. He found it too hard, making polite chitchat with people who never wanted to talk to him in any case. After the accident, he hadn't been able to go to work for a week either, until Helen had almost dragged him there. 'Your staff need you.'

It was still ringing. He picked it up now, heard a slight delay and then the warm, familiar tone of Katie. 'Dad! How are you? Is it still boiling over there? It's *freezing* here. I'm actually wearing a thermal vest, like a mountaineer!' It was her usual rapid-fire way of speaking. 'What about you? Are you going okay?'

'Not bad,' he said. 'Your mum's out. Do you want to leave a message or call back? Is everything okay?'

'Everything's great. I'm just getting organised for Christmas. I want to set a time for our call. I don't want to ring when you're both off singing carols or in case you've headed down to the beach.'

'Nowhere near a beach this year. Vineyards, I think, rather than the sea.'

'What?'

'We're going away for Christmas. Your mother's idea. We're going to stay somewhere in South Australia. We're heading off on Christmas Eve. We'll be away for about three days, I think. A place called Cla—'

'You can't!'

'What?'

'You can't go away. Look, I'll call back. I need to make a phone call. I'll ring back as soon as I can. Bye.'

Ten minutes later, Helen was just coming in with the shopping when the phone rang again. Tony hadn't had a chance to tell her about Katie's call yet. He answered this one too. It wasn't Katie calling back. It was Liam, calling from Barcelona.

'Dad? What's this about you going away for Christmas? You never go away for Christmas.'

'We are this year. Hold on. I'll get your mother.'

Tony watched as Liam obviously said the same thing to Helen. She smiled. 'And hello, darling. Yes, your dad and I are well. No, I know we don't normally —' she laughed. 'I hadn't realised you and Katie were so set in your ways. Why? We needed the change in scenery. We're driving there on Christmas Eve. It's about five hours away —' She turned to Tony, astonished. 'Liam's just hung up on me.'

Guest 4

'Mrs Kaminski? Hello, this is Glenda, your daughter's temporary secretary in Melbourne. Yes, it was very nice to talk to you last week too. Mrs Kaminski, I hope you don't mind me interfering, and I am perfectly aware I am stepping over many boundaries and breaking many long-established secretarial rules, but frankly, I see my job as being one of putting out fires and finding solutions to otherwise insurmountable problems. Do you have a minute to talk? It's about Christmas. Your daughter and Christmas, to be precise. I've had an idea.'

Guests 5, 6 and 7

Try as she might, June couldn't get the picture of Belle and Chloe turning up at the bakery out of her mind. She told her husband all about it.

'It's not fair, Bill. Those little kids, being used like pawns between their parents. Holly's exhausted. I'm sure she does most of the mothering, and the fathering, while those two selfish parents of hers do nothing but shout at each other. I said to her, I'd like to knock their heads together. They're as bad as each other, playing games, using the kids as weapons. Do you think they're even aware of the effect all their fighting is having on their children? If they only knew Holly and the little girls were thinking of running away —'

'So tell them.'

'I just wish there was some – what did you say?'

'Tell them. Maybe they should know.'

'What, just march up to them both in the street?'

'That might be a bit public. You could find out where they both work, couldn't you? Though maybe it's better to go to their house, talk to them both at the same time.'

'When Holly's there? I couldn't. She'd be so embarrassed.'

'Then lure her out of the house somehow. Lure all three of them out. Get tickets for the cinema down the road. I saw a poster for that new kids' film opening up. Tell her you won a family pass, but the film's really not for you, so you want her and Belle and Chloe to have the tickets. And when the three of them are at the film, go to the house and say your piece.'

June stared at her husband in amazement. 'You're good at this scheming, aren't you?'

'I've been living with you for years,' he grinned. 'I learnt from a master.'

'You really think I should talk to the parents?'

'I don't know. But I do know you won't rest until you've done something.'

Two nights later, June and her husband were in their small, old car, trying to find a parking space near Holly's house. Bill was driving. When he'd offered to come with her, she'd accepted immediately. She felt sick with nerves, even though it had all unfolded as Bill had suggested. She'd bought a family pass to the film and presented it to Holly with the elaborate story her husband had suggested. It had to be used by that evening, she said apologetically. 'Perhaps your parents would like to go with you?' June asked, her fingers crossed that they wouldn't.

'I don't think so. They don't go out much,' Holly said. 'Not at the moment, anyway.'

'Trouble at home again?'

Holly had just nodded.

Bill found a place to park around the corner from Holly's house. Their car stood out among the others on the street. It felt strange to be in this part of town. She wished she'd dressed differently too, not come straight from work in her bakery uniform. She was starting to have second thoughts about even being here. But then she remembered Holly's desolate expression, remembered Belle and Chloe turning up like that, and her resolve strengthened. What was the worst thing that could happen? They'd start shouting at her too? Tell her to mind her own business? So let them, she decided. She had a few things she wanted to say back to them herself.

Bill wished her luck. She took a moment to breathe deeply before she made her way to Holly's house. She'd never been here before. She'd found the address in Holly's employment file at the bakery. She gazed around, amazed at the size of the houses. It was like a different world to the one she and her husband had raised their family in. These weren't houses. They were mansions. On this street alone there were more than six two-storey buildings, each with their own large gardens, high fences, remote-controlled gates and garages that were bigger than June's house. She walked up their driveway, looking through the railings of the tall fence. The garden was obviously landscaped. There were even sculptures visible. And was that seriously a fountain? She knew Holly's parents were both very successful in their fields, her father an architect, her mother a university academic. There was money to burn, that much was clear.

June remembered the night Holly had finally opened up and told her everything about her family life. Not just about how bad her parents' relationship was. She'd told June how angry they were at her choice of career. How 'very, very disappointed' they were in her for choosing not to go to university. Their disbelief that she wanted to train as a pastry chef, to stay working in June's bakery. They'd been embarrassed enough that she worked there part-time after school, they told her. They had friends who bought cakes from that shop. What would they think to be served by Holly? They'd put pressure on her for weeks to change her mind, to apply for university instead. They'd tried anger, silence, everything, until they'd realised her mind was made up. She'd have moved out, she told June, if it hadn't been for Belle and Chloe.

'But surely they've come round to the idea now?' June had asked. 'They've tasted your cakes, haven't they? Realised you have a real talent for baking?'

'Mum doesn't eat cakes. And Dad didn't say much any of the times he tried them.'

'But they must be happy to see you doing something you enjoy?'

'They're never happy,' Holly had said.

The walk towards the entrance gate seemed a kilometre long, not a hundred metres. There was an intercom in the wall beside the elaborate wrought-iron gate. June hadn't phoned ahead. She hoped Holly was right, that they would be at home. If not, she'd just have to miraculously win some more cinema tickets for another night and make this trip a second time . . .

She pressed the button. Almost a minute passed before there was a crackle and then a man's voice.

'Yes?'

'Mr Jackson?'

'Yes.'

'This is June, Holly's boss from the bakery. I wonder, could I have a word with you and your wife?'

'Why? Is something wrong?'

June answered truthfully. 'Yes, I think so.'

The gate slowly opened and June walked up the drive.

Chapter Fourteen

Jim Quinlan stood in the middle of the crammed charity shop, shaking his head in disbelief. There wasn't an inch of spare space, either in the shop itself or in the back room. Every available spot was piled high with cans of food, toys, plum puddings, boxes of biscuits, chips and lollies, even rolls of wrapping paper. 'It's like Santa's warehouse in here. Lola, you're amazing.'

'It's nothing to do with me. It's the people in the Valley.'

There had been enough donations in the two days since the sign had gone up to fill more than fifty Christmas hampers. They hadn't won the window display competition. That had gone to the video shop for a funny display in the shape of Santa made from empty DVD cases and tinsel. But it hadn't mattered. The biggest front-page picture in that week's paper had been the charity shop's Christmas campaign. Lola had deliberately absented herself from the photo session. Word would have spread around town that Bett was going back to work on the paper and Lola didn't want anyone accusing her of media favouritism. Instead, Margaret, Kay and Patricia had lined up beside the window, holding empty plates, sad expressions on their faces. A little theatrical, perhaps, but it had got the message across.

Kay was quoted in the article, explaining that they'd been in touch with the hospital, the schools, the churches, the police as well as the service clubs, the Lions, the Rotary people, anyone they could think of, to ask who might be in most need of what she called 'a little help at Christmas'. She'd also invited anyone in need to slip a note into the charity shop, during or after opening hours, listing their address and the ages of the people in their family, and they'd be looked after too.

'It will all stay confidential, but no one needs to be ashamed to ask for our help. We know there are many generous people in the Valley who will donate not just food, but small presents for kiddies, even decorations for the tree. We'll gather everything here at the shop, then make up the Christmas hampers in time for delivery on Christmas Eve.'

That had been the plan, at least. However, the donations were coming in so quickly and in such quantities that there was no longer any room in the shop. There'd been an emergency committee meeting called – without Mrs Kernaghan's knowledge – to discuss possible storage solutions. Lola had let the talk wash around her initially, occupied with her own thoughts of Christmas – in particular, which rooms she was going to allocate to her special Christmas guests. The family in the family room, of course, but would she put the others in adjoining rooms, or spread them all around the motel? Spread them around, she decided. The businesswoman from Melbourne had requested the quietest room in the motel, so she'd be in room fifteen. The very relaxed man from Broken Hill who said he didn't care where his room was could be in room eight. The nice couple from Victoria could have —

'Lola? What do you think?'

She blinked. Her three friends were looking at her with concerned expressions. 'What on earth's wrong? Did I doze off?'

'No, but we have been asking your opinion for the past five minutes and you've been miles away.'

'What was the question again?'

'What are we going to do with all the donations? We can hardly move as it is, and we've already had two calls today from the schools. They've done gift-gathering days among their students and they've got what they said are dozens of boxes to bring down tomorrow. We're going to have to move all the clothes out at this rate.'

Lola peered out into the shop. Kay was right. You couldn't even get to the racks for all the donations. 'We'll just have to move them somewhere else. The donations, I mean, not the clothes.' She laughed merrily.

Patricia, Kay and Margaret exchanged glances. 'Yes, Lola. We did reach that conclusion ourselves. But to where?'

'I'd have thought that was perfectly obvious,' she smiled.

Which was where her son Jim had come in. He stood in the shop now, doing some mental arithmetic, before nodding. 'I think we can manage it. The function room is the best spot. You'll not only have plenty of storage room – if we arrange it properly, you'll have all the room you need to assemble the hampers too.'

Lola beamed. 'Darling, I knew I could depend on you.' Not that she'd been waiting on his answer. She'd already told the committee that the function room at the Valley View Motel would make the perfect storage place. And if the donations overflowed that, which they threatened to do, well, they could take over a few of the empty bedrooms too, couldn't they? Not that she'd mentioned that possible scenario to Jim just yet. 'And don't worry about the logistics. Luke has already rounded up a group of his friends to do all the moving for us. Marvellous!'

After farewelling Jim, she returned to the back room to confirm the good news. She could hear the three of them giggling even before she got to the doorway.

They were all gathered around the computer. It was pushed into a corner now, surrounded by the hamper goods. Kay was perched on a box filled with cans of sliced peaches donated by one of the local supermarkets. Margaret was beside her, leaning on a crate of wooden toys that a local craftsman had dropped in the day after the newspaper story appeared. Patricia was behind them, hemmed in between many jars of jam and several dozen bottles of Clare Valley riesling.

'What's so funny? Don't tell me it's another cat video?'

Kay laughed. 'Cats are so last year, Lola. Look at this website.'

Lola manoeuvred herself with some difficulty past a large bag of plastic toys and a bumper box of salt and vinegar potato chips until she was in front of the screen too. Expecting a freeze-frame of sneezing pandas or children falling off swings, she was surprised to see a full-screen photo of herself, wearing bright-red lipstick and a red fake flower in her hair. It had been taken at their impromptu Melbourne Cup luncheon that year. She hadn't had time to dress up. 'You rude ladies. Laughing at me like that. And me so old.'

'We're not laughing at you, Lola. Watch this. It's the most amazing website.' Kay pressed a button and they all waited. There was a flash of colour, then a drum roll and then, to a jaunty organ version of The Kinks' 'Lola', the photograph of Lola on screen began to change, slowly but unmistakably getting younger, her skin smoothing and becoming wrinkle-free, her jawline firming, her eyes brightening, the image going back and back through time until the screen was filled with a baby's face that somehow still looked like her – red lipstick, red flower and all. Both had stayed constant throughout all the changes.

'Oh, my good God!' Lola said, laughing. 'I'm adorable! It's like magic. How on earth did you do it?'

'It's based on some kind of FBI missing person technology,' Kay explained as she pressed the 'Watch Again' button. 'Luke showed it to us yesterday. All we had to do was scan in a photo, choose a song and the website did the rest. Wait until you see Patricia's. She looks more like a monkey at the end than a baby.'

Patricia was nearly crying with laughter. 'It's true, I do.'

They watched Lola's again, then Patricia's, Kay's and Margaret's, amazed and laughing at each equally.

'Does it work in reverse?' Lola asked. 'Can we scan in a photo of a child and see them as an adult?'

'Of course,' Kay said. 'I've done all my grandchildren already. If it all comes true, two of the boys are going to be bald by the time they're fifty and one of the girls is definitely going to be a supermodel. She's only three. Do you think I should put a bet on her future career?'

Lola produced the photo of Ellen that she always carried in her purse. It took Kay only a few minutes to scan it, load it on to the program, enter Lola's choice of song, then sit back and press 'go'.

Lola could hardly believe her eyes, or ears. To the sound of Ellen's favourite of Lola's old bedtime songs, 'Don't Sit Under the Apple Tree', her great-granddaughter changed from a sweet twelve-year-old to a pretty fourteen-year-old, into a beautiful twenty-year-old, growing older, older, into her late twenties, her early thirties . . .

'Stop, please,' Lola called. 'Stop it there.'

Kay paused it. On the screen was a woman in her thirties. A woman who was the spitting image of Anna.

'Good heavens,' Margaret breathed. She'd known Anna too. 'That's extraordinary.'

It was more than extraordinary. It was almost frightening. It suddenly didn't feel like a fun game to Lola any more. There were now too many memories rushing at her. Sad ones, happy ones – too much of every kind. She made a show of looking at her watch, pretending to be surprised at the time. 'I'm sorry to leave, but I think I'll call a taxi rather than wait for Luke,' Lola said. 'Goodbye, everyone.'

There was an exchange of worried glances, but no one stopped her. 'Goodbye, Lola,' they chorused.

In her room that evening, classical music playing on her small radio, a glass of gin and tonic on her bedside table, Lola was feeling much better. She'd changed into her favourite pink silk pyjamas and was lying on her bed, leafing through one of her photo albums. It was something she liked to do when she was rattled by life. She'd been rattled by life today. She found it soothing to be reminded of all the people she'd known, the places she'd lived, and most of all, to gaze at pictures of the family that still filled her life. Looking through her albums from cover to cover, either front to back or back to front, always made her feel safe and loved and, yes, fulfilled. She needed that comfort now.

She had been silly to overreact to the computer program. She'd already phoned Margaret to apologise. Margaret had interrupted to apologise first. 'We didn't think, Lola. We're sorry. We should have realised that Ellen would remind you of Anna —'

'Of course you shouldn't have. It was great fun. Such amazing technology. I was just a bit tired.'

It was true. She was a bit tired. A bit sad. A bit melancholy. It had been a good day in parts, too, of course. She had to try to think positively as well. She'd been happy to see all the donations coming in. Proud of Jim for offering to store everything at the motel. But it had still been a day of sad emotions, as every day of her life had been, she conceded now, good thoughts giving way to sad thoughts, back to good thoughts, layer on layer on layer . . .

Were human beings like trees inside? she wondered. If someone were to cut her in half, would they see all the rings representing her eighty-four years on earth, all the emotions she'd felt throughout her life? Thin grey rings when times hadn't been so good? Wide colourful rings when her year had been filled with joy and laughter, fun and family? What would the rings covering her short marriage be like? Thin and dark and unhappy? No, not completely, because Jim had come from that same marriage. If there were dark rings representing that time, there would also be the flashes of light that Jim had brought into her life. As Anna, Bett and Carrie had too. They'd be instantly visible, as great splashes of bright colour representing all the joy and fun they'd given Lola. Ellen's arrival. More colour and light. That silly feud over Matthew would be there too, dull, unhappy markings and colours, until Lola had plotted to bring them together again, with the musical she'd written – that would definitely be there too, displayed as cheerful colours. And then dark ring after dark ring reflecting Anna's sudden illness and too-quick death. Nothing but shadows and dull colours for what had felt like forever . . .

Except that wasn't true, Lola realised now. There had been some happy moments amidst their sadness about Anna, as she, and the rest of her family, searched for some kind of meaning, for any crumbs of happiness available. Laughter over shared memories of the singing Alphabet Sisters. Pride in Anna's work as an actress. Tears, but happy tears, at remembered acts of kindness and generosity from Anna. The best of times, the worst of times. That was the truth of all life and all lives, Lola knew. Nobody went through life seeing only bright colours and warm light. Sorrow ran alongside joy, despair beside happiness, fear beside confidence. And best of all – or was it worst of all? – you never knew when the light might suddenly switch off, when the colour might turn to monochrome. But you also never knew when that dim light might begin to glow, when something good and happy might appear, when it was least expected and, sometimes, when you needed it most. Like the arrival of Delia, Freya and George, followed by the twins . . .

She shouldn't have been so unsettled by the website today. They'd all often remarked how much Ellen looked like her mother. Of course an adult Ellen would resemble Anna even more. It had still been a shock.

Lola turned her attention back to the photo album on her lap. There'd be no surprises in here. She knew it was filled with pictures of Anna. Not just Anna, either, but all three girls, the whole family, at all stages of their lives. She flicked slowly through the pages, starting from the back of the album, enjoying the feeling of turning back time again, watching the three girls get younger, watching Jim's hair grow full, Geraldine's turn from grey to brown, her own from its current white to original deep chestnut. Back and back she went, passing dozens of images of herself and Jim in front of every motel or guesthouse they had ever managed or lived in together. It had been their ritual, a photo taken on the first day and a photo on the last. She watched Jim grow shorter and younger with each photo, his cheerful expression and sturdiness evident no matter what age he was.

Towards the front of the album, she found herself in the Irish section. She hadn't brought many photos with her when she'd emigrated. There was one of her family house in Kildare, a big house in the countryside with an oak tree at the front gate. One of herself with her parents on her wedding day, sheltering under umbrellas. It had been a typically damp Irish summer day. One of her and her husband Edward standing in front of the church in their wedding clothes, and another of the two of them more casually dressed, taken on the boat to Australia in the late 1930s. She'd kept those for Jim's sake rather than her own. She preferred not to be reminded of her husband. The final photo was of herself as a child in Kildare, pictured standing between her parents. She touched their faces. She hadn't seen them since the day she'd left for Australia as a twenty-year-old. They'd been dead now for more than fifty years. She barely remembered them. It was sad, but it was the truth.

And so there it was, she thought. A life lived backwards in less than five minutes. A life of almost eighty-five years reviewed that quickly. No, that wasn't all. In the pocket at the front of the album was an envelope of extra photos. Twenty or so images she hadn't had room to display in the album, but still wanted to keep. She flicked through them now too. There were more motel shots. Extra funny ones with Anna, Bett and Carrie from their days as the Alphabet Sisters singing group. She had other, separate albums devoted entirely to those days. These were just the spare photos, but it was good to see them again too, to remember those happy days.

The final photo in the pack did surprise her. It was of a man in his early thirties, with kind dark eyes, a shy smile, his black curly hair combed into neatness. The photo was nearly fifty years old, but Lola could remember exactly where it had been taken. Not only where, but what had happened the morning it was taken, what had happened after it was taken, what the weather had been like that day, even that there had been a slight breeze. It had been one of the happiest days of her life. If that time were to show up on one of her inside tree rings, she knew it would be all golden colours and warm light.

His name was Alex Lombardi. She'd been seeing him for four months by the time the photo was taken. They had met in Melbourne, in the most ordinary fashion, standing beside each other in a queue at their local supermarket. He'd remarked on the fine weather. She agreed it was a glorious day. He noticed her accent and asked about it. She noticed his accent and asked about it. They walked out of the store together, talking. Fifteen minutes later, they were still standing outside the store, still talking. She learned that he worked two streets away in Carlton, assistant manager with an Italian food-importing company. She told him about her guesthouse, two streets in the other direction. Three days later they met again, once more at the supermarket. That time he asked her to join him for a coffee. The next day she invited him to join her for a tea. It was a relationship founded on varying strengths of caffeine, they agreed a month later, when they were seeing each other every day. It moved easily, beautifully, even thrillingly, in Lola's opinion, from coffee- and tea-drinking and talking to lovemaking and talking. She suddenly understood why women sought romance. Everything she had with Alex was everything she hadn't had with her husband. Alex listened to her, amused her, entertained her, admired her. She wasn't completely in love with him. Not yet. Something was holding her back, some inbuilt caution. But she was as close to love as it was possible to be.

On the day the photo was taken, she and Alex had given themselves an afternoon off. Jim was away on a school camp. She had no bookings and for the first time ever, she hung a 'Sorry, no vacancies' sign in the window. Aged in their thirties and behaving like children wagging school. They packed a picnic and caught a tram to the beach in Brighton. They swam, sunbaked, read to each other, swam again. Ate their picnic. Kissed. Kissed many times, between the conversation and the laughter, so at ease with one another, so happy in each other's company.

Who decided they shouldn't go back home that night? Her or him? Perhaps they decided at the same time. They called it research. It was important that Lola knew what her competitors were up to, he said. So they booked into a guesthouse near the beach, smoothly and easily calling themselves Mr and Mrs Lombardi. The woman at the front desk didn't care whether they were married or had just met on the tram, they could tell, but it added an extra glow to their mood. They asked her to recommend a good Italian restaurant nearby. She shrugged and told them the food was better in the pub.

Lola found herself smiling now, remembering every moment of that night. Enchanted, it was the only word to describe it. There had always been so much to talk to each other about. There hadn't been any unease or caution in their lovemaking that night, either. It had been as luxurious, as loving, as special as always. Passion, laughter, conversation. They hadn't slept at all. It hadn't mattered.

Life wasn't so cruel for them to be separated immediately on their return to their real lives the next day. They were granted another six months of happiness after that, more dinners, laughter, even fights, followed by more conversation and lovemaking. Lola knew it was getting serious. Alex had told her how he felt. She had told him how she felt. She watched him with Jim, saw his kindness to her son, and knew that all would be well there too. It was a golden time.

Until Alex came to the guesthouse one morning, unexpectedly. He usually phoned before he visited. He thought it was only good manners. Just one more addition to the many things she liked so much about him – his intelligence, his gentleness, his humour, his looks, his touch. His eyes.

His eyes.

She'd known as soon as she looked into his eyes that morning that the news was bad. 'I have to go home. Back to Italy. There's a problem in my family.'

She'd already heard about his complicated family background.

His father had died when he was only twelve. An older brother had taken charge of the family business, supporting their mother, several elderly aunts, many cousins. The brother was the one in trouble now. He'd been in a serious car accident, and wouldn't be able to work for six months at least. Alex was needed at home.

'Forever?'

'I don't know, Lola.'

'It'll be hard to come back.'

He didn't need to reply. She saw it in his expression. This wasn't a brief trip back. They both knew that.

Yet his news didn't bother Lola as much as she'd expected. She knew this wasn't going to be the end of her and Alex. She'd already moved countries once in her life, from Ireland to Australia. She could go from Australia to Italy, surely? She'd learn the language. Jim would learn it too. It would be an adventure for all of them.

Over the next week, as Alex made his preparations to leave, she waited for him to ask her to come and join him. She'd given it long and careful thought. She would say yes.

He didn't ask her.

On his last night, she was the one who brought it up. She asked him outright. Could she and Jim join him, follow him, after he'd settled back home again?

Again, his eyes gave her his answer, before he spoke. 'Lola, I'm sorry.'

'I see,' she said. She didn't flounce away, didn't cry, didn't get upset. She just felt very, very sad.

He took her hand, held it tight, raised it to his lips. She saw he was as sad as she was.

'Why not?' she said, trying one last time.

'You're a married woman.'

'I am?' Even this many years later, she remembered that she'd smiled, thinking he was joking. 'Where's my husband? I seem to have mislaid him.'

He didn't smile back. In that moment, she regretted ever having told him the truth about her background. In the ten years since she had left her husband, she had lived a lie, telling everyone, yes, even her little son, that she was a widow, that her brave soldier husband had been killed in the war. She'd reached the conclusion very early on in her days as a single mother with a young son that a widow would receive a much better reception than a runaway wife. It may have been the 1950s, moving into the swinging sixties, but in the rural areas of Australia where she and Jim usually found themselves, attitudes were still old-fashioned.

She'd told Alex she was a widow too. Until one night, ironically, after several glasses of very good Italian wine, he had asked her for more details about her husband. She told him everything. About their wedding in Ireland. The emigration to Australia. Her rapid realisation that the man who had seemed so kind and charming at home in Kildare was in fact a bully, a weakling and, worst of all, a drunkard. How he had started to shout at her. Shout at Jim. How he had hit her one night. Threatened to hit Jim. How she had lived in fear until the day she'd realised that her life didn't have to be like this and she'd left him. She hadn't seen him since. He could be dead or alive for all she knew. At the time, Alex had listened in that intent, focused way he had. Asked her questions. Told her how brave she was. Made it clear he understood how difficult it must have been. At the time she'd basked in his praise. Now, she'd have done anything for him not to know the truth.

He tried to explain. 'My family are very traditional, Lola. Very Catholic.'

'So were mine. I still remember my Hail Marys.' He didn't smile. She tried again. 'Alex, they don't need to know the truth. No one else does. Only you. People don't ask. They accept what they're told. We'll just tell everyone in Italy I'm a widow. For all I know, that may be the truth now.'

'It's too late. I've written about you to my brother. I told him everything about you.'

'Everything?'

'Everything.'

'Can we pretend I'm someone else you've met in Australia? Someone new?' She was only half joking.

'Who looks like you and has a son the same age? And an Irish accent?'

He was right. His honesty helped. She saw in that moment that her dreams of a life together were just that. Of course she and Jim couldn't pack up everything, follow him across the world. Of course not.

They were still holding hands. 'Will you write to me?'

'Of course,' he said.

'Will you be gone long?'

'I've told them I'll stay for six months. A year at the most.'

'And then?'

'I'll come back.'

'To Australia?' To me, she meant.

'As soon as I can.'

In the first three weeks, there was one letter from Italy. Brief and overwhelmed. The business was in a mess. His brother was in worse health than he'd been told. She wrote back to him, a long letter, with photos and stories, trying to cheer him up, letting him know how much she cared about him. She received a brief post-card in return. She wrote another letter. Then another. Six months passed. Nothing. Seven, eight. Two weeks before a year was up, she finally received a second letter from him. She had stayed in the same guesthouse, longer than she'd wanted to, because she didn't want to change address. She didn't want to risk a letter arriving there for her after she'd gone, and never finding its way to her.

She only had to read the first line to know the rest. He wasn't coming back. He couldn't. Not now that he was engaged to the daughter of his mother's oldest friend.

Lola had put the guesthouse on the market the next day. She and Jim were in a new town and new guesthouse within a month. She hadn't written back. She couldn't. If she had, the letter would have been filled with lies, telling him she under-stood, that she wished him and his fiancée well and many years of happiness together. She hadn't felt those things. All she'd felt was broken-hearted. She could have written and told him that, she knew, but what was the point? What would it have changed about their situation? So she'd said nothing back to him at all. If he ever did write to her again, she hadn't received the letter.

Lola touched the photo of Alex again now. It would be fifty years next month since they'd had that day on the beach together. It seemed extraordinary to think of all that had happened since. Herself and Jim making move after move, growing older, Jim meeting Geraldine, the arrival of the three girls, more moves, their performing days, until they came to a halt, a mostly very happy halt, here in the Clare Valley. So much had happened right here, in this motel, as well.

She thought of her husband now too. All these years later, she at least knew what had happened to him. She'd heard from his sister out of the blue, not long after Anna's death. He had died back home in Ireland, after a life spent travelling around Australia and then through America. A drinker to the end, she was sure of it. She'd felt sad for his family, but not a moment of regret that she and Jim had left him when they did. She was now, truthfully, a widow.

And Alex? What had happened to him? Had he had a long happy marriage? Many children? Or a short, unhappy marriage, no children? Was he even alive still? If he was, would he still have that good heart, or would the trials of family life have beaten it out of him? Would he still have those kind, dark eyes, or would their light have dimmed too? She gazed down at the photo, smiling again. For years she hadn't been able to look at him without feeling a pang of sadness, even a flash of anger for what might have been, what had been lost between them. Now, this long afterwards, it felt . . . it felt only good to see his face. She felt curiosity, not sadness. Where was he now? she wondered. Had he had a happy life, a good life? What would he look like all these years later?

She reached for her phone and dialled a local number. 'Luke, it's Lola. Could you please pick me up earlier than usual tomorrow? And show me how to do something on the computer?'

'It's easy,' Luke said in the back room of the charity shop the next morning. 'See, just place the photo here, press this button and *voila*, it's now a digital image. That means we can do stuff with it on the computer.' He quickly typed something on the keyboard and there on the screen was the website Lola's friends had been using the day before.

'An old flame, Lola?' Luke asked, looking up at her with a nice smile.

'Yes, as a matter of fact.'

'Want to see if you had a lucky escape?'

'That's it exactly.'

'Did you both have a special song you'd like to play while it does its magic?'

They had had a song of their own – 'Catch a Falling Star' by Perry Como – but she wasn't going to ask Luke to find and play it. Some things needed to remain private. 'No. Silence is fine, thank you, Luke.'

The site quickly worked its photographic wizardry again. 'Ready?' Luke asked.

'Ready,' she replied. She asked Luke to run the program as slowly as possible, then pulled her chair in close to the screen as the images started to appear.

She knew there was no way of knowing whether this was what would have happened to Alex. He might have died young and handsome. He could have grown old and fat. Been bald by the time he turned fifty. But the computer program took the optimistic approach. As the images appeared on the screen, his face kept its shape, his skin stayed the same light tan, even his hair stayed thick, with just a smattering of grey here and there . . .

Beneath the image, a small box displayed the age of the subject: seventy-seven, seventy-eight, seventy-nine . . . She asked Luke to stop the program at the age he would be now – eighty-three. If nature had been as kind as the computer program, if he was still alive – all those ifs – then Alex was still a handsome man. Elderly, yes. Wrinkled, yes, but the image on the screen had the same kind eyes, the same shy smile. Beside her, Luke stayed silent. She was grateful for his sensitivity. She patted his hand.

'Thank you, Luke.'

'Does he look like you imagined?'

'Even better,' she said.

'Would you like a print-out of that last photo?'

'You can do that?'

'I can do anything.'

Another click of the mouse, a whirr of the printer and there it was in her hand, a colour print of the photograph.

'I'm so glad I've lived this long,' Lola said to Luke. 'And I used to think the invention of television was incredible. Not to mention skyscrapers. The wheel. Fire . . .'

Luke grinned as he closed the program down. 'Is there anything else I can do, Lola? Would you like me to try and find out where your friend is now?'

Lola laughed. 'Could you? Yes, please. Would you ask him to meet me for lunch here tomorrow?'

'I mean it, Lola. Do you want me to try to find him?'

'How on earth will you do that? You don't even know him.'

'Lola, haven't you listened to anything I've been teaching you for the past year? This box thing is called a computer. It's connected to an amazing invention called the internet that stretches all around the world and —'

'Yes, Luke, very droll. I mean it. How could you possibly find him?'

'On the internet. There are thousands of websites to help find people. Not just by googling them, either. You remember what I taught you about googling?' At Lola's nod, Luke went on enthusiastically. 'There are "find your family" sites, "trace your ancestry" sites, hundreds of ways of tracking down people, all over the world.'

'But he's probably still in Italy. You don't speak Italian, do you?'

'No, but the computer can. There are hundreds of translation sites. Lola, I'm serious. I'm happy to try and find him if you want me to.'

'But he might be dead by now. He probably is. It's a miracle I'm still walking and talking.'

'Maybe he is. I can find out for sure, if you want. That would be where I'd start, if you don't mind me being so ghoulish.'

'Ghoulish?'

'Dead people are the easiest to find. Most cemeteries register all their —' he searched for the word.

'Inhabitants?'

He smiled. 'Yes, them. They're registered online these days. Nearly everything's online these days. I helped my boss's wife find her great-uncle last month. He'd fought and died in France and she wanted to find out where he'd been buried. It took a while but I found him. Not just his exact location in the cemetery, either. I even found an aerial photograph of it. I'm sure I could find your friend. I just need all his details, every single thing you can remember about him.'

Lola remembered a great deal. Luke wrote it all down. Alex's full name. His birthday. His mother's name. His place of birth. His occupation. His last known address . . . She hadn't kept his letters, but she'd always remembered the address.

After he'd finished making notes, she sat back, folded her hands in her lap and waited.

Luke noticed. 'Lola, I'm sorry. I won't be able to find him right now. It might take me days of searching. Weeks even. Especially when there are two languages involved.'

'Oh, of course,' Lola said, feigning a laugh. 'What was I thinking! That you'd be able to conjure him out of thin air just like that!' It was exactly what she'd been thinking. And hoping.

'I'll do what I can, as quickly as I can, Lola. I promise.'

She patted his arm. 'You're a good, kind man, Luke. A good, kind man.' He was. Just like Alex had been.

It was only after she'd said goodbye that she realised she'd missed another opportunity to talk to Luke about Emily. Next time, she vowed.

CHAPTER FIFTEEN

'Hello, Dad! Did you have a good day at work?'

'Hello, Ellen.' Glenn stopped at the door, immediately suspicious. 'What's wrong? Have you broken something? Has Lin left?'

'No, everything's fine. She's cooking dinner. I've even done my homework.'

'You do know Denise and Lily are coming tonight?'

'Seven o'clock, isn't it?'

'And that's okay? You're sure?'

'It's fine.'

'What did Lola say to you? Has she bribed you to behave?'

'Kind of.'

Glenn sent up a silent prayer of thanks. He wanted to pick his daughter up in a hug, thank her. But instinct told him to play it carefully. 'That's great. I'll just go and change. I'm soaked with sweat. The sooner this storm breaks the better.'

'Can I get you a cool drink?'

'I'd love a lemonade, thank you.'

'Coming right up.'

Glenn couldn't resist. He rang Lola from the bathroom, hoping the noise of the running water would mask the sound of his voice. 'What did you say to Ellen? Because you should hire your speech out to troubled parents the world over. She's like a new girl.'

'I didn't tell her anything she didn't already know.'

'You're not going to tell me what you did say, are you?'

'No,' Lola said. 'Some things are best kept secret between a great-granddaughter and her very elderly great-grandmother.'

'Thanks, Lola.'

'Any time, Glenn. Let me know how it goes. I want Ellen's version of tonight and then I want the truth.'

'I'll ring you tomorrow. Will you let me know the best date for her to arrive as well?'

'I'm just juggling a few things here. I'll get back to you about that as soon as I can.'

'I owe you, Lola.'

'No, you don't. We both love her. It was the easiest thing in the world to do.'

All evening, Glenn could see Denise and Lily watching Ellen with something like amazement. A cross between wariness and amazement, in fact. *This* was the she-devil who'd been hiding in her room, shouting at them through doors, who'd refused to come out, who'd turned down their Christmas invitation? She couldn't have behaved better or been nicer. Her manners were impeccable. She asked questions, answered their questions. She took Lily into her room after dinner and even from the living room Glenn and Denise could hear the two of them laughing as they played something – innocent pop videos, Glenn hoped – on Ellen's computer.

'I don't know what you've done, but you should market it,' Denise said.

'I'm sorry it's taken this long. And been so hard on you.'

'It's been hard on everyone, I know. You're sure she won't join us for Christmas?'

Glenn had never been more sure of anything. Much as he loved seeing Ellen behave like the old Ellen, he knew even a mention of the island holiday could take them right back to square one. Possibly to some place even more troublesome.

There were more giggles.

'I'll just check they're getting on okay,' Glenn said.

Ellen and Lily had a large photo album on the bed between them and were looking at his wedding photos. Laughing at his hairdo, specifically. Glenn knew his daughter wasn't just showing off his funny hairstyle. She was showing off her mother.

'It was the happiest day of your life, wasn't it, Dad?'

'It was a beautiful day,' Glenn said carefully.

'Your wife was very pretty, Glenn,' Lily said politely.

'Yes, she was.'

'Lily's mum and dad got divorced when she was only three, Dad, did you know that?'

Keep smiling, Glenn told himself. She's trying. 'I did know that, Ellen, yes.'

'I'll bring photos of their wedding day next time I visit,' Lily said. 'He looks even funnier than your dad. I only see him twice a year. He lives in America, but he's bald now. I think he polishes his head.'

'Polishes it!'

'With furniture polish!'

The two of them shrieked with laughter again. Time to go, Glenn thought. It was a relief to return to Denise's company.

Two days later, in her room at the motel, Lola had the rare and frankly unpleasant realisation that she had nothing to do. She'd been so busy all week and now here she was, with a whole hour to herself and nothing to do in it. She ticked off her mental list. Ellen – sorted. Window display – sorted. Christmas secret – all underway.

There was nothing more to do now in regard to her Christmas guests until they started arriving. She could hardly wait. Though there was of course still the minor matter of booking the airline ticket for Ellen. Something kept stopping her from doing that, and she still wasn't sure what it was. Sixth sense or another new hope? She'd spoken to Ellen and Glenn after the most recent dinner with Denise and Lily. It had all gone swimmingly, apparently. Ellen sounded very proud of herself and after some prodding, had confessed that Denise's daughter was 'okay'.

'Too young for me but she's not as bad as I thought.'

'And Denise?' Lola had asked.

'Okay. But not as pretty as Mum. Or as nice. Or as funny.'

'No one ever will be,' Lola said.

Glenn had reported positive results too. Astonishing results, in fact. Denise had apparently even asked if he was sure Ellen wouldn't like to join them for Christmas.

'Don't push your luck just yet,' Lola had advised. But she had tucked the idea away herself. It would mean she wouldn't have Ellen at the motel as her Christmas assistant, but if the worst came to the worst, surely her guests wouldn't mind pitching in and helping her themselves? Wouldn't that make it even more of a Christmas to remember for them all? And really, when it came down to it, they were getting free accommodation, weren't they? It was only fair that they do a little something to earn their keep.

There'd even been good-ish news on the Mrs Kernaghan front. She'd taken as much credit as possible for the reworked charity shop window, even setting up an interview with the local TV station in Port Pirie. The other ladies were outraged, but Lola had doused their flames of fury.

'It's good publicity for the shop and our Christmas hampers,' she said. 'That's all that counts, no matter how and who gets the publicity.'

'But did you see her on the TV, Lola?' Kay had said. 'Showing them around the shop as if she was Coco Chanel?'

More like Coco the clown, Lola had privately thought.

'And then that bit of her sitting at the computer pretending to write the note for the window!' Margaret added. 'She doesn't even know how to use the computer!'

'We'll get more donations. More items for our hampers. Focus on that, not on her,' Lola had advised.

She'd been right. The donations had doubled in quantity after the TV segment went to air. They also got something else unexpected. New volunteers for the shop. Whether it was the Christmas spirit kicking in, or the lure of the computer setup, Kay had reported a tenfold increase in retired people wanting to work shifts in the shop. Not just retired people, either. They'd had a few young people get in touch. Come the new year, Lola suspected she and the other ladies would be lucky to get a shift at the shop – or on the computer – at all.

The only little bugbear in Lola's mental roll call remained her granddaughters and their still-simmering row. She hadn't seen either of them that week so far, but she'd spoken to both. Carrie had done her usual whingeing about Matthew and the children but had refused to talk about Bett.

'I've done all I can with her, Lola. If she's going to get huffy about anyone offering even the tiniest bit of advice, then there's nothing I can do.'

Bett had been no better. She'd spoken in the fake cheery voice Lola knew she only used when she was in danger of bursting into tears. She'd also spoken in strange clipped sentences. How are things with the twins? Lola had asked.

'Fine! Great!'

'And Daniel?'

'Great!'

'Have you had a chance to talk?'

'Every night. It's all great!'

Both Carrie and Bett were unhappy, Lola knew it. They were

so clearly keeping their distance, not just from her, but from each other too. It made her so sad. What would it take to get them talking to each other again? Should she lock them in a room together and not let them out until they were friends?

That was it! The solution was so obvious Lola was amazed it had taken her so long to come up with it. It was a matter of logical thinking, outlining the problems inherent in the situation and letting the solution rise slowly to the surface. Problem one. What needed to be done? Carrie and Bett brought together on a project. Problem two. What else needed to be done? The Christmas hampers assembled. Possible solution to both problems? Carrie and Bett assembling the hampers together! Any obstacles? Just one. Their children. Their five children. Their five handfuls of children.

The solution? A team of experienced babysitters, of course.

Lola picked up her mobile phone and started making some calls.

Twenty minutes later, it was all organised. Her friends had agreed immediately. 'Many hands make light work.' 'The more the merrier.' 'Five of them, five of us. It's an equal battle.' It took her only ten minutes and two admittedly begging calls to her granddaughters to get them to agree, too.

The next morning, before the sun had turned up its heat to high, her plan was underway. There they all were – Lola, Patricia, Margaret, Joan and Kay – in the living room of Bett's house, looking after not just Zachary and Yvette but also Carrie's three for the day. Gazing around the room, Lola decided it looked like a social experiment – a combined crèche and an old folks' home.

She didn't voice her thoughts, mind you. Kay in particular was sensitive about getting older.

Meanwhile, ten kilometres away, in the function room of the motel, if everything Lola had set in train was starting to unfold, Carrie and Bett were hopefully making up the first of two hundred or more Christmas hampers, finding themselves chatting, laughing and growing closer as each minute passed . . .

That was the idea, anyway. Lola could only hope things were going better at the motel than they were here in babysitter land. She put her hands over her ears again as Zachary gave a loud squeal.

'What's happened to babies these days?' Margaret said, as she jiggled a wailing George in her arms. 'Mine were never as noisy as this, I'm sure of it.'

'Or as athletic. What is Bett feeding the twins? Royal jelly?' Kay asked. She was trying to change Yvette's nappy and struggling with her wildly waggling legs. She'd also narrowly avoided an impromptu shower in a liquid other than water when she'd tried to change Zachary's nappy ten minutes earlier. 'Now I know why I only had one daughter,' she said.

Lola glanced at her watch. They'd been minding the five children for less than fifteen minutes. Just six hours and forty-five minutes to go.

She stood up with a groan. 'Cup of tea, anyone?'

'This is a job for a dozen people, not two,' Carrie said sulkily, looking around the motel function room. 'It's like a supermarket in here. How on earth are we supposed to get it all done in one day? Lola made it sound as if she just needed us to do a bit of packing, not run a wholesale warehouse.'

'The sooner we get started, the sooner it'll be done,' Bett said. She could feel Carrie mimicking and mocking her words behind her, but fought against her instinct to turn and shout at her. The atmosphere between them was already bad enough. They could at least try to get through one hour without fighting.

Bett knew what Lola was up to. Subtlety had never been their grandmother's strong suit. The musical four years earlier had got the sisters talking again and Lola obviously thought a day packing these Christmas hampers together would do the same. Wishful thinking, in Bett's opinion. She was already steeling herself for one of Carrie's lectures on childrearing. She'd seen the look on Carrie's face that morning, when Carrie came to her house to drop off her children and pick up Bett.

She had done her best to tidy up, but Carrie and her X-ray vision seemed to notice every hastily shut cupboard, dirty counter and dusty windowsill. Lola's gang, as Bett thought of them, were fortunately already there. For ladies of a mature age, they were surprisingly giggly. If it hadn't been so early in the morning, she'd have suspected they'd all been drinking. They'd also been very carefree about Bett's and then Carrie's instructions regarding their children's needs. Lola had eventually interrupted.

'Darlings, please! Between us we've reared enough children to fill a football team, if unisex football teams exist. Off you go to do those hampers and don't give us a second thought. You can ring, but only twice during the day, okay? We'll call you if anything happens. And besides, if anything does happen, Margaret's got a first-aid certificate, haven't you, Margaret?'

'Me? Well, I donate blood to the Red Cross —'

'So you're not squeamish? Perfect!' Lola said. 'Off you go, girls. See you at six!'

Six p.m. Many long hours away. Bett suppressed a sigh and wished she wasn't feeling so tense, in her temples, her back, her whole body. It had been another bad night with Daniel. Both so polite to each other, on the surface everything perfectly normal, except for the fact she felt constantly on the verge of tears and continually guilty about forcing him into going part-time. She'd tried Lola's suggestion of a daily walk. Oh, they'd walked. They'd also fought, all the way down their country road, for a kilometre of the Riesling Trail that followed the path of the old railway line and all the way back home. There didn't seem to be any common ground between them any more. No safe areas of conversation. She'd tried apologising again, tried to explain, but Daniel had interrupted.

'Bett, you've got your way, so now we get on with it. It's that simple.'

'But it doesn't feel right.'

He stopped. 'So you don't want me to go part-time in the new year now?'

'Yes, I do. I mean, no! No, I don't.'

He started walking again. 'You don't know what you want, so you can't expect me to know either.'

It was true. He was right. She didn't know anything any more. She'd expected to feel different, feel better. She just felt terrible in a new way.

Not that she'd let on to Carrie about any of this. During the drive to the motel, Carrie had spoken in a deceptively innocent tone. 'So Lola tells me you're going back to work sooner than you expected.'

'Mmm. I've done a few hours already. It'll be one day a week in the new year.'

'And Daniel's going to go part-time then too? Look after the twins as well?'

'Mmm.'

Great, she wanted to hear Carrie say. *What teamwork.* Instead, her sister radiated disapproval. Bett had taken a breath, about to explain why they were going to try it, how lost she'd been, how she'd felt like she was drowning, but Carrie made a performance of turning up the radio and singing along – in perfect tune, Bett acknowledged – to a pop song. That had been the end of any more car conversation.

'So, how shall we do this?' Bett said now.

Carrie shrugged. 'You tell me.'

Bett kept her temper with difficulty. 'We could work out a system. Take it in turns, maybe – one of us packing, the other gathering the items, that kind of thing.'

'Fine.'

Stay calm, Bett, stay calm. 'Unless you've got a better idea, of course?'

'I don't really care how we do it.'

'That's a great attitude, Carrie. Full of charity. What about we just ring the recipients up and tell them to come and pick what they want themselves? Is that what you think? Save you the bother?'

'God, you are snippy today. Finding juggling work and home life a bit tricky, are you?'

Forget trying to stay calm. 'Fuck off, Carrie.'

'Don't take your unhappiness out on me.'

'You selfish, conceited —'

'Oh, grow up, would you? Name-calling at your age? I've had it with you, Bett. I've done all I can to help you, offer advice, give you praise —'

'*Praise?* Praise? You've done nothing but undermine and criticise me from the day the twins were born. From before then, even, when I was pregnant – I wasn't eating properly, I wasn't exercising enough. No wonder I had such a hard labour. I hadn't prepared well enough. No wonder the twins weren't sleeping properly. On and on and bloody on. I don't *need* you to tell me what a bad mother I am, Carrie, all right? I can see that perfectly well for myself. So mind your own bloody business, would you? You and Perfect Matthew and your three perfect children can go off and live your perfect lives and leave me and Daniel and our kids alone.'

Carrie's expression didn't change. 'Have you finished?'

Bett nodded.

Carrie turned back to the hampers. 'So let's get on with

this, will we? As you pointed out, the sooner we get started, the sooner it's done.'

'So you're just going to ignore everything I've said?'

'Oh, no, Bett. I'll remember every ridiculous, immature word of it. But I haven't got anything to say back to you. The only reason I'm here is as a favour to Lola. Let's get started, will we?'

Would it be ridiculous and immature of her if she were to pick up the tins of peaches and start throwing them at Carrie? Bett wondered. If she were to toss the bottles of olive oil at her too? Open the windows of the function room and tip all the donated toys out into the car park? Bett wanted to do all that and burst into tears too. What was *happening* to her lately? She'd lost all reason, all patience, all sense of proportion. And now, she'd lost face as well. Carrie was there, smug and calm, enjoying the high moral ground, already leafing through the large pile of paper slips. Bett was the one with the red face and mutinous expression.

Lola's underlying plan to get them talking definitely hadn't worked. Which left only the hampers to get ready.

In clipped tones, they devised a method. Carrie would read out the recipients' details, the number of family members and their ages. Bett would fetch and carry the items. They'd swap places after an hour.

They got started. Luke and his friends had arranged everything in neat groups. Toys, foodstuffs, decorations, miscellaneous gifts. Despite her own unhappiness, Bett found herself admiring people's generosity. She hadn't donated anything yet herself, even though she'd written a short article for the paper about the donations. She would, as soon as possible. Had Carrie donated anything? she wondered. About to ask, she changed her mind. She wasn't sure she could bear hearing that Carrie had donated a thousand dollars' worth of top-quality biscuits or cakes or toys, when she and Daniel could barely afford to pay their own bills, let alone help out people in greater need than them.

If she'd been working with anyone else, she'd have had plenty to say, she knew. Perhaps even speculated about who some of the recipients were. It had all been done as anonymously as possible, although Lola and two other of her shop ladies knew the full details, so they could arrange the deliveries on Christmas Eve. The slips just had the bare details. Bett waited as Carrie leafed through another pile.

'We have to do them all, Carrie. It's not a matter of picking the best ones,' she said.

'You're right,' Carrie said. 'I am sorry.'

Her words were pure politeness on the surface, chosen to hurt underneath. 'Thank you, Carrie,' Bett answered, in tones equally saccharine.

'A family of four, mother thirty-four, father thirty-nine, two boys aged eight and ten.'

Bett moved up and down the rows of goods, choosing and delivering them back to Carrie, who began packing them into a box.

'Two boys, did you say? What would they like?'

'I don't know, Bett. I'm not their mother. I don't know them.'

'Your generous nature is astounding me. Such sympathy for other people's troubles.'

Carrie just rolled her eyes.

That time Bett didn't hesitate. She threw the can of peaches she was holding directly at her sister. It missed her by inches, flew over the pile of boxes and landed with a crash on the bar area behind them, knocking over a row of glasses. The shattering noise filled the room.

'That's enough, you cow!' Bett shouted. 'You think I want to be here with you either? With you and your bloody smugness, seeing how perfect you look, and knowing how wonderful your children are and your marriage is? Well, I don't! Because you're absolutely right about me, Carrie. I *am* a hopeless mother. I *do* feed my children the wrong food. They don't sleep because I'm not putting them to bed at the right times. And you know what else? My marriage is falling apart. I don't talk to Daniel about anything any more. We either fight or we don't talk. He can't seem to do anything right either. But I can't expect you to understand, can I? Not Mrs Perfect, with her Perfect Husband who does everything around the house —'

'No, he doesn't.'

'— and yes, I know what else you're thinking, I've probably made a huge mistake wanting to go back to work so soon, I don't know — What did you say?'

'I said that no, Matthew doesn't do everything around the house. He's useless, actually.'

'But he cooks. Cleans. You told me —'

'I was lying.'

'Lying?'

Carrie nodded.

'Why?'

Carrie shrugged.

'You mean he doesn't cook dinner four nights a week? Give the kids their baths every night?'

Carrie laughed. 'No.'

'Do your kids sleep through every night?'

'No.'

'Eat everything you put in front of them?'

'No.'

'Get on with each other all the time?'

Carrie laughed again. 'No.'

'But you told me they did. You've done nothing but tell me —'

'I was hoping if I kept saying it, it might come true.'

Bett could hardly believe what she was hearing. 'So you're finding it hard too?'

A nod.

'Really hard?'

Another nod. 'Of course. Not always, though.'

Bett waited.

'There are lots of good times. Like when they're asleep and I've opened a bottle of wine.' She became serious. 'Bett, what planet have you been living on? Of course it's tough. You just have to concentrate on the good times. Lie to yourself if you have to. I do it all the time. You also have to remind yourself – constantly – about how cute or funny they can be. Think positively. Remember how much you love them, even when they're being sick or screaming or wide awake in the middle of the night. You must have had to do that already?'

Bett nodded.

'Then you know what I'm talking about. Doesn't your heart just fill up at the sight of them sometimes? You've felt that too, haven't you? In the mornings, especially? That's always my favourite time.'

Bett nodded again, remembering Yvette and Zachary just that morning. 'When you first go into their rooms and they see you, do you mean? And they're so excited and happy?'

Carrie nodded. 'Exactly. I just wish they'd stay there like that, happy and half-asleep. Just for a few years. Or even for an hour now and again, long enough to give me time to do some washing. Or vacuum. Or cook something more interesting than fish fingers.'

'You have trouble getting things done too?'

Carrie rolled her eyes.

'Why haven't you told me any of this?'

Another shrug.

Bett didn't know whether to scream or cry. 'Carrie, I've been going crazy. Completely crazy, seeing you doing everything so perfectly, and knowing I was failing at everything, at every single step. But if you're not being the perfect mother —'

'No one is, Bett. There's no such thing.'

'Then there's hope for me, isn't there?'

'For God's sake, Bett. What magazines or websites have you been reading? Everyone finds it tough. Because it is tough. Wonderful but tough.'

'But why don't people talk about it more?'

Carrie held up one of the Christmas hamper slips of paper. 'Why are these anonymous? Why did people drop the forms in after hours or put them in the post? Because they're embarrassed, ashamed? Because they felt they'd let their families down, themselves down, that they should have done a better job? That's how I feel sometimes about being a mother. And I bet just about every other mother in the world feels the same way sometimes too. It's hard, Bett. Hard for everyone. You and me included.'

'So why have you been such a bitch to me lately?'

'Me? You started it. I was just trying to help, give you a bit of advice now and again.'

'Now and again? You've done nothing but —' Bett stopped herself. She might never have a conversation like this with her sister again. 'Carrie, if I ask you a few questions, will you answer them honestly?'

'Maybe.'

'Does Matthew ever cook?'

'Once in a blue moon and it's always sausages on the barbecue.'

'Does he do much housework?'

'I think he put a plate in the dishwasher once. Oh, no, he

didn't. That was me again. Can I ask you a question? Do you and Daniel really fight?'

'All the time lately. About everything.'

'And what about? You know . . .'

'Sex?'

Carrie nodded.

Bett pulled a face. 'Never again. Ever.' They both laughed. 'I'm exaggerating. Yes, but rarely.'

'I need a word that means rarer than rarely. Barely? Don't care-ly?' Carrie gave a quick smile. 'Another question. Why have you decided to go back to work so soon? I thought you wanted to spend the first year at least with the twins.'

'I do. I did. But —'

'You're not sure any more?'

'I've only done a few hours back so far. It was great. It felt so easy.'

'But?'

'I also felt guilty the whole time. That I should have been home with the twins and doing housework. And I don't think that going part-time is what Daniel really wants, either. But it's too late now. We've discussed it over and over' – she allowed herself the lie – 'and we've made the decision.'

'Why is it too late now? Why don't you wait until you've done a few full days in January? If you still don't like it, tell your editor it was a trial and you're sorry, it hasn't worked out for you. If they need to, they'll find someone else. It's a local paper, Bett. It's not like you're the head of the UN.'

'You have such a turn of phrase, you know that?' But there was no sting in Bett's words.

'I know,' Carrie said, smiling. 'I'm perfect in so many ways. As for Daniel, it's not too late for him to change his mind either, is it? He can tell his boss he was overtired and hadn't thought it through properly. That's probably true anyway, isn't it?'

Bett could only agree.

'See, I do know everything.' Carrie grinned suddenly. 'I'd better stop there or you'll throw more peaches at me. That was very childish, by the way. You're older than me, you're supposed to set a good example.'

'Sorry, Carrie.'

'Forgiven. And forgotten. For now, anyway. Come on, we'd better get back to work. We haven't even finished ten boxes yet. Lola will kill us. Forget about political correctness, too. Give the boys the balls and cricket bats and the girls the dolls and teddies. And give them *all* lots of chips. Little kids love chips.'

By lunchtime they had put forty hampers together. At first they had worked in almost silence again, Carrie reading the details, Bett fetching, before swapping over. As the filled hampers began to take over a corner of the room, they talked more about each of the recipients. It wasn't only families asking for help. There were hampers for several elderly people, single men, single mothers. Bett and Carrie wondered about the elderly ones, particularly. Had they needed food or had it been to make sure they had a visit, even briefly, from someone at Christmas time?

Their conversation took winding, twisting turns. They talked about Anna. About Lola. About their parents. They talked more about their children, tentatively at first, the subject weaving carefully in and out of other, easier topics. Bett introduced it again, confessing she was worried that Zach was sucking his thumb. Carrie told her Freya had too, for a while. They swapped stories about baby food. Carrie admitted her children often ate chicken nuggets as well as fish fingers.

'I thought they only ever have home-cooked, organic food?'

Carrie shook her head. 'They even have breakfast cereal some nights.' She grinned, a sweet, cheeky grin. 'Don't tell Matthew, will you?'

They rang Lola in the early afternoon. Bett had trouble hearing her. There was a lot of noise in the background. It was hard to tell if it was laughing or crying. 'Is everything okay there?'

'We couldn't be happier. We're all just great. You won't be finishing earlier, by any chance, will you?'

'Have you had enough? Do you want us to come home?'

Lola gave a clearly fake laugh. 'Of course not. We haven't had this much fun since . . .' She trailed off. 'But don't feel you need to stay away on our account. If you do finish earlier than you thought, do come back. I'm sure the children must be missing you.'

'You told us to take as long as we liked. That you'd be fine till six at least.' Bett winked at Carrie.

'It's just there are so many of them. Babysitting is one thing. Babies-sitting is a whole new ball game.'

'But they're fine?'

'The children? They're wonderful. It's the five of us I'm worried about.'

Bett reported the conversation back to Carrie. 'Are you okay to keep going? You're not missing your three too much?'

'Are you joking?' She picked up another slip of paper. 'The next one's for a family of five. Mother, father, three boys aged eight, six and five. So how about you get them —'

'Bats, balls and lots of chips, I know. Coming right up.'

Lola had been only half joking during her phone call with Bett. It had been a rocky morning, to say the least. But slowly, the adults had started winning the battle of the babies. By lunchtime, it was almost peaceful in the house. It was just a matter of allocating tasks, Lola realised. Sharing out the children. Working out where everyone's strengths lay and focusing on those, to use the business jargon she'd picked up from reading the *Financial Times* online.

Her four friends certainly had many skills to bring to this particular babysitting table. She should have guessed Kay would have the magic touch with babies. All those years of delivering dairy cows.

'You're like a baby whisperer,' Patricia said, watching amazed, as first Yvette, then Zachary fell asleep in her arms.

Margaret was the cook of the group. She'd taken four-year-old Delia into the kitchen with her as she checked the cupboards and refrigerator for contents and supplies. 'Would Bett mind if

I did some cooking, Lola? It doesn't really suit me to sit around doing nothing but watch babies all day.'

'I'm sure she wouldn't mind at all.'

'I'm just going to nip into town and get a few ingredients. Her freezer's nearly empty. I bet I can fill it before she gets back.'

Lola pressed money onto her. 'My family, my expense.'

Patricia had been in the laundry. She came out now. 'I'll make a start on the curtains and the floors too. She's not into all that organic stuff, is she? I love a good scrubbing day but I like my bleach and my sprays. None of this bicarb soda and vinegar carry-on.'

'Except for the windows and the mirrors,' Kay said. 'Nothing works better than newspaper and vinegar for a streak-free finish.'

Lola gazed at her friends. When had they got these advanced degrees in domestic arts? She certainly wasn't going to start complaining. She cheerfully handed over more dollars.

Joan came in from inspecting the garden. She wasn't impressed. Her own garden was a regular winner of local contests. 'Bett and Daniel wouldn't mind if I did a bit of work out there, would they?'

'If they notice, they'll be delighted. If they don't notice, we'll tell them.'

Joan walked up to Lola and held out her hand. 'Please, sir, may I have some more?'

Lola and Patricia stayed with the children. The other three

were back from town within the hour, laden with bags of ingredients, cleaning products and punnets of seedlings.

Margaret opened all the windows in the kitchen before she got started. It was another hot day, but a cool breeze started drifting through the rooms, carrying the scent of baking cakes, simmering casseroles and rising scones with it. Delia proved to be an excellent helper, stirring mixtures and sifting flour under Margaret's careful eye.

The temperature made it a perfect day for cleaning, too. The washed floors dried in minutes. The clothes dried on the line before it was time to hang out the next load. Patricia got little Freya to help her by handing out the clothes pegs.

From her vantage point as Minder of the Smaller Children in the living room (she'd decided it really wouldn't hurt them to view a little bit of television, it was so educational these days, after all), Lola watched her friends in amazement. 'You're all like a many-armed housework machine. What have I unleashed?'

'Girl power,' Patricia said.

'I feel ashamed. Helpless old thing that I am.' They'd insisted she wasn't to do any of the physical work.

'Helpless, my foot,' Kay said. 'Today is all about playing to our skills, isn't it? What about yours?'

'All I know how to do is dress up,' Lola said, jiggling Zachary in her lap. Yvette was lying on a lambswool rug at her feet, kicking her legs in the air. 'Shall I start with this little fellow? Put him in a chiffon babygro?'

'And give him a Liberace complex for the rest of his life?' Patricia said. 'No, you're the musical one.'

'Great idea,' Margaret said. 'Sing, Lola, sing.'

So she started singing. She sang every song she could remember. Songs from her favourite musicals. Songs from her Irish childhood. She even sang the song that had been her and Alex's song, 'Catch a Falling Star'. It had been in her head ever since her conversation with Luke. She hadn't told her friends about Alex yet. Luke had promised not to breathe a word about it either. If he found any definite information, she would tell them, she'd decided. Perhaps. Eventually. If he didn't, then there'd have been no false expectations or interest raised.

Her friends made some impolite comments and did some obvious wincing at her singing – she told them they were just jealous that she knew so many tunes – but the babies appeared to like it.

'Either that or they're tone deaf,' Kay suggested.

At five thirty Lola gazed with pleasure around her. They were all sitting in the living room, holding a child apiece. The floors gleamed. The windows shone. The washing line had been filled, emptied and filled again, all afternoon. The linen cupboard was now full of fresh-smelling towels, sheets and pillowcases. The babies' chests of drawers were restocked with their little singlets, babygros, socks and bibs. Even Bett and Daniel's clothes had been washed, ironed and put away. The hot wind and burning sun of December in South Australia made life difficult for humans but it couldn't be faulted for optimum drying conditions, they all agreed.

In the kitchen, Margaret had made casseroles, soups and apple pies. The freezer was now filled with neatly labelled home-cooked ready meals. Outside, Joan had followed the shade around the garden, with great help from little George, plastic bucket and spade in hand. She'd weeded, trimmed edges and planted the hardy summer plants she'd bought that afternoon. Her work wouldn't be evident for some weeks, even months, but she'd drawn up a map of what she'd planted and where, as well as a simple list of instructions for Bett and Daniel.

When Bett rang to say they were on their way home, Lola didn't tell her what they'd been up to. 'Ready when you are,' she said.

Bett's mouth fell open when she walked in. She didn't need to have anything pointed out to her. She kept uttering short phrases as she toured the house. 'The floors . . . the windows . . . the laundry.' She opened the chests of drawers in the bedrooms. 'Oh my God. Folded clothes.' She looked out at the garden. 'Oh my God. No weeds.' She turned to all five of them as they followed her into the kitchen. 'How did you do this? When did you have time?'

'Many hands make —' Lola and Kay began in unison.

'Casseroles and cakes!' Bett said, opening the freezer. 'Oh my God. And scones and bread and soup.' She looked more over-whelmed than shocked now. 'Thank you all so much. I can't believe it. I must owe you a fortune.'

'Not a cent,' Patricia said. 'Your grandmother bankrolled us.'

'If I'd known this was what you'd all be up to, I'd have

suggested we do the babysitting at my house,' Carrie said, not managing to hide her envy.

Lola knew her youngest granddaughter well. 'Don't worry, darling. We're basing ourselves at your house tomorrow.'

'Tomorrow?'

Lola reached into her Glomesh handbag and pulled out another big bundle of the charity hamper slips. 'You and Bett didn't think you'd finished, did you?'

Chapter Sixteen

Guest 1

'What's up with you?' Neil snapped.

'Nothing.'

'You haven't taken your eyes off me since I got home.'

'Just surprised to see you outside your room, I guess.'

'Haven't you got work today?'

Rick shook his head. 'I called in sick. I've got —' His mind went blank. 'A disease.'

'A disease?'

'Not a serious one. But I need a couple of days off.'

Neil nodded. 'Who are you expecting?'

'What?'

Neil repeated the question.

'No one,' Rick said.

'So why do you keep looking towards the door?'

'I thought I heard the postman.'

'Mate, are you okay?'

'I could ask you the same question.'

'I'm fine.' Neil's shutters came down.

'You want to go for a bit of a walk? A quick drink, or anything? Just hang out?'

'What about your disease?'

'I'm feeling better. What do you reckon? Head out somewhere?'

'No, thanks.'

'Do you want to talk about anything?'

'No, thanks.'

Neil was heading for his room. Rick had to keep him out here, keep him talking. He asked the first question that came to mind. 'So, any plans for Christmas Day?'

'No.'

Keep talking, Rick. Keep talking. 'I'm going home. To my family. We always get together at Christmas time. It's a chance to see each other, you know. To catch up on everyone's news. To let everyone know how much we mean to each other.'

'Great,' Neil said. He went into his room and shut the door.

All Rick could think about were the tablets he'd seen in Neil's bedside drawer. Was that what Neil was planning to do? Overdose on sleeping tablets?

He couldn't just sit back and let him go. He went across and hammered on Neil's door.

'Mate?'

'What?'

'Can you open the door?'

It took some time, but Neil eventually opened it.

'Everything okay?' Rick asked.

'Yes. What do you want?'

'Can you, um . . . Can you loan me twenty bucks?'

'I don't have it.'

'Did you have trouble at Centrelink today?'

'Yes.'

'Do you need some money? I can help you out.' He reached for his wallet.

'I thought you wanted twenty bucks off me.'

'I do. Not for now, though. For next week.'

Neil shut the door.

Shit, Rick thought. Now what could he do? Neil's mother had said she'd be there as soon as she could. She lived three hours away, though. It would be two o'clock at least before she got there.

She'd been a combination of shocked and relieved when Rick rang and told her what he'd seen on Neil's computer. 'I knew something was wrong, that he was planning something. My poor baby. We have to stop him, Rick. Please, stay there with him, keep an eye on him, please. Don't let anything happen to him before I get there.'

He'd promised. But he didn't know what to do or how to do it. If Neil hadn't been in earshot, he'd have rung a helpline, the Samaritans, or someone else. They'd know what to do, wouldn't they? Give him advice? But it was all about talking with them, wasn't it? He didn't know if talking was what Neil needed right now. Who else could he call, though? The cops? That was it. He'd ring the cops. He went outside the front door, hoping that if he spoke in a low enough voice, Neil wouldn't hear. He dialled 000. 'Hi,' he whispered when the call was answered.

'Police, fire or ambulance?'

'I'm not sure. Who looks after possible suicides?'

'I'm sorry?'

'I think my flatmate is going to kill himself. I don't know for sure, but his mother's been worried about him for weeks and now I am too. It's not a prank call, I promise.' He explained it all quickly. That his flatmate had booked a one-way ticket to some place in the middle of nowhere. That he hadn't left his room in ages except for today to get some dole money. That all he'd been looking at on his computer for weeks were suicide sites.

'What's his mental state now?'

'Bad. Depressed.'

'His life?'

'Pretty bad. There's not much going on for him. I just thought he was going through a bad patch, you know. Keeping to himself. His mother's on her way, but what if she's too late? What do I do?'

'Where is he now?'

'In his room. He's got loads of tablets in there.'

'Does he know you've called us?'

He looked over his shoulder. 'I don't think so. His windows are shut and the blinds are down.'

'Go back into the house, keep talking to him. What's your address?' Rick gave it. 'We'll get someone there as soon as we can.'

Back inside, Rick went straight to Neil's bedroom door and knocked. 'Mate?'

'What? Jesus, can't you leave me alone?'

'I need some help.'

The door was flung open. 'With what?'

Rick glanced around the room, his mind suddenly blank. 'The curtains.'

'For fuck's sake.' Neil shut the door again. 'Just leave me alone, would you?'

Rick spoke loudly into the door. 'Neil, I think you should know, I've accidentally called the police. They'll be here as soon as they can.'

The door flung open again. 'You've what? Why?'

'They want to talk to you.'

'About what?'

'About how things are going for you.'

'Since when do the cops give a shit about how I am? Since when does anyone give a shit?'

'Lots of people do.'

'Like who?'

'Me, for a start.'

'Oh, yeah.'

'I'm your mate. I've been worried.'

'Sure. I've hardly spoken to you in weeks. You wouldn't know what to be worried about.'

'Mate, what's happened to you?'

'Nothing.'

'Are you . . . ?' Rick tried again. 'You're not . . .'

'What?'

'Planning to do anything stupid, are you?'

'Like what?'

'I don't know.'

'Like what?'

'You know.'

'What?'

Rick couldn't say the words. He shuffled his feet. He managed a quick glance down at his watch. Only five minutes had passed. It could be an hour before the cops got there, let alone Neil's mother. He didn't know how much longer he could handle this.

'So can I go now?' Neil's voice was heavy with sarcasm and annoyance.

'No!' Rick practically shouted. He decided to tell him the truth. 'Mate, your mother's worried sick about you. She's been worried sick for weeks. I went into your room today when you were out. She begged me.'

'You *what*?'

'I went though your stuff. She was worried you were on something, drugs or drink —'

Neil just stared at him.

'Then I went onto your computer —'

Neil's expression changed then, relaxing slightly. 'You don't know the first thing about computers.'

'No, I don't. But my sister does. She gave me a quick lesson over the phone.' He didn't want to go into what he'd found. This was going badly enough as it was. 'Mate, don't.'

'What?'

'Don't do it. Please.'

'Why don't you just mind your own fucking business?'

'You were going to do it, weren't you? You really were. You were going to get on a bus and go to some motel and —' He stopped there.

'Thoughtful, aren't I? I could have done it here but I didn't want to leave you with any mess.'

'How the hell were you going to do it?'

'Tablets.'

'But why?'

'Why not?'

'I mean it. Why?'

'Because I've had enough.'

'Had enough of what?' Rick searched desperately for a way to keep him talking, to make it okay. Where were the cops? Where was Neil's mother? Searching desperately for something, anything, to say, he tried a joke. 'Had enough of being locked in your room day after day? No wonder. It stinks in there.'

There was a moment when a flash of anger appeared in Neil's eyes, then it was gone. 'Jesus, never go into counselling, will you?'

Keep him talking, Rick. Keep him talking. 'Mate, you just have to get out more —'

'You don't understand.'

'No, I don't. I'm sorry, Neil. I thought you just wanted some time to yourself.'

'I do. Right now.'

'Don't do it. Please.'

'Who'll care if I do?'

'Your mum. Your sister.'

'Yeah, like they spend all their time getting in touch with me.'

'They do. You just never take their calls. I'll care too. You're my friend.'

'Some friend. I'm useless, mate. I can't even find a job.'

'You haven't even tried. You sent out, what, two applications? Jesus. It took me ten goes before I got my job.'

'It's not just work. Ever been dumped? Have any idea how that feels?'

'At least you've had a girlfriend. I haven't even got that far.'

'What does that mean?'

'What do you think?'

'You're a virgin?'

'Shut up.'

'Are you?'

'Shut up, I said.'

'Jesus, I thought I had it bad.' It was the first time Neil had even come close to smiling.

A knock sounded at the door.

'Is that for you or for me?' Neil said.

'Police,' a voice called.

'Sorry, mate,' Rick said. 'It's for you.'

The policeman and the policewoman were still there an hour

later when Neil's mother arrived. She must have broken every speed limit, Rick realised. She didn't knock, didn't call out. She just opened the door and ran inside, almost knocking her son out of his chair with the force of her hug. 'No, Neil. Don't do it. Please don't do it. We love you. We'll help you. We'll make it better, I promise you. Just don't do it. We'll fix it all for you. Whatever we have to do, we'll do it, I promise.'

Ten minutes later, the front door opened again. It was Neil's younger sister. She came straight over to her brother, hugged him, held him close. Rick hovered in the background. He'd stayed in the kitchen, trying not to eavesdrop as the police counsellors had slowly coaxed the story from Neil. They'd done this before, Rick could tell. Their questions were kind, understanding. When Neil started to cry, Rick took himself out to the back yard. His friend didn't need a witness to that. He'd only come back in when the policewoman had appeared at the back door, asking if he'd like a cup of tea.

As Rick stood by the door now, Neil looked over. He was at the centre of a group of people. His mother still hadn't let go of his hand. His sister was touching his shoulder.

'Anybody else about to arrive?' Neil said to him. 'What did you do, mate? Send up a bloody flare?' But there was no anger in his words.

The policeman stood up. 'We've lots of people you can talk to, Neil. Remember that. You're not alone.'

'You're bloody right,' his mother said. 'I'm never leaving him on his own again.' She wasn't trying to be funny, but they all laughed.

Rick walked the policeman and woman to the door. He felt a bit weird now, embarrassed somehow. He waited until they were all outside, standing on the footpath. 'Sorry if that was a false alarm. I didn't know what else to do, who to ring.'

'You did the right thing.'

'Will he be okay?'

'He's talking. He knows people care about him. That's a good start.'

Back inside, the positions hadn't changed. Neil's mother was still huddled close to him, holding his hand. His sister looked like she'd been crying and was now holding tightly to his other hand. Time to get out of there, Rick decided.

'I better head off,' he said, awkwardly. 'Have some shopping and stuff to do.'

'Thank you, Rick,' Neil's mother said. Neil's sister thanked him too.

Neil was looking down at his feet. Rick didn't know if he'd be there when he got back. He had a feeling his mate would be heading home with his mum for a bit. For Christmas, maybe even longer. There was something he needed to say to him before he left.

'Neil, sorry about going into your room like that.'

Neil looked up then. He gave his friend a smile. The first one Rick had seen in a long time. 'Don't worry about it, mate,' he said.

Guests 2 and 3

'I don't think you've got the camera in the right place, love. Move it to the left again a little bit. That's it. There we are.'

Helen sat down on the chair beside her husband. Sure enough, there they were, the two of them, tiny on the computer screen. She waved at the small camera, and the version of herself on the screen waved back. Tony waved. His tiny version waved back too.

'What do we do now?'

Tony checked the instructions he'd printed out. 'According to this, we just wait until they ring us.'

'I still can't work out how they're going to both appear at the same time.'

'You make it sound like a magic trick. It's called skyping, Helen.'

'You'd never heard of it before Katie explained, so don't you get all high and mighty with me.' She gave him an affectionate nudge as she said it. 'You're sure we don't have to do —'

A musical ringing tone sounded, followed by the appearance of another small box on screen with a moving image inside.

'It's Liam!' Helen said. Another ringing tone and another box appeared. 'Katie, we can see you too!'

'Hi, Mum. Hi, Dad. Can you hear me okay too?' Liam asked in an echoey voice.

'Hi, everyone. Can we all see and hear each other?' Katie said, just as echoey.

After a few pauses and speaking-over-each-other moments, the four of them found their rhythm. Helen couldn't believe it.

She thought emails were incredible enough. Now look at this, herself and Tony in their living room, talking to their daughter in London and their son in Barcelona, all of them visible on screen at the same time.

Tony was just as bowled over, she could see. He couldn't stop waving at them. Katie and Liam waved back to him each time, both of them laughing.

Liam eventually put a stop to it. 'We know you're there, Dad. We can see you. You don't have to wave every time you talk.'

'It's just *incredible*,' Helen said again. 'Thank you both so much.' The camera and instructions on how to install and operate Skype had arrived via Katie weeks before, but it was only today that they'd set it up. Tony hadn't been interested before. Katie had organised today's call too, telling her parents what time they should be sitting at the computer for a trial run.

'And it really doesn't cost anything?' Tony asked.

'Not a cent,' Liam said.

Helen leaned forward, drinking in the sight of her two children. It was the next best thing to having them at home. 'So could we do this on Christmas Day? I bet our motel will have a computer we can use. Can you take your laptop to that country house, Katie? Would it work there? Will you have yours handy, Liam? It'd be so wonderful, as if we were all in the same room together.'

'We could do that, I suppose, couldn't we, Liam?' Katie said.

'I suppose so, Katie. We have the technology.'

'But we won't need to,' Katie said. 'Will we, Liam?'

271

'No, Katie, we won't.' They both had the giggles now, saying each other's names too often and too formally.

'Although I suppose we could still skype each other. But it would be pretty stupid, Liam, wouldn't it?'

'It sure would, Katie, wouldn't it?'

Helen was now completely confused. 'What are you two going on about?'

Katie grinned. 'Didn't I give it away on the phone? All my talk about how hard it might be for you to ring me, so you'd have to wait for me to ring you? When do I ever turn down a chance for you to pay for the call? Didn't you guess I was up to something then?'

'Haven't you guessed even now?' Liam said.

'It's your own fault your surprise is ruined, though, you know,' Katie said. 'I don't know what got into you both, acting all out of character like that, booking spur-of-the-moment getaways. Look what we've had to do. You were supposed to just get a phone call from the airport on Christmas Eve.'

'I hope you'll get your money back from that motel. Though I suppose we could all go there together.'

'No way, Liam,' Katie said. 'I'm not flying halfway across the world for a week in some fleapit of a country motel. I want my own bed and Mum's home cooking.'

'Oh, yeah. Mum's home cooking and Dad's beer fridge. Bring it on!'

Helen looked at Tony. He just shook his head too. 'Kids, please. What are you talking about?'

'Poor ageing parents,' Katie said. 'Shall I speak more slowly? Explain in simple terms? Mum, Dad, the reason you can't go away for Christmas is because Liam and I are coming back home for Christmas. We're arriving Christmas Eve, on separate flights but within an hour of each other. So could you please come to the airport and pick us up?'

'You're coming *home*?'

'Here?'

'Both of you?'

'Surprise!' Katie said.

'Surprise!' Liam echoed. 'Those parents of ours are pretty quick, Katie, aren't they?'

'They sure are, Liam.'

Katie started waving at the camera again, mimicking her father. 'So is that okay, Mum? Dad?'

Liam started waving too. 'Can you cancel your holiday and come and get us instead?'

Helen felt Tony's hand grip hers. She turned, and saw his eyes had filled with tears. She felt that rush of love for him once more.

Katie spoke again. 'Mum? Dad? Can you pick us up?'

Helen squeezed Tony's hand in return. It looked like she'd have to answer for the both of them. 'We sure can,' she said.

Guest 4

'And your final meeting is six p.m. in the boardroom downstairs. I've arranged catering as requested.'

Martha looked up from her BlackBerry. 'What meeting at six?'

'I discussed it with you last week. A delegation from the union. It's later than you'd like, you said, but one of the delegates is coming from interstate so you said you would make an exception in this case. There's been unhappiness about some of your new contracts and you said, and I quote: "For God's sake, they're never satisfied, those people. Get them in, Glenda, and do it as late in the afternoon as possible. They'll want to get home so that should keep it short and sharp."'

It sounded exactly the sort of thing she'd say. Why couldn't she remember it, though? 'Okay, Glenda, thanks.'

'And I'll tell the caterers to wait for the nod from you before they bring in the refreshments, is that right?'

'What?'

'You said it was a good trick you'd learnt from your mentor. Keep the delegates hungry, but make sure they can smell the food. Promise at the start of the meeting you'll feed them once an agreement is reached. It's called the carrot and stick approach, I believe.'

Again, it sounded like the sort of thing her mentor would have said, but Martha couldn't remember saying it herself. She rubbed her temples. It had been a long week. A long, hard week. All worth it, of course. She'd landed two new contracts and looked like securing another before the Christmas break, but she increasingly felt like she was pushing a boulder uphill, trying to stay focused as everyone else went into giddy, pre-holiday mode around her.

Except for Glenda. Apart from that early disagreement,

when Glenda had crossed the line in regard to Martha's situation with her family, she couldn't fault her temporary secretary. The office had never run so smoothly. Was it a bad thing to hope that her usual secretary might get pregnant on honeymoon, decide to resign and leave the desk open for Glenda to work here full-time?

Martha added the meeting time to her BlackBerry diary. 'That's fine, Glenda, thank you.'

'I'll meet the delegates in reception, get everyone settled and then ring for you to come in, yes? I think that's the best approach psychologically. It gives you the position of power, if they're waiting for you.'

'Fine, yes.'

'Besides, you've got that conference call with your state managers from five thirty. You did have that down for four p.m., but I had to reschedule. It's running closer to your six o'clock meeting than I would have liked but it was the best time slot available.'

Martha couldn't recall discussing that meeting either. She glanced down at her diary again. There it was. 'Fine, thanks. I'll keep that one to under thirty minutes. Any other business? You've confirmed all my Christmas arrangements?'

Glenda nodded. 'Motel confirmed and car confirmed. I've used your preferred chauffeur company and requested a silent driver. Pick-up on Christmas Eve at Adelaide airport, returning on Boxing Day.'

Martha could feel Glenda's disapproval radiating across the desk, but at least she'd stopped airing her opinions so forcefully.

There hadn't been any more talk about her mother calling, or any more re-enacted phone messages. There'd been no mention between them of Christmas at all, apart from one moment the previous day. Martha had come outside and found Glenda at her desk, adding the finishing touches to what looked like the wrapping of an elaborate Christmas present.

Glenda had glanced up at her and then continued. 'I'm on my morning tea break, Miss Kaminski, in case you think I am doing this on work time. It's also my own sticky tape. I never take my employer's stationery for personal use.'

Martha watched for a moment. Glenda's desk was piled with what looked like more than a dozen tiny knitted figures. She was placing them gently, one by one, into a bright-red box. 'What is it?'

Glenda gave her a brief, pitying look. 'A Christmas present.'

'Yes, I can see that. Did you make them yourself?'

'To the last stitch. I'm as good a knitter as I am a secretary.'

'You knit? Really?'

'I also sew, embroider and am an excellent cook. I also like making toys. These are for my grandchildren.'

'You've got grandchildren?'

'Two. My only son's daughters. He and his wife and the girls live in New York at the moment. I miss them every day. They miss me every day too. We'd rather be together at Christmas and we will be next year. In the meantime, I've made them these. I'm couriering them today.'

'Can I take a look?'

Glenda handed them to her one by one, an entire menagerie

of colourful knitted animals – a koala, a kangaroo, a rabbit, a giraffe, an elephant, a platypus, all perfectly made. Last out of the box was a knitted doll. It was a female figure with grey cotton wool hair, glasses and a big red felt smile. Martha looked at the doll, then at Glenda, then back at the doll.

'It's you, isn't it?' Martha said.

'Cute, aren't I?' Glenda said, taking it back and putting it in the box too. 'If I can't be there myself, I want to be there in effigy.'

'You wouldn't fly to New York and join them?'

'There's nothing I'd love more than to be with them for Christmas. Unfortunately, I'm terrified of flying.'

The phone rang then, and their conversation came to an end. But Martha had realised why Glenda seemed so obsessive about reuniting her with her family. Projected emotions, obviously. What was it with some people and Christmas time? It was just one more day of the year, after all.

The working day passed in its usual fast procession of meetings, emails, decisions and spreadsheets. Her conference call at five thirty was straightforward, finishing at five fifty-seven p.m. She took a moment to freshen up in her personal bathroom before going downstairs to the boardroom and her final meeting for the day. She didn't look her best, she knew that. There were shadows under her eyes and she needed a haircut. She'd schedule one in next week. She applied a quick layer of foundation, a touch-up of pale lipstick. She didn't need to make any 'I'm a powerful businesswoman wearing red lipstick' statements for this meeting with the union. She met them often enough, usually when a new representative took over her company's portfolio and wanted to flex some muscles. She would listen, she would take notes – in fact, she'd get Glenda to come in and take the notes for her – and then she would coolly, calmly and clearly remind them that she strictly adhered to all current market conditions, always had done and would continue to do so. It was true. She also kept a careful eye on the conditions offered by similar agencies, to ensure her own company led the pack. 'Be tough, but be fair,' as her mentor had always said.

Her intercom buzzed. It was Glenda. 'Everyone's in the boardroom waiting for you, Miss Kaminski.'

'Thank you, Glenda. On my way. I'd like you to be there to take notes, please.'

'I'm sorry, but I can't.'

'I beg your pardon?'

'I finish at six p.m., unless I've been given prior notice. Agency rules. And one minute before isn't enough prior notice. I'm sure you'll cope admirably. Have a good evening. See you tomorrow.'

Martha came out of her office. Glenda's desk was tidied and her handbag gone. No matter. She wouldn't bother with notes. What would any of the union reps say that she hadn't heard before?

She had the lift to herself. The corridor on the floor below was empty too. Ahead of her, the boardroom door was shut. As she came closer, she got a waft of cooking smells from the boardroom's adjoining kitchen. It was standard practice to order sandwiches and coffee for these meetings. This smelt more like roast potatoes and plum pudding. She hoped Glenda hadn't got carried away with the Christmas spirit when she was briefing the caterers.

She opened the door and stepped inside. 'Thank you all for coming. I won't keep any of us for long.'

Martha stopped still. There weren't six union representatives waiting for her in their seats around the gleaming boardroom table. There were only four people. Her mother, her father, her brother and her sister. On the table was a dinner setting for five. Champagne glasses. Santa serviettes. There was even a decorated Christmas tree in a corner of the room.

She took an involuntary step back. 'What the hell —?'

'Happy early Christmas, Martha!' all four members of her family chorused, as if they had been drilled.

She was speechless. She couldn't seem to move. She just stood there, staring at them. They were all wearing party hats. Even her father.

Her sister spoke first. 'You wouldn't come to us so we've come to you,' she said. 'Hi, Martha. It's great to see you again.'

'Hello, Martha,' her mother said, with a big smile.

'Happy Christmas,' her brother said, waving.

'Happy Christmas,' her father echoed. He wasn't smiling but he wouldn't have been there if he didn't want to be.

But no way. No *way* was she going to be pushed into this. Her BlackBerry buzzed in her hand. It was Glenda calling.

'Please don't even think about leaving. Everything's ready on warming plates there behind you. A full turkey dinner and there's plum pudding too. They've all gone to a lot of trouble to be here this afternoon so I hope you'll show some good manners. Your mother's a very nice lady. She also told me that it was your father who was your mentor for all those years. So follow his lead today. I liked him too.' Glenda hung up before Martha beat her to it.

'Will I open this?' her brother said, holding up a bottle of champagne. He didn't wait for the go-ahead. The cork went flying out of the bottle. The champagne fizzed and foamed. His sister and mother sprang forward with their glasses just in time.

Amid the fuss, her father stood up and pulled out the chair beside him. 'Please, Martha, take a seat. Here, beside me.'

For the first time in three years, she did as she was told.

Guests 5, 6 and 7

Holly had splashed out on a taxi home from the cinema. Her little sisters were tired. They'd also had so much popcorn and ice-cream she wasn't sure they'd be able to cope with the stop-start journey on the bus. They'd loved the film, though. So had Holly. It was so cheerful, full of elves and carols and lots of other songs. Belle and Chloe hadn't stopped singing the theme tune since.

'Will I let you all out here?' the taxi driver asked, pulling up to the gates.

'That's great, thanks,' Holly said, handing over a twenty-dollar note. It was fifteen on the meter. 'Please, keep the change. Happy Christmas.'

She helped the two girls out, then reached up and entered

the combination. The gates slowly opened. As the three of them walked up the drive, Holly wished she could blame the sick feeling in her stomach on the ice-cream and popcorn. It was the unease she felt every time she came home from a night out. She wished there was some way of knowing beforehand what she'd be walking into. A fight? A stony silence? Closed bedroom doors? Sometimes her parents slept in the same room, but not if they'd been fighting badly. Sometimes Holly wished their house wasn't so big. If there weren't so many spare bedrooms, would they be forced to share and forced to sort out their problems?

Not for the first time, she tried to imagine how it would be if things were normal at home. If she and Belle and Chloe were to walk in and find their parents sitting companionably in their living room, watching TV together, or reading the paper, having a glass of wine or a cup of tea, looking up like normal parents. 'Hi, girls! How was the film?'

They walked in. Their mother came down the stairs towards them, still dressed in her work suit, her makeup and hair impeccable. She wasn't smiling.

'Hello, girls. How was the film?'

'Great!' Belle said.

'Will we sing you all the songs?' Chloe asked.

'Not tonight, no. It's late. Off to bed, please. Holly, can you come into the living room with me?'

'But I promised to read to them.'

'Not tonight. Girls, upstairs please.'

Chloe frowned. 'But Holly always —'

'Now!'

They ran up the stairs. Holly followed her mother into the living room, feeling that nausea again. She was so attuned to the mood in the house she knew something had happened. It wasn't something good, either. Her father switched off the large-screen plasma TV as they both came in. He was still in his work clothes too – a rumpled linen suit – his expensive Italian shoes kicked off beside him.

She looked at her parents. 'What is it? What's wrong?'

'Shut the door, please, Holly.'

She did. They both took a seat. She stayed standing. She shook her head when her father gestured towards the sofa.

'We had a visitor tonight,' her mother said.

Holly waited.

'June. Your boss.'

'June? June was here?'

Two nods.

'But why?'

'That's what we'd like to know. What have you been saying to her?'

'Nothing,' she lied, quickly.

'Oh, really? That's not what June said. What happens in this house is our business as a family, Holly. *Our* business.'

They weren't just angry, she realised. They were furious. She could see it in their body language, their expressions, hear it in their voices.

Her mother kept talking, her tone icy. 'Perhaps you'd remember that in future. And perhaps you'd also tell your interfering boss that much as we appreciate her taking the time to come and remind us of our responsibilities as parents, we will run this family in the manner we choose, and we won't be bullied into anything by someone like her.'

There was so much that Holly could have said. She didn't dare say a word of it.

Her father took over then. 'Your June also went to great pains to inform us that you and the two girls were thinking about running away at Christmas. We told her it was ridiculous, of course.'

Holly found her voice. 'It's true.'

'I'm sorry?'

'We were going to run away. We didn't want to be here for Christmas.'

There was an exchange of glances between her parents.

'Holly, sit down,' her mother said. 'Now.'

Holly had just taken a seat when the door flung open. Belle, then Chloe ran in. Belle went straight to her big sister. 'Holly, can you help us find that —'

Their mother interrupted. 'Girls, didn't I say —'

'No!' Holly was surprised by the volume of her own voice. 'Please, let them stay.' She needed to have them near her while she caught her breath and tried to work out what was happening here tonight.

'It's nine o'clock —'

'Please.'

Chloe and Belle took up their usual positions, one on either side of Holly.

Their mother started again, in the voice Holly had never liked, the one she used when Holly knew she was angry but pretending she wasn't. 'So, Belle and Chloe, I hear you've been planning a bit of a secret. A surprise Christmas trip away, without us.'

Belle's mouth opened. Chloe's did too. 'How did you find out?'

'Let's just say a little bird told us. She told us a lot, in fact. So we told her something too. That you weren't the only ones who'd been planning a Christmas surprise. And so your dad and I think we'd all better have a family meeting and get these surprises out into the open.'

'Ours is a great secret,' Chloe said, before Holly could stop her. 'Christmas at the Valley View Motel. For free!'

'Without us, though?' her mother said. 'Wouldn't you miss us?'

'You can come too,' Belle said earnestly. 'But only if you're good and you don't mind sleeping in boxes.'

Holly couldn't take her eyes off her parents as they both pretended to laugh. It felt like she was watching a performance. 'What was your Christmas surprise?' she asked them, still wary.

'Will we tell them now?' their father said, looking at their mother. She nodded.

'We had a trip planned for you all for Christmas too.'

'Really?' Belle said.

'To where?' Chloe said.

There was just a brief pause.

'Disneyland,' their father said.

'*Disneyland!*' Both girls ran to their parents, shouting questions. When, where, how?

Holly watched, still with that strange detached feeling, as her parents answered Belle and Chloe's questions as best they could. As best they could when they didn't know the answers. Holly would have bet all the money she had that they hadn't been planning anything like a trip to Disneyland. This was a result of June's visit. It had to be.

She'd find out tomorrow exactly what had happened tonight. She knew they would have tried to intimidate June, not physically, but with words. She could almost hear them. 'Oh, Holly exaggerates. She's very highly strung. The only thing we've been fighting about is where to take them for Christmas!'

Perhaps she wouldn't ask June for the details. Watching her sisters now, so excited, begging for more details, perhaps all that mattered was that June's visit had made even some, temporary difference.

Belle turned back to her then. 'Do you mind if we don't go to the Valley Motel this time, Holly? Maybe we could go next year instead? I'm sure that lady we email won't mind, will she?'

Holly tousled her little sister's hair, going along with it all too. 'I'm sure she won't. Not if we explain we're off to Florida instead.'

'I think we'll go to Disneyland in France, not Florida,' her mother said.

'Florida's supposed to be better,' their father said.

'You're an expert on Disneyland, are you?'

'It's the main one.'

'But we could base ourselves in Paris if we went to the French one. See the Eiffel Tower.'

'It's the middle of winter. It'll be freezing. Florida will be much warmer.'

'It's a longer flight.'

'Oh, like an extra two hours is going to matter. That's just crazy. What do —'

'Stop it! Stop fighting!'

They all turned. It wasn't Holly who'd spoken. It was Chloe. Her smile had disappeared. She now just looked upset. 'Please. Stop.'

'We're not fighting, Chloe,' her mother said. 'We're discussing.'

'You're fighting. And it gives me a stomach ache. And Belle too.'

Holly stood up. 'Time for bed, girls.' She knew her sisters too well. This would turn to tears any minute now. 'Come on. I'll tuck you in.'

'Holly, come back down when you're done, please?' It was her mother. It wasn't a request. It was an order.

She nodded. She'd pay for telling June so much, she knew. If not tonight, then in the future. But as she walked up the stairs with her sisters, she realised something else. She didn't mind. Something had happened tonight. A subtle, tiny shift in power in favour of herself, Belle and Chloe.

She would come back down and face whatever it was her parents planned to say to her. If she found the courage, there was plenty she could say in return. But there was something else she had to do first.

As the girls cleaned their teeth, she sent a text to June. *Thank you.*

The answer came back immediately. June must have been waiting.

Any time, it said.

CHAPTER SEVENTEEN

In her room, Lola resisted the urge to ring Luke. He'd had the information about Alex for four days now. Surely he'd been able to find out something? Her impatient nature was coming back to bite her and not just because Christmas was almost upon them. If this was a film, she had a horrible feeling it would end badly, a split screen of two old people running towards each other on a railway platform or an airport concourse, arms outstretched, calling each other's names, before one of them dropped dead from a heart attack. But they *were* old. There wasn't time to waste.

She was embarrassed to admit her mind had been playing tricks on her since the possibility of finding Alex again had arisen. She'd imagined all sorts of scenarios. Calling Jim, Geraldine and the girls together to make an announcement. 'I'm going to live out my days in Tuscany with a very dear, very old and very handsome Italian lover of mine.' Another time she'd pictured Alex arriving in Clare, to an instant rekindling of their feelings and their instant relocation to a charming, cosy house just outside the town, overlooking a dam, three vineyards and the racecourse.

What had happened to her? She was worse than Emily day-dreaming about Luke. If Alex was still alive, he could be a long way from being well enough to travel to Clare. He could be on to his second, third or fourth wife by now. Although, as Italy was as Catholic as Ireland used to be, divorce might have been difficult. Perhaps he was still with his first wife, both of them plump from all the fine food and pasta and bread, sitting out under a vine-covered verandah surrounded by pink-cheeked grandchildren, red and white checked tablecloths, raffia-covered bottles of wine . . . *Stop, Lola.*

But if he was still alive, if he was still well, did he ever think of her? she wondered. Had he ever sat down to write to her, or asked a computer-literate friend to try to find *her* on the computer?

She couldn't wait for Luke to come back. She'd try to do a bit of research herself. It took only a few minutes to set up the laptop and wait for what had so far proven to be a very reliable broadband connection to kick into life. The search engine page came up. Using two fingers, carefully spelling his full name, she typed it in and pressed search.

Five and a half million results. Good Lord! Had it been this simple, all these years, to find him? She clicked on one page, then another, her mood changing from optimism to pessimism. There were thousands of people with his name out there. She didn't have the skills to weed them out. And suddenly she didn't have the inclination either. Before she was drawn any further into the web, she quickly clicked to shut all the pages down, and turned the laptop off again too.

She was being silly, being so interested in Alex's whereabouts, turning him into her knight in shining armour, her rescuer. She knew what was really going on. She was reacting belatedly to Jim and Geraldine's news. For all her apparent cheerfulness about getting in touch with old folks' homes, being happy to stay in Clare, the truth was . . . yes, the truth was she was terrified. Once upon a time, she'd relished change, revelled in it, loved moving, the adventures it opened up, the challenges and also the rewards. She'd encouraged all her granddaughters to travel as much as possible, even giving them plane tickets as twenty-first birthday presents, practically pushing each of them onto the planes herself.

Now, though, the last thing she felt like doing was packing up and starting again. The motel was what she'd called home for the past twenty years. She knew every inch of it, literally. She'd cleaned it all often enough in the early days. She had memories of so many guests, so many parties, big and small, including her own gala eightieth. Conversations with her three girls, when they had all lived there together, moving in and out of different rooms, depending on which ones were available. So many talks with Jim, in the kitchen or out under the trees. Chats with little Ellen, too, on the park bench that looked over the vineyard-covered hill opposite the motel, in the days when Bumper, the motel's pet sheep and in-house lawnmower, had been her constant shadow.

So many memories of Anna too. She had died here at the motel, just two rooms away. Lola walked past it every day. It gave her another reason to remember Anna, on top of all the other memories that were sparked here every single day.

Were Jim and Geraldine right? Was it time they all left Anna's memories in peace, moved on, mentally and physically? Perhaps the three of them were the ones who needed that distance the most. Bett and Carrie were so overwhelmed by the present that they didn't have the luxury of spending time in the past, though Lola knew they grieved for their sister constantly too.

And what about Ellen? Little Ellen, who had sounded so happy to know she was coming back to the motel. Was that a mistake on Lola's part? Or was it a good thing to bring her back one more time, before the motel changed hands and became some new family's place of memories?

Lola returned to the desk and turned the laptop back on. It only took a moment to send the email.

Ellen? Are you there?

Five minutes later there was an answer.

Lola! Yes! Are you?

Lola smiled. She wished it was possible to talk to Anna like this, send her occasional emails too, receive them in return, rather than relying on those imaginary conversations where she had to play both parts.

Darling, can you talk for a minute?

Of course.

Was it her news to share? Should she wait until Ellen got there and tell her then? No. Act, and act now! She dialled Ellen's number and got straight to the point.

'Darling, I think you should know something important before you arrive. I could wait until you were here, but you might be upset by it. I want you to have as much time to think it over as you can.'

'What's wrong? Are you sick? Lola, what is it?'

'I'm not sick, darling. I'm sorry. I should have said that at first. No one is sick. We're all very well. It's about the motel. Ellen, I think you should know that your granddad and grand-mother have decided to sell it. They want to move from Clare and buy a business somewhere else.'

'What about you? Are you going with them?'

'No, I'm not. I'm staying here in Clare.'

'Are Carrie and Bett staying?'

'So far, yes. But I don't know if that will be forever.'

'That's all right, then.'

'You don't mind about the motel?'

'No.'

'Really?'

'I love being there, but it makes me sad too.'

'Will it be too hard for you to come back this time? To be here without your dad? You can change your mind if you want to, if you'd rather spend Christmas in Hong Kong.'

'No!'

'I just thought you should know before you got here. It has

particular memories for you and I didn't want you to be upset.'

'I'm fine. Thanks for telling me.'

'You're a good, grown-up girl, my Ellen.'

'Dad doesn't always think so.'

'Yes, he does. He just doesn't like it when you shout and sulk.'

'Don't you start!'

Lola smiled. 'See you soon, darling.'

'I can't wait!'

Lola and Glenn confirmed Ellen's flight arrangements the next day. She'd arrive the evening before Christmas Eve. Luke would go down to Adelaide to collect her. The hardest thing for Lola was not letting on to Jim and Geraldine, or Bett and Carrie.

As it was, they were all so busy helping with the Christmas hampers she suspected they wouldn't have heard her if she did mention Ellen. It was just as well the motel wasn't booked out. Eleven of the fifteen rooms were being used to store everything. Even so, Lola wasn't sure they would have enough hampers to supply the requests that had come in.

Every morning whoever opened up the charity shop found a little collection of white notes waiting inside the door. Sometimes they were just facts – names, address (always with CONFIDENTIAL) written alongside, ages of children. There had been a few heartbreaking letters, people going into detail about the difficulties they were facing. It was so sad, Lola thought. From the outside, the Valley looked like the most idyllic place in the world, with its gentle hills, beautiful vineyards, stone cottages. An easy lifestyle, plenty of sports facilities, nice houses, shops . . . But no person and nowhere on earth was immune from heartbreak or unhappiness. Lola had learned that herself the hard way. One letter had made her especially sad. A young lone father, bringing up two children after his wife had left him for another man. There had been a lengthy discussion about his letter in the shop.

'How can a woman leave her kids like that?' Kay asked.

'She might have fallen desperately in love,' Margaret said. 'That might have taken over all her maternal feelings. Maybe when the first flush wears off, she'll come back.'

'How can the kids ever forgive her?' Patricia wondered. 'Being abandoned by their own mother?'

'Maybe they'll find more solace in the fact their father raised them on his own,' Lola said. 'That's a pretty good role model to have.'

They had just sorted that morning's requests for help into order when the door opened. It was Mrs Kernaghan. Lola half expected to hear crashing organ music and the screeching of bats. It was the first time she'd been in the shop since she'd claimed credit on TV for the Christmas hamper idea.

'I do apologise for my absence. I've had to deal with a number of pressing engagements. How is the appeal going?'

Lola tried not to react as she felt a pinch from Kay on one side and a nudge from Patricia on the other.

'We're inundated, Mrs Kernaghan,' Margaret said. 'It's shocked us all how many people in our area are in need.' She held up a bundle of the slips. 'These are just today's.'

'Don't believe all of them, will you?'

'I'm sorry?'

'You heard me. Don't believe all of them. It's important to check each request for authenticity. I know human nature. If something is going for free, you can bet people will cheat and lie to get some of it.'

'Mrs Kernaghan!'

'I wish it wasn't true, but it is,' she said firmly.

'You're wrong in this case, I'm afraid,' Lola said. 'We've had the sorrow of reading so many of the requests. I don't think people would stoop that low.'

'Then you don't know people as well as I do. We held a charity fundraiser in one of our fashion stores several years ago to raise money for a local woman whose child was dying of cancer. More than ten thousand dollars was donated. Photos were taken. The local TV station even did a story on her. It turned out it was all lies. The child didn't have cancer at all. The mother had half starved him and shaved his head, just to con people into giving her money.'

'I think that's an urban myth,' Kay said hesitantly. 'I'm sure I read that same story on the internet.'

'Me too,' Patricia said. 'I thought it happened in America.'

Mrs Kernaghan looked a little flustered. 'One's memory plays tricks when one is as busy as I am. But the principle is the same. People will do anything to get something for free and I would bet —'

'Ten thousand dollars?' Lola offered.

'— that not all of your cries for help are authentic.'

'And what do you suggest we do, Mrs Kernaghan?' Lola asked. 'Call around to each of the addresses and ask to see their bank accounts? Check their fridges for food? Their cupboards for Christmas presents? Make sure they really do need help before we give them anything?'

Mrs Kernaghan either didn't notice or chose to ignore Lola's sarcastic tone. 'Let me see some of those requests. I've got to know a lot of people since I moved here. I'm sure I can help sort the wheat from the chaff.'

'No.' The other three spoke in unison.

'I'm on the committee too.'

'This is a sub-committee,' Lola said, fighting an inclination to hide the slips of paper down the front of her dress. 'We've sworn confidentiality. People's pride is at stake.'

'Don't believe everything you see, hear or read. That's all I'm saying. Be vigilant,' Mrs Kernaghan said, picking up her hand-bag and sweeping out again.

'Maybe she's right,' Kay said, once they were all sure she'd truly left. 'How can we know that everyone who's asked for help really needs it?'

'If they don't, the fact they've stooped to pretending they need charity shows they need some kind of help,' Lola said. 'And if they do get a hamper, they'll surely have a better Christmas than they might have had. Which was the whole idea, wasn't it?' But she could still see Mrs Kernagan had planted a seed of doubt. Damn her, Lola thought.

Lola was in her room watching the news that night when there was a knock at the door.

'Luke!' she said. 'What a lovely surprise.'

'I'm sorry I didn't ring before. I didn't want to get your hopes up. Can I come in?'

'Of course.'

He had his laptop under his arm. 'I'd use yours but this one's even faster. Not that I've given you inferior equipment.'

'Of course you haven't. Have you got some news for me?'

'Something to show you, rather than tell you.'

She watched, impatiently but admiringly, as he set up the laptop, clicked on the keyboard and surfed on the internet until there, on the screen in front of them both, was a photo. An unmistakable photo. But one she'd already seen. Alex, aged in his eighties.

'That's the one I gave you, isn't it? Have you done an even better job with that program?'

'It's not your photo, Lola.' Luke was smiling from ear to ear. 'It's the real thing. I've found him, Lola. That's him, isn't it? Your Alex.'

Lola moved closer. It was clearly him. The same-shaped face, kind eyes. Brown skin, with many lines. Of course there were lines. He was an old man now, as she was an old woman. 'But how did you do it? So quickly? Luke, I can't believe it. Where is he? Rome? Tuscany?'

'Moonee Ponds.'

'*Moonee Ponds?*' It was a suburb of Melbourne. An ordinary suburb of Melbourne. 'How did you —? Where is —?' She had so many more questions now, she couldn't complete a single one.

'Lola, it was so easy. I couldn't believe it. It was almost a disappointment. Once I got going, it only took me a few hours. Everything's easy these days. All the newspapers are online, service clubs have websites, even people your age have Facebook pages.'

Lola had heard about Facebook in some detail from Ellen. She'd listened attentively enough but had frankly been none the wiser afterwards. All she knew was that it was a very modern way of keeping in touch, and it sounded very complicated. 'Alex is on Facebook?'

'No. That was just an example. I found him through his local Italian-Australian Association. It took a bit of digging – his is a pretty common name – but I came across two photos, one from five years ago, the other a year ago, and I would have sworn it was him. But I didn't want to show you unless I knew for sure. So I rang the association. And they gave me a number for him.' Luke was smiling, so proud of all he had achieved.

Lola, however, was horrified. 'You spoke to him? You spoke to Alex himself?'

'Not to him. His daughter. He lives with her.'

'His daughter?' Why was her heart beating faster? Why did she suddenly feel a mixture of nerves and excitement. 'Not his wife? You're sure it was his daughter?'

'I'm sure, Lola. He's widowed. His wife died nearly fifteen years ago. His daughter told me everything, once I explained who I was and why I was calling.'

'Who did you say you were?'

'I lied a bit. I'm sorry, Lola. I got caught on the hop a bit.'

'Luke, what did you say?'

'I said I was your grandson.' He hurriedly continued. 'I said that you had gone into a nursing home and had started to go a bit funny in the head and go down memory lane, and you kept talking about this Alex as if he was really important to you, and how you'd met years ago and there was something you wanted to say to him before you died, and that I'd promised you I'd do whatever I could to find him . . .' Luke trailed off. 'I'm really sorry, Lola. I got a bit carried away.'

Lola was doing her best to stay calm. 'Can I please get this straight? You told Alex I'd gone funny in my head and was in a nursing home?'

'Not Alex, his daughter. She was very nice, but she did say she hadn't ever heard of you.'

Why did that hurt Lola, even a tiny bit?

'But she verified all the other facts you'd told me. That her father had lived in Melbourne in the 1950s and 60s. That he'd gone back to Italy, for about thirty years. She also told me that she'd been born there, and that he'd moved back here about ten years ago, after his wife died. He lived on his own for a bit, but for the past four years he hasn't been well, so he's been living with her and her family. In Moonee Ponds.'

'He's an invalid?'

'Not from what she said. I asked if it was possible to speak to him and she said he was out playing bridge, or maybe it was bowls, but if I left my number she'd ask him to call me. So he must be fairly fit if he can do that. I mean, I know bowls isn't exactly windsurfing and bridge isn't bungee jumping, but —'

'I get your point, Luke. Has he rung you back?'

'No, not yet. But I left your number as well as mine. And he'd ring you, not me, wouldn't he? Once he got the message from his daughter?'

Lola suddenly dropped her phone on the floor. Luke laughed. 'Lola, isn't that what you wanted? Me to track him down so you could talk to him?'

'No. Yes. I just —'

'Didn't think I'd be able to find him this quickly? Lola Quinlan, you're talking to a computer whizkid here. Anyone else you need tracked down? Shergar?'

'The kidnapped Irish racehorse? How do you know about him?'

'Wikipedia,' Luke said.

'Luke, thank you so much. And this might sound silly, I know, but can I please ask you to —'

'Keep all of this to myself too? Of course, Lola. My lips are sealed.'

Lola's phone rang. They both stared down at it on the floor.

'Lola, answer it!'

She seemed to be frozen on the spot.

Luke picked it up and read the display. 'It's Bett.'

Lola took it and answered. 'Bett, I can't talk now. I'll call you back. Sorry. Bye.'

Luke bit back a smile. 'I'd better go. I'll leave you to it. Goodnight, Lola. Good luck. Happy talking.'

'Thank you, Luke. For everything.'

It was only after he'd driven off that she realised she still hadn't asked him about Emily.

That night she didn't move more than three metres from her phone at any stage. She took it with her into dinner, despite her own rule about no mobile phones at the table. She carried it as she sat on the park bench talking to Jim after dinner, reassuring him once again that she was happy to stay in Clare, that it had been her own free will and choice and that he wasn't to give her a second's thought. She retired to her room earlier than usual, ostensibly to watch the news. What she did was watch her phone. It still didn't ring.

She rang Luke from the bedside phone. Yes, he assured her. He'd given Alex's daughter the right number. Yes, her mobile phone number would work from Melbourne. Yes, he had been clear that Lola was an old friend, and yes, Alex's daughter had sounded like she was sober and reliable and knew how to take down phone numbers.

'I could always give you his number,' Luke said. 'You could ring him.'

Lola hit her palm against her forehead. How could she have been so stupid? 'Yes please, Luke.' Her hand was trembling as she wrote down the number.

For the next fifteen minutes she stared at the row of figures. She stared at her phone. The number. The phone. What had happened to her? Where had the 'Act and act now' impulse gone, now she really needed it? Why didn't she just ring him? What was she afraid of?

She knew. She was afraid that he wouldn't want to talk to her.

This was ridiculous. She was an old, old woman, behaving like a silly, silly teenager. She was worse than Emily, carrying a torch for Luke for all these years and yet not doing anything about it, waiting for the planets to align or the moonbeams to shine or something to happen to bring her dreams to life without any effort on her part. The real world wasn't like that. Lola knew that better than anyone. If you wanted something to happen, you had to help make it happen.

She had Alex's number. She could ring him this minute, rather than sit here waiting for him to ring her.

So why didn't she?

The phone was still in her hand when she fell asleep that night.

She was woken by a call the next morning. 'Alex?'

'Lola? It's Bett. What did you call me? Ali?'

'I was saying hello. Hello, Bett.'

'You're chirpy this morning. I thought you were going to ring me back last night?'

'Sorry, darling. I had an early night. I was tired. All those hampers, you know —'

'Of course. I was just ringing to say thanks. And also to ask if I could come and talk to you about something. An idea I've had.'

'You're not leaving Daniel again, are you?'

Bett laughed. 'Not today, no. My marriage is back on steady ground, thanks to you. You and your friends, more to the point. That's what I wanted to come and talk to you about. My neighbour's babysitting the twins this morning. Can I be there in ten minutes?'

She'd hung up before Lola had a chance to say yes or no.

Lola couldn't risk Alex ringing while Bett was there. It wasn't a conversation she could have in front of another person, even a beloved granddaughter. So she turned the phone off, but not before checking her voicemail was working. Perhaps this might be better – he would ring, leave a message and she'd be able to gauge from what he said and how he sounded how things might be between them.

As soon as Bett came in, she kissed her grandmother on the cheek and launched into the reason for her visit. 'Lola, I want to say thanks and I also want to say sorry. I know you think Carrie and I should have behaved much better than this, but you helped us a lot, more than you realised. Everything has felt so much easier and clearer since you and your friends came to our houses.'

'I'm so glad, darling. So what have you decided to do?'

'I'm still going to try working one day a week next year. For sanity and to get me out of the house. But going part-time in January isn't going to work for Daniel, we've both realised that. He's spoken to his boss again and he's going to stay full-time.'

'So what will you do with the babies when you're both at work? Bring them into the office with you?'

'Our bosses are relaxed, but not that relaxed. Lola, is it true there's been a rush of new volunteers for the charity shop since you launched the Christmas hamper appeal?'

'Dozens, yes.'

'Do you and Patricia and Kay and Margaret feel it's time to move on, in terms of your charitable deeds?'

Lola's lips twitched. 'Go on.'

Bett gave her a sheepish smile. 'Lola, I've told all my friends about that day in my house. Carrie's told all her friends too. You saved our lives. If we go to the cupboard, there are clean clothes. To the freezer, there's dinner. It's nice to look out at our gardens, not guilt-inducing.'

'I'm so glad,' Lola said smiling. She knew exactly where this was headed.

'Did you all enjoy it too?'

Lola thought about it before she answered. Yes, they had. It was more fun than being in the charity shop together. More relaxed. There hadn't been the bother of any customers to serve, for starters. And there was something so satisfying about putting someone else's messy house to rights. Much more satisfying than doing one's own housework, they'd all agreed. 'It was great fun,' she told Bett. 'And your children are delightful company.'

'Lola, I know you know what I'm going to say. You haven't stopped giving me that smile you give when you know what I'm up to. But here's our proposition anyway. Come the new year, if you're all keen, we want to hire the five of you. It wouldn't be enough, I know, but I'd pay you whatever I'd earn in a day's work at the paper. Cover all your costs and give you whatever was left over, too. It would be worth every cent of it, to come home and you'd have all been there and worked your magic. Carrie would pay you too, more than me, probably. Other friends of mine said they'd sell their wedding rings to pay for your services.'

'Let me get this straight. From January, you and Carrie —'

'Us for starters, but there's a long waiting list of others too, if you were all up to it —'

'— want five elderly women to come to your houses once a week —'

'Or once a fortnight. Or once a month. Once a *year* if that's all you can manage.'

'And mind your babies, fill your freezers, clean and garden and the rest of it. For a token sum.'

Bett nodded. 'I know you can't speak for the others, but in principle, do you think they might be even a bit interested?'

Lola already knew what her friends' answers would be. The days were sometimes very long for everyone now they were all retired and living alone. As for being paid, of course they wouldn't expect that. Lola herself would secretly cover the cost of ingredients, garden plants and cleaning products. Any money the girls paid them could go straight into the charity shop fund.

'We'd have to call ourselves something, though,' Lola said. 'Give it dignity, a formality . . .'

'You'd do it? You really think you all would?'

'If we found the right name, yes. I think perhaps we all would.'

Bett smiled. 'What about the Merry Widows?'

'How cheery. Let me talk to the others, Bett. Not just about the name, about everything. I'll call you back as soon as I can.'

'I'm going to see Mum and Dad now. Will I come back after that?'

'Good heavens, you are keen.'

'Desperate, not keen. Thank you, Lola. Even if you say no.'

Lola not only had a positive answer for Bett when she came back. She had a name. Kay had coined it.

'We'd be some kind of crack team, is that what you mean? We'd come in, babysit, cook, clean and conquer? Like some kind of, I don't know, Baby Squad?'

Bett laughed out loud. 'That's it exactly. You'd be the Baby Squad.' She hugged her grandmother. 'Thank you, Lola, so much. I don't know how you do it, but you always make things better for me.'

Lola hugged her just as tightly. It was like having the old Bett back, happy, relaxed, with time to talk. Lola had missed their talks so much. She suddenly wanted to tell her everything, about

Jim and Geraldine selling up, about her secret plans for Christmas, about Ellen's visit. About finding Alex, most of all.

She patted the small armchair beside her. 'Darling, come and sit here with me for a minute, would you? It feels like so long since you and I had one of our good old catch-ups.'

'It feels so long because it *has* been so long. I'd love that.' Bett had just sat down when her mobile rang. 'Sorry, Lola. It's my neighbour, Jane. I won't be a second.' She answered the call. 'Hi, Jane. Oh, no. No, that's fine. Don't worry. I'll be back as soon as I can.' She was already standing before she finished the call. 'Lola, I'm sorry. Yvette has fallen and cut her lip. It's not serious but Jane can't stop her crying and Zach is upset now too. I'd better get back. Was it anything important? Can I ring you later?'

Lola found the brightest smile she could. 'It wasn't important at all, darling. You head home, quick as you can.'

If she had been a paranoid kind of woman, Lola thought the next day, she would be starting to think the planets were conspiring against her. Alex not ringing. Bett not being able to stay to talk. And now her entire Christmas plans falling like dominoes, one after the other. It had started with two emails, waiting there for her when she logged on to her laptop computer first thing after breakfast.

Dear Ms Quinlan,

Re: Christmas booking

We regret to inform you that we are no longer able to take up your wonderfully generous offer for a free three-night stay in the Valley View Motel. My husband and I have had the great surprise of our two (overseas-based) children announcing they're flying home to spend Christmas with us. So we're staying put and I must confess, so happy to be doing so! We wish you the very best for the festive season and hope to come and stay with you in the Valley View Motel one time soon. It sounds like a wonderful place.

Yours sincerely,

Helen and Tony Brooks

Dear Ms Quinlan,

Re: Booking for Martha Kaminski/Christmas

I wish to cancel a booking made in the name of Martha Kaminski for the nights of December 24, 25 and 26. Ms Kaminski will now be joining her family in Queensland for the Christmas break.

I understand from Ms Kaminski that it was in fact a free offer, but should this inconvenience you in any way, please be assured we will of course recompense you. Please accept our apologies for any difficulty this cancellation may cause.

We wish you the best for Christmas and the new year.

Sincerely,

Glenda Sorenson

PA to Martha Kaminski

It didn't stop there. Lola had just finished her shower and was getting dressed for the day when there was a knock at the door. It was Jim, with a slip of notepaper. 'I've just taken a message for you, Lola. Someone called Mrs Harris. It was hard to hear everything she said, she was a bit teary, but it sounded like something to do with her son and Christmas? What are you up to? I thought you said there'd been no bookings.'

'Nothing to worry about. Thank you, darling. I'll call her back.'

Lola was on the phone for nearly half an hour. The woman was alternately tearful and joyful. Lola was shocked to learn what the woman's son had been planning to do at the motel. It hardly seemed possible. Lola tried to recall the emails she'd received from him. She'd thought him the most relaxed of her guests. And yet . . .

'He's with us at home now, here with his sister and me. We can't take our eyes off him. I'm sure it's driving him crazy but to think, to even think for a minute that he was going to . . . I know they say it's often a cry for help, that not everyone goes through with it, but if it wasn't for his flatmate . . . It's just so terrible. I keep thinking what might have happened, what he might have done, but he'll be okay now. I hope he'll be okay. He knows how much we love him, and he's going to go and talk to some doctors, and I know he'll find work soon. He's so clever with his hands. You should see the sofa he fixed up for me, and he's so young. He's got his whole life ahead of him. He'll meet someone else. She wasn't right for him . . .'

What a sad world it was sometimes, Lola thought after she'd said goodbye. Who ever knew what pain another person was going through?

Two hours later, Jim put a second call through to her room. 'Another one for Lola Quinlan, proprietor,' he said. 'Another one about Christmas. What exactly are you up to, Lola Quinlan?'

'A lot less than I thought,' Lola said truthfully. 'Thank you, darling. Please put the call through.'

A moment later a young woman came on the line. 'Is that Lola Quinlan? Lola, this is Holly Jackson. I was booked to stay with you over Christmas. With my two sisters. We won a free stay?'

Lola frowned, reaching for her notebook. From memory, her fourth set of guests was a family, mother and daughters, not three sisters. 'I'm sorry, Holly. I must have made a mistake. I have you down as a family booking. You don't sound old enough to have daughters.'

Her caller sounded anxious. 'I'm not. I'm very sorry. I told a bit of a lie about that. And I told another lie too. I'm seventeen, not thirty-five. And I'm even sorrier for this late notice, but we can't take up your free offer after all. Our parents have made other plans for us.'

Lola was confused. The three children had been coming to the motel without their parents? She fought against her natural curiosity to ask more. The girl, Holly, sounded upset enough as it was. 'Well, never mind at all. Are you going somewhere nice instead?'

'I don't know for sure. It might be Disneyland. If they can decide between Paris or Florida. Or we might end up staying at home. I don't know yet.'

'Well, I hope you have a very happy Christmas together wherever you are.'

'I hope so too,' Holly said.

Lola hung up, reached for her Secret Christmas notebook and crossed out their names too. What had happened to her great Christmas idea? Where would she find any guests now?

A thought flashed into her mind. Did she actually *want* any new guests now? Was she feeling just the slightest bit of relief that she wouldn't have to do all that cooking and cleaning and fetching and gathering in this heat? Not that she would have been doing it all herself, but still . . .

She had a sudden mental picture of waking up on Christmas morning and a glorious nothing stretching out in front of her. Just her own company, all day long. Her own company and Ellen's too, of course . . .

But was there any point in Ellen coming now? Would it make more sense for her to come in the new year, when everyone was there? When they could all make a true celebration of her arrival? When perhaps Glenn could even join her for a few days? At the end of Ellen's stay, mind you. They'd want her to themselves first.

Lola's mind started ticking over. Who knows, perhaps after the success of Denise's last visit, just perhaps Ellen wouldn't think it was the very worst thing that could possibly happen in the entire world if she was to spend Christmas on that luxurious island with her father and Denise and Lily . . .

There was no time like now to find out.

She picked up her bedside phone, glad to have this diversion. She knew herself well enough. The more she did to keep herself busy, the less time she had to mull on the fact that Alex still hadn't rung. She had checked her mobile again and again, especially after she'd hung up from her other calls, just in case something had gone wrong with her ring tone and his call had come in silently. She'd been disappointed each time. There hadn't been any missed calls or any messages left on her voicemail. She'd gone through every possible scenario. He was waiting until after breakfast. After lunch. After dinner. She searched for every reason except the one that was the most obvious. He hadn't rung because he didn't want to talk to her.

She'd just dialled Ellen's number in Hong Kong when her mobile rang. She hung up on Hong Kong and snatched up her phone. 'Lola Quinlan.'

'Lola, hello. Any word yet?' It was Luke.

Her heart slowed. 'No, nothing, I'm afraid. And refined lady that I am, I've decided to wait for him to call me first.'

'I'm so sorry, Lola. I promise I gave his daughter the right numbers. Just in case you were worried about that. I said them twice and she read them back to me.'

'It's fine, darling. He's an old man. Nearly as old as me. Perhaps he's still searching through his memory bank, trying to remember who I am. He'll call in his own good time, I'm sure of it.'

She wasn't sure of it. The only thing she was sure of was her decision not to ring him. She realised she couldn't bear it if his reaction wasn't a good one. If she were to ring him and he was cool on the phone, or distant, it would feel like time travelling, taking her right back to how she'd felt when he first returned to Italy. If he wanted to call her, he would. If he didn't, he wouldn't. It was as simple a situation as that. And sadly, as each hour passed, it was becoming clearer that he didn't want to call her. So there was nothing she could do but live with his decision, as she had lived with his decision all those years earlier.

Doing her best to push all thoughts of him out of her mind, she rang the Hong Kong number again. She had a nice exchange with Glenn's housekeeper Lin and then her granddaughter came on the line. 'Hi, Lola! How are you?'

'Healthy as a young trout, darling.' Lola had always vowed to tell Ellen the truth as much as possible. She did her best now. 'Ellen, I'm going to get right to the point. I'm ringing because I think your Christmas plans are about to change. But I want you to know this hasn't been the plan all along, me plotting to somehow get you to stay there for Christmas, to go away with your father. I promise. This has all come as a surprise to me too.' She explained that her need for a kitchen slave had disappeared, with the cancellation of all of her Christmas guests. 'I want to see you so much, my dearest Ellen, but I don't want you to be rattling around here in the motel with just me for company.'

'But what about you rattling around there on your own? Won't you be lonely?'

Lonely? The more Lola thought about it, the more she knew that being on her own for Christmas would be idyllic, not lonely. She knew she'd enjoy thinking about her son, her granddaughters and their families, even Ellen, happily having their own, different Christmas celebrations in different parts of the country and the world. She'd have her feet up. She'd read all day. Or watch TV all day. Drink gin all day. Yes, even spend all day listening to those Christmas radio programs, as she'd joked with Jim. 'I won't be lonely for a second, darling. I promise you. Not at Christmas. But by New Year, yes, I will be desperate for company. So I'm ringing to ask if you would possibly consider changing the dates of your trip. Would you even think about going away with your Dad, Denise and Lily for Christmas, and then coming here to me for New Year? I want the truth, please. Tell me exactly how you feel and whatever you decide, we'll work around it.'

There was silence for a moment and then Ellen spoke again, her voice calm. 'I think that would be okay. As long as I know I'll be coming to you for New Year.'

'I'll be waiting with bells and whistles. And it won't just be me, darling. Your entire family will be here waiting for you.'

'And I won't have to do any washing up at all then, either, will I?'

'Not even a teaspoon. You're sure, Ellen?'

'I'm sure, Really-Great-Gran.'

'You're a darling girl. I'll ring your dad, will I?'

Glenn was overjoyed, in his matter-of-fact way. 'Lola, how did you manage this?'

'I don't really know,' she said honestly. 'I actually didn't plan it. It all seemed to happen of its own accord. But we still get to have her for New Year, promise me that?'

'Of course.' He laughed. 'And I still get to celebrate that with her too. She'll be back here in plenty of time for Chinese New Year. Thanks, Lola. I don't know how you did it but I'm glad you did.'

CHAPTER EIGHTEEN

The day before Christmas Eve, Lola was at the forecourt of the motel, standing in the shadiest spot she could find. She'd waved goodbye so many times that morning her arm was hurting. First Carrie, Matthew and their three children had driven up to say goodbye.

'We'll ring on Christmas morning, Lola. Thanks for everything! Enjoy yourself!'

Daniel, Bett, Zachary and Yvette were next. They were all red-cheeked and fractious-looking, Bett and Daniel more than the twins. 'You don't think the Baby Squad would come away with us, do you?' Bett whispered to Lola as they hugged goodbye.

Jim and Geraldine were the last to go. Geraldine gave Lola a barely touching kiss on the cheek. Jim hugged his mother tightly. 'This feels all wrong,' he said. 'Leaving you alone like this.'

'Darling, we've been through all this. Besides, you'll have forgotten all about me by the time you get to Sevenhill.' It was the next town to Clare, only seven kilometres away.

'We'll ring on Christmas Eve and Christmas morning,' Jim

said as he climbed into the driver's seat. They were taking Geraldine's car, leaving Jim's behind.

'I hope I'm here,' Lola said cheerily. 'I may have taken off on a driving holiday myself by then. Keep an eye out for me in your rear-view mirror, won't you?' She experienced a brief feeling of glee to notice Geraldine's suddenly worried expression.

Jim still didn't drive away, winding down the window for one last exchange. 'We'll only ever be a few hours away. We can come back if you need us at any time.'

'If I need help thawing my TV dinner, you mean?' Lola laughed. 'Jim, would you please just go? Or I'll have burned to a crisp standing here saying goodbye over and again.'

'You're sure you won't be lonely?'

'I don't know. You won't leave me alone so I can find out.'

'Happy Christmas, Mum,' he said then, finally starting the car.

'Happy Christmas, darling. Happy Christmas, Geraldine.' She got one warm loving smile and one frosty one in return. No change there.

Thank God, she thought, as they finally drove out of her sight. Alone at last. And for four days at least. She and Jim had made the decision together to declare the motel closed for the Christmas period. There was the chance someone would come, but for the sake of a few dollars, Jim didn't want her to be worrying or waiting around. So they'd added a new sign to the one on the main road, advising they were closed for renovations and wishing everyone a merry Christmas. Jim had recorded a similar message on their answering machine. Lola herself would deal with any email enquiries that might come in.

She'd decided to spend Christmas Day on her own. She'd had plenty of invitations, of course. Kay, Margaret, Patricia and Luke, even Emily and her family. She'd turned them all down, nicely but firmly.

Their responses had been identical. 'But you can't be on your own. Not at Christmas.'

She could be and she wanted to be. It really was just one more day of the year, she explained each time. A day with far too much pressure on it. She liked her own company. She didn't have a huge appetite these days. She'd make herself a cheese sandwich, a large gin and tonic and perhaps have some good chocolate for dessert. She'd watch TV or listen to the radio or even read, being sure to stay inside out of the heat, cool and content and comfortable. At the end of the day, if she felt like it, she might make herself an especially large gin and tonic, and go and sit for a while on her park bench, enjoying the cool of the evening.

She wouldn't – she would *not* – keep looking at her phone, wishing it would ring.

She spent Christmas Eve with the charity shop ladies, overseeing the delivery of the Christmas hampers. They'd galvanised a team of drivers, picking men and women they knew would be discreet, people who would simply drop off the hamper with a smile and warm Christmas greeting, without passing any comment or judgement on the recipients. There had been two hundred and twenty requests in the end, and easily enough donations to fill them. Each hamper had been overflowing with goodies, in fact. Some families were receiving two hampers full of Christmas cheer. Perhaps not all of the requests had been authentic, but Lola decided she didn't mind. The goodness the people in the Valley had shown far outweighed any deception that had gone on.

As the delivery day drew to a close, once again, she was forced to deflect another stream of invitations. People seemed truly horrified that she was spending Christmas on her own. 'Do you want to even drop over to our house for leftovers?' one asked.

'We can all drive up and see you for an hour or two,' another said.

'No!' Lola said. 'No, thank you,' she corrected. 'I'm doing an experiment. Seeing if I still eat too much on Christmas Day even when I'm on my own. I would hate an unscheduled visit to upset my finely tuned calculations.'

'You'll ring if you get lonely, won't you?' Kay asked again, as she said goodbye.

'I certainly will,' Lola said. I certainly will not, she thought.

She refused to look at her phone that night. What was the point? She knew now that Alex had decided not to call her. 'Oh, well,' she said aloud. She did her best to ignore the voice inside her that was much more unhappy.

She woke to a hot, blue-skied Christmas morning. Hotter even than the forecast. She felt it as soon as she pulled open the curtains. That swirling wind was back too. She could tell by the shifting and swaying of the gum trees on the hillside opposite. Definitely a day to be inside by the airconditioner.

She did everything she wanted to do and nothing she didn't. She didn't get dressed until midday. She watched a movie. She ate her cheese sandwich. She took calls from her family and friends, keeping them as brief as possible. 'I'm fine. I couldn't be happier. Now off you go and enjoy yourselves.' They all seemed happy and cheerful. She was glad.

Ellen rang from the island. She sounded bright, too.

'You're having fun?' Lola asked. 'You're okay?'

'It's great,' Ellen said. 'We've had presents, and been for a swim, and we're about to have lunch. Board games afterwards. Dad and me versus Denise and Lily.'

It was difficult for Lola to reconcile this Ellen with the spitfire of a fortnight earlier. 'I'm very proud of you.'

'So far, so good,' Ellen said cheerily. 'As long as they let me win the games.'

Lola was secretly glad she hadn't turned too goody two-shoes.

'And you'll still send me a photo of your Christmas Day outfit, Lola, won't you?'

'Of course I will,' Lola promised. 'Don't I always?'

It was tricky enough taking the photo. In previous years she'd had Bett or Carrie handy to be the photographer. Today she made two attempts using the camera's remote button and managed a photo of the carpet both times. Eventually, she took a photo of herself in the mirror. It wasn't perfect – the camera in front of her face spoiled the effect slightly, but she knew Ellen would get the general idea. Lola was very proud of today's outfit. If she'd known Mrs Kernaghan's email address, she'd have been tempted to send the photo to her too. She'd taken her inspiration from Mrs Kernaghan's window display, after all. In terms of the colour scheme, at least.

She was wearing a long floating green satin skirt on which someone – not her – had embroidered red stars. She'd teamed it with a multicoloured chiffon overshirt and a very large, very long silver scarf that she'd tied as a belt. She had green bangles on one arm, red ones on the other, flashing Christmas wreath earrings and a seasonal necklace made of Christmas decorations looped together into a three-strand necklace. It was her jaunty Santa hat that set the whole outfit off, though, she knew.

'I've toned down my look this year,' she wrote to Ellen in her email. 'No point pushing out the boat when I'm the only one here. Wait till you see what I've got planned for New Year's Eve!' She followed Luke's written instructions, downloading the photo from her camera to the computer, and then attaching it to her email. 'Off you go,' she said aloud, pressing 'send'.

Nothing happened.

'Off you go this time,' she said again.

Still nothing.

She checked the cable. Fine. The connection. Not fine. Drat, she thought. Of all days for the internet to go down. She really wanted Ellen to see the photo today.

What could she do? She didn't want to ring Luke, even

though she knew he was home in Clare with his mother. Not on Christmas Day. Even computer whizkids needed one day off a year. It might be easy to fix but it could also be tricky, and she knew Luke wouldn't leave without sorting out the problem. No, she didn't want him using up hours of his day on her.

She went to the office and tried the motel computer. The same problem. Was it something to do with that fierce wind? Perhaps the email and the photo were having trouble flying through the air or whatever it was they did to get around.

No matter, she decided. She had another computer trick up her sleeve. She also had the keys to Jim's car. She was a good driver, despite what people thought about women of her age still having licences. Besides, hardly anyone would be on the roads this time of the afternoon on Christmas Day. She also had the keys to the charity shop. The internet connection there was very reliable. A much better setup than her own, too. She might even watch a few YouTube clips of old musicals once she'd sent her photo off to Ellen. That always cheered her up. Not that she needed cheering up. She was absolutely fine. Not in the least bit lonely.

Not in the least. And she'd only checked her mobile phone for messages a few times. Six, at the most.

The main street was almost empty. There was only one car parked at the northern end. It was very, very hot, she realised. Even if it hadn't been Christmas Day, the temperature would have kept people inside and off the road. She could see mirage-like shimmers on the asphalt ahead. The trees lining the street barely gave off any shade. She drove on past the shop and around the corner to the coolest spot she could find. She could be inside for an hour or so, depending on what clips she found on You-Tube. She didn't want to come back to a baking car.

The Santa hat she was wearing wasn't great at keeping the sun off her face. She kept her head down and stayed close to the cool of the buildings as she hurried towards the front door of the charity shop. The display area was still empty, but the sign asking for donations had been replaced with dozens of A4 sheets of paper covering the front door and the entire window, all bearing the same two words. 'Thank You.'

She went inside and shut and double-locked the door behind her. Not that anyone would be trying to get in, but it was a habit she'd developed whenever she was in the shop on her own after closing time, counting the day's takings. It was already warm inside, after only a day without the airconditioning being on. The shop was closed now until the new year.

It felt nice to be there on her own, she realised, as she turned on the computer, heard its familiar hum and watched the screen come to life. Yes, the internet was working fine here. She quickly connected the camera, downloaded the photo and sent her email off to Ellen. That should give them something to laugh at if there's any tension there at all, she thought.

She'd just logged out of her email account and was about to go onto YouTube when she heard something. A noise out the back. There was only a small walled yard there, where they kept spare cardboard boxes and the shop's mop bucket and rubbish bin. She stood up and peered through the little window that looked into the yard. The gate in the wall was moving.

'Who's there?' she called, her voice barely a whisper. Another banging noise. The gate moved again. As if someone was on the other side of the wall, trying to kick their way in.

To where? To here? To the shop? But why on earth would someone do that? On Christmas Day? There was nothing here to steal. All the money was gone, banked on Christmas Eve. There were just a few racks of second-hand clothes, a couple of shelves of old books and DVDs.

And a full computer setup. A computer. A camera. A colour printer. A scanner.

She heard voices.

Her hands started to shake. Whoever was outside wouldn't expect anyone to be there. They'd have chosen this lazy hot time on Christmas Day for exactly that reason. But how would anyone have even known it was here to steal?

The answer came to her immediately. Mrs Kernaghan's TV segment. She had sat in front of the computer, proudly demonstrating what a state-of-the-art setup they had. She'd actually used the term 'state-of-the-art'. None of them had thought for a moment it would make them a target. They were a charity shop. Who would steal from a charity shop?

The voice came from just outside the window. 'Hurry up, mate.'

She had to hide. She couldn't stop them. Once she would have tried. Grabbed something, a broom, an umbrella, tried to scare them off that way. But she was old. She was frail. Where could she go? What should she do? Ring for the police? There wasn't time. She could see them both now, two young men, inside the yard. They were starting to force open the door to the shop itself.

She only had a minute, less. Quick, Lola. Quick. Think. The changing room. It had a door, a lock. They wouldn't expect anyone to be in there. They wouldn't even look, would they?

They wouldn't hurt her if they did find her, would they?

She got herself into the changing room and locked the door only seconds before she heard the back door fly open. It slammed against the wall. 'Fucking hell. Keep the noise down,' she heard one of the men say. The same voice? A third voice? Were there more than two of them?

'Jesus, look at it. This must be worth a fortune.'

'We'll find out,' the other said.

'It's still on.'

'Just pull out the plug.'

'Someone's left a handbag behind too.'

'Grab it.'

Lola started to shake even more. Why hadn't she picked up her handbag? Her mobile phone was inside it. Her camera. The keys to the car. The keys to the shop. The keys to the motel. She nearly called out. *Please don't take my keys.* She didn't. She held her breath. They were quiet now, busy. She heard the computer being dismantled, shoved into cardboard boxes. She'd heard them drag several inside. The leftover cardboard boxes from the Christmas appeal. She heard the back door and back gate open, shut, open again as they went in and out. They were quick. Effi-cient. *Go. Go, get out, leave. Please, just take it, just go, just go . . .*

She heard one of them come back inside, into the shop itself. She heard the sound of the wire hangers being pushed along the racks. Heard the till being opened. The familiar ping of its bell set her shaking again. He was less than two metres away from her. *Go, go, just go, please, just go . . .*

'Jesus, mate. Get out of there. Someone will see you.'

'It's Christmas Day. No one's around. I need some new clothes. Give us a minute.'

'It's second-hand crap. Get out of there.'

Lola was now shaking so violently her teeth were chattering. How could they not hear her? She couldn't control it. Not just her hands, her whole body was trembling. She was so scared. Scared they'd find her. Scared what they'd do if they found her. She started to pray, to God, to Mary, to baby Jesus, to all the saints, to her parents, to her ex-husband, to everyone she could remember. *Help me, help me, help me. Go, please go. Go. Take everything you want. Just go.* She heard the back door slam. Heard something else screech shut in the backyard. The gate. It was strong, made of steel. They must have forced it open and forced it shut again. A moment later, their car started. It had a noisy exhaust.

It was ten minutes before she could move. Another five min-utes before her hands stopped trembling enough to open the small flimsy lock that had kept the changing room door shut. If

326

they had tried it, if they had pushed it even slightly, it would have opened. The thought of being found so easily, the thought of them pushing back the door and seeing her there, in the corner, set off more shaking. She had to hold onto the door, the racks, take support from wherever she could to make her way across the shop to the back room where there was a chair. She nearly fell twice. Her legs could barely hold her up. She had to get out of there. She had to ring someone, anyone.

She couldn't. They'd taken her bag and taken her phone. There wasn't a landline in the shop.

She'd have to go out on the street, flag someone down.

She couldn't open the front door. She'd double-locked it. The keys were in her bag.

She tried to bang on the door, get someone's attention that way. She was still shaking so much she barely made a noise.

She tried to tear at the signs covering the front window, the signs saying 'Thank You' over and over again. She'd helped tape them up herself. She couldn't seem to tear any of them off. Her hands were useless.

Outside, the street was quiet. No cars, no people. It was Christmas Day. Everyone was at home.

She'd have to use the back door. She went out into the tiny yard. It had to be forty degrees or more out there, the temperature heightened by the white paint on the walls. The door to the shop slammed behind her as she went out. She tried the gate. It wouldn't budge. Whatever they'd done when they kicked it open and kicked it shut would need more than her strength to fix.

Stay calm, Lola. Stay calm. Go back inside and think. Stop shaking and think.

She pulled at the back door. Pulled again. It was stuck. No, it couldn't be. Again, and again. The handle was so small, and her hands were now sweating so much she couldn't get a grip on it. She took off her hat, the ridiculous Santa hat she was still wearing, and tried using that. It just slipped off the handle. She kicked the door with her sandalled foot. She did nothing but hurt her toe.

She was stuck in the yard. In the sun.

'Help!' she called. 'Please, someone. Help me!'

Who would hear her? The shops on either side were shut for two days.

'Help! Please! Can anyone hear me?'

How could they? There was no one nearby to hear.

'Please! Someone! Anyone! Help me!'

The only sound was the cicadas, tick-tick-ticking in the heat.

CHAPTER NINETEEN

Moonee Ponds,

Melbourne

The noise in the living room had reached ear-splitting levels. There was a game of chasey going on, the four children weaving their way at high speed between the dining table, the sofa, out the back door into the garden and then onto the deck, coming perilously close to knocking over the card table laden with drinks each time. In the kitchen, a group of women were laughing over a bottle of prosecco while they mixed salads. At floor level, two toddlers were taking it in turns to pick up blocks of Lego and throw them at each other. Outside in the barbecue area, three men were in charge of cooking the plates of marinated fish and chicken.

In a comfortable armchair at the end of the open-plan kitchen and living room, an elderly man sat back, eyes closed, oblivious to the noise and the chaos around him. He had his iPod plugged in, with the soothing tones of Bach beautifully blocking out the squeals, the shouts, the running feet and the slamming of the back door as the twenty members of his family went in and out, sending in a blast of Christmas Day heat each time.

Fifteen minutes earlier, his daughter had asked if he'd like anything: a glass of wine, a beer, some sparkling water?

'Water would be lovely, thank you, *cara*.'

She'd gone over to the kitchen to get it, got caught up in a conversation with her sister and two sisters-in-law and forgotten about him, he realised now. No wonder. She'd been flat-out busy all day. All week, in fact. It was no easy feat to cook Christmas lunch not just for her own family, and for him, but her husband's extended family as well. She'd been making lists and muttering to herself for days now. He'd get the water himself. He'd been waited on hand and foot enough as it was.

'You all spoil me,' he'd said to her earlier when she settled him in his favourite chair and made sure he had the latest edition of *Il Globo* to read.

'You're our dad. It's our job to spoil you.'

Before going over to the fridge he took a moment to take in the whole scene around him. To think he was responsible in some way for all of these people being gathered here today, all from different countries and backgrounds, here in Australia. The idea of it overwhelmed him sometimes. They'd done a count one day, his daughters and his sons-in-law, and they'd got to nine, *nine* countries represented in some way in just his one family. Italy, of course, through him and his ancestry. His wife too, God rest her soul. But after that, the Lombardis had turned international. His oldest daughter, Italian-born and raised, had gone travelling after university and while in France, met a young man studying winemaking. An Australian, of Hungarian and Spanish descent.

His other daughter had stayed closer to home, but married a Swedish man working nearby, whose father was from Stockholm but whose mother was German. It had continued into the next generation too. His oldest granddaughter, half-Italian half-Australian in ancestry, now completely Australian in accent, was dating a Vietnamese man she'd met at university. His grandson was engaged to a young New Zealander. And somehow, all of them, every branch of his large family tree, had ended up living here in Melbourne, within twenty kilometres of each other. The Italian side coming through, his daughter always said. We stick together. Family is everything.

He'd never have thought, all those years ago when he returned to Italy, that he would be back here. It was like he'd been given four lives, he often thought. His first twenty-four years in Italy. Ten years in Australia. Italy again for nearly forty years. And now back in Australia again.

His daughter Rosie, now in her early fifties, had moved here with her Australian winemaker husband soon after they were married. Her two children had been born here. She'd begged him to come and join her family after her mother died. 'Please, Papa, while you're still young enough. If you wait any longer, you'll be too old to enjoy it when you get here. You used to love Australia, didn't you? You'll love it again.'

He had loved it. It had been filled with good memories for him. Sad times too. But precious ones. Work he had done. Places he had seen. People he had met. A woman he had loved.

He'd spent a lot of time in recent months thinking back

over those days in Melbourne. His daughter had taken him on a day trip down through Brighton and so many memories had returned as they had coffee at one of the beachside cafes. He'd almost spoken to Rosie about that time, but he'd stopped himself. He knew from experience that his daughters didn't like to think of him as having had any romantic life at all before he had met their mother.

He wondered whether all this memory-revisiting was part of growing old or a subtle hint that the end was nigh? He hoped not. He was only eighty-three. He ate well, exercised as much as possible, worked outdoors in the garden when he could. Sudden cardiac arrests or road accidents aside, he might have another decade ahead of him.

If he didn't die of thirst now, that was. He glanced over. His daughter was still laughing, standing at the bench with a glass in one hand, a salad fork in the other. He reached beside him for the stick he needed to use more and more, and made his way over to the fridge.

She spotted him. 'Papa! You're banned from the kitchen. Back to your chair!'

'Banned from the kitchen, not from the fridge. A glass of water isn't out of the question, surely?'

'Oh, God. I forgot. I'm sorry. Here, let me get it.'

He touched her cheek. 'I can manage a glass of water for myself, *cara*.'

The fridge door was covered in bits of paper, postcards, work rosters, swimming pool opening hours, all secured by colourful magnets. As he opened the door to get the bottle of water, one of the magnets fell off, sending a flutter of paper towards him.

He started to reach down and was beaten to it by his daughters. He managed to retrieve two pieces of paper himself, without too much groaning, and made a show of pinning them back on the fridge, making a mock bow when the women congratulated him far too effusively. He was beginning to think his family regarded him as a useless old pet.

He did manage to get to the fridge magnet on the floor before them. Rosie collected them, insisting that travelling friends send her the most outlandish ones they could find. This one was from Munich, an over-sized stein of beer, three sausages and what was supposed to be sauerkraut but looked more like slugs in a bowl. Putting it back on the fridge, he noticed his own name on one of the slips of paper stuck there. Underneath, two other names, with phone numbers beside them. Lola. Luke.

Lola?

He turned to his daughter. 'Rosie, is this your writing? Did you take this message?'

She looked over his shoulder and put her hand to her mouth. 'Papa, sorry. I meant to tell you. I've lost the plot this week. I don't know what I've done or what I need to do. Honestly, next year I'm taking early holidays. It's impossible to work and prepare for Christmas at the same time.'

'I'm always like that at Christmas, whether I'm working or not,' her sister-in-law said, starting to laugh. 'Remember last year? I completely forgot to defrost the turkey and we had to get the hairdryers out —'

'Rosie, the message?'

'Papa, sorry. I got a call last week. This lady's grandson rang looking for you. Apparently you used to know her years ago? What was it, Lily or Lola?'

'Lola,' he said. 'It was Lola. She rang here, do you mean? Lola rang me?'

'You remember her? Sorry. I said to the guy that I'd never heard you mention her.' She quickly filled him in on her conversation with Luke – that Lola was in a nursing home, hoping to get in touch with people from her past or something like that. She winked at her sister-in-law. 'An old girlfriend, Papa?'

He didn't answer, but kept looking down at the paper with the two phone numbers.

She reached past him and poured the glass of water. 'It's not too late to ring, is it? You can wish her happy Christmas. Use the phone in the hall if you like. At least you'll be able to hear in there.' She turned back to her sister-in-law and laughed. 'God, I'd forgotten all about the hairdryers! Is that why we said we'd never do turkey again?'

In the quiet of the hallway, Alex put on his glasses, picked up the phone and slowly and carefully dialled Lola's number.

On the road between Clare and Sevenhill, Lola's handbag was lying in a clump of dried grass, under the wire fence. Nothing had been taken from it but her purse. The phone and camera were deemed too old, the rest of the contents dismissed as 'old lady stuff'. The phone started to ring. Once. Twice. Three times. There was no one nearby to hear it or answer it.

In Clare, Luke and his mother had finished their Christmas dinner, done the washing-up and were now in their airconditioned living room about to watch a movie. They'd been sitting outside on the verandah, but it had got too hot, the gusting wind only adding to the discomfort. Later, once it cooled down a bit, Luke planned to go and visit friends across town. They not only had a great selection of PlayStation games but a swimming pool in their backyard.

He'd just pressed play on the remote control when his phone rang. 'Sorry, Mum. Won't be a sec.' He answered it. 'Luke speaking.'

A hesitant voice spoke. 'Hello. I hope you can help me. I'm trying to reach Lola Quinlan. My name is Alex Lombardi —'

'*Alex?* Hello, Alex! This is Luke. God, Lola will be so glad you've rung —'

'Is she all right? You told my daughter she's in a nursing home?'

Luke gave a sheepish laugh. 'Actually she's not, no. Sorry. She's absolutely fine. Fit as a fiddle still. Amazing, actually. She's up at the motel today, but I can give you her mobile number if you want to try that first?'

'The motel?'

'The Valley View, here in Clare.'

'I'm sorry, where are you both?'

'The Clare Valley. South Australia. Vines and hills and a lot of heat today. Happy Christmas, by the way.'

'Happy Christmas to you too. I rang her mobile but there was no answer, just voicemail. I rang it three times and still no answer.'

Luke frowned. 'That's not like her. Maybe she's mislaid it. Alex, I know she really wants to talk to you. Can I try and track her down for you?' They agreed a plan – Luke would call Lola at the motel and pass on Alex's number to her again. 'She'll call you as soon as she can, I'm sure.'

'What on earth's going on?' Patricia asked after he'd hung up. 'Who was that? What are you and Lola up to now?'

'I can't answer that, Mum, sorry,' Luke said. 'It's classified Lola information.' He rang Lola's mobile himself first. It just rang out, eventually going to voicemail. He left a brief message. He rang the Valley View Motel number next. No answer there, either, just Jim's recorded message that the motel was closed for renovations and wishing everyone a Merry Christmas.

'That's weird,' Luke said. 'I wonder where she is.'

'She could be fast asleep. Or out hill-walking. You know Lola. She said she wanted to be left alone today to do exactly what she wanted when she felt like it.'

'But she'd want to know he rang. I know she would.'

'Who *is* he?' Patricia asked again.

'I'm sorry, but I really can't say. It's Lola's story, not mine.

Mum, do you mind if I drive up to the motel, just to see if she's okay and give her the message?'

'Of course not.' She stood up. 'If you don't mind if I come with you. I've never liked the idea of her being on her own on Christmas Day.'

On the way they tried to remember which room she was staying in at the moment. Either eleven or twelve, they thought. They knocked on both. No answer. They peered through the windows as best they could. Nothing. They knocked on all the other rooms too. No answer there, either. They looked in through the dining room window, the kitchen window, into Jim and Geraldine's manager's house windows. Nothing and no one.

'What if —?' Luke started to say what they were both thinking. What if something had happened to her? What if she was lying unconscious in her room? What if that was why she wasn't answering their calls or door knocks?

'We can't jump to conclusions. I spoke to her this morning. She was in fine form. Where else could she be?'

Luke rang Emily's house. Patricia rang Margaret, Kay and Joan. No, none of them had spoken to Lola since their happy Christmas calls that morning.

'She must be in her room. Having a nap or a bath,' Margaret said. 'Where else could she be?'

'Could you ring the taxi company? Check if she got a lift anywhere?' Kay suggested. 'Maybe she went to visit Anna.' They all knew that Lola made regular visits to Anna's grave in the Sevenhill cemetery.

Luke rang the taxi company. No, they hadn't collected Lola that day.

He and his mother were still at the motel, trying to work out how to break into Lola's room when two other cars arrived. Margaret, Joan and Kay were in one. Emily was in the other.

'You didn't have to come,' Patricia said as they walked towards her. 'I'm sure she's fine.'

'Of course she is,' Margaret said, trying to look cheerful. 'I just wanted to wish her happy Christmas again.'

It was Emily who noticed that Jim's car was missing.

'He and Geraldine are on a driving holiday,' Kay said.

'But they've taken Geraldine's car,' Emily said. 'I waved to them both the day before yesterday. Can Lola still drive?'

'When it suits her,' Margaret said. 'But where would she have gone?'

They decided to split up. Kay, Patricia and Margaret would go to the Sevenhill cemetery to see if Lola was visiting Anna's grave. Luke and Emily would try the charity shop. It was the only other place they could all think of. Margaret gave him her keys. 'Ring us if she's there.'

Luke drove in his old Corolla.

'She'll be all right, won't she?' Emily said.

'Of course. Mum's probably right, we're all overreacting.'

There was silence for a minute and then Emily spoke again. 'Lola's great, isn't she?'

'Brilliant,' Luke said. 'She's the coolest old lady I've ever met.'

'Me too,' Emily said.

'I'm not sure about her clothes, though,' Luke said.

'I love her clothes!' Emily said, turning towards him, outraged. 'Lola without her clothes would be, well, not just without clothes, but not Lola, if you know what I mean.' She was now bright red.

Luke laughed. 'I'm teasing you. Her clothes are really cool. She's a whizz on the computer too. Much better than any of the other ladies.'

'She could beat some of the winemakers hands down as well, with her palate,' Emily said. 'She's my number-one tester for any of my new drinks.'

'I love those drinks you do. I've got a great palate too,' Luke said. 'Can I be your number-two tester?'

'Sure,' Emily said. If it was possible to turn an even brighter red, she managed it.

Luke parked right in front of the charity shop. Their car was the only one on the street. 'She mustn't be here,' he said. 'I guess she's at the cemetery after all.'

Emily had gone around the corner to look up the side street. The car was there. 'That's it, isn't it? That green one?'

It was, Luke agreed. 'She'll have her feet up in the back room, watching old musicals on YouTube, you wait and see,' he said, as they approached the charity shop. He tried the door. It was locked.

They both knocked. 'Lola?' Emily called. 'Are you in there?'

They tried to peer in, but all the thankyou notices made it impossible to see more than a few shadowy outlines.

Luke knocked again. 'Lola? Are you there?'

'Didn't Margaret give you her keys?'

It was Luke's turn to go red. He opened the door and let Emily go in first. She fanned her face. 'It's like a sauna in here.'

'It's like a sauna everywhere,' Luke said. 'Lola?'

No answer.

'Don't say we've just missed her,' Emily said. 'Could she have gone out the back door?'

They reached the curtain separating the shop from the computer area. Luke pulled it back. Lola wasn't there. Nothing was there, except a bare table and one chair.

'Bloody hell,' he said. 'Where's the computer gone?'

Emily stopped short behind him, just as shocked. 'No one took it home for Christmas? For safekeeping?'

Luke shook his head. 'We've always left it here. Every weekend. It was as safe here as anywhere else, we always thought. Right on the main street.'

'Maybe Lola's borrowed it?' Emily said. 'That could be why she's here?'

'She wouldn't know how to unplug it all. And where is she?' He called her name again, going out into the shop, looking behind the racks, the counter, in the changing room. 'Nothing else is taken. Just the computer stuff.' He called her name again. No answer.

Emily was checking under the table, as if she would find all the equipment there. 'Who would steal from a charity shop? At Christmas?'

Luke came back out into the shop, his phone to his ear. 'Mum, we're at the shop. Lola's not here and nor is the computer, the printer, none of it . . . Stolen. I'll call the police in a sec, yep. No, the front door was locked, nothing forced. The back door's locked again too.' He tried to open it. It was shut fast. 'I'll check the gate. They must have got in that way.'

He asked Emily to hold the phone while he fumbled with the bunch of keys Margaret had given him. After three false tries, he found one that fitted into the back door lock. It turned but the door didn't open. 'Something's wrong with it,' he said.

'Something's wrong with the back door,' Emily reported to Patricia. 'Hold on. Luke's going to give it a kick.'

It took him three heavy kicks to loosen it. On the fourth kick, there was a crashing sound as the door flung open, smashing against the wall outside. The heat streamed in. Emily dropped the phone as she and Luke saw the same thing at once.

Lola huddled in a corner of the yard, her face and body covered by a silver scarf.

As they rushed to her side, she lifted it up and gave them a weak smile.

'Luke and Emily. I'm so glad to see you both.'

Between them, they helped Lola to Luke's car. She insisted she was fine, just hot and thirsty. The scarf had saved her, she kept saying. But she could barely stand, they could both see that. She was talking too quickly, not making complete sense, telling them about Ellen and photographs and two men and the computer being taken, how sorry she was, how she could have tried to stop them, but there were two of them, so she'd hidden, and her bag was gone, her phone – they took her camera too, she thought . . . She suddenly broke off and gazed at them both. 'How did you know I was here? How did you find me?'

'It was Luke,' Emily said. 'He rang everyone.'

'But why? How?'

'Later, Lola,' Luke said, with a glance at Emily. 'I'll explain it all later.'

'Don't worry, Lola,' Emily said. 'We're here now. We'll take care of you.'

'Emily's right, Lola,' Luke said. 'You're safe now.' His voice was calm, but his expression was as concerned as Emily's. 'Heatstroke?' he mouthed to her.

'I think so,' Emily mouthed back.

Despite Lola's protests, Luke told her gently and firmly that they were taking her to the hospital.

Emily knew the sister in charge of the emergency room. While Luke helped Lola with her admission details, Emily filled her in on what had happened.

'Nearly three hours out in that heat? At eighty-four? She's lucky she's alive.'

'She'll be fine, won't she?'

They glanced over, in time to see Luke and the admissions clerk laugh at something Lola said. She'd rallied since they'd brought her into the cool of the hospital. 'It's some kind of miracle, but yes, I think she will be. How on earth did you know she was there?'

Emily told her all she knew. 'Luke got a call. An old friend of Lola's was looking for her. When she didn't answer her phone we all went searching.'

'She's a lucky lady. That old friend might have saved her life.'

The reception area in the hospital was soon crowded with Lola's friends. They divided the phone calls between them. Margaret rang Bett, Kay rang Jim, Patricia rang Carrie.

Margaret went into Lola's room to share the news. All of her family were on their way back home.

Lola wasn't happy. 'No. I'm fine. I'm fine. Please, tell them to stay where they are. They need a holiday.'

'I said that's what you'd say. But they insisted.'

'And I insist even more insistently that they don't come back. Please, Margaret, call them again.'

'You're not supposed to use mobile phones in a hospital.'

Lola gave her a glare. Margaret passed over her phone.

Lola spoke to Jim first.

He was adamant. 'It doesn't matter what you say, Lola. We're on our way back already.'

'No. Jim, please, don't. I'm better off here than I was even in the motel. People everywhere, even if some of them are dressed as nurses and doctors. I'm fine. I really am fine.'

'We're only two hours away. We'll see for ourselves and then if we really think you're fine, we'll go away again.'

'But you won't. You'll get in a fuss. And Geraldine will be cross.'

'Geraldine won't be cross. We'll see you tonight.'

Bett had already started packing up the car. 'Oh, sure, Lola. As if we can carry on with our holiday and forget you're in hospital.'

'I'll be out of here within an hour. Your parents are already on their way. If you come back too, I won't talk to you. I mean it, Bett. I'm fine. Nothing bad happened.'

'It could have.'

'It didn't. Darling, please, be practical about it. I'm surrounded by friends. If anything does happen to me over the next few days, which it won't, I'm in the best possible company. Everywhere I look there is someone staring back at me as if they're willing me to drop dead.'

Around her bed, Margaret, Kay, Joan and Patricia all looked at their feet.

Lola winked at them and kept talking. 'You'd only have to join a queue to come and gaze at me in a worried way, Bett. I'm fine, darling. F. I. N. E. Old, but fine. See you in three days' time, as we arranged, okay?'

Carrie was more matter-of-fact. 'Lola, Dad says you sound pretty good, all things considered, and he and Mum are on their way back already. Do you want us there as well?'

'No, darling. I really don't.'

'Thank God for that. That car trip here was a nightmare. I'd hate to turn around and do it again already.'

'That's my girl,' Lola said. 'See you next week.'

After a series of tests and examinations, Lola was pronounced well enough to go home that night, once the doctor gave her a final check. He was due to call to her room before six p.m. There was a discussion that almost turned into an argument about where she should go after that – to Margaret's, Kay's, Joan's or Patricia's. Lola put a stop to it herself.

'I'm going to my home. The motel. You can all please visit me tomorrow but I will be very happy in my own room tonight. Jim and Geraldine will be there too, remember.'

'But won't you be scared in your room on your own?' Kay asked. 'After what happened?'

Lola was refusing to dwell on what had happened, or what might have happened. She was fine. She was safe. She was well. She was also already too conscious of spoiling all her friends' Christmas Day celebrations. 'It takes more than that to scare me. Please, all of you, off you go home. My friends Luke and Emily will take me home, won't you, dears?' Two nods. 'Tomorrow I'd adore some company, so I insist you all come and have a game of cards or bridge or a large glass of gin with me. Tonight, however, I will go back to my own room, lock my door, hop into bed and sleep, perchance to dream. That's a quote from *Hamlet*, by the way. I'm demonstrating my mental agility with the spontaneous quoting of Shakespeare.'

She finally convinced her friends to leave. Only Luke and Emily remained in her room. Was this the moment she'd been waiting for? she wondered. She'd already noticed the two of them talking and laughing with each other that afternoon. Every cloud – in this case, their rescue mission – had a silver lining indeed. Perhaps, just perhaps, she didn't need to say anything more. Perhaps, if it was meant to be between them, it would unfold in its own good time.

But it wouldn't hurt to give it a little nudge along, would it? 'Emily, dear, would you please go and ask the nurse if it will be okay for me to have a gin tonight? They're insisting I rehydrate. I just want to be sure that means all liquids, not just water.'

Once Emily was out of earshot, Lola fixed Luke in her sights. 'Luke, there's a lot to ask you, but just for now, just quickly, while we have a moment alone together —'

'Lola, please, I need to tell you something first. While we're on our own —'

She held up her hand. 'I'm the one who nearly died today. My turn first. I'll be quick, we haven't got long.'

'Lola, I mean it. I need to tell you something important, it's about A—'

'Luke, please, listen to me. I just have one simple question. How do you feel about Emily?'

Up came his blush. 'She's lovely. I've always really liked her. She's so easy to talk to. But Lola —'

'As a friend or as something more? Please excuse my bluntness. She'll be back any second.'

The blush deepened. 'I don't think she'd be interested in me. I've wanted to ask her out for ages but I haven't in case she said no.'

Lola timed it perfectly. Over Luke's shoulder, she could see Emily coming along the corridor towards her room. 'Emily say no if you were to ask her out? Emily? Turn you down?' she spoke a little more loudly with each word. 'I don't think that will happen. Emily thinks you're the bees' knees. Don't you, Emily?'

Both Luke and Emily were now a blazing, burning bright red. Lola shut her eyes. 'Now, I'm just going to lie here and have a little rest to myself before the doctor comes. So how about you both go out into the garden or take a little stroll into town and hopefully by the time you come back to collect me at six you'll have had the chance to talk about all sorts of things, including where you might go on your first date.'

Luke and Emily had just stepped outside the front door of the hospital when his phone rang. He took it out, didn't recognise the number, but answered it.

'Luke? This is Alex. Lola's friend. I'm sorry to bother you again, but were you able to contact Lola?'

'Alex!' Excusing himself and moving out of Emily's earshot, he hurriedly told him everything that had happened that day. 'We have you to thank. If you hadn't been trying to ring her —'

Alex interrupted, his tone urgent. 'Was she hurt? Did they do anything to her?'

'She's fine,' Luke said. 'Really, she is. She's incredible.'

'Can I talk to her?'

'Of course. Of *course*.' He explained to Emily that he'd be right back.

In her room, Lola was still lying on the bed, her eyes shut.

Luke spoke softly. 'Lola?'

She kept her eyes closed. 'Yes, darling.'

'I'm sorry to disturb you, but I've got someone on the phone who wants to talk to you.'

'Who is it, pet?'

'It's Alex.'

Lola's eyes opened wide.

CHAPTER TWENTY

Lola had just settled into her motel room when she heard a car drive up. Moments later, her son was at the door. He walked in, and gave her one of the biggest hugs he'd given her in years. Geraldine followed him in. She didn't hug Lola, but she touched her hand gently, before offering to go and make them all tea. Lola gratefully accepted.

'That's the last time I leave you alone for Christmas,' Jim said, pulling up a chair to his mother's bedside. 'Not just for Christmas. For any day.'

'Don't be silly, Jim. Did you find a new guesthouse?'

'Lola, forget the guesthouse. What were you thinking going down there like that? Can't you see how dangerous that situation was? What might have happened?'

'I could have been attacked, do you mean? Could have died out in that yard? Yes, Jim. As you and Geraldine could have died if you'd had a car accident rushing back to see me. As Bett might die if she's eaten by a shark during her beach holiday. Or Carrie might die if she, I don't know, has an allergic reaction to her face cream.'

'Lola —'

'Jim, my little Jim, I didn't die. You don't need to scold me like a child. I am fine. Truly. I moved around the yard with the shade. I called for help as often as I could. I had my scarf to protect me. Yes, granted, I was getting very thirsty and that mop bucket wasn't at all comfortable to sit on, but I felt sure I'd be rescued eventually. And I wasn't scared. I had someone to talk to and keep me company —'

'To talk to? I thought no one could hear you?'

'I talked to Anna the entire time. I told her that it was up to her to send someone to find me, and would she please make it snappy, that I was damned if I was going to end my days in some shabby yard at the back of a shop. I told her I'd much rather go out with a gin in my hand and a song in my heart.'

'And did Anna talk back?'

Lola smiled. 'You think I'm delirious, don't you? No, darling, she didn't. I do both parts when I talk to Anna. Which I do often. I've done it since she died. It gives me great comfort. It would give me even greater comfort if she spoke her own lines sometimes, but perhaps I'd be more shocked than delighted if she did. I'm not sure I believe in ghosts. I'm not even sure if I believe in heaven. But I do believe she is somewhere, and she is happy, and for the sake of not knowing a better word for it, then I'll call it heaven for now.'

Jim wasn't in the mood for a theological discussion. 'All I can say is thank goodness for Luke and Emily. How on earth did they know you were there? Why did they go looking for you in the first place?'

Lola hesitated, then decided to tell him the truth. Her conversation with Alex still felt like her own special secret, but Jim needed to know the facts. Quickly and concisely, she explained all that had happened to lead Luke and Emily to her today. Jim listened intently.

'You don't remember Alex, do you?' she said afterwards. 'I wondered if you would, but you were only a little boy at the time. He was a very dear friend of mine, Jim. After your father died' – she was still amazed at how easily she had kept up that lie, and how little it mattered that it had been a lie all those years – 'Alex was the only man I ever really loved. If he hadn't had to go back to Italy,' she paused, 'well, who knows what might have happened.'

'And are you going to see him again? Meet up with him? After all these years?'

Lola laughed. 'You sound very protective, darling. Worried in case he is after my vast, sorry, my non-existent fortune?'

'No. Worried in case he's not good enough for my mother.'

'I'll wait and see. He and I need to have a few more conversations first. If the time is right, and if it also feels right, I'll fly him in and parade him in front of you for your inspection and approval. Or fly all of you over to Melbourne to inspect him in his natural habitat.'

'I got a fright today, Lola. When I first got the phone call from Kay.'

'They had me on death's door and all of that?' At Jim's nod, Lola smiled. 'They did seem a bit excitable. Too much sherry in their Christmas trifles, I suspect. But I'm a long way from death's door yet, Jim, I hope. And you too, I hope even more. So let's cheer ourselves up, fill our days with wine and song, and oh, yes, start thinking about a special event coming up. In – let me just check my calendar – about six days' time.'

'A special event?'

'I suppose special guest might be a more accurate word to use. We'll prepare room nine, I think. Or perhaps seven. That gets beautiful morning light, doesn't it? No rush about deciding yet, though. You and Geraldine have to go back and finish your driving holiday first, after all. And find a new place to live. As do I. We are in for a busy end-of-year, aren't we?'

'Lola, what are you talking about now? Special guest? I thought you said Alex wouldn't be coming yet.'

'He's not. It's far too soon for him and me. Darling, weren't you listening to a word I said? This is a really, really special guest. A twelve-year-old one from a far and distant land, coming to celebrate the start of a new year with us all.' She smiled as it dawned on him. 'Yes, Jim. Ellen.'

She told him everything that had been going on with Ellen and Glenn in Hong Kong. Afterwards, Jim insisted on cancelling his holiday. How could he leave Lola alone again, not knowing what she might get up to next?

Lola insisted he go. They compromised. He and Geraldine would stay that night and if Lola was still in fine enough form the next morning, then they would continue their break. He was worried that her apparent good humour was all the adrenaline rushing through her veins. That as soon as she stopped, as soon as it all sank in, she would collapse.

'You really don't have any faith in the restorative effects of a well-mixed gin and tonic, do you, Jim?' she said, as he prepared it for her.

'Lola, you don't have to joke with me. I know it must have been a frightening day.'

'It was, yes, but now the fright has passed. Thank you, darling, for rushing to my rescue, even if the rescue had already been done. I will sleep easy knowing you're here tonight. But not tomorrow night. I want you out of my sight by then.'

She waited until he had gone before she lay down and once again closed her eyes. She didn't even take a sip of her drink. It took only a minute before the tears she'd been holding back all day started to well up and make their way down her face.

She turned up the music on her radio to cover the sound of her sobbing. Her tears ran unchecked. What a terrible, terrible day that had been. She'd never been so frightened in her life. From the moment she'd heard the two men start to break in, until Luke and Emily appeared, she'd truly believed her time had come. She wasn't ready to die. She had so much she still wanted to do, so much to think about, so much to tell her son, her granddaughters, her great-grandchildren. If the worst had happened, if the two men had found her, attacked her . . . She started to shake again at the thought. She had an active imagination at the best of times, but in recent years she'd read too many reports of elderly women being bashed, or worse, assaulted in different ways . . . *Stop it, Lola!* It hadn't happened. Through some miracle or luck, they hadn't found her. And through some miracle or luck, a chain of events had unfolded and Luke and Emily had rescued her from the yard before she'd suffered anything more serious than a bad thirst and an uncomfortable behind from sitting perched on a mop bucket for too long.

It had almost felt like being at her own funeral, having everyone rush to her side like that, their concern, their phone calls, all of them telling her how awful they'd have felt if anything had happened to her, how much they cared about her. Tomorrow that might make her feel good. Tonight it just made her want to cry even more.

And then, on top of everything, to have spoken to Alex.

Nothing about the circumstances had been ideal. But just to hear his voice! It was as if the years had turned back, as if she was that young woman in Brighton and he was the young man, ringing as he so often had, to invite her to meet him for coffee, for a meal, for a few hours away together. He still had a trace of the Italian accent amid the perfect English. His voice sounded older, but of course, he was older.

They had only spoken for five minutes. She could recall every word, but right now, she didn't want to think over each sentence, investigate them for more meaning. He'd said two words, several times, that had meant the most to her. *I'm sorry.*

It was as if he had been waiting all those years to say them. The words she'd wanted to hear when she first got his letter telling her that he couldn't come back.

I'm sorry.

She hadn't expected their first conversation to go straight to the heart of their friendship. But she was glad of it. She matched his honesty with a question of her own.

'Were you happy with her, Alex?'

'I was, Lola. We had a good life. Two beautiful daughters.'

'Tell me about them.' She didn't want to hear about his good life with his wife, not yet.

He told her about Rosie and Lucia. About his grandchildren. About the decision to move back to Australia ten years earlier, after his wife's death.

To anyone else, she would have expressed sympathy. Now, she stayed silent.

He spoke again. 'And you, Lola? Have you been happy?'

Did he mean had she remarried? Had more children? They knew nothing about each other, she realised. It was too soon to share everything. Not the right time, either. She kept her answer simple and truthful. 'Most of the time, yes, very. Sometimes, no.'

'The perfect life, then?'

She'd smiled into the phone. 'Yes, I think so.' She heard another voice then, someone calling him. *Papa*. It was Christmas Day, after all. A family day. 'You should go, Alex.'

'Can I ring you again?'

She thought about it for several long seconds. Was it foolish to make a connection with him again, after so many years? What would they have to say to each other after any initial exchange of news? Would every conversation be filled with regret for their separate lives? Perhaps. But there was only one way to find out.

'Of course,' she'd said.

He'd asked if he could call at six thirty the following night. Old Alex wasn't so different from young Alex, so courteous, so precise with his arrangements.

'I'll look forward to it,' she'd said.

The last of her tears slowed now at the thought of him. She wasn't being silly. She knew they wouldn't be able to turn back time. She knew they wouldn't be able to recapture their lost years. But that afternoon, when she had been at her most scared, she'd made a promise to herself. It had been an hour into her ordeal, outside under the hot sun, trying to stay calm, to remain positive, to have hope. She'd turned to Anna.

'I'm in a bit of a fix, Anna.'

It's not an ideal situation, Lola, no.

'Am I going to get out of here?'

Of course you are. And when you do, you have to make sure to seize every moment you can, enjoy every second you're given, and regret nothing. Promise me, Lola.

'I promise, Anna.'

She knew it hadn't been Anna reaching out to her from the grave. She'd been talking to herself. But she would still do as she'd said. Not dwell on sad times. Keep looking forward. Grab every experience she could, while there was still time and while she still had her wits about her. She'd keep that promise, if it was the last thing she did.

CHAPTER TWENTY-ONE
New Year's Eve

'One, two, three, four, five . . . How many of us are there, Really-Great-Gran?'

'Thirteen, darling. Oh, you've done a lovely job folding the napkins, Ellen, thank you. Are they swans or pigeons?'

'Lola! They're bishops' hats.'

'Sorry, darling. My eyesight has got so bad lately.'

'If you take off those glasses you might be able to see better.'

Lola took off the diamante-framed oversized glasses she'd been wearing for the past hour. They'd been a Christmas gift from Carrie. Lola thought they went very well with the feathered and jewelled fascinator Bett had bought her. They'd all opened their presents to each other just that morning, as soon as Daniel had arrived back from the airport with their guest of honour, Ellen. The dining room of the motel had been a hubbub of noise since, filled with every member of the family: Jim, Geraldine, Bett, Daniel, Zachary, Yvette, Carrie, Matthew, Delia, Freya and George – and Ellen, of course. Lola had revelled in every squeal, shout and exclamation, content in her chair in the centre of the room, with the perfect view of the Christmas tree in the corner and the blue sky and vineyards through the window.

It was as if Ellen had been there with them for weeks. She'd fitted back in so quickly and easily. She was taller, thinner, growing more like Anna every day. Her face was as beautiful as ever, the scar barely visible these days. Ellen was certainly no longer self-conscious about it. She was like a little dragonfly, Lola thought, flitting from person to person, playing with her cousins, talking to her grandparents, hanging onto her aunts' hands, coming back to Lola herself each time. 'I'm not even tired, Lola, and I've been awake for hours!'

Later, when it was a bit cooler, they'd all go to visit Anna and have their customary glass of champagne in her honour at the graveside. For the time being, Lola was keeping Ellen busy setting the table under the trees, on the spot where she had planned to serve the Christmas lunch-that-never-happened. She hadn't told her family about her thwarted plans. Less said the better, she'd decided. They'd all started watching her like hawks as it was. As if she was going to take a notion to get herself locked into a sun-baked yard again.

Not that such a thing would ever happen again. The day after Boxing Day, once word had spread around town about the robbery and what had happened to Lola, the shop's handyman had been in to repair the broken door and to fit a different bolt to the yard gate. Lola herself had been interviewed by the police. The computer equipment hadn't been found and wasn't likely to be, unfortunately. Whoever had stolen it, locals or otherwise, would have already sold it on or were using it themselves, the police thought. Just as unfortunately, the loss wasn't covered by any insurance. The committee had made a decision not to take out contents insurance the previous year. It hadn't seemed worth it – the only contents were second-hand goods, after all. But less than a week on from the robbery, before the shop had even reopened after the Christmas break, every piece of equipment had been replaced, free of charge. Margaret had taken the first of the calls, then Kay, then Patricia. Person after person ringing to donate computer parts and equipment. They'd unanimously put Luke in charge of everything. He was their computer guru, after all.

For the time being, Luke was storing everything at his mother's house. It was already taking up most of one of the spare bedrooms: a nearly new computer, a second-hand camera, a printer and a scanner. 'We got a new one for Christmas. You're welcome to this old one,' one of the donors had said. The donations had kept coming in, even after they had more than enough to rebuild the charity shop setup. So many donations, in fact, that it looked like they'd be able to set up another Mission Control in the local old folks' home and possibly the library as well.

Lola had been to the old folks' home the previous day, allegedly to inspect a location for the computer equipment. The truth was she had been inspecting possible new living arrangements for herself.

She knew Jim would have been horrified if he'd known. The day he and Geraldine had returned from their driving holiday – two days earlier than expected – Jim had come to her room to see how she was.

'Darling, you know how I am. You've rung five times every day.'

He'd told her that he and Geraldine had seen several guest-houses they'd been interested in, but that they had decided to put their moving plans on hold.

'Why?' Lola said, already suspecting the answer.

'After what happened to you, we just don't think we need to be in any hurry.'

'What nonsense,' she said. 'If anything, it should give you more reason to move. The Valley is clearly a hotbed of crime.' She took pity on him then, and smiled. 'Darling, nothing happened to me. How many times do I have to tell you? Please, go ahead with your plans. Move tomorrow, if you find the right place, and I'll manage the sale of the motel for you. In the meantime, I'm having great fun trying to decide where I'll rest my weary bones once you're both gone.'

She'd spoken to the sister in charge of the old folks' home. She'd even read their brochure, from cover to cover. It had a great deal going for it. It was clean and bright and she knew lots of people there. She had been on the verge of having her name added to the waiting list when Margaret called to the motel for an afternoon game of cards in the dining room.

Between games, Lola told her everything about Jim and Geraldine moving. 'I'm thinking the best place for me is the old folks' home,' Lola told her.

Margaret had immediately disagreed. 'I can't see you there at all. You need your independence.'

'For now, perhaps. In a year or so, all I'll need are waterproof sheets and a bib.'

'Lola, stop it. I'm going to ask you something and I want you to think about it, not just say no immediately. Why don't you come and live with me? I've plenty of room in my house. All at ground level, too. No steps. I'd love your company.'

'Margaret, I'm an old lady.'

'I'm headed that way myself.'

'I'm not getting any younger. Or sprightlier.'

'Thank God for that. I have enough trouble keeping up with you as it is.'

'But you've lived alone for years. An occasional visit from me is one thing, but as a permanent fixture?'

Margaret laughed. 'Lola, I'm not a student asking you to come and share my bedsit. I've *heaps* of room.'

It was true. Lola had been to Margaret's many times. It was a large house with four bedrooms, in a lovely part of town, looking over hills and vineyards.

'You want to be my landlady?'

'Yes, and I'd inspect your room every Sunday. Lola, of course not. We'd be flatmates.'

'Like Felix and Oscar in *The Odd Couple*?'

'I hope not. You're not obsessively tidy or extravagantly messy, are you?'

'Neither. I'm extremely housetrained.' She'd had to be, all

these years of living in motel rooms and having to be ready to move out at a moment's notice if a paying guest wanted the room. 'I'd pay you rent, of course. At the going rate.'

'What on earth would I do with rent money? Spend it on drugs? Lola, you could contribute towards the food and the bills, but why would I charge you rent? Seriously, isn't it the perfect solution?' Margaret launched into a very persuasive sales pitch. They were old friends. They were both widows. They had plenty in common – books, music, people, their soon-to-be-launched Baby Squad. The house had two living areas, a large garden. They also knew each other well enough to be able to say if something was annoying them about the other, surely?

She'd told Margaret she wanted to sleep on it. She'd gone to her room, lain on her bed, talked about it with Anna, had a quick nap and then rung Margaret to accept her offer. She'd move in at the end of January, they decided. It would give Jim and Geraldine the freedom to really plan their next step. She'd tell everyone after the new year celebrations. For now, she and Margaret would keep it to themselves.

'What would you like for entrée, Lola?' Ellen had now finished folding serviettes and was in waitress mode, going from family member to family member taking orders. 'Prawn cocktail or melon and ham?'

'Prawns please, darling. Thank you.'

Lola watched, smiling, as Ellen went over to Bett and Carrie next. The two sisters had been talking and laughing most of the morning. It was good to see them getting on so well. It wouldn't last, of course, but a ceasefire, however temporary, was always welcome. Perhaps once the Baby Squad got into full swing they might use some of their new spare time to meet for coffee. Lola doubted it, mind you. In her experience, from her own time as a young mother and many decades of watching other mothers at work, spare time was a thing of the past until the children were in their twenties.

'Cold drink, Lola?' It was Geraldine. She had been surprisingly solicitous since her and Jim's return. The thought that Lola had nearly died? Or the knowledge that freedom was just a few weeks away? A combination of both, perhaps.

'Tonic water would be lovely, thank you, Geraldine. I don't really like the taste, though, so perhaps you'd put a drop or two of gin in it as well. And some ice. And some lemon.'

Lola could have sworn she nearly saw Geraldine smile.

See, Anna. I'm trying. So is she.

Good girls, Anna said.

Jim came in, carrying the portable phone. 'Call for you, Lola.'

Ellen frowned. 'We're about to have lunch. You won't be long, Really-Great-Gran, will you? Who is it?'

'It's her boyfriend,' Bett said with a smile.

'He rings every day. Sometimes twice,' Carrie said.

'*Boyfriend?*' Ellen's voice went up an octave.

'Wrong word, Ellen. Sorry,' Bett said. 'He's too old to be her boyfriend.'

'Her old-man-friend?' Carrie suggested.

'What's he like?' Ellen said, eyes shining. 'Is he cute?'

Lola ignored all of them and took the phone over to a corner of the room.

'Hello, darling,' she said.

EPILOGUE

Four months later

'Are you okay, Lola?'

She smiled at her son sitting on the plane beside her. 'I'm fine, darling.'

'Not too tired? It was an early start.'

'I enjoyed it.' Bett and Carrie had collected her from Margaret's house at six a.m. The sun had started to rise as they came into the town of Auburn, around the sweeping bend of the road, sending shafts of soft light onto the vineyards and the olive trees. They hadn't spoken much. In the back seat of the car, by choice, Lola had enjoyed the quiet murmur of their voices.

Jim and Geraldine were waiting at the airport check-in. It had been less than an hour's drive for them from their new guesthouse in the Adelaide Hills. They'd been there for six weeks. They hadn't sold the Valley View Motel yet, but this new opportunity had been too good to pass up. They'd leased the motel for the time being. Lola had driven past it that morning on the way to Adelaide. She hadn't felt sad to see it. She'd said her goodbyes three months earlier, shed several quiet tears and then turned her energy to making her new house her home.

It was the first flight she'd taken in ten years. It was so beautiful to look out the window, see the sky, the land, the sea, the incredible blue sea, as they lifted off from Adelaide airport.

After a while, she rested her head back and shut her eyes, thinking over all that had happened in the past few months. That's why it was important to live for as long as you could, she thought. You never knew what might happen to change everything, for good or for bad.

Beside her, Bett squeezed her hand.

Lola patted her hand in return. 'Dear Bett,' she said.

She reached down to her handbag and unfolded a piece of paper from inside. It was an email from Ellen that had arrived the previous night. Her Top Ten Tips for a Carefree Flight. If anyone was qualified to give that advice, it was Ellen. She'd taken more flights in her almost thirteen years than all of them put together. Most recently, less than a month ago. She and Glenn had come back to Sydney to live. Lola had been so happy to hear the news. They'd get to see Ellen not once a year, but once a month at least. It was just a short flight from Sydney to Adelaide.

Ellen had already been back to the Clare Valley since her new-year visit, staying for a week in February when Glenn first got news of the job in Sydney and was over for meetings. He was now in charge of the entire Australasian operations of his advertising agency. It felt right to come home, he'd said. Ellen had stayed at the motel while Glenn went house-hunting and school-hunting. He'd found a house with enough room for four.

Denise wouldn't be moving in immediately. She had her own business in Hong Kong to wind down first, and she also wanted Lily to finish her school year.

They'd all been concerned about Ellen's reaction to the news. 'It will be absolutely fine,' she said when Lola asked her, and when Bett, Carrie and Geraldine asked her too. She'd picked up the saying from Lola, they all knew that.

'If you keep saying it often enough, it usually comes true,' Lola had told her.

She'd had trouble getting Ellen's email off her computer the evening before, but Luke had called around and in that calm way of his, fixed the problem, downloaded the email and got the printer working again too. Lola and Margaret both had computers in their rooms. It made sense. The last thing they wanted to do was fall out over who got to spend more time online.

Emily had come with Luke. They went most places together these days, whenever Luke was back in Clare, that was. It looked like being more often. He'd been offered a job in the town's main electrical shop, setting up his own computer department.

'It's all going well between you?' Lola managed to ask Emily when Luke went out to his car to get a spare cable.

Whoosh. Her face turned red.

'I'm glad to see it,' Lola said, smiling. 'So it's serious, do you think?'

More colour rushed into her face. She nodded. 'It's like he's my best friend, except he's a boy,' Emily said, with a kind of amazement. 'We can talk about anything.'

'What a lovely way to be,' Lola said.

Patricia approved of Emily, Lola had been glad to see. As the mother of an only son herself, Lola knew better than most how she might feel about Luke's first serious girlfriend. 'I like her a lot,' Patricia confided. 'Not that I'd say anything if I didn't.'

'We don't need to say anything,' Lola had laughed. 'We do it all with meaningful glances, apparently.'

Lola had reported it all back to Margaret after Luke and Emily left. The pair's budding relationship had been just one of their many conversation topics these past few months. Their living arrangement had worked out better than either of them might have hoped. There had been occasional glitches, of course. Only to be expected, they'd agreed. Two independent women under the same roof. They'd hit on the best way of dealing with them early on. A note left on the kitchen table. 'I'm just no good at confrontation, Lola,' Margaret had said. 'If I had to say it to your face, I'd get in a tizz.'

The problems and the notes had been very mild so far, Lola thought. Their main issue was that Lola was, well, just a little more untidy than Margaret. *Please don't forget to put the milk back in the fridge after you've used it*, Margaret had written once. *Please put the phone back on the cradle after you've finished talking*.

'You're going to find me a handful when I really start losing my marbles and forgetting things, Margaret. I can see the notes now. *Lola, please remember to dress yourself before leaving the house. Lola, have you got your teeth in? Lola, please don't start on the gin before breakfast*.'

Lola had left Margaret only one note, a month after she'd moved in. She'd woken up, gazed out of her window and realised that she felt happy. Safe. Content.

Thank you so much for having me. Sorry about the milk, she'd written.

She'd liked the view from her motel room. The view from her new room at the back of Margaret's house ('It's our house, Lola,' Margaret kept saying, but Lola wasn't used to saying that yet) was twice as beautiful. A glimpse of a dam. A sweep of hillside. A stretch of gum trees. At night time there was the sound of kookaburras. In the morning there were magpies. There was a willy-wagtail that played on the lawn each night. She and Margaret liked their own company, and both had plenty to do outside the house between the Baby Squad and their occasional shifts at the charity shop, but they liked each other's company too. They kept to themselves in the morning, but often met for lunch, and if they felt like it, they'd spend the evening either watching TV or reading or listening to audio books. More often than not, though, they were entertaining.

They had a lot of visitors. Margaret's gate had a slight squeak so they always had warning. Margaret offered to oil it, but Lola stopped her. She loved the sound of it, the anticipation, not knowing who was about to arrive. 'If I can't have a herald blowing a trumpet to signify a new arrival, the squeaky gate will do just fine,' she said.

She'd also had her own phone installed in her room. She'd spent a lot of time on the phone recently. Alex had rung most nights. Sometimes just to say hello. Sometimes to tell a story. Sometimes she rang him.

Early on, they'd cleared the air completely between them. There had been more apologies and explanations from Alex. Acceptance from Lola. There could have been anger, perhaps. She knew that. She could have asked him more questions. 'Why didn't you come back for me?' But they were too old for that. They'd had their lives. Good full lives. What more could either of them have asked for?

In another call, Lola asked him to list all his physical ailments. 'This will be the only time I ever want to hear about them, so please do feel free to go into as much detail as you like.'

He did. She heard that he had hip problems, was on three different sorts of tablets, had had a couple of skin cancer scares, and his hearing wasn't the best these days. She'd sympathised and then told him, in warm but firm tones, that she never wanted to waste any more talking time on medical matters. 'That's why God invented doctors, Alex. To keep friendships like ours alive.'

He read to her sometimes, or she read to him. She was half-way through reading him a Robert Ludlum thriller. He'd sent it to her for her eighty-fifth birthday in February. She was enjoying his reading of an Agatha Christie novel.

He knew all about her family. About Anna's death. About Carrie and Bett's relationship. About Lola's relationship, or lack of relationship, with Geraldine. She knew about his family. That Rosie worked too hard. That Lucia was having a few marital problems. They talked about their friends. He asked about Margaret, Kay, Patricia and Joan. She asked him about the weekly gatherings at the Italian-Australian Association. Their conversations weren't always long. Sometimes they lasted less than five minutes, or even shorter. 'Lola, it's me. I'm doing a crossword. What's a six-letter word for a wading bird?' 'Alex, it's me. What was the name of that opera you were telling me about?'

They hadn't met in person. What was the rush? they'd decided. Why go to all the bother of flights and driving and sitting in airports just so they could see each other and talk? They already knew what each other looked like. Yes, perhaps they would like to have held hands, perhaps even kissed, but really, at their age, what else?

'Talking is the new sex,' Lola said to Bett. Bett looked quite shocked.

'There's plenty of room for him to stay here too,' Margaret said, the week after Lola moved in with her. 'If you want him to come and visit. There's another spare bedroom.'

'He wouldn't need it. He'd sleep with me.'

Margaret had looked a bit shocked too. What was it with these young people?

Lola had enjoyed telling Alex about the Baby Squad too. Not that she was in charge of it any more. They'd been meeting at the charity shop one afternoon to see if any of the other retired ladies or even a few of the men might like to become squad members, when Mrs Kernaghan swept in. She'd become very vocal with her ideas, suggesting that they think about copyrighting the name Baby Squad and drawing up a list of rules and regulations. One week later, they'd opened the *Valley Times* to find a long article and interview with Mrs Kernaghan extolling the virtues of the squad, how it was all about the older generation sharing knowledge with the younger generation, fostering community links and adding to the health and wellbeing of generations of women. 'Charity is all very well, but it has to start at home, literally,' Mrs Kernaghan was quoted as saying. 'What could be more important than giving the young mothers and children of our beautiful Valley all the help we can?'

Bett hadn't known anything about the interview. 'I think she wrote the article herself,' she said.

Bett was still working at the newspaper one day a week. She'd come to a paid arrangement with her neighbour Jane to mind the twins while she worked. The Baby Squad still did regular housework raids on her house, though. Daniel was full-time at his job. The new setup was doing them both good, in Lola's opinion. Bett was herself again, bright-eyed and happy. When she spoke about the twins, it was to share funny stories, and not with a look of fear and panic. She still complained about Carrie. But then Carrie still complained about her, too.

'Can't you just complain directly to each other?' Lola said once. 'Cut out the middleman?'

Carrie and Matthew were fine too, Lola knew. A marriage on traditional lines, Carrie the housewife, Matthew the breadwinner. It wouldn't have been Lola's choice, but it seemed to suit them. In the past month, Carrie had also started selling make-up on the side. 'Marvellous idea! Play to your strengths,' Lola had said when Carrie called around to Margaret's – to Lola and Margaret's – to give them a free demonstration of the products. She'd been a bit too light-handed, Lola had thought – what was the point of wearing make-up if the effect was subtle and 'barely there', as Carrie had put it, reciting the lines. Lola had reapplied a few more layers after Carrie left.

In recent weeks, the weather had started to turn cooler. After the long hot summer, the autumn was spectacular, the vines bright red and orange. She'd described it to Alex. They often spoke about the places they'd both lived in and visited, cities he'd been to around the world, or towns in Australia she and Jim had worked in. Places they'd both like to visit. 'Where will we go this week?' she'd ask. She'd pick a city, Venice or San Francisco. Next time they spoke he'd have a few facts about each place to tell her.

In the past month they'd spoken more about meeting up in person. In the Clare Valley or in Melbourne? Melbourne, they decided.

'Wouldn't it be fun to go to Brighton one more time?' he'd said. 'Re-enact that day we had, perhaps?'

Alex told her that his daughter Rosie had said she'd collect Lola from the airport and drive her and Alex anywhere they wanted to go. Rosie had said the same thing to Lola, when she answered the phone once. Lola liked the way she called her father Papa. 'Papa always met me whenever I came home from any trip, and he always drove me to any place I needed to go, too. It'll be good to return the favour.'

The flight to Melbourne was only an hour long. She should have come long before today. Should have, could have, would have. Didn't. And there it was. She couldn't change anything. She couldn't make time stand still, go backwards or slow down and let her savour good times. She just had to go where it took her.

'Stop saying sorry,' she'd said to Alex during their fifth, or perhaps it was their sixth, phone call. 'We can't change anything. Let's just be glad we've got this chance to talk again.'

But if it was possible, of course there were things she would change in her life. Anna's death, first and foremost. If there'd been anything she could have done to stop that happening, she'd have done it. It still made no sense. Nothing had ever seemed so unfair, for Anna, for Ellen. For any of them.

And if she could stop the pain she knew Alex's family would be feeling now, she'd have liked to have done that too.

Rosie's call had come before ten a.m., three days earlier. Lola had spoken to Alex the night before, for an hour. They'd discussed politics, argued about religion, talked about their families and finally said goodbye.

'Talk to you again tomorrow,' he'd said. 'Goodnight, Lola.'

'Goodnight, Alex.'

They didn't say 'I love you', but she knew she loved him and she knew he loved her. When you got to their age, you knew these things.

The call had come in on her mobile phone. 'Lola, it's Rosie.'

'Rosie!' Her voice sounded strange, as if she had a cold. 'Darling, are you all right?'

'It's Papa. Lola, it's Papa. He's —'

'He's what, Rosie?' *Please be sick, Alex. Be sick, be in hospital, be in an ambulance, be anything but —*

'He's dead.' Rosie was crying so hard she could barely speak. 'He died in his sleep. I went down this morning and he —'

Lola waited. She didn't breathe, didn't move. She just waited.

Rosie couldn't stop crying. 'Lola, I'm so sorry. I'll have to call you back.'

Lola stayed where she was. For the next hour, she sat there on her bed, the phone beside her, waiting for Rosie to call back. She didn't cry. Not yet. She didn't go out to the kitchen, though she could hear Margaret moving around, hear the kettle boiling. As she waited for Rosie to ring again, she sat still, listening to all the sounds of life around her. The birds outside her window. A tune playing faintly on the radio. She wouldn't cry. She wouldn't. Not yet.

Rosie was only slightly calmer when she called back. 'I'm so sorry, Lola. I'm so sorry.'

Lola chose to believe she was apologising for crying. 'You mustn't say sorry for that. Of course you have to cry. You have to make all the noise you can about your papa, laugh and shout and cry and —'

'He was so happy these last few months. He was happy anyway but he was different happy. He loved talking to you so much. Thank you, Lola.'

'You don't have to thank me. It was the easiest thing in the world.' She said it out loud then for the first time. 'I loved your father very much, Rosie.'

The words triggered Rosie's tears again. 'I don't want him to be dead, Lola. I want him here. I want him back.'

She was saying all the things Lola couldn't yet, putting words to her feelings. It made it easier to hear Rosie say them, to be the one saying the soothing things, to tell her that Alex had said so many times how much he loved his daughters, his whole family, how proud he was of them, the joy they'd brought him.

'Will you come to his funeral, Lola? Please. So we can meet you?'

'Of course,' she'd said.

She cried alone, many times, during the three days that followed that call. She cried for all that would be lost to her and Alex now, the conversations, the memories. She cried for their lost years. For the lonely nights that she knew would now lie ahead.

She also cried tears of gratitude. For the unexpectedness of life, bringing them back together again, even briefly. For all the small, seemingly unconnected events that had come together to allow her and Alex to reconnect. She traced it back and back, marvelling even through her grief. If Patricia and Luke hadn't moved to Clare five years earlier, none of this would have happened. If Luke hadn't become interested in computers, it wouldn't have happened. If he hadn't set up that system in the charity shop for them all, if he hadn't installed that photographic program, if Lola hadn't kept that photo of Alex, if Luke hadn't known how to use the internet to find people, if Alex hadn't tried to ring her on Christmas Day . . .

So many tiny steps coming together to make so many other wonderful things happen. Was it fate, or magic, or both?

As the flight attendant announced they would soon begin their descent into Melbourne, Lola felt a touch on her hand.

'You okay, Mum?' Jim asked.

'I'm fine, darling, thank you.'

She leaned forward and watched through the window as Melbourne appeared in the landscape beneath them. She pictured the scene in the airport, Rosie waiting at the gate, checking the monitors for their flight arrival. She had insisted on coming to collect them. 'Papa would kill me if I didn't,' she'd said.

The next day, after the funeral, Ellen and Glenn would fly into Melbourne airport too. That had been Bett's idea. They were all staying in the same city-centre hotel for three nights. They'd go and see a musical one night. Take a tram ride one day. Perhaps a museum, an art gallery. They would also take a day trip to Brighton together. Bett's idea again. In the past three days, Bett had been a constant presence by Lola's side, listening to her talk about Alex, the man she'd known all those years ago, the man she'd connected with again, too briefly. About all she had loved about him, had been loving again, about what their plans would have been if they had managed to meet in person again.

'Let's still do them,' Bett had said. 'In his memory.'

Lola knew that today would be a very sad day, for Alex's family, for herself. But there would also be laughter too, she hoped.

Shared memories of him – a loved father, grandfather, friend. Perhaps there would even be new friendships made, between her family and Alex's family. And who knew what small event would happen today that would set all sorts of others in train in the future? In the way something as small as a brief conversation in a supermarket queue with Alex fifty years ago had somehow led to her being here, on this plane, her son on one side, her granddaughter on her other side, about to land in Melbourne for his funeral.

Yes, life really could be extraordinary, Lola thought. She gazed around the plane. All these people here together, so ordinary on the surface, but who knew what each of them had done in their lives or hoped to do in the future? She knew a little of what was going on in Bett's head, in Jim's head, in both their lives, but surely they had their secrets from her too? If she was able to ask every single passenger what their greatest hope in life was, or their greatest fear, would there be hundreds of different answers? She was sure of it. And what about all the hotel guests she had met in her life? People she'd had the briefest of dealings with, a greeting at the reception desk, a casual conversation in the dining room? All those different lives and loves and fears and hopes and dreams. Perhaps it was as well people kept their inner lives secret. Imagine the cacophony if all their hopes and dreams and worries were being broadcast. 'Will I ever fall in love?' 'Will I get the job I want?' 'Will I have children?' 'Will I be rich?'

What would be the most common thought? she wondered. 'Will everything be all right?'

There was no way of telling. Lola knew that from experience. But yes, the chances were everything would be all right. It was just a matter of taking the good with the bad – not only in life's experiences, but in the people you met, in the luck you had, in the thoughts you had. There was no secret to a perfect life, because there was no such thing as a perfect life. It was a matter of finding a place for yourself in your own particular galaxy, a spot in your own solar system of family and friends. The freedom to move in and out of each other's orbits, pull towards each other sometimes, away from each other at other times.

That was how it had been for her, Lola realised. For all of her family and friends, too. All of them leading their own separate lives, yet always staying connected. All of them alone, with their own fears and worries and hopes, yet finding comfort, entertainment and, yes, love, in the closeness of others.

The plane began its descent. Lola took Jim's hand and then Bett's hand in hers and squeezed. She felt their squeezes in return.

She didn't know what today would bring, but after eighty-five years, she could predict it a little. There would be sadness and sorrow, but perhaps there would be some happiness and joy too. They would all meet new people. Hear stories. Share thoughts. Eat a little, drink a little.

Lola shut her eyes, knowing one thing for sure. Moment by moment, layer by layer, new memories would be made today, for all of them. And what more could anyone ask of a day – or of life itself – than that?

ACKNOWLEDGMENTS

My big thanks to:

John Neville, Noel Henny, Padraig O'Sullivan, Anthony Murphy, David Healy, Rachel Tys, Marylou Jones, Frances Brennan, Kate Strachan, Dominic McInerney, everyone at the Clare Library in South Australia, especially Heather Lymburn, Candice Ellis, Charles Cooper, Lurlene Simpson, Trish Jones; Val Tilbrook, Claire Giles, Alda Jones, Suzanne Uphill, and all the Friends of the Library, Mayor Allan Aughey, Jo Kelly and all at Melrose Rural Women's Gathering.

My two families, the Drislanes and the McInerneys, and all my friends, with special thanks to Max Fatchen, Austin O'Neill and Lee O'Neill.

My agents: Fiona Inglis, Jonathan Lloyd, Kate Cooper, Gráinne Fox, Christy Fletcher and Anoukh Foerg.

My publishers around the world: everyone at Penguin Australia, especially Ali Watts, Arwen Summers, Gabrielle Coyne, Bob Sessions, Peter Blake, Louise Ryan, Sally Bateman, Carol George and Debbie McGowan; Trisha Jackson, Helen Guthrie, Ellen Wood, David Adamson and all at Pan Macmillan in the UK and Jen Smith and everyone at Random House in the USA.

My big thanks, as ever, to my sister Maura for all the help, laughs and encouragement she gives me.

And finally, and as always, my love and thanks to my husband John.

THE ALPHABET SISTERS

If you enjoyed LOLA'S SECRET, you might
like to read the prequel, THE ALPHABET
SISTERS, first published in 2004.

Anna, Bett and Carrie were childhood singing stars – the Alphabet
Sisters. As adults they haven't spoken for years. Not since Bett's
fiancé left her for another sister . . .

Now, Lola, their larger-than-life grandmother, summons them
home for a birthday extravaganza and a surprise announcement.
But just as the rifts begin to close, the Alphabet Sisters face a test
none of them ever imagined.

An unforgettable story of three women who learn that being
true to themselves means being true to each other.

'Big-hearted family saga set in Australia, Ireland and London'
Daily Express

The first chapter follows . . .

CHAPTER ONE
London, England

'Your sister is married to your ex-fiancé?' Jessica's voice rose to such a pitch Bett Quinlan half expected the light bulbs to explode. 'We've worked together for nearly two years and you tell me this now?'

Bett knew right then she had made a big mistake. 'It didn't ever really come up until now.'

'Something like that doesn't need to come up. That's something you tell people within minutes of meeting. "Hi, my name's Bett, short for Elizabeth. I work as a journalist in a record company and my sister is married to my ex-husband."'

'Ex-fiancé,' Bett corrected. She tried to backtrack. 'Look, forget I mentioned it. I'm fine about it. She's fine about it. He's fine about it. It's not a big deal.' Liar, liar.

'Of course it's a big deal. It's a huge deal. And they'll both be at your grandmother's party? No wonder you're feeling sick about it.'

'I'm not feeling sick about it. I said I was a bit nervous about going home for it, not sick.'

'Tomato, tomayto. Oh, Bett, you poor thing. Which sister was it? The older one or the younger one?'

'The younger one. Carrie.' Bett felt like the words were being squeezed out of her.

'And what happened? Were they having an affair behind your back? You came home from work early one day and caught them at it in your marital – sorry, engagement – bed?'

'No, it wasn't like that.' Bett stood up. She'd definitely made a mistake. That afternoon at work she'd decided to invite her friend and colleague Jessica back for dinner to tell her the whole story. She'd hoped it would help make this trip back to Australia easier. Prepare her for people's reactions again, like a dress rehearsal. But it wasn't helping at all. It was excruciating. She ran her fingers through her dark curls, trying to take back control of the situation. 'Can I get you a coffee? Another glass of wine?'

'No thanks. Don't change the subject, either. So did you go to the wedding?'

'Would you prefer tea?'

Jessica laughed good-naturedly. 'Come on, Bett. You brought it up in the first place. Think of it as therapy. It can't have been good for you to go around with a secret like this bottled up inside you. Did you go to the wedding?'

Bett sat down again. 'I didn't, no.'

'Well, no, of course you didn't. It would have been too humiliating, I suppose.'

She blinked at Jessica's bluntness.

'Did your sister use the same wedding invitations? Just cross out your name and put hers instead?'

'That's not very funny.'

Jessica gave a sheepish smile. 'Sorry, couldn't resist. So who was the bridesmaid? Your older sister? Anna?'

'No, she wasn't there either.'

Jessica frowned. 'None of her sisters were there? What? Did it cause some huge fight between all three of you?'

In a nutshell, yes. 'It was a bit like that.'

'Really? You haven't spoken to either of your sisters since the wedding?'

'No.' Bett shifted uncomfortably in her seat. 'Or seen them.' Not since the weekend of the Big Fight. Which had followed the Friday of the Revelations. Which had followed the Weeks of the Suspicions. 'Not for three years.'

'Your grandmother's party will be the first time you've seen your sisters in *three* years?' At Bett's nod, Jessica gave a long, low whistle. 'This is more complicated than I thought. No wonder you went so weird when that fax from your grandmother arrived.'

'I didn't go weird.'

'Yes, you did. Have you got any photos of your sister and your fiancé together?'

'Why? Don't you believe me?'

'Of course I do. I just need to get the whole picture of it in my head, so I can give you all the advice you need.'

'I'd rather you didn't –'

'Please, Bett. You know how much I love looking at photos.'

That much was true. Jessica was the only person Bett had ever met who genuinely enjoyed looking at other people's holiday photos. She wouldn't just flick through a packet of snaps either, but would inspect each one, asking about the subject, the setting, the film speed used.

Jessica was being her most persuasive. 'I'm sure it will help you. This way I'll know exactly who you're talking about.'

'Thanks, anyway, but –'

'Bett, come on. You've told me half of it. I may as well see the rest.'

'Look, I –'

'Please-please-please . . .'

Bett gave in, picking up the small photo album lying on top of the bookcase in the corner of the room. At least it would take Jessica only a few minutes to get through them. She had left South Australia in such a hurry three years earlier that she hadn't taken any of her photos with her. The only ones in her album were those her parents and Lola had sent with their letters.

As Jessica gleefully started turning the pages, Bett retreated to the tiny kitchen with the dirty dishes, feeling sick and steam-rolled. Thirty-two years old and she still hadn't learnt how to stand up for herself. For a fleeting moment she wondered how her sisters would have reacted in the same situation. Anna would have given Jessica a haughty stare and chilled her into silence. Carrie would have tossed her blonde head and told her laughingly and charmingly to mind her own business. But not

Bett. No, she'd just felt embarrassed about having said too much and then handed the photo album over anyway. She decided to blame the wine they'd had that night for this sudden need to show and tell all. Nine parts alcohol, one part truth serum.

She came back into the living room and picked up a music magazine, trying to pretend she wasn't watching Jessica's every reaction as she pored over each photo. For a while the only sound was pages turning, interrupted by Jessica asking the occasional question.

'Is that your mum and dad?'

Bett glanced at it. A photo of her parents, arm in arm in front of the main motel building, wearing matching Santa hats, squinting into the sunshine. They'd sent it in their Christmas card the previous year. 'That's right.'

Jessica read the sign behind them. 'The Valley View Motel. Is that where you grew up?'

'We moved around a lot when we were younger, but that's where they are now.'

Jessica nodded and turned the page. 'And this is Lola? The old lady wearing too much makeup?'

Bett didn't even have to look at the photo. 'That's her.'

'Would you look at those eyebrows! They're like caterpillars on a trampoline. She was your nanny, did you tell me?'

'Sort of.' Nanny always seemed too mild a word to describe Lola. She'd certainly minded them as children. With their parents so occupied running the motels, it was Lola, their father's mother, who had practically brought up Bett and her two sisters – but she was more a combination of etiquette teacher, boot-camp mistress and musical director than nanny.

'Is she wearing fancy dress in this next photo?'

Bett glanced over. It was a picture of Lola beside her seventy-ninth birthday cake, nearly twelve months earlier. She was wearing a gaudily patterned kaftan, dangling earrings and several beaded necklaces. Nothing too out of the ordinary. 'No, that's just her.'

Jessica kept flicking the pages, and then stopped suddenly. Bett tensed, knowing she had reached Carrie and Matthew's wedding photo. Bett had wanted to throw it away the day she received it, but had stopped herself. She hadn't wanted her grandmother to be right. It was Lola who had sent the photo to her, enclosing a brief note: 'You'll probably get all dramatic and rip this up but I knew you'd want to see it.'

'This is them?' Jessica asked.

'That's them.'

Jessica studied it closely. 'Carrie's very pretty, isn't she? And he's a bit of a looker too, your Matthew. Nice perm.'

At least Jessica hadn't said what people usually said when they remarked how pretty Carrie was: 'You don't look at all alike, do you?' As for her other remark . . .

'He's not my Matthew. And it wasn't a perm. He's got naturally wavy hair.'

Jessica grinned. 'Just seeing if you defended him.' She turned the page and gave a loud hoot of laughter. 'Now we're talking.

I've been dying to see proof of the Alphabet Sisters. Look at you with that mad head of curls.'

Bett tugged self-consciously at that same head of curls, now at least slightly less mad. Lola had sent her that photo, too. It had arrived with just a scrawled note, subtle as ever. 'Remember the good times with your sisters as well.' It had been taken at a country show in outback South Australia more than twenty years previously, at one of the Alphabet Sisters' earliest singing performances. Anna had been thirteen, Bett eleven, and Carrie eight. Bett could even remember the songs: 'Song Sung Blue', 'Swing Low, Sweet Chariot' and a David Cassidy pop song. Just minutes after the photo had been taken, a fly had buzzed its way straight into Anna's mouth. Her shocked expression and sudden squawk had made Bett and Carrie laugh so much both of them had fallen off the small stage, a wide plank of wood balanced on eight milk crates. The memory could still make Bett laugh.

Jessica was inspecting it very closely. 'You were a bit of a porker back then, weren't you?'

The smile disappeared. 'Well, that was nicely put, Jess, thanks.'

Jessica was unabashed. 'I always believe in calling a spade a spade. And you were a plump little thing. Look at that little belly and those rosy-red cheeks.'

Bett didn't need to look. That little belly and those rosy-red cheeks had never gone too far away. She was about to ask Jessica if she still thought she was a porker – she had gone up and down in weight so many times she hardly knew what size she was – but Jessica was too occupied with the photo. She was taking in every detail, the flicked fringes, the matching dresses, the bad makeup – all Lola's handiwork.

She glanced up at Bett. 'Not exactly the Corrs, were you?'

Bett laughed despite herself. 'I bet they didn't look that good when they were teenagers either.'

'I bet they did. Have you ever wondered if there's a fourth Corr sister, a hideously ugly one they keep locked away?' Jessica looked at the photo again. 'You're not very alike, are you? Even apart from the appalling eye makeup and the different hair colours. Unless they're wigs?'

'No, all our own work, I'm afraid.' Anna had straight black hair, Bett's was dark brown and Carrie's dark blonde. She presumed her sisters' hair colours hadn't changed in three years. She'd find out soon enough. In less than two weeks, in fact. Her stomach gave a lurch.

The fax from Lola in South Australia had arrived at Bett's work out of the blue, just the one line. If Bett didn't come home for her eightieth birthday party, she would never talk to her again.

Bett had rung her immediately. 'Lola, don't do this to me, please,' she'd said, straight to the point as soon as her grandmother answered. 'You know what it'll be like.'

'Elizabeth Quinlan, stop being such a baby. You're scared of seeing your sisters. So what? I'm nearly eighty and I've got a lot more to be scared of than you have. I could die any moment. Now, hang up, book your ticket and get here as soon as you can. I've got something I want you to do.'

Lola had obviously taken her extra-strength bossy tablets that day. 'I can't drop everything just like that, Lola. I've got a life here now.'

'And you've got a grandmother in Australia who has missed you very, very badly and wants to see you again.' Her voice had softened. 'Please, Bett. Come home. For me.'

Bett had thought about it for two days, veering between excitement and dread at the idea. One image had kept coming to her. Lola, standing in front of the motel, beaming at her, waiting to give her a hug. In the end Bett had compromised. Yes, she would come back for the party, but it would be a lightning trip. She'd arrive in South Australia the day of the party and then leave as soon as possible afterwards.

Lola hadn't been at all pleased. 'But I need you here for longer than that.'

'I can't, Lola. I've got a life here,' she'd repeated firmly. It had been a strange sensation. She wasn't used to standing up to her grandmother either.

Beside her, Jessica was going through the album again. 'It's a tricky one, that's for sure. No wonder you're so nervous. Your first meeting with your sisters and the happy couple in three years, all of you in the same motel, not to mention the added tension of a party . . .'

Bett nodded, waiting for her friend's sound advice, the helpful comments.

Jessica shut the album with a snap. 'I'd say it's going to be ferocious.'

Sydney, Australia

Anna Quinlan knew that outside the sun was shining. That less than a kilometre away the waters of Sydney Harbour were probably glinting in the sun, to a soundtrack of ferry horns, gull cries and tourist-guide commentaries.

But it could have been the Sahara Desert outside. She'd been trapped inside this coffin of a recording studio for three hours now, trying to get the voice exactly right for a new range of kitchen sponges. She'd decided the client was not just from hell, but from somewhere much deeper, hotter and even more unpleasant.

She peered through the glass of the studio window again, counting to ten as she caught sight of him. He looked like a suit-wearing spotty child who surely couldn't have driven himself to the studio today. He didn't seem old enough. She snapped back to attention as Bob, the producer/technician, pressed the button on the intercom so his voice came into her headphones.

'Anna, Henry feels you are really getting there, but he wonders whether you could combine the laugh in your voice from that first take with the kind of bubbling tone you did on the one before that last one, and add a little more lightness to the whole thing.'

Henry leaned forward, speaking into the microphone as though he was an MC at a football-club presentation night. 'Yes, loved that bubbly sound, Anna. Just perfect for our demographic. You don't mind, do you?'

Mind? Mind that she had spent three hours saying one sentence in dozens of different voices? Mind that the preschooler in the suit had tried to describe the mindset of a kitchen sponge – a kitchen sponge! – to her? 'It's determined, it's energetic, it's fun . . .'

No, it's not, Henry, she'd thought. It's a three-inch square of detergent-soaked sponge with a scouring pad on one side that you do dishes with. It isn't Russell Crowe.

She bit her tongue. Whatever you do, Anna, don't let them see you're upset. Keep cool, keep smiling, keep up the front. She'd learned that lesson after years of unsuccessful auditions for parts. No one wanted a moody actress. It was much better to be tagged as a thorough professional, even if it was sometimes mistaken for haughtiness. And at least Henry had definitely decided that the sponge was female. Today's booking had been set up, cancelled, then set up again while Henry, his advertising agency and his market-research team argued over the best gender for their new sponge.

Anna looked at Bob for help. He was just chewing, as normal, and hitching up his trousers, unfazed, also as normal. She knew he didn't care how long the client took. He charged an hourly rate.

Some of her frustration must have shown on her face. Bob took pity on her. He spoke again, surreptitiously inclining his head towards the client. 'Anna, perhaps it would help if you visualised yourself in the sink, getting psyched up to help your housewife – sorry, homemaker – clear all those dirty dishes. And there's one particularly greasy pot that's going to need special energy, but you know it will be worth it to scrub like mad until every spot is gone.' Another barely noticeable nod at the client. 'Whenever you're ready. Tape's running.'

It worked a treat. Staring through the glass, seeing her sharp bobbed hair and immaculate makeup reflected back at her, Anna imagined Henry evolving into a dirty, grease-spattered saucepan. She imagined herself as the sponge, leaping out of nowhere and scouring his face until every spot and blackhead had disappeared, shouting all the while in a voice that was a combination of Mary Poppins and kamikaze pilot. She leaned towards the microphone. 'Let me at it! I'm the clean machine!'

Henry's pimply face broke into a huge smile. 'That's it. Perfect. Thanks, Anna.'

She had just leaned down to her bag when his voice came in again. 'But would you be able to do it one more time? I think it needs just a touch more softness, to convey the moisturiser we've included in the washing-up liquid.'

*

An hour later Anna was driving out of the studio carpark. The voice of the sponge was now lodged in her head and she knew from experience it would stay there for the next few days or until a new character's voice took its place. Last month her internal voice, her mind voice, had varied between a kitten stuck up a tree (for a cat food commercial), a warm-hearted nurse in an old folks' home (health insurance) and a cake waiting to be iced. That had taken three hours to get right too, before Bob stepped in once again with her motivation. 'Imagine you're the cake, Anna, okay? You're scared. You don't know which brand of icing you're about to be iced with but you sure as hell want it to be high quality. So we need a combination of fear and anticipation and . . .'

Her seven-year-old daughter, Ellen, loved it, of course. She treated Anna's repertoire of voices like a human jukebox. Lying sleepily in bed listening to a goodnight story, she'd pick and choose the voices. 'Mum, can you read this one like the Zoomer Broom?' The Zoomer Broom featured in an animated TV commercial where the ordinary household broom metamorphosed into something Harry Potter could have used for Quidditch, babbling nonsensically all the while. Ellen's other favourite was the ocean pie, a gurgly underwater voice.

Anna parked on the street across from the hospital, ten minutes late. Hurrying towards the lift, she composed her face, already hearing the disapproving tones from her neighbour, who had grudgingly agreed to collect Ellen after school and bring her here to the clinic for her latest appointment. The lift door opened and Anna spied her little daughter in the distance, standing up on a chair near the nurses' station, chatting to one of the staff. In the dozens of hospital visits since Ellen's accident, she had got to know all the nurses very well. Anna tensed, as she always did when she remembered the trauma of those first months. She decided it was time Ellen had a good spoiling: she'd give her whatever she wanted for dinner, let her watch whatever video she wanted, and then read her all the stories she wanted, as well.

By nine o'clock Anna's patience was wearing a little thin. Ellen had been alternately tearful and cranky all evening, insisting on pizza, then not eating any of it, and not settling on any one video but wanting to watch specific scenes out of five different ones. Anna had finally had enough, speaking more crossly than she intended, which set off the tears again. She then read two extra stories, purely out of guilt, hardly finding the energy for the different voices.

Ellen still wouldn't settle, hopping in and out of bed. She stood in the doorway of the living room now, tears on her face. 'Is Dad home yet?'

Anna kept her voice mild with effort. 'No, darling, he's not.'

'Where is he?'

'At work, I think.' She thought. She didn't have a clue where Glenn was. He didn't ring and tell her any more if he was going to be late, or if he was going to be home at all, in fact.

'Can you read me another story, then?'

'Sweetheart, you've had enough stories. It's time to sleep.'

'I can't sleep. I'm scared again. I keep remembering.'

The doctor's voice came into Anna's mind. 'There will be some post-traumatic stress and recurring fear, but it's important you learn to listen without making too much of it. Children are children and very skilled at knowing which buttons to press.' So what was she supposed to do? Ignore Ellen's tears? Tell her to get over it? Of course she couldn't. She pulled herself up out of the deep sofa. 'All right, Ellie. You hop back into bed and pick another story. I'll be there in a moment.'

By the time Anna got to the bedroom, Ellen had changed her mind. 'Can I have a tape instead? Can I hear Really-Great-Gran's tape?'

'Again? You sure you don't want a story tape?'

Ellen lay back and shook her head. Her dark hair fanned out on the pillow.

The tape had arrived from Lola more than two years earlier, with a note to Anna attached. 'This is for you to play to Ellen. I'm still having no part of this nonsense between you and your sisters but I'm not losing a great-granddaughter because of it. Please play her this tape so I'm not a shock each time she meets me.'

Anna put the tape in, then lay on the bed beside Ellen, stroking her hair back from her face as Lola's voice filled the room. Her still strongly Irish-accented tones were clear and precise.

'Hello, Ellen. This is your great-grandmother speaking. Now, my little dote, I've been giving a lot of thought to what you should call me and I think I've come up with the best solution.

Your scoundrel of a mother started calling me Lola when she was just a child and her two sisters followed suit, but you need a different name for me, I think. And not just Great-Grandmother. I'm much better than great. So, my darling, I would like you to call me Really-Great-Gran from now on. Okay?'

There was a pause on the tape.

'Are you listening, Ellen?' Lola asked.

'Yes,' Ellen answered sleepily beside Anna.

The voice on the tape continued. 'Good girl. And are you happy with that? Happy to call me Really-Great-Gran?'

'Yes, Really-Great-Gran,' Ellen answered in the pause. She knew this ritual off by heart.

'Good girl. Now, I'm going to tell you a few stories about your mother and your grandfather, but first I'm going to sing you one or two of my favourite songs. So settle back and relax.'

Relax? Anna bit her lip as Lola started warbling 'Don't Sit Under the Apple Tree' in her falsetto voice. The last thing Lola's voice would make you do is relax. She could clear a room in seconds. Ellen didn't seem to mind. Lola could have been singing a sweetly tuned nursery rhyme, the way Ellen was reacting. Her lids were getting heavier by the second, her lips mouthing the words along with her great-grandmother's slaughtered version. Anna smiled, remembering the song. It was one of the first ones Lola had taught Anna and her sisters. There'd been a row over who got to sing the high notes. Carrie had won, hadn't she? Or was it Bett? It certainly hadn't been her, cursed with as deep a singing voice as her speaking voice. She'd always sung the bass parts.

Lola reached a shrieking crescendo, then paused on the tape, as if expecting her performance to be followed by rapturous applause. 'One of my favourites, Ellen, and one of your mum and aunts' favourites too. As is this one. Are you comfortable? Sing along with me, darling.'

As Lola embarked on 'The Good Ship Lollipop' Anna glanced down. Ellen was fast asleep.

Back in the living room, Anna poured herself a glass of wine and pressed the TV remote control. She stared at the screen, trying to pick up the plot of the thriller, fighting the desolate feeling inside her that seemed to be rising closer to the surface each day. One phrase kept occurring to her. *I'm lonely*. Lonely. Yet she had friends in Sydney, didn't she? People she could meet for coffee? And hadn't there been joint friends, other couples who came over for dinner or who they met in restaurants occasionally? Not any more. They had all slipped away the past year or so, like extras in a film, Anna thought, silently stealing away and leaving the main action to unfold. She couldn't blame them. Who would want to be around to see how she and Glenn treated each other these days?

The TV program changed to advertisements and Anna noticed without pleasure that it was her voice coming out of the mouth of the animated mobile phone on the screen. She'd done that one two years ago now and here it was back again.

She put down the glass and rubbed her face with her hands. Who was she fooling? She didn't want to talk to Glenn or any Sydney friends or colleagues. She wanted to talk to her sisters again. She wanted Carrie to sympathise with her. She wanted Bett to cheer her up with some madly melodramatic account of how bad her day had been. She wanted to tell them both how awful things had become with Glenn, especially since Ellen's accident, but how wonderful Ellen herself had been, most of the time.

She could ring her mother or father at the motel, but she'd never really confided in either of them. It had always been too hard to get the timing right. They'd be either in the kitchen cooking for house guests, or out in the bar or doing the accounts, or any of the hundred things both of them always seemed to be doing. She could ring Lola, but lately those calls hadn't been having the calming effect they used to. For the first year or two after the big fight, Lola had been understanding, trying to see each of their points of view, as she always had. Understanding had turned to exasperation. 'This is ludicrous. I'm ashamed of the three of you, carrying on like this.' She'd tried the frosty approach for a while. 'I'm not talking to any of you while you persist in this ridiculous carry-on.' But then Lola had missed their phone calls too. 'Just because I'm talking to you doesn't mean I've forgiven any of you.' But for the past six months there had been silence on the subject. Perhaps she'd realised, as Anna herself slowly had, that that was that. It had gone on too long now for things to change.

A scream on the TV made Anna jump. A young blonde

detective was being chased down a dark street by two men in suits, her face in close-up, fear-stricken. 'Oh, shush, would you,' Anna said aloud. 'You're just acting, for God's sake.' She put the remote control on the shelf under the coffee table. As she did she noticed the mail in a pile, wrapped inside the free local newspaper. How long had that been there? She picked it up and checked the date – more than two weeks old. How many times had she asked Glenn not to leave the mail there? Is this what it had come to? Each of them deliberately doing the things they knew most annoyed the other?

She flicked through the bundle. Bills. Advertising material. A fundraising letter from Ellen's school. And a thick cream envelope. She turned it over, recognising the handwriting immediately. Puzzled, she tore it open. It was an invitation. She read it again. No, not an invitation. A summons.

Clare Valley, South Australia

Lola Quinlan turned her gaze away from the vineyards visible through the window of the Valley View Motel dining room and back to the table where her youngest granddaughter was sulkily folding serviettes. 'Did I tell you what happened in the charity shop this morning, Carrie? A young woman, around about your age, perhaps a bit older, came in and said, "Could I try on that dress in the window?" And I said, "Yes, of course, but I'd much rather you used the changing room."'

Carrie didn't smile or look up. 'You've been telling that one for years, Lola.'

'Good jokes never die, you know. What did the zero say to the eight? Nice belt.' She glanced at the elegant gold watch on her thin wrist and stood up. 'Time for *Days of Our Lives*. I'm not going to offer you any help because you're doing such a marvellous job of it yourself. And you know how important I think it is for you young people to see a job through from start to finish.'

Carrie ignored her, not looking up as her grandmother came closer.

'Carrie, are you ignoring me?'

The younger woman kept her head down.

'That's fine, but don't frown like that, darling. It's very bad for the skin. If you're going to sulk, at least do it with a smile on your face. Or try doing those exercises I showed you, the ones that firm your chin. See, like this.' Lola started grimacing, stretching her lips sideways, then into a tight pout; out, then in again. 'Twenty of those a day and it's like a gym workout for your face, so I read. A little alarming for any passers-by, but that's the price we pay for endless beauty, isn't it?'

Carrie started to smile.

'That's more like it,' Lola said. 'And I know what you're thinking and, yes, I am a wizened interfering old bag of bones and quite happy to be like that.' She leaned over and kissed her granddaughter on the top of the head. At five foot nine, her posture still excellent, Lola towered over Carrie. 'But I still love you, you know.'

'If you really loved me, you wouldn't have –'

'Yes, I would have.' Lola collected her handbag. 'Will you be staying on for dinner tonight? Thursday, schnitzel night.'

'No, I'll go home, I think.'

'How are those renovations going?'

Carrie and her husband had bought an old farmhouse several kilometres south of the Valley View Motel the year before. 'Fine. Slowly.'

Lola was watching her. 'And how is Matthew, Carrie?'

Carrie turned back to the serviettes. 'He's fine. Up to his eyes in sheep manure and vet magazines as usual. You know the sort of thing.'

'You're getting on all right, are you?'

'Yes, thanks.'

'Really?'

Lola was like a human sniffer dog, Carrie thought, still not looking up. Line up a row of people and she'd sniff out each of their problems instantly. Not this time, though, Carrie decided. The days of confiding in her grandmother were well and truly over. 'Really. It's a bed of roses, in fact.'

'Rubbish. No marriage is a bed of roses. That at least was one of the positive things about Edward dying so young. We might have missed out on the good times but we missed out on some of the bad, boring times as well.' Lola was amazed, as always, at how easily the lies about her husband tripped off her tongue. 'Tell me, do you ever get bored with Matthew, Carrie?'

'Tell me, do you ever think you're overstepping the mark with your questions, Lola?'

'Oh, good Lord, yes. But people are usually so shocked, they've answered me before they've had time to think twice. Do you know what I found out this morning? That Mrs Kennedy is stepping out with her son-in-law's father at the moment. Talk about keeping it in the family. Having a grand old time, she told me.'

Carrie felt a rush of combined affection and annoyance, her usual reaction to Lola's behaviour. 'That's the only reason you're still working in that charity shop, isn't it? It's nothing to do with helping the poor or keeping yourself busy.'

Lola made an elegant gesture with her hand. 'If people choose to tell me things, there's nothing I can do about it. I see it as my gift to society: helping people unburden themselves of their problems.'

'Digging the dirt on them, you mean.'

'I noticed you changed the subject, by the way. Don't think that's the end of it.'

'I don't know what you're talking about.'

'Oh, I think you do. Now, then, I must be off. I'm going to call on your mother in the kitchen and beg some afternoon tea. I really do have the perfect set-up for an old lady, don't I? A son and daughter-in-law with their own motel and restaurant and a granddaughter who is the sweetest in the world.' Lola gave

Carrie another kiss, then swept out of the room, leaving a faint trace of expensive perfume behind her.

Alone in the dining room once again, Carrie worked quietly until she had folded the last of the serviettes. With a loud sigh, she leaned back in her chair. One hundred paper swans surrounded her. This time in two days the room would be transformed for a wedding reception, the paper swans swimming elegantly up and down the rows of long tables. She'd already strung up the fairy lights the bride had requested. She'd ordered the special candles from Adelaide and they were due to arrive any moment. The bridal arch had proved tricky for a week or so. It would all come together, though. She'd done it enough times to be sure of that.

She sat back and flicked at one of the paper swans with her finger. It toppled, falling against the swan beside it, which also toppled. Within moments a whole row of them had fallen, domino-style. She could have jumped up and stopped them but instead watched idly as the last dozen or so flipped and rolled onto the unswept floor.

She didn't care. At that moment she was sick of it all. She was sick of her job. She was sick of the motel. She was sick of the fact people made such a mess while they were eating that they needed serviettes in the first place. She was feeling especially sick about her grandmother wanting to throw a birthday party for herself and insisting that Bett and Anna attend.

'But why, Lola? Why now? It'll ruin everything,' Carrie had said that morning, hoping she wasn't giving too much away. 'All that tension.'

'I've given you all three years to sort it out and you haven't even got to the starting gate. So I'm taking charge once and for all. I've written to both of them as well. Insisted they come or else. So they will, I know.'

Carrie opened her mouth to protest but one of Lola's quelling looks had blasted her way and she shut it again.

Scooping up the paper swans now and ignoring the state of some of their wings, Carrie replayed the conversation yet again. If only Lola had turned eighty a few months ago. A year ago, even. But no, it had to be now. And she had to insist on throwing a party. A huge party.

'You wouldn't be happy with a nice family dinner, you and me and Mum and Dad?' Carrie had suggested hopefully.

'Of course not. I could die any day and I want to go out with a bang. And I want Anna and Bett to see the explosion. Besides, I've got something very important I want the three of you to do for me.'

'Important? What's wrong? Lola, you're not sick, are you?'

'Don't pry, Caroline. I said I want to talk to the three of you about it. Once I have the three of you in the same room together again.'

The three of them. The three of them who hadn't spoken to each other for years, let alone been in the same room. Or the same town. Or the same country even. And whose fault was it?

Hers.

Who did everyone blame?

Her.

But now it had all changed, hadn't it? The reason none of them had spoken to each other in that time no longer existed. Which would make this reunion of Lola's even more hideous and humiliating and horrible than it would normally have been.

Carrie took her anger out on the last of the paper swans, crumpling it up in her hand and then immediately feeling guilty. 'Sorry, swannie,' she said out loud, smoothing the serviette and readjusting the little paper beak. It now looked like it had been in a washing machine. She tucked it away in her pocket. The way her luck was going this one would end up on the bride's place-mat and she'd cause a scene. Carrie had already spent enough hours calming the young woman, as she'd fretted about everything from the number of prawns to be served in the prawn cocktails to the mathematical probabilities of it raining on her wedding day.

Carrie had wanted to snap at her more than once. 'You think the wedding day is stressful? Try getting through the marriage.'

She jumped as the bell at reception rang once, twice, a third time. Right now she'd had enough of guests, too – especially guests who rang the bell more than once. She walked out, plastering a smile onto her face, knowing it was just several teeth short of a grimace. At least she was exercising her facial muscles. Lola would be pleased.

'Good afternoon,' she said to the waiting couple, her voice sickly sweet. 'I'm very sorry to have kept you.'

extracts reading groups
competitions books new
discounts extracts
competitions
books
new
events books
extracts
new reading groups
interviews
events extracts
discounts
new books events
events new
www.panmacmillan.com
extracts events reading groups
competitions books extracts new